THE DARK GUEST

SARAH HAMAKER

Seshva
Press

ISBN: 978-1-958375-00-6

Cover design by 100 Covers.

Editing by Liz Tolsma

❀ Created with Vellum

WHAT OTHERS ARE SAYING ABOUT THE DARK GUEST

"Once I started reading *The Dark Guest*, I could not put it down. The story captures the reader in the first chapter and doesn't let go until the last. Sarah Hamaker has created wonderful characters to root for as she takes them on a dangerous, twisty journey to the truth."

—Patricia Bradley
Author of The Natchez Trace Park Rangers Series

～

"Sarah Hamaker has crafted a novel that makes you think long after you've turned the last page. *The Dark Guest* draws past sins into the present and highlights the freedom that only true repentance brings."

—Jodie Bailey
CBA Bestselling Author

～

"This book drew me out of my reading slump and into its sticky web of spies and Cold War intrigue. In this high stakes tale, the well-crafted characters overcame their pasts and fought for the truth to come to light using code breaking and investigation to bring it all to a satisfying conclusion. Highly enjoyable."

—Lisa Phillips
USA Today Bestselling Author

"Filled with engaging characters, page-turning intrigue, and a sweet romance, *The Dark Guest* is a riveting political thriller you won't want to miss."

—Kelly Goshorn
Award-winning Author of *A Love Restored*

～

"Sarah Hamaker has done it again! *The Dark Guest* is an edge-of-your-seat suspense that kept me turning the pages well into the night. She's managed an exquisite blend of danger, action, espionage, and double-crossing that kept me wondering who was who. Yet in this great story where you never know who is telling the truth, she's woven in a magnificent hero and a true-to-life heroine, as well as a love story for the ages. In a time when most main characters are picture perfect and physically impeccable, hers are neither. I couldn't put this book down until I finished it, and you won't, either. Highly recommended."

—Donna Schlachter
Author of *Always a Wedding Planner*, *Double Jeopardy*, and other mysteries and suspense

～

"As the threads of the mystery come together and the suspense builds, *The Dark Guest* becomes a book you can't put down. Engaging characters and a beautiful romance make Hamaker's book one you will remember long after you finish reading.

—Nancy J. Farrier
Author of the Driftwood Cove Series

"Destroy, O God, the dark guest within whose hidden presence makes my life a hell."

From "The Dark Guest" prayer in *The Valley of Vision: A Collection of Puritan Prayers and Devotions*

CHAPTER
ONE

"You have date tonight?" Rainer Kopecek smiled from his seat by the window, which overlooked the manicured lawn of the Happy Hill Assisted Living Facility.

Violet Lundy returned the old German's smile as she removed the pillows from his bed. "Only if you're available."

He cackled with glee. "If I were only—"

"Forty years younger." she finished his sentence before stripping the bed and tossing the sheets into her cart. "I don't mind being alone."

"Ah, you are much too young to give up on love. Too pretty as well."

"You sound like a matchmaker." She snapped a fresh sheet on the twin bed, then sprinkled a little lavender on it to help cover the strong disinfectant odor that permeated all the laundry. Of all the residents at the facility, she liked Mr. Kopecek best because of his optimism.

"Nothing wrong with that." He waggled a gnarled finger. "I would like you settled before I meet my Maker."

"I thought you were going to live as long as Methuselah." She chuckled. "So I have plenty of time."

He shrugged his shoulders. "Life, it can be cut short. You should not wait too long to find someone."

Violet smoothed on the top sheet and thought about how Patrick had demonstrated all too clearly how fragile life was. To change the subject, she nodded at the framed photograph of a glowing bride and handsome groom that graced the bedside table. "Not everyone can be as lucky as you and Verna."

The old man's eyes misted as he followed her gaze to the picture. "Ah, well, we had twenty-six good years together before she died."

After fluffing his pillow, Violet dusted the dresser top. "You must still miss her very much."

Mr. Kopecek stared at the photograph. "We have now been apart longer *zhan* we were married."

Violet touched his shoulder. Mr. Kopecek never failed to notice her as a person, not just someone who cleaned his room. He had a way of drawing her into conversation. She always did his room last so she could visit after her shift ended.

"Have I told you how we met?" Mr. Kopecek winked.

He had shared about his wife on numerous occasions. "You know I love to hear it."

As Mr. Kopecek relayed the familiar events, Violet straightened his clothes in the closet, some of which hung like drunken sailors on the hangers. She poked her head out and caught his eye. "Mr. Kopecek, why is your closet in disarray? Were you looking for something?"

He motioned her to come closer. Violet moved to his chair.

"It was not me. Someone went through my things," he whispered. "But no one will find it. I have hidden it."

His low voice coupled with his German accent prompted her to lean down in hopes of better understanding him.

"You will help me?" His hand clutched hers, and his breathing quickened. "Because the time has come to right a past wrong."

Violet covered his wrinkled hand with hers. "I will help you if I can."

"No matter what happens to me, the truth must come out." He squared his shoulders and tapped his chest with his forefinger. "I withstood the best the Stasi could throw at me. If I would not break then, I will not now."

Violet hid the uneasiness that crept up her spine by squeezing his hand to express her support. Mr. Kopecek had hinted that his life in East Berlin had its dark side, but he had never revealed anything more troubling than stories about soap shortages. "Tell me what you need."

"I knew you would help." He puckered his lips as if eating lemon. "Ms. Siddons humors me as if I do not know what I say." His rheumy eyes met hers. "But I do. I know why I will not be left in peace. It is because of *Der Volf.*"

"The Wolf?" Mr. Kopecek had been saying strange things lately, but she had thought it a symptom of old-age memory loss. After all, the man was eighty-six. Now, though, with his voice firm and his eyes beseeching, perhaps he wasn't losing his mind after all.

"Yes, *Der Volf* has risen from the dead. Now I will be silenced." He gripped her arm with his other hand and pressed his fingers firmly against the flesh. "I know too much about the days of old."

She patted his hand even as her own pulse quickened by the urgency in his tone. For whatever reason, he thought danger lurked nearby, and she needed to reassure him of her support to calm him down. "You know I would do anything for you, Mr. Kopecek."

He relaxed his grip. "You are *gut* girl and will make some man a good wife. Get married soon. Have many children, which God did not grant to us."

Violet let out a breath. He often peppered his speech with God, something that made her a bit uncomfortable, since she hadn't been talking to the deity lately. At least he'd forgotten all about the closet and what he wanted her to do for him. She started to pull her hands away when he tugged her closer.

He whispered in her ear, "Verna loved to walk in *zee* rain."

Startled at the non sequitur, she leaned back. He seemed to expect her to say something, so she repeated the sentence softly. Before she could ask for an explanation, someone rapped on the door, and Violet jumped. Mr. Kopecek's manner had affected her more than she'd realized. "Come in." Violet straightened up and turned to face the entrance.

Daura's sturdy frame filled the doorway. "Mr. Kopecek, time for dinner." The aide entered the room. "It's Swiss steak night."

"My favorite." Mr. Kopecek glanced at Violet. "Remember what I said. You will know what to do when comes the time."

Daura reached down and helped him to his feet, saying over her shoulder, "See you tomorrow, Violet."

Once Mr. Kopecek and Daura left the room, Violet gathered her cleaning supplies. She turned off the light and closed the door. What exactly did Mr. Kopecek want her to do?

After clocking out for the evening, she paused to take a careful look around the parking lot before getting into her vehicle. Mr. Kopecek's talk about a wolf must have shaken her more than she realized if she was looking for a bogeyman in a brightly lit lot outside of an assisted living home in the relative safety of Fairfax, Virginia.

His last words played again in her mind as she started the car, along with the puzzling fact that while he talked about his wife frequently, Mr. Kopecek had never once mentioned Verna liked to walk in the rain. She would have to ask him tomorrow what he meant—and why he needed her help.

VIOLET'S STRANGE CONVERSATION WITH MR. KOPECEK MADE HER RELUCTANT to go directly home after work. Stepping into A Cuppa Coffee, she breathed in the strong aroma of roasted coffee beans and pastries. A cup of tea and a *pain au chocolat* would soothe her troubled thoughts. She moved to the pastry counter and eyed the last remaining chocolate croissant. Her mouth watered in anticipation of biting into the flaky pastry. As she smiled at the barista standing ready to take her order, another employee reached into the pastry case and plucked up her croissant with tongs to place on the plate held in her other hand.

"What can I get you tonight?" The barista's words drew Violet's attention back to her order.

"A large to-go cup of Earl Grey tea." She nibbled on her lip. "Any chance you have another *pain au chocolat?*"

The barista glanced at the pastry case now devoid of the chocolate-filled croissant. "I don't see one. Did you want something else?"

"No, thank you."

The barista rang up the order and accepted payment, then another employee handed Violet the hot drink.

At the condiment counter, she added a splash of cream and a packet of raw sugar. Turning to leave, Violet spotted the croissant residing uneaten on a plate at the table of a handsome man around her age. His brown hair brushed the collar of his button-down Oxford shirt. The man pushed his glasses back up on the bridge of his nose and took a sip of his steaming beverage before returning his attention to the pile of papers in front of him. Mr. Kopecek's words about not being alone echoed in her ears. Her rather solitary existence didn't put her in the path of many men, eligible or not. A surreptitious glance at his left hand, which rested on the table as he bent over the papers, revealed no wedding ring. Maybe a man who liked chocolate croissants would be worth getting to know.

Before she could talk herself out of it, she wove her way through the tables to stop at his booth. At first, the man didn't notice her, and Violet's courage fled like a flock of birds startled by a predator. But just before she could take a step back, the man raised his head, and her eyes locked with his warm brown ones. She'd never noticed before just how attractive a pair of eyes could be.

"May I help you?"

Violet froze, heat rising in her cheeks. All thoughts of fleeing or anything else vanished in an instant as a spark ignited the air between them. She caught her breath in a half gasp. "Well, er, you see, you have my pastry."

Dr. Henry Silverton gaped at the young woman standing in front of him before shifting his gaze to the croissant on the plate by his left hand. "This is yours?"

"No." The woman shifted, and her long, auburn hair slid over one shoulder in a cascade that reminded Henry of a waterfall. "I meant I wanted to have a *pain au chocolat,* but it looks like you bought the last one."

"I see." Henry most certainly did not see, but he definitely wanted to continue talking to the pretty young lady. If only he were good at small talk, he would find a way to make her smile. He suspected she had a lovely one. "I haven't eaten it. Do you want it?"

The woman flushed a deeper red and clutched her beverage cup so tight, Henry feared it might split from the pressure.

"That's very nice of you, but I couldn't take your pastry. I mean, I shouldn't have bothered you. I'm sorry for having disturbed you while you're working. Have a good evening." After the flurry of words, she fled the coffeehouse before Henry could protest.

If he were an able-bodied man, he would have jumped up and run after her to get her name and perhaps her phone number. But such a feat was beyond his capabilities. At least she hadn't appeared to see his crutches propped up in the corner of the booth. For once, he had been able to enjoy an encounter with a member of the opposite sex that didn't involve pity. Even if he had known her name or had a way to contact her, once she discovered he wasn't a whole man, their relationship would end like all the others. Best to stick to studying the Cold War. At least the historical facts he dealt with didn't cause disappointment.

CHAPTER

TWO

Henry stared at the open document on the computer screen. Blank. Just like his mind. He took off his glasses and rubbed his eyes. His book deadline hung like the sword of Damocles over his head, but the words wouldn't come, not when a pair of green eyes and a head of auburn hair continued to invade his thoughts. Chapter twelve in his seminal work on the building of the Berlin Wall remained a mystery, along with the young woman's name from the coffeehouse.

His meticulous outline covered what needed to be in the chapter. However, the opening eluded him, and with it, the rest of the chapter.

Maybe a walk in the garden would break his writer's block—and refocus his attention on his work. He rose from his chair and reached for his crutches, slipping his hands through the cuffs and onto the handles with practiced ease. In his lurching gait, he maneuvered around stacks of books on the floor of his home office, down the hallway, and out the back door into his little bit of paradise within the city of Alexandria, Virginia.

The frozen ground crunched beneath his boots. Come spring, the tiny square of earth would be abloom with color, but now it resembled something from T.S. Elliott's *Wasteland*. Five minutes in the frosty air was all he could take, and he trundled back inside for some hot tea to revive both his cold hands and his sluggish mind.

As the oolong tea brewed, Henry thumbed through his mail. He had acquired the bad habit of ignoring the post for days at a time. A glance at the postmark on a flyer revealed he had neglected to review it for more than a week. Positioning himself by the trashcan and recycling bin, he dispensed with most of the mail by pitching the circulars and catalogs into the recycling container and the junk mail in the trash. Bills went into one pile, while personal correspondence —of which there was less and less these days, a deplorable condition since Henry much preferred the handwritten word to computer-generated typefaces—went into another. After filing his bills and setting aside those needing immediate attention, he used a decorative African letter opener to slit the three remaining envelopes.

The first two concerned invitations from friends to join them and a "lovely friend" at different charitable events, which he tossed aside to decline later with a brief note. He had no intention of meeting any more eligible young women, not after the disasters of recent memory. Henry couldn't stand the pity or forced cheerfulness most women displayed when realizing his face—which friends and family referred to as handsome—accompanied a broken body that couldn't stand upright without the use of crutches. If only his mother would stop pressuring his sister to fix him up because she wanted to see her youngest settled.

A smile tugged at the corners of his mouth. If only he'd gotten the phone number of the woman from last night, he might find the courage to try again.

He slid a letter out of the third envelope and read the opening paragraph before registering the words scribbled on the page. The signature *Rainer Kopecek* provided no additional clues as to the writer's identity. He blinked and started over slowly from the beginning.

. . .

January 30

Dear Dr. Silverton,

I have read with great interest your book on the East German secret police, The Stasi in East Berlin. *Yours is one of the few scholarly works that managed to capture more than the facts but also the feel of that troubled time. What you got wrong, I will address in another letter, if time permits me.*

There is something else on my mind. You mentioned a ghost figure, a person whom some perceived to be a double agent who betrayed the Stasi to the United States.

I can confirm the existence of this person, called Der Wolf. *He is a dangerous individual who guards his or her identity with force. However, you also had one very important detail wrong.* Der Wolf *wasn't double-crossing the Stasi.* Der Wolf *was first an agent for the United States who then spied for East Germany.* Der Wolf *is a traitor to this country.*

You mentioned in your book that this shadow individual had been reported killed around the fall of the Berlin Wall. You did your homework and had several reputable sources to corroborate this, although no one could tell you the true name of the ghost. So I do not blame you for cementing more lies where this person is concerned.

I too thought Der Wolf *had died. Then recently, I saw* Der Wolf *alive in a very unexpected place. By your writing, I know you are a man dedicated to the truth. Come and see me at Happy Hills Assisted Living in Fairfax, and I will tell you what I know.*

But I must warn you. Der Wolf *will fight exposure. I am already in danger, and I have put you in* Der Wolf's *crosshairs as well. Since I am old and I feel that my time on earth is growing shorter, it does not matter as much for me. But you must be careful.*

Trust no one.

Auf Widersehen,

Rainer Kopecek

. . .

HENRY FROWNED AS HE PUT DOWN THE LETTER. HE TOOK GREAT PRIDE IN HIS research, in getting the facts right. His triple checking of evidence with multiple primary sources, many times from the mouths of the people who had lived the events he studied, drove his editor crazy.

The unnamed double agent had intrigued him from the first tantalizing mention in documents uncovered in the Stasi archives. Sources cultivated within the ex-spy community confirmed the existence of such a person, but no one would provide details. All were adamant, on both sides, that the agent had been an East German who passed along Soviet secrets to the United States.

Henry mulled over Rainer Kopecek's letter. Based on the phrasing and German words, he surmised the old man had probably lived in East Berlin during the Cold War. The name rang a bell, but he couldn't pull up the reference. He reached for his car keys. Since his chapter wasn't coming along, he might as well drop by the assisted living home to see Kopecek. For if the letter writer was to be believed, Henry might have a chance to rewrite history.

CHAPTER

THREE

Violet dashed across the employee parking lot. Of all the days to oversleep, she had to pick the day of the Virginia State Health Inspector's quarterly visit. She had wrestled with her bed sheets most of the night, having a hard time falling asleep. Mr. Kopecek's words replayed in her mind to the point of exhaustion. One moment, she believed it was the old age talking and the next, she was sure he was cogent. If she were honest, the memory of her embarrassing encounter with the handsome man at A Cuppa Coffee also contributed to her lack of sleep.

She picked up her pace, shoving thoughts of stopping by the coffeehouse after work to see if the man was a regular. Kathy Siddons would have a conniption if the rooms weren't done on time. Violet pushed the doors open and stopped short at the scene before her. A man in a double-breasted suit and shiny shoes stood talking with the director, who held a handkerchief in her hand, a sure sign someone had passed away. Siddons had a heart harder than shellac and only pretended grief when a resident died. To her, they were not people but rather goods to be serviced, then replaced when they expired. But appearances mattered, so the woman put on a show of sadness whenever there was a death.

Violet bowed her head to ease past Siddons. If she had any luck, she would make it down the hallway and into the employee area without being noticed.

"Violet, a moment, if you will." The older woman's grave face made her cringe inside.

She turned and tried not to look like she had been caught with her hand in the cookie jar. "Yes, Ms. Siddons?"

The petite woman could manage an unhappy appearance even on a good day. Violet mirrored her Debbie Downer countenance.

"I'm afraid I have bad news." Siddons blotted under her eyes.

Violet raised her eyebrows and waited. She had learned early on that to interrupt her was to invite the wrath of the gods.

"Mr. Kopecek died last night." A flicker of what Violet swore was relief crossed the director's face.

Then her words sunk in. "What?" Violet should keep her mouth shut, but of all the residents she had expected to pass away soon, Mr. Kopecek was not even on the list. Mrs. James with her endless health complaints or Mr. Anderson with his bad heart, but not sweet Mr. Kopecek. "What happened?"

Siddons turned to the man beside her, who consulted a folder in his hand.

"It appears he died in his sleep," he said.

"How do you know that?" Tears welled up, and for once, Violet let them fall. She usually didn't give the director the satisfaction of seeing when she was upset, but this time, Mr. Kopecek's death hurt too much to worry about the other woman's reaction.

"Dr. Wallace examined the body," Siddons interjected. She smiled at the man. "Dr. Billings was out on a call, so we were lucky Dr. Wallace could come by and sign the death certificate for us."

"You work with Dr. Billings?" Violet barely glanced at the man, her grief at her friend's death overshadowing the oddness of having a stranger instead of the home's regular doctor put an official end to Mr. Kopecek's life.

"Yes, we're colleagues." Dr. Wallace turned to the director. "Now, if there's nothing else, I must be going."

"Thank you for your assistance. I'll show you out." She threw a warning glare at Violet to get to work, then left with Dr. Wallace.

Violet hurried down the hall to Mr. Kopecek's room. The sight of the empty bed tugged on her heart with a physical ache. Seeing the old man every day had brightened her otherwise bleak existence. It might be a life lived by her own choice but one that she wished could be different nearly every day. Now she wouldn't have him to fill the loneliness of her job.

She stepped into the room, and her shoes crunched on broken glass. The contents of the bedside table, including the photograph of his wedding day, lay shattered on the floor. Plucking the frame from the floor, she gazed at the marred picture of Mr. and Mrs. Kopecek.

"Sad, isn't it?"

Violet turned around to see Daura in the doorway, her brown eyes glistening.

"He sounded so chipper last night," the aide said.

"It's such a shock." Violet swiped tears from her face. "The doctor said he died in his sleep."

Daura nodded. "Mr. Kopecek appeared peaceful, like he hadn't struggled."

"You saw him?"

"I was the one who found him. I'm working a double today, and he was my first check when I came on at six. I'm sure gonna miss that man and his stories."

"Me too." Violet wrinkled her brow as she surveyed the disheveled room. "But what about all this mess?"

"Ms. Siddons said he must have knocked it over earlier trying to get his glass of water."

"Then why didn't he call for a nurse?" She wanted to believe Mr. Kopecek had been sharp until the end, but the chaos in the room told a different story. Violet shook her head. It didn't make any sense. "Do you think he was losing his mind?"

"He did say some strange things about wolves coming to get him."

"Yeah, he talked about a wolf with me as well." Violet studied the wedding photo of the Kopeceks in front of a grey cinderblock building. Verna, dressed in a brown suit, held no flowers as she posed beside her beaming groom. The love of the pair outshone their dismal surroundings.

Daura poked her head into the hallway. "Boss lady coming. I'll see you later."

No sooner had Daura slipped out than Siddons stopped by the room. "Oh good, you should start here first." She hovered in the doorway. "We'll need to have his things removed and the room thoroughly cleaned. That's your number-one priority today."

Violet brushed her fingers across her damp cheeks. "Did Mr. Kopecek list anyone to notify?"

"His file doesn't have any relatives listed." The other woman adjusted the collar of her tailored dress. "Seems he was alone, which will make things easier."

For you. Violet kept her eyes on the picture, not wanting her boss to see the contempt in her eyes. "What will happen to his things?"

"For now, I'll have Lem bring some boxes for his clothes and personal belongings. Our attorney, Mr. Davidson, will be by later this morning to talk about what arrangements need to be made." Siddons sighed. "Mr. Kopecek should have left instructions or a will with Mr. Davidson, as we require of all our residents. I only hope he made provisions for his death before his mind started to slip."

Violet bit her lip to keep from defending Mr. Kopecek. Any change in routine brought out the bear in the director, and Violet didn't want to be the catalyst to unleash that beast. No one was safe when she went on a rampage. To her relief, Siddons simply left the room.

Once the director's heels clicking down the corridor could no longer be heard, Violet let tears slide down her cheeks. If the last thing she did for Mr. Kopecek was to take care of the things he loved so much, she would do it as homage to a man who had eased her way at Happy Hills. She carefully placed the broken frame on the stripped bed and slipped out of the room for her cleaning supplies.

When she returned and swept under the bed, she found *The Stasi in East Berlin* by Dr. Henry Silverton. A memory of Mr. Kopecek sitting in his chair reading this book brought a fresh spurt of tears to her eyes. Brushing them away, she flipped through the pages, pausing to look at the penciled notations jotted in the margins. The German words made no sense to her, and she started to close it when one phrase jumped out at her.

Der Wolf.

It couldn't be a coincidence that Mr. Kopecek's last words to her had been about that same animal. Suppressing a shiver, she snapped the book shut and tucked it into a box before continuing her cleaning. If only she could reason away the thought that Mr. Kopecek had tried to warn her of a very real danger, but his unexpected death made it difficult to dismiss his words as the ravings of an old man.

HENRY MANEUVERED HIS CRUTCHES THROUGH THE SLIDING DOORS AT THE front entrance of Happy Hills Assisted Living Facility. A musty smell overlaid with disinfectant permeated his nostrils, nearly teasing a sneeze out of him. The front desk was deserted, so he moved down the hallway, stopping to ask an elderly woman shuffling behind a walker the location of Rainer Kopecek's room. Her rather garbled instructions sent him off in what he hoped was the right direction.

After a few turns, he paused in front of room 253 and read the name plate next to the nearly closed door. *Rainer Kopecek.* Now that he was here, he wasn't sure what he would say to the gentleman. He probably should have called first to ascertain if Kopecek was well enough to talk. The letter from him seemed coherent enough, but the meaning behind the words had been less than clear. Henry squared his shoulders and rapped on the door frame.

The door flung open, and a familiar face with green eyes flashed up at him. The woman from the coffee shop glared at him, her hair hidden underneath a bandana. Then her expression crumpled into grief as recognition flared in her eyes. "May I help you?"

Blinking at the sudden change from anger to sadness, he gathered his senses together. "I'm, um, looking for Rainer Kopecek."

She glanced down, sucking in a deep breath, before returning her gaze to his. "He died last night." That brought on a fresh spurt of tears, and her hand came up to brush away the moisture.

"He's dead?" Whatever he had expected, it hadn't been this.

She nodded.

"What happened?"

"I'm not sure." She sniffled and reached into the pocket of her apron. Pulling out a tissue, she blew her nose. "I can't believe he's gone."

"Was he sick?" Henry thought about the letter with its warning, and he fought back a shiver.

"No, he seemed fine yesterday. The doctor said he died of natural causes." She pressed the tissue to her eyes. "I'm sorry, this is quite a shock to me as well as the rest of the staff."

Henry frowned. "So there was nothing unusual about his death?"

"Why are you asking these questions?" The woman drew in a shuddering breath. "Do, I mean did, you know Mr. Kopecek?"

"No, I didn't but I—"

"Sir, excuse me." A woman dressed in a suit interjected herself into the conversation. The short woman's countenance wavered between annoyance and ingratiation, as if trying to size up who he was and if he was important enough to be pleasant to. The woman's gaze shifted to the young woman. "What's going on here?"

"Nothing, Ms. Siddons." The younger woman spoke before Henry could volunteer an explanation. "I was just finishing up in here." She backed into the room and shut the door firmly in their faces.

Ms. Siddons turned to Henry. "Sir, I see you don't have a visitor's pass. We ask all of our visitors to check in at the front desk. I'll walk you there to get your pass." Ms. Siddons indicated the direction with a wave of her hand and waited until Henry started down the hallway.

"Which resident are you here to see?" She shot him a sideways glance that lingered long enough to make him uneasy.

"Mr. Kopecek." Frustration mounted at once again not getting the younger woman's name and not being able to extract more information on Rainer Kopecek before Ms. Siddons showed up.

"I see." Ms. Siddons pulled her mouth into a semblance of a sad face. "Did my employee tell you the sad news?"

Henry could see the woman's heart wasn't in the performance. His own heart ached at the thought that a man's passing elicited such disingenuous emotion from someone who obviously was in charge. "Yes, but she didn't tell me what happened. Was Mr. Kopecek ill?"

They reached the reception area where a middle-aged woman dressed in a bright flower print dress now sat behind the desk.

Ms. Siddons turned to him. "How did you know Mr. Kopecek?"

Henry vacillated between telling a white lie and the truth. As usual, the truth won out. "He sent me a letter recently, and I was hoping to talk with him about it."

"Ah, I see." Ms. Siddons folded her hands together. "I'm sorry you didn't get a chance to speak with him." Her posture stiffened. "If you'll please excuse me, there's paperwork regarding Mr. Kopecek's death I must attend to. I'm sure you understand."

"Of course." Henry nodded, and the older woman walked away. He would have to do more digging on Rainer Kopecek. Perhaps it would lead him to another encounter with the lovely young woman who so obviously cared about Kopecek.

Convenient the man had died before Henry could speak to him about the contents of the letter. And if there was one thing Henry knew for certain—coincidences like that rarely happened naturally.

～

THE MAN WHO CALLED HIMSELF DR. WALLACE WAITED FOR THE CELL PHONE call to connect. Things had gone mostly according to plan, but with The Wolf, *mostly* wasn't good enough.

"Any problems with the death certificate?" The voice on the other end of the cell phone hummed with power.

Dr. Wallace slunk in the car seat. "No, I was able to convince them Dr. Billings had sent me and signed the certificate *natural causes.*"

"Will he be cremated? I don't want a body around in case someone asks questions later." The Wolf spoke crisply, conveying impatience with this task.

Dr. Wallace swallowed hard. "I don't know. All records relating to after-life instructions are at a local attorney's firm."

"Why did you not know this?"

"There's no way I could have known ahead of time." Dr. Wallace tapped his fingers on the steering wheel, then caught himself. "I researched the job as thoroughly as I could. I assumed the wills and such would be kept in the director's office."

"I see." The Wolf drew out the syllables. "Is there anything else you would like to add?"

"You didn't give me enough notice to worm my way inside to find out for sure." As soon as the words left his mouth, he feared he'd said too much. The Wolf didn't tolerate excuses. And those who failed to deliver the right results at the right time suffered the consequences.

"I suppose under the circumstances, you have done what you could. You'll be paid in the usual way. Dispose of this phone. And Wallace?"

"Yes?" Dr. Wallace sat straighter.

"Occasionally, because of extenuating circumstances, I allow a pass when someone I've hired deviates from my explicit instructions. I won't be so generous next time."

CHAPTER
FOUR

Violet sat on the edge of the club chair in the director's office. Siddons, who lounged in a leather armchair, tapped out a staccato rhythm on the smooth polished surface of her executive desk. Violet had only entered the inner sanctum once during her final interview for the cleaning position, and she wasn't happy to return. Her instincts warned her to stay far away from the director, and subsequent encounters over the three years she'd worked at Happy Hills hadn't altered that feeling.

"Do you know why you're here?" Siddons paused her finger tapping and raised her eyebrows.

No doubt this was one of her infamous trick questions. Violet took the safest route available. "Daura said you wanted to see me."

Siddons resumed tapping and blew out an exasperated breath. "Yes, well, that's true. But do you know why I asked you to come to my office?"

Violet kept her expression innocent and inquiring. With some effort, she managed not to roll her eyes. Her patience had been stretched to the breaking point with Mr. Kopecek's death yesterday and that strange encounter with the man from the coffee shop. She had trouble believing now he had even stopped by to ask about Mr. Kopecek. Her fresh grief had made her less than cordial, and she still didn't know his name or how he knew Mr. Kopecek.

Now she had to deal with Siddons, a woman who ran her little kingdom like a queen lording over her servants. If only she could work in her chosen field instead of here as a cleaner, but then again, her life consisted of *if onlys*.

She met Siddons's gaze. "That's why I'm here—to find out why."

"Violet, you—" A sharp rap on the door demanded her attention. "Yes, come in."

Her secretary, a hefty matron in her fifties with bouffant hair, opened the door. "Mr. Davidson is here."

"Show him in, please." Siddons smoothed her hair and stood.

Violet rose too. She'd never had an opportunity to meet the Happy Hills attorney, but she recognized his name as someone the residents both trusted and admired.

"Good morning, Mr. Davidson. I wish your visit could have been under less sad circumstances." Ms. Siddons sidestepped her desk to shake the hand of the older man who carried a briefcase and wore an air of one used to giving orders.

"Mr. Davidson, may I present Violet Lundy, one of our cleaners. Violet, this is Mr. Kopecek's attorney." Siddons motioned Violet to be seated as Mr. Davidson took the other club chair and the director returned to her desk.

Mr. Davidson cleared his throat. "Has Ms. Siddons told you why I needed to speak with you?"

Violet shook her head.

"I drew up Mr. Kopecek's will." The lawyer paused. "I'm very sorry that he died. I liked him."

Violet's heart constricted. Here, at least, was someone who would mourn the passing of Mr. Kopecek.

"You're mentioned in his will," Mr. Davidson said.

"Me?" Violet couldn't imagine why Mr. Kopecek had included her in his will, unless perhaps he'd left her a little memento. Her heart warmed at the thought that their talks had meant something to him too.

"Ms. Siddons, is there someplace Ms. Lundy and I can go to discuss her legacy?" Mr. Davidson didn't appear to notice how the director attempted to look busy shuffling papers on her desk.

"Certainly. You may use the conference room." She rose and moved around the desk. "I'll walk you down."

He smiled as he stood. "No need. I remember the way."

Violet slipped out of her chair to follow Mr. Davidson from the office. Once in the corridor, he led the way down a short hallway to an empty room.

"Here we are." The attorney opened the door and motioned her to precede him into the room. Closing the door behind him, he sat across the table from her.

She bent her head down at her folded hands. "I can't believe Mr. Kopecek left me something. I also can't believe he's dead." She raised her eyes. "He seemed so alive two days ago."

Mr. Davidson put on a pair of reading glasses. "I gather his passing was unexpected."

"Very, at least from my perspective. He was fine when I left that night around six." Violet shoved memories of their friendship from her mind. She wasn't ready to relive their time together, but snippets of their conversations kept returning to her mind as she boxed his things.

"My condolences. It sounds like you'll miss him."

Violet nodded, her throat tight with suppressed tears.

The lawyer pulled some papers from his briefcase. "This is Mr. Kopecek's last will and testament."

Violet furrowed her brow, her mind finally lighting on what had been niggling at it since the lawyer walked into Siddons's office. "Isn't this a little quick to be reading the will?"

Mr. Davidson peered over his spectacles at her. "Mr. Kopecek left explicit instructions that his will be read as soon as humanly possible after his death."

"Oh." Violet rubbed her hands together in the cooler room. Siddons turned the heat off in here unless a meeting was scheduled. "Then shouldn't the other recipients be present for the reading?"

"You are the sole beneficiary."

Violet gaped at him, remembering to close her mouth only after several seconds passed. "There's no one else in his will?"

"That's correct." Mr. Davidson picked up the papers. "I think you will understand more after I read the will." He cleared his throat. "This is the final will and testament of Rainer Kopecek, currently a resident of Happy Hills Assisted Living Facility. I hereby leave all my worldly goods, including but not limited to papers, personal effects, money, dividends, bonds, jewelry, and books, to Violet Lundy."

Violet heard the words, even comprehended them, but still didn't understand why Mr. Kopecek would leave her everything. Sure, she had talked to him daily while cleaning his room, but she wasn't family.

"Ms. Lundy? Are you okay?" Mr. Davidson eyed her from across the table.

"Yes, I'm surprised, shocked really." With effort, she focused her attention on the matter at hand and not on the fact that once again, death had reached into her life in an unexpected way. "I expected Mr. Kopecek to leave his possessions to a relative, no matter how distant."

"Mr. Kopecek told me specifically all his relatives were deceased." He paused, and his voice softened. "He considered you like a grand-daughter."

A tear slid down her cheek, but she held the rest at bay. No sense showering the attorney with her sorrow. She had gotten out of practice in controlling her emotions in public, but the hard-earned skill came back to her, and she tucked away her grief like folding a handkerchief. Violet forced her lips to form the words for which Mr. Davidson seemed to be waiting. "What, exactly, did he have besides the contents of his room?"

Mr. Davidson pushed a piece of paper across the table. "Here are the totals of his financial assets as of yesterday."

Violet exhaled, the numbers swimming momentarily before her eyes. So many zeros. She glanced away, then back at the paper, but the numbers stayed firmly the same. A quick calculation in her head with some rounding, and she arrived at an astounding final amount. "Are you saying that Mr. Kopecek left me close to half a million dollars?"

"Yes. Most is tied up in investments and such."

Violet skimmed the accounts listed, but the numbers wavered on the page. She tamped down the elation that swelled within her that she could finally be free to disappear wherever she wished. Surely her family wouldn't find out about the legacy. She didn't want to think about what would happen if they did.

"I know this is a lot to comprehend," Mr. Davidson said. "I'll inform Ms. Siddons that you are the proper recipient of Mr. Kopecek's estate. My office will contact you soon about transferring the accounts to your name."

Violet folded the sheet of financial assets in half, hiding all those zeros from prying eyes. "Thank you."

"Before I go, do you have any questions?"

Only one popped into her mind. "When was this will written?"

Mr. Davidson glanced at the legal document. "Almost eighteen months ago."

"I see." Violet didn't see, but she wasn't sure what she expected to learn about the date. She stood. "I appreciate your coming down here in person."

The lawyer rose. "It was my pleasure. I will have a copy of the will sent to you. Is your address still Merriweather Way in Fairfax?"

She nodded.

"Mr. Kopecek was a delightful person." Mr. Davidson replaced his glasses in his shirt pocket.

Violet followed him to the door. "Did you know him well?"

"We would chat by phone every few months." Mr. Davidson held the door open for her. "He would call over the flimsiest excuse. I knew he just wanted to talk. I didn't mind because we had such interesting conversations."

Violet kept pace with the attorney down the hallway. "Did you talk with him recently?"

"About six weeks ago he called to include the addendum that you know about the legacy as soon as possible after his death."

Violet shivered at the thought Mr. Kopecek might have known his passing was imminent. Two months ago was when he began to say strange things, odd phrases featuring animals. "How did he seem to you?"

Mr. Davidson paused in the lobby. "You know, he seemed agitated about something, kept saying that he had to keep *it* safe from The Wolf. I know Ms. Siddons believes that his mental capacity was diminishing, but I disagree. He was in his right mind when he wrote the will, and he was in his right mind when I last spoke with him."

Violet let out a breath, her shoulders sagging. "Thank you. I appreciate your telling me that. I was worried about him because the staff was starting to treat him like he was losing his mind." She reached into her pocket for a tissue and dabbed at her eyes. "He was trying to tell me something, and now I'll never know what it was. Thank you again, Mr. Davidson."

The lawyer handed her a business card. "Please call if you have any questions."

She tucked it into her cleaning apron. To think Mr. Kopecek had all that money and yet he chose to live in Happy Hills.

It was almost as if he was hiding—like her.

CHAPTER

FIVE

S enator Iris Morrison fingered the tiny scar on her neck. Cosmetic surgery had rendered it nearly invisible, but sometimes, the remembered pain brought to mind its former angry, red line. High necklines hid the disfigurement from sight, but she often thought of the night a knife sliced her flesh.

She returned her attention to the two newspaper clippings sent to her office in the Russell Senate Office Building on Capitol Hill yesterday in a sealed envelope marked personal. A faint postmark indicated it came from Washington, DC, but that didn't mean anything.

A small mention in the *Fairfax Times* caught her attention—a death notice. The obituary stated that Rainer Kopecek, age eight-six, had died of natural causes at the Happy Hills Assisted Living Home in Fairfax, Virginia, on February 15.

Iris hadn't heard the name Kopecek for years, hadn't wanted to remember those times in East Germany when the wrong word to the wrong person could result in destruction of an entire family. The second article touted Dr. Henry Silverton's latest treatise on the Cold War, *The Stasi of East Berlin*. Like many who had lived or worked near the Iron Curtain, she had read the book with interest. The sender had slashed across the notice, "Chapter eight is of special interest." She didn't need to reference the book to remember what chapter eight disclosed—an accounting of how a double agent codenamed The Wolf died in East Berlin hours before the Wall fell.

She was pleased that old contacts had not betrayed the identity of the double agent, sticking to the story that the turncoat had started out on the East German side before switching to the United States. The scholar had gotten many things right in his story. Iris tapped the clipping with her red-tipped fingernail. Only a handful of people knew the truth. Now one was dead.

Dr. Silverton would have to be watched to ensure he didn't accidentally uncover the truth. She reached into a drawer and pulled out a new, prepaid cell phone. Before she dialed the number, she debated whether to include a follow up on Kopecek to make sure the old man hadn't left any evidence behind that could implicate The Wolf. Probably nothing to worry about, but Kopecek, while not formally trained in espionage, had had what the Americans liked to call a dog in this fight. But Kopecek had made trouble, and his wife had not been allowed to slip through the cracks. Ah, well. It didn't do to dwell on what might have been. Better to focus on what the future held.

Iris keyed in the number and waited for the call to connect. "It's me. I need you to check out two people. Dr. Henry Silverton and whoever inherited the estate of Rainer Kopecek. The usual workup. I'll contact you again in forty-eight hours." She ended the one-sided conversation and slipped the phone back into the drawer. She might be overreacting, but where The Wolf was concerned, you couldn't be too careful.

HENRY REREAD THE WORDS HE'D TYPED ON THE LAPTOP SCREEN. THE illusive chapter twelve started to take shape, but he couldn't fully concentrate on how the Stasi's extensive network of informers impacted the everyday life of East German citizens, not with Rainer Kopecek's letter poking out from underneath his research. With a sigh, he reached for it to study it again.

Who was Rainer Kopecek? He couldn't find any reference to the man in any of his research so far, and an Internet search turned up zilch. It was like the man didn't exist. Or rather didn't want to exist, which gave credence to his letter. Henry rubbed his neck and stretched his arms above his head. Maybe if he typed in Kopecek into the Stasi archives, that might pull up something. Germany had recently started scanning the more than a hundred miles of files the Stasi had documented on East German citizens during the Cold War. Those files were available to only scholars in a searchable online database.

Henry jiggled the mouse, entered his name and password, and waited for the page to appear. Trust the Germans to come up with a surprisingly efficient website. *Kopecek* returned hundreds of hits. He tried *R Kopecek* to narrow down the field and found only three entries. The first one, dated in the 1950s, concerned a man in his sixties, which couldn't be the Rainer Kopecek of today, given the man would be more than a hundred years old if still alive.

Henry skimmed the second entry, this one dated in the mid-1970s. A reference to Gunther and Christel Guillaume piqued his interest. The married East German spies had infiltrated West Germany and gathered intelligence for East Germany for years before being caught during the same time period. One sentence mentioned Kopecek: *R Kopecek informed the agent that one of his neighbors had recently returned from a mysterious trip, but the investigation revealed the neighbor to be one of our own delivering a package to Guillaume.*

Sitting back, Henry closed his eyes and sifted through the reams of knowledge stored in the files of his mind. He knew the Stasi encouraged ordinary citizens to inform on family, friends, neighbors, employers, indeed anyone and everyone. That was one reason the

27

East Germans had been so successful in stamping out any trace of rebellion. The old records contained thousands of such lines showing human depravity at its worst. He hit the print button and moved on to the final document.

This time, more than one Kopecek had a mention.

On November 10, 1982, Verna Kopecek requested permission to travel to West Berlin to visit her ailing mother. Subsequent research revealed that VK does indeed have a sick mother reportedly on her deathbed. No known dissidence from VK or husband R Kopecek, who has informed on suspicious circumstances in the past. Inclined to grant permission for VK only to visit for a few days.

Henry printed the document. When he pulled it off the printer, a faint, handwritten addendum caught his eye. *Permission denied per W, 12/11/82.*

Strange that only a day later, the answer switched to *no*. He'd read dozens of similar records and couldn't recall a single one that flip-flopped from *yes* to *no*. Any hint of concern resulted in reams of documentation outlining why the person couldn't be allowed to leave. Of course, usually the answer was *no* from the start, but the few that had been *yes* stayed *yes*.

Reading the short paragraph again, Henry jotted down a list of questions that needed answering before he could guess why Rainer Kopecek had contacted him. Topping the list was exactly who was Verna Kopecek and why was her exit visa denied. Maybe Gunther Richter would have some insight into this mystery.

HENRY SIPPED HIS TEA AND WAITED FOR GUNTHER TO FINISH READING THE printouts from Henry's morning sleuthing. He'd been surprised Gunther had been available to meet for afternoon coffee at A Cuppa Coffee, Henry's favorite shop. Its location across from George Mason University made it convenient for Henry to slip away between classes.

The older man still had a full head of silvering brown hair, appearing to look much younger than his seventy-five years. Gunther tapped the faint writing on the document mentioning Verna Kopecek. "What do you make of this *W*?"

That had bothered Henry too. "I first thought it must be Markus Wolf, but he was never involved with the Stasi's day-to-day operations."

"He didn't concern himself with such mundane things, not with his work infiltrating West Germany with his own network of spies," Gunther agreed. "He was legendary for his unorthodox methods of ferreting out secrets, but somehow I don't think Markus is the *W* here."

Henry sighed. Things would certainly be simpler if the East German spymaster Markus Wolf had penned that note, but his own research confirmed what his gut instinct told him. Wolf wouldn't be concerned with exit visas, not when he had the whole West German government to bring down.

"Did you see the 1998 CNN documentary *Cold War?*" Gunther picked up his coffee cup.

Henry nodded. "Not surprising that Wolf expressed no remorse for his actions."

Gunther raised an eyebrow. "None of us who lived in East Germany then thought he would regret one iota of his programs." He set down his cup. "He might not have been involved with the Stasi directly, but he certainly knew—and approved—of their methods."

"One quote from that documentary stuck with me." Henry visualized Markus Wolf, square glasses magnifying unrepentant eyes that gazed straight at the camera. "Wolf said, 'One may wonder at times if the end justifies the means. It would certainly be the simplest thing to say, "No, certainly not." But that wouldn't be the full truth. With intelligence methods, you can't apply the same yardsticks as with ordinary morals.'"

Gunther frowned. "He was that kind of man. None of us on the other side were sorry when he died, especially since he was never punished for his role in spying against West Germany."

Henry remembered the efforts to bring Markus Wolf to justice, which culminated in a suspended two-year sentence in 1997. "I guess I was grasping at straws to think this W could have been Markus Wolf."

"Oh, you weren't too far off." Gunther finished his coffee.

"What do you mean?" Henry's heartbeat quickened. He sensed Gunther had something that would take him in a new direction, one that would hopefully tie into Rainer Kopecek's letter.

"You're looking for a Wolf all right."

CHAPTER
SIX

Violet lugged the last box of Mr. Kopecek's earthly possessions into her third-floor, one-bedroom apartment. She locked and bolted the door before shoving the box with her foot to join the other eight in the center of her living room.

After going through the pockets of all his clothes, she had donated them to Goodwill straight away, along with his shoes. Everything else had gone into one of these boxes that now sat like statues on the worn carpet.

Her surge of adrenaline gone, she flopped onto the couch and stared at the boxes. It didn't seem fair that a man's entire life could fill so little space. Although she shouldn't be too surprised, given what she had gleaned about his life in East Berlin the few times he had mentioned it. She'd even browsed the history section in the library to read a bit about the Cold War and East Germany because of Mr. Kopecek. Day-to-day tasks lost their importance when a person was more concerned with feeding their family or surviving the latest purge.

A faux white-throated sparrow sang out the ten o'clock chime on her wall bird clock. There was no time like the present to take a closer look at what was in the boxes. When Violet had told Siddons about Mr. Kopecek leaving her his things, the director had nodded and said that would make things easier. After she had cleared out Mr. Kopecek's personal effects, Violet worked on readying his room for its next occupant. But this morning, Siddons accosted her in the hallway claiming Violet broke the facility's code of conduct by being named Mr. Kopecek's heir. Siddons then fired her on the spot.

Violet shuddered at the memory of Siddons accusing her of cozying up to Mr. Kopecek for his money. She was immensely glad Mr. Kopecek had freed her from having to work for a woman like Siddons, all business and no compassion, all prickles and no love, all hardness and no grace. His legacy would allow her to stop living the hand-to-mouth existence of the last five years. Too bad she had so few dreams to fulfill. But the loss of a job that had filled her hours worried her. She'd counted on it for more than an income. The pleasant distraction of the residents and the rigorous physical work of cleaning helped her sleep most nights without nightmares. Now that the job was gone, Violet feared its loss would open the door for the past to intrude at night once more.

She knelt beside a box, opening the flap to take out books. Some were in German, some appeared old, and a few were modern histories about East Berlin, including one whose name she recognized. *The Stasi in East Berlin* by Dr. Henry Silverton. She flipped the book over and read the back cover blurb. She remembered Mr. Kopecek reading this volume in December. He often talked to her about his reading, but when she questioned him about this book, he furrowed his brow and asked her a strange question relating to whether one should awaken sleeping dogs that would be hungry and ferocious.

She hadn't known what to say. Her own secrets reminded her of a pit bull with one paw on a bone. But he'd merely smiled a very sad smile and patted her on the hand, telling her not to worry about an old man thinking about his past. And she hadn't, until he was gone, and she wondered if she should have realized just how frail he had been.

Violet returned her attention to the book, opening it to skim through the pages. Light pencil marks and notes in the margins were written in what she presumed to be German dotted some chapters, while others were clean. She started to set the book aside when the dust jacket slid off. A handsome man on the inside back sleeve stared back at her. Blinking, Violet studied the author, who was a dead ringer for the man she'd not-quite-met in A Cuppa Coffee and encountered again outside Mr. Kopecek's room. At least now she had a name for the man who haunted her thoughts. Dr. Henry Silverton had light brown hair brushed back off his forehead and dark brown eyes.

The brief bio outlined his doctorate at Georgetown University in history, his specialty in the Cold War, particularly East Germany, and his professorship at George Mason University, where he was a tenured professor in the history department. *The Stasi in East Berlin* had been nominated for one of the top history prizes and had received praise from scholars and book reviewers alike. Dr. Silverton had written two other books on East Germany and was working on another tome about the Berlin Wall.

Mr. Kopecek would have had much to talk about with Dr. Silverton, given the latter's interest in East Germany and the fact Mr. Kopecek had lived there under communism. With a smile, she tapped the book. Maybe she should ask the professor to translate the notes Mr. Kopecek had written in the margins of Dr. Silverton's book. That would make their meeting again seem more natural. And after two embarrassing encounters with the professor, she wanted to have a normal conversation with him.

She refocused on the task at hand. This would take all day if she continued to be sidetracked. But that could be a good thing, since she had nothing else to do. She set aside the few mementos she wanted to keep, like the Kopeceks' wedding photograph and a few books they had discussed together. She was fitting the last book back into a box when her landline phone rang. Standing on feet that tingled from sitting on them too long, she picked up the handset on the fourth ring. "Hello?"

Nothing, only the faint sound of breathing.

She tried another greeting to no avail. Great, just what she needed. A telemarketer call. One more reason she should have said no to the bundle of services the telecom salesperson had pushed on her, but the lower monthly payment had convinced her to accept the landline along with internet and streaming. "I'm hanging up now."

"Violet Lundy?" The caller's tone of voice had a silky edge to it, one that masked whether the person was male or female.

Her heartbeat quickened. The mere mention of her name shouldn't send a tingle down her spine—after all, telemarketers often had the name of the recipient as part of their call script. "Speaking."

"Ms. Lundy, consider this a friendly warning. The Wolf is stirring in the lair. Be very careful you don't draw the animal's attention."

CHAPTER

SEVEN

Henry picked up the phone and dialed Happy Hills Assisted Living Facility. With any luck, he would be able to find out Rainer Kopecek's next of kin. "Hello, may I speak to someone regarding Rainer Kopecek?"

"I'm sorry, sir, but we can't discuss our residents." The receptionist spoke quickly.

"I know you can't, but since Mr. Kopecek died on Tuesday, he's technically no longer a resident." He crossed his fingers that she wouldn't hang up on him.

"Who's calling?" Her voice had a wary tone to it.

"Dr. Henry Silverton."

"Oh, you're a doctor. I thought you might be a reporter or something." The woman's tone changed to respect. Henry started to correct her misunderstanding as to what kind of doctor he was but decided to see if his title would open the door to the information he sought.

"How old was Mr. Kopecek?" Henry stared at the words that wavered ever so slightly across the page. He'd guessed the writer was elderly, but he had no idea Mr. Kopecek would die before Henry could talk with him about his extraordinary letter.

"Are you a relative?"

"No."

"I'm sorry, I can't tell you that."

Henry knew a roadblock when he saw it. After all, he came across them often enough in his research. Something about Kopecek's letter grabbed his imagination, but that could be the still unfinished chapter twelve talking. Another question occurred to him. "May I ask you one more question?"

"You can, but I'm not sure I can answer it."

"Did he leave a will?"

"Since it will be public soon enough, I'll tell you he did." This time, the woman's voice sounded downright cheerful. "No one expected what was in it."

The line fairly hummed between them. He might as well hear what she was obviously dying to tell. "Oh?"

The woman dropped her voice. "He left all his money and possessions to one of the room cleaners, if you can believe that. The director about had a cow, she was that upset. Called Violet all kinds of names and fired her on the spot. Although I doubt Violet cared, given the size of Mr. Kopecek's estate."

"You don't say." Maybe the roadblock had a way around it after all. "This Violet, she got everything, all his papers and such?"

"That's right." The woman's voice returned to normal. "I'm sorry, sir, I can't help you with anything else."

Henry picked up on the cue that someone had approached and the receptionist wouldn't tell him anything else. He thanked her and hung up. Now that the possibility of papers or other information dangled in front of him, Henry had to follow the lead, even if it might take him down a rabbit hole. It shouldn't be too hard to find out who Violet was. Maybe if the odds were in his favor, she would turn out to be the pretty woman who had been in Kopecek's room the day he stopped by the home.

CHAPTER

EIGHT

Violet approached the door of her apartment, arms weighed down with reusable shopping bags. For the first time, she'd ignored the food prices and picked up whatever caught her interest. Setting the bags on the welcome mat, she inserted her key into the lock, pushed open the door, and picked up her bags to enter the tiny foyer.

After shoving the door shut with her hip, she turned and dropped the bags with a thud. The apartment was strewn with torn pieces of paper, fabric, wood, and glass. She sucked in a deep breath. A photo of a bloody classroom flashed into her mind, and she tamped down the image firmly. No need to go there, not now. No blood here, just the remnants of rage.

Every box from Mr. Kopecek had been upended and the contents destroyed. Stuffing leaked out from the sofa cushions, drapes hung in tatters, and the coffee table lay in a broken heap. Books, spines ripped and pages torn, littered the floor. She peeked around the corner and winced at the chaos in the kitchen—cabinets open, glass and plates shattered on the countertops and floor, cans punctured, and food boxes poured out. Tears burned her eyes as she stared at the total annihilation of her possessions.

Whirling around, she stumbled out of the front door and blindly reached into her handbag. Leaning against the wall, she yanked out her phone and punched in 911.

ONLY SIX O'CLOCK, BUT IT FELT LIKE MIDNIGHT GIVEN HOW TIRED SHE WAS. The crime scene crew had come and gone, but the police officers remained. There had been no fingerprints but hers and Mr. Kopecek's. On the top step outside her apartment, Violet started to rub her eyes, then remembered her fingers still bore traces of fingerprint ink.

The officers had also taken many photographs and promised to canvass her neighbors to see if anyone had seen or heard anything. She could have told them to save their breath, as no one here would talk to the police about anything, much less a crime. This lack of interest in other residents was what had initially drawn her to the complex.

"Can you tell if anything is missing?" The tall, black detective inexplicably named Brown asked her.

"No." She shifted on the wooden step. "My jewelry's still here, and so are the coins from my change jar, although the glass is broken. And all the books and papers from Mr. Kopecek are destroyed." She brushed a tear from her cheek, not caring if she left a streak of ink. The loss of what Mr. Kopecek had left her hurt more than the destruction of her property. "Aside from that, I can't tell what anything even is anymore. It's all trashed together in a heap of rubble." Her furniture and kitchenware hadn't been top quality, but they'd been hers. The violence of the destruction worried her, but she didn't want to share that with the officer.

"Do you have friends or family you could stay with tonight?" Brown folded his notebook and tucked it back into his breast pocket.

Violet shook her head. "I'll go to a hotel for the night and tackle the cleanup in the morning."

"Sounds like a good idea." He handed her a business card. "Call me if you think of anything else or if you find something is missing while you're cleaning up."

She tried to smile, but her lips refused to cooperate. "Thank you."

Brown stared at her, his head cocked to one side. "You look familiar."

Her heart beat faster. "I must have one of those faces. The responding officers said the same thing."

Brown nodded. "That must be it. Take care, and do call if you think of something."

"I will." She stood to watch him join his partner at the foot of the stairs. The pair climbed into the unmarked police sedan and drove off.

She re-entered the apartment to fully assess the damage. Fingerprint dust covered every available surface. Blowing out a breath, Violet considered simply coming back in the morning with garbage bags because nothing was salvageable.

"Violet! What happened?" The portly apartment manager wheezed in the foyer of the apartment and leaned against the wall, his forehead sweaty despite the chilly February air. "The assistant called me with news of police cars."

"I had a break in, Stan." She waved a hand at the chaos. "The intruder trashed the place."

The man eased further inside. His eyes narrowed, and he pointed his stubby finger stained with tobacco at the far wall. "Is that a hole punched through the drywall? It looks like a man's fist made it."

She followed the pointing finger. "I think it is."

"You're not going to get your deposit back unless that's fixed." His double chin quivered. "I can tell you that right now."

Her lease would expire in two months, and by the expression in the manager's eyes, she would not be welcome here any longer. The apartment had served its purpose, but now that she had money, she could find a more upscale place to hide.

"Stan, I filed a police report. My renter's insurance and the complex's insurance will cover the damages."

Her landline phone rang somewhere within the apartment. She tossed him a tight-lipped smile and slung her canvas tote over her shoulder. "Now if you'll excuse me, I've got to find my phone in this mess." She moved past his bulk as he shifted back. Another step put him out of the apartment. The phone rang a third time as she closed the door.

She groaned as another peal shattered the quiet. The handset lay somewhere beneath the avalanche of stuff. She followed the sound, then paused by her broken bookshelves. The ringing stopped, then started again. Violet closed her eyes and listened, pinpointing the location to the far corner. She opened her eyes and saw a mound of torn throw pillows. Ah, ha.

She plucked up the receiver and punched the talk button. "Hello?"

"May I speak to Violet Lundy?"

Violet leaned her aching forehead against the wall. All she wanted was for this day to be over, not deal with some stranger. "Who's calling?"

"Dr. Henry Silverton."

The receiver slipped in her hand, and Violet tightened her grip while pushing off the wall with her other hand. "I'm Violet Lundy." After the mysterious phone call she'd received, she wasn't sure she liked having Dr. Silverton call her out of the blue, even though a while ago, she would have welcomed the contact.

"I heard you're the heir to Rainer Kopecek's estate."

She bit back a gasp, anxiety creeping up her back. "How did you know that?"

"I'm sorry. I should have explained. Mr. Kopecek sent me a letter dated January 30th. I think we might have met, well not exactly met, when I stopped by Happy Hills to talk with him."

"What do you want?" Given the destruction of her apartment, she wasn't about to volunteer information to this man when she couldn't verify his identity. Violet pressed the heel of her hand against her forehead.

"Do you have his papers and books?"

"Yes." No harm in telling him that, given the items were now in bits and pieces.

"May I look through them?"

"Why?" Surely a history professor wouldn't have trashed her apartment, then called her to ask to see the very things he'd destroyed. Her head pounded as she tried to sort out what to do.

"I think he was trying to tell me something about The Wolf."

If she wasn't so tired, she would ask what he meant by The Wolf. It was curious how often that animal turned up in her life these days. "That won't be possible."

"Please, it's important."

Under different circumstances, Violet might have respected his persistence. Now she just wanted to end the call and find a place to sleep. "It's not that."

"Then what's wrong?"

"Someone broke into my apartment and trashed it."

"Are you alright? Have you called the police?"

The concern in his tone coaxed a tear to her eye. It had been a long time since a stranger had expressed anything approaching sympathy for her. "I'm okay, and I called the police. They just left."

"Do you have someone to help you put your place back together?"

She bit back a laugh. "There's no need. Whoever did this left nothing untouched."

"I'm sure there are some things you can salvage."

"No, not a thing. Everything, the dishes, drapes, books, furniture, clothes, and mattress have been shredded, broken, or ripped apart."

"What a terrible thing to have happened. When you say everything..."

"I mean everything. All Mr. Kopecek's things too. Utterly ruined." Her canvas tote slid off her shoulder and landed on the floor. Reaching down to pick it up, she suddenly remembered that not everything had been lost.

"There was one thing I had with me from Mr. Kopecek's estate that wasn't destroyed."

"That's good news. What was it?"

"Ironically, it's a copy of your book."

CHAPTER
NINE

Henry replaced the receiver in its stand and rocked back in his chair. After learning of Kopecek's death, he had almost dismissed Kopecek's letter from his mind, but something wouldn't let him leave it alone, and he had used the online white pages to find Violet Lundy's number to ask if he could look through Kopecek's things.

He spent the remainder of the evening staring at the computer screen. By eight o'clock, he had netted a measly five hundred words on chapter twelve. He usually knocked out three times that, but his mind remained clogged with what Kopecek meant by The Wolf.

He was beginning to see wolves among the sheep if he connected a burglary and a dead traitor merely on the fact that someone who had lived in East Berlin left a stranger his belongings. To finish his book on deadline, he would need to solve the mystery. The total destruction Violet described spoke of an angry person, one who might stop at nothing to get what he wanted.

He couldn't imagine Violet being the target of what surely was a random crime. Closing his eyes, he conjured up a picture of the woman. With an old-fashioned name like Violet, she probably was a middle-aged matron who could scrub out a stain with baking soda and vinegar. But instead of continuing with that mental picture, he substituted the younger woman he'd encountered in the coffeeshop and again outside Kopecek's room. Maybe she was the person he sought. The fact that the woman didn't sound older than mid-thirties gave credence to that hope. But then people were always telling him how old he sounded on the phone. Must be his precise diction. Nobody spoke like that anymore, least of all his students.

His phone rang, breaking into his mental portraiture. He answered it without checking caller ID. "Hello?"

"Dr. Henry Silverton?"

"Yes." Henry sat up straight, his attention sharpening at the tone in the caller's voice, not too friendly, not too distant, somewhere in the murky middle. "Who is this?"

"The *who* isn't important."

"It is to me. I don't converse with people who won't identify themselves."

"Then don't say a word. Just listen." The man—or was it a woman? The voice could go either way—lowered his voice.

"I'm listening." Henry reached over and silently switched on a recorder he used to tape research interviews.

"You're opening a line of inquiry that should be left closed. Some things need to stay in the darkness. Rainer Kopecek is one of them."

His pulse jumped. "Are you threatening me?"

"It doesn't have to be taken that way. I'm just giving you a friendly warning." The caller chuckled, but it wasn't a warm sound. Instead, the laughter doused Henry's peevish inquiry like Gatorade poured over a football coach after the winning touchdown.

"If you're such a friend, then tell me your name." Henry had dealt with his share of cutthroat academic politics, but nothing more serious than who was getting tenure and who had been passed over.

"There's no need for that. I'm an admirer of your work and would hate to see your academic career cut short just when it is showing such promise. We might not be in East Berlin, but that doesn't mean its secrets won't still hurt you."

HENRY GLANCED OVER AT THE GROUP OF TWENTY-FIVE JUNIORS AND SENIORS in his Cold War seminar course. "The East German leadership saturated East Berlin and East Germany with more spies than any other country in history." He leaned on his lectern, his crutches propped against a special holder on the side. "To put it in perspective, the Nazis had one spy per two thousand citizens. In Russia, the KGB had one spy per 5,830 citizens. Anyone care to guess the ratio of Stasi spies-to-citizens?"

Janelle Turner, a slim black history major, raised her hand. "Five spies per one thousand citizens."

Henry shook his head. "Anyone else?"

A few other students called out ratios, but none were right. "Good guesses, but you're not even close to the truth. The Stasi had one spy per 166 citizens—and that's not counting the extensive network of informers."

"Why so many?" Janelle looked up from her laptop. "Isn't that many spies overkill?"

"You're not the first to think that, but you've missed what the East Germans were attempting to accomplish. Not only were they embracing communism and all that entailed, but they were also trying to establish total control over their citizens—including their thoughts, hopes, dreams, and desires. With its spies and informers, the Stasi poisoned every aspect of life in East Germany. Friends betrayed friends. Wives betrayed husbands. The family was constantly threatened by informers."

"But why did so many people inform on their family and neighbors?" Ethan Drummond, a political science senior, straightened slightly to ask the question before slouching further in his chair.

Given that Ethan never sat up straight, Henry often thought his backbone must be made of spaghetti.

"Because the system deprived everyone but those in high authority of basic needs and wants. People stood in line for hours for a loaf of stale bread. The economic conditions were frightful. The merchandise produced by East Germany was inferior in quality, quantity, and fashion to that available in West Germany. You could be denounced for a pair of jeans or the latest record by a popular Western band."

The students closed their laptops and slid tablets into backpacks. Henry glanced at the clock and saw class time had ended. "Next week, come prepared with two pages on how living under such a regime would impact your day-to-day life."

He smiled at the groans and balanced on his crutches by the lectern as he slid his papers into his messenger bag.

"Dr. Silverton?"

Henry peered over his shoulder at the young woman who stood clutching a large shoulder bag. Then he blinked. The green-eyed woman from the coffee house and assisted living facility, the one who had started to haunt his dreams, was summoning his attention. With a quickening pulse, he acknowledged her inquiry. "Yes?" He quickly shoved the rest of his things into his bag and turned to face her.

"I hope you don't mind my coming by after your class. The history department secretary told me you would be finishing up here, and I thought we should talk in person."

He wrinkled his brow. "Are you a student here?" Maybe he could get her name and phone number through the student directory if his courage fled before he could ask her directly.

The woman twisted her lips into a wry smile. "No. That was another lifetime." She reached into her bag. "I have some questions about your book, *The Stasi in East Berlin*."

The copy she held appeared well-read, the cover beat up and sticky notes jutting out from the pages at odd angles. The department secretary must have thought she was a fan. He could just see the matchmaking wheels turning in the sexagenarian's mind. A pretty young woman with a copy of his latest book would surely catch his eye. This time, he wouldn't berate her for telling the attractive young woman where to find him. "How can I help you?"

"I think I should start with introducing myself." She held out a slim hand, and he slipped his right hand out of the crutch cuff to grasp hers. "I'm Violet Lundy."

TEN

Violet stirred sugar into her large cup of Earl Grey tea and tried not to stare at the man on the other side of the table at A Cuppa Coffee. It had been forever since she'd noticed, really noticed, a man. Dr. Silverton was even more handsome than she remembered, with his brown hair brushed back from his forehead and his piercing brown eyes framed by dark chocolate rectangle glasses. All that brown should have been boring, but on him, it accented the strong jaw line and broad set of his shoulders. He wasn't at all what she expected, and somehow the difference pleased her. The crutches only added to the mystique, making him seem more accessible and down to earth.

"Here you go, Dr. Silverton." The coed waitress set the cup of tea on the table in front of him and beamed.

"Ah, you remembered the cream. Thank you, Brandy." Dr. Silverton arranged his crutches out of the way.

"Do you need anything else?" The waitress shifted on her feet, her desire to please this man pulsing off her body. Good grief. Violet must get out more if she'd forgotten how silly young women could be around handsome men. Not that she was much older than this girl, but somehow the eight year or so age difference seemed like a half century.

"No, this will do."

Still, Brandy lingered for a few seconds longer before turning and bouncing back to her station behind the counter, her ponytail swinging in time with her hips. Violet watched Dr. Silverton, who ignored the performance, picked up his cup, and took a sip. "You're not at all what I expected."

His opening gambit surprised her further. Violet set down her spoon. "I'm not?"

"No." Dr. Silverton fixed his eyes on hers. "You're younger, more attractive. I pictured you as a middle-aged matron with short graying hair." He paused. "Your name does not match your appearance."

A laugh escaped her lips. "It doesn't?" This professor was becoming more interesting by the minute.

He shook his head. "No. Violet as a girl's name went out of favor years ago. Nearly everyone with that name is older. Much older."

Violet shifted in her chair, the lie rising to her lips as naturally as if she were spilling the truth. That's what happened when you told something over and over again. The old-fashioned name had hidden her well these past five years. "My mother had a thing for the flower. At least that's why she said she picked Violet."

"Ah, I see. My dad was a Shakespeare aficionado. *Henry V* was his favorite play." He shrugged. "So I've got an old man's name too."

She smiled. "I think I read somewhere that Henry is on the upswing again for boy's names."

"Perhaps, but it's a big name for a youngster to fill." His eyes behind the glasses clouded, but then he blinked. "I'm sorry, that was probably too personal, grilling you about your name." He eyed his cup. "I've never been very good at small talk. Which is why I flubbed our first meeting."

Violet bit her lip. It had been a long time since anyone had even cared to ask anything about her beyond the niceties. She had gotten so used to talking in generalities about the weekend or the weather, she, too, had forgotten what a real conversation was like. That was why she had liked chatting with Mr. Kopecek so much. He teased her about her lack of a love life, but he also seemed to genuinely care about her as a person. Now another man was expressing interest in her beyond the superficial, although in Dr. Silverton's case, it was probably more academic than personal. "It's okay. I was a little forward, practically demanding your pastry."

He took another drink of tea and refolded his paper napkin. "Ah, well, we've been properly introduced now. Tell me, what was Rainer Kopecek like?"

Violet toyed with her cup handle. "He was very sweet. We would talk about books and sometimes his wife. I will miss him."

"How was his mind?"

Her ire rose at the indignity of one more person questioning dear Mr. Kopecek's sanity. She'd heard enough rumors floating around Happy Hills those last few months before his death about his possibly having dementia or Alzheimer's. While at work, she had to keep silent about her decidedly non-medical opinion about Mr. Kopecek, but now she didn't have to watch her language. The words came out with heat. "Mr. Kopecek wasn't losing his mind, if that's what you're asking. He might have said some strange things lately, but he wasn't senile."

Her sharp tone didn't seem to offend the professor, as his posture stayed relaxed. He leaned across the table. "Oh?" He dropped his voice to a whisper. "What strange things?"

Violet studied him, seeing only interest in his gaze. The caller's voice warning her to be careful flashed into her mind. She would see what Dr. Silverton knew before sharing Mr. Kopecek's words. "I think I'd like to see the letter he wrote you first."

"Fair enough." He reached into the inside pocket of his tweed blazer and handed her an envelope addressed to Dr. Henry Silverton. Violet recognized Mr. Kopecek's handwriting, her finger tracing the slightly shaky letters. She slid the single sheet of paper out.

"I only opened it last Friday." A sheepish expression crossed his face. "I don't always take time to look through my mail on a regular basis. It stacks up sometimes."

His eccentricities continued to pile up like his correspondence. Violet read the letter, her eyes lingering on the similarities between what Mr. Kopecek had written and what he had said to her. The mention of a wolf, The Wolf to be precise, sent a shiver down her spine despite the warm restaurant. If Mr. Kopecek trusted this man, she would too. "He talked to me about a wolf during the last few weeks before he died. And now his letter makes reference to a spy with the codename The Wolf." She refolded the letter, slid it back in its envelope, and handed it back. "Do you think Mr. Kopecek knew something about this person's true identity?"

Dr. Silverton finished his tea. "That's what I'm trying to find out." He glanced around the restaurant, nearly deserted this time of the afternoon, and beckoned her to lean toward him as he shifted closer to her across the table.

Violet raised her eyebrows but complied.

"I'm afraid Mr. Kopecek has started something that could be very dangerous." His eyes stayed on hers, concern emanating from their depths in the steadiness of his gaze. "I received an anonymous phone call from someone warning me to not investigate the matter anymore."

Violet sucked in a breath, her heart rate accelerating. "Me too," she blurted out before she could stop herself.

"Someone called you?"

She nodded. "Yes, after the break-in." She bit her lip. "Now I wonder..." She trailed off, not sure how to put into words her fear.

He finished the thought for her. "If Rainer Kopecek was murdered?"

CHAPTER
ELEVEN

"What do you mean her apartment was trashed?" Senator Iris Morrison paced at Lincoln's feet in the deserted memorial, phone to her ear. The afternoon rain kept enough tourists away to allow for privacy.

"Just what I said." The man on the other end sharpened his tone. "When I got to the Lundy woman's apartment, cop cars were everywhere. I asked what happened, and someone told me her place had been burglarized. The police report says the entire contents were broken, ripped to shreds. There's nothing salvageable."

Iris slipped into the shadows as a group of Asian tourists wandered into the memorial out of the wet, late-afternoon rain. "Then whatever they were after wasn't found."

"Hard to tell since nothing could be identified, according to the investigating officers."

"You talked to them?" Iris hissed into the phone. "You should know better than to take that risk."

"Hold on, I didn't talk to them. I asked an old buddy of mine to forward a copy of the police report. It was pretty thorough."

She closed her eyes, relief coursing through her body. It was risky enough just trying to find out what Kopecek might have told the Lundy woman, but it would be even more dangerous to be out in the open about it. "What about the professor?"

"He's exactly what you'd expect. Pure academia. No wife, no girlfriend, no pets. His parents are missionaries in the Central African Republic, have been for years. In fact, he grew up over there. He has an older sister whose husband works for the National Security Agency, but I doubt there's a connection. Nothing there to show that he'll be a problem for The Wolf."

"Maybe not." Iris tucked herself farther back into the corner by Lincoln's right arm as a group of teenagers poured into the hall. She lowered her voice to stay as invisible as possible. "But as long as they're not looking into Kopecek, everything will be fine." The man sighed, and Iris tightened her grip on the phone. "What is it?"

"Lundy and Silverton had coffee together yesterday afternoon."

She bit back a groan and lowered her voice. "What did they talk about?"

"Don't know. The coffee shop was practically deserted, so I couldn't snag a table close enough without arousing suspicion. But they did look rather cozy, leaning across the table to chat."

Tension worked its way up the back of her neck to the base of her skull, triggering the start of a headache. "Keep an eye on them. I'll call you when I can." She ended the call and dropped the phone into her pocket. Iris slipped out of her hiding place and wound her way through the pack of teens, resisting the urge to glance over her shoulder to ensure she wasn't being followed. But as she made her way down the steps, her heels clipping on the wet stone, she couldn't repress a shudder. The Wolf had awakened, and now no one was safe. Rainer Kopecek's death had set into motion a series of events that would likely lead to more destruction.

Possibly even her own.

~

VIOLET GROANED, DISORIENTED IN THE DARKENED HOTEL ROOM. SHE fumbled for her phone on the end table as its ring tone advised her that she should "Get Happy." Not a chance of that happening after she'd discovered yesterday afternoon that Dr. Silverton also had received a threatening call about The Wolf. She had stayed up late reading *The Stasi in East Berlin* to see which parts had garnered remarks by Mr. Kopecek. The pattern that emerged showed notations only alongside paragraphs mentioning spies, traitors, and a mysterious agent called The Wolf.

A sliver of bright sunshine spilled onto the carpet from the nearly closed blinds. This morning, the fear that had gripped her last night at the thought of The Wolf or his minions coming after her seemed silly. Sure, her apartment had been thoroughly trashed and she had received that weird phone call, but that didn't mean a dead agent had the ability to reach beyond the grave and haunt her today.

Judy Garland admonished her to stop worrying about her troubles, and Violet finally picked up her phone. "Hello?"

"I can't believe you didn't send your brother greetings on his birthday."

She so didn't need this today. "Hi, Mom."

"Don't you *Hi, Mom* me. You know how lonely he is, so far away from everyone. For you to be so callous as to forget his birthday, well, I don't know what to say." Her mother's tone told Violet she was in for a long harangue about her shortcomings as a daughter and a sister, with the nonexistent grandchildren thrown in for good measure.

"I'm sorry, but I've had a—"

"I don't care to hear your sorry excuses." Her mother's words cut across her like a sword slashing off the heads of sunflowers. "Nothing in your life should be more important than sending birthday wishes to your brother, not with him being so restricted in his movements."

Even though she knew it was useless, she couldn't let her mother's statements go unchallenged. Five years—well, really more like twenty-eight years, but who was counting?—of the obvious being pointed out hadn't made a dent in her mother's belief in her son. "After all this time, you still can't face the fact that Patrick's not the man you think he is. When are you going to realize that he is not, and has never been, a nice person?"

"You know I don't approve of some of his choices, but now he needs his family more than ever."

The finality in her mother's tone closed the subject more firmly than dirt on a coffin lid. Violet rubbed her forehead, trying to remember if she'd eaten dinner last night. No, her last meal, if it could be called that, had been a cup of tea with the professor. His warm brown eyes flashed in her mind, but she couldn't think about Henry now, not with her mother on the Patrick warpath yet again. "What do you want?"

Her mother's tone turned wheedling. "The fifth anniversary is coming up, and I thought we would all go see Patrick. You know how he gets around that time of year. I think it would be good for him to see us."

Violet bit back an explosive *no,* knowing it would only incite a bigger argument with her mother, one she wasn't up to having today. "What does Dad say about it?"

Her mother sighed. "You know your father. He's not thrilled with the idea, but he'll come around."

You mean you'll hound him until he does. Since what her mother referred to as "Patrick's incident" happened five years ago, Violet had erected a barrier between herself and her mother, a high wall that her mother had yet to breach with her guilt-inducing comments and her strong personality. "Mom, I've got to go. Bye." Violet ended the call and turned off the ringer. If her mother called back, she didn't want to know.

As she padded to the shower, Violet wished she could turn off the tiniest twinge of hurt that came from the fact her mother hadn't bothered to wish her daughter a happy birthday too.

~

VIOLET WAITED IN THE LOBBY OF THE FUNERAL HOME, THE SOMBER SETTING A perfect match to her mood. Having to pick up Mr. Kopecek's ashes so soon after her mother's phone call had darkened her already solemn frame of mind. Mr. Kopecek told her often that he wished for his remains to be scattered in the Potomac River, the closest thing to the River Havel that bisected Berlin. She arranged for the funeral home to provide a plain cardboard box, a fitting tribute to a man to whom possessions weren't as important as the people who used them.

"Ms. Lundy." A pale man dressed in a muted gray suit approached. "I'm Stanley Gibbons, the manager of Everely Funeral Homes. Would you please come this way?"

Violet followed the man down a softly lit hallway and into another room, this one appointed with groupings of club chairs and loveseats.

"If you'll have a seat, we will be right out with Mr. Kopecek's remains."

Instead of sitting, Violet roamed around the room. On the walls hung reproductions of paintings. Closer inspection revealed each painting's theme centered around death, from *Romeo at Juliet's Deathbed* by Henry Fuseli to *The Death of Leonardo da Vinci in the arms of Francis I* by Ménageot. Mr. Kopecek would have approved of such a diverse group of prints, and that pleased her.

Soon the door opened, and another gentleman appeared carrying a small box. Violet's eyes welled.

Carefully handing her the ashes, the man asked, "Is there anything else we can do for you, Ms. Lundy?"

She shook her head, her throat too constricted to speak.

"Then please take your time." The man withdrew, closing the door behind him.

Violet clutched the earthly remains of Mr. Kopecek and exited the building. Better to get on with the scattering of his ashes before she completely broke down and couldn't drive for her tears. Once in the car, she blew her nose. The trip to Lady Bird Johnson Park off the George Washington Parkway went smoothly, and she arrived there mid-morning. Situated on an island in the Potomac River, it was the perfect place to scatter Mr. Kopecek's ashes. He would have approved of its quiet, contemplative design. This time of year, no other cars dotted the parking lot, and she hurried down the path through the tunnel to the island.

Picking a secluded spot by the water, she hugged the remains to her chest and let her tears fall. When her crying subsided, she took a deep breath. "Mr. Kopecek, I'm sorry you're gone but glad you're with Verna at last. I miss you. Godspeed in your eternal rest."

Her head bowed, she whispered a short prayer of thankfulness for having known Rainer Kopecek. He had given her life purpose when things had seemed bleak and hopeless. Now he was gone, and all she had left were her memories and his cryptic notations in a book. She wiped her eyes. Time to let him go.

Opening the cardboard container, Violet gently tossed the contents into the water. The finely ground dust drifted away on the current. If only her disquiet about his death would smooth away as easily.

CHAPTER

TWELVE

"Do you want to tell me about her?"

Henry raised his eyebrows and stared across the living room at his brother-in-law Keith Madison, who wore a much too innocent expression as he stood at a table mixing drinks. "I knew I shouldn't have said anything to Sissy."

Keith laughed and squeezed slices of lime into the sparkling water before carrying the two glasses to the sofa where Henry sat. "You know your sister can't keep a secret."

"I know." Henry sipped the water, letting the carbonation tickle his mouth. "I wouldn't have said anything, only she caught me off guard, and I spilled the beans of my meeting with the young woman."

The next potential Mrs. Silverton had yet to arrive at the Madison residence. Henry never kidded himself that his older sister wasn't trying to find him a wife with these dinners. But he could relax now with Keith before what was surely going to be an excruciating evening.

Keith cast him a knowing glance. "Does this woman have a name? That was the one thing Sissy didn't weasel out of you."

Henry sighed. "Can we change the subject? It was one cup of tea, and I'll probably never see her again, so there's no point saying her name, because then—"

"Sissy will badger you about her for weeks," Keith raised his glass in a salute. "That's my lovely and sometimes obstinate wife."

"Only sometimes?" Henry grinned. "I've known her longer than you, and she's always been stubborn."

"That's true. At least her other attributes outweigh her few faults."

"I could debate you on the *few*, but what's the point?" Henry sank a little bit more against the cushions, the tension of the last few days slowly draining away. Time spent with his sister and her husband was usually worth the effort it took to sustain dinner conversation with another blind date.

"Smart man." Keith set down his glass. "I wish I could tell you more about tonight's candidate, but I haven't met her."

Henry frowned. "You haven't?" Usually Keith vetted the young women Sissy suggested for her brother.

"Nadia, who was supposed to come, had to go out of town on a family emergency, and it was just going to be three of us, but you know Sissy."

Henry's stomach tightened. Sissy in her planning stage was bad enough, but when she winged it, his sister had an even worse track record. "Please tell me it isn't her manicurist."

Keith coughed, a sound suspiciously close to a laugh, and Henry shot him a look that said it wasn't a funny memory. The previous time Sissy's carefully planned date for Henry had cancelled the day before, she had convinced her pedicurist to come instead. The evening turned awkward when the woman announced she had a husband and two children in Vietnam. The woman had thought Sissy wanted her to give pedicures after a dinner party, not take part in the festivities.

"I think Sissy learned her lesson after that," Keith said. "But I must warn you Sissy met tonight's date at her shop."

"A customer?" Henry glared at the ceiling. He most definitely wasn't the type of man that a woman who shopped at his sister's exclusive boutique at the upscale Fairfax Corner shopping center would find attractive.

Keith shrugged. "I think so, but she assured me the woman—I can't remember her name—would be perfect." He paused. "There's some story about her that touched Sissy's heart. You know what a soft spot she has for the underdog."

Henry nodded. His sister's championing of those without a voice was one of the things he loved about her, but before he could comment, the doorbell rang.

Keith rose. "I'll get it."

Henry reached for his crutches and pushed himself to his feet, turning to face the doorway as the murmur of voices drifted down the hallway. His sister came into the room from the kitchen and kissed him on the cheek.

She whispered in his ear, "I think you'll like her very much."

Henry tried to smile, but truth was, he was getting tired of meeting women once. The ones he wanted to spend more time with had no interest in someone with limited mobility, while the ones he wasn't interested in sometimes kept calling him. Sissy always approached these dinners with such optimism, and he wished he could share her belief that his future would indeed have a wife in it.

Keith came back from the front door and paused at the threshold to the living room, his body partly blocking the woman from Henry's view. Then Keith moved into the room, a young woman at his side. Her tan skirt swirled above knee-high boots, and a yellow sweater set off the red highlights of her auburn hair. Henry's mouth went dry. If he hadn't been braced on his crutches, he would have collapsed onto the couch.

Violet Lundy stood beside Keith, her expressive eyes rounded in shock. She seemed to be as surprised as he was. For once, Henry wasn't upset with Sissy's matchmaking proclivities. This might turn out to be her best dinner yet.

~

VIOLET BARELY HEARD THE INTRODUCTIONS HER HOST, KEITH MADISON, performed. She had accepted Sissy's kind invitation to dinner yesterday because she didn't want to eat alone in a restaurant. This morning, after her mother's phone call spoiled her mood, she had debated calling with her excuses, but at the last minute, she had wanted to be among strangers. Now she stared at the man Sissy had described as her "bachelor baby brother."

Violet heard the silence and realized with a jolt that neither she nor Henry had acknowledged the introduction. "Oh, sorry, but we've met."

Henry gave a small smile. "We had coffee yesterday afternoon."

Sissy clapped her hands, her blonde bob swaying. "So this is your mysterious coffee date?" She turned to her husband. "Oh, how funny."

"Yes, well, it was only coffee. Or rather tea." Henry shifted on his crutches as a pinkish red crept like ivy up his cheeks.

"Dr. Silverton was kind enough to help with some research I'm doing." Violet had never seen a man near her own age blush before, but the realization Henry had mentioned their meeting to Sissy and Keith distracted her. He probably hadn't said what they talked about if he hadn't given her name, but the thought that someone else knew about their encounter sent a fissure of fear down her spine. The less people who knew about Mr. Kopecek and The Wolf, the better, as far as she was concerned.

"Oh, you don't have to call him Dr. Silverton." Sissy crossed over and looped her arm through Violet's. "Henry will do just fine." She led the way into the dining room, calling over her shoulder, "Come along, you two. Dinner's ready."

CHAPTER

THIRTEEN

Violet spooned the delicate chocolate mousse into her mouth, savoring the airiness of the whipped dessert. Dinner had gone surprisingly well, given its awkward start. Henry managed to deflect his sister's attempts to ferret out how they knew each other with enough of the truth to satisfy her curiosity. The topics discussed as they ate tender lamb stew with barley centered on the more conventional, such as recent books read, movies seen, and places visited.

She placed her spoon in the empty dessert dish and turned to her hostess. "Thank you, Sissy. This was delicious and exactly what I needed."

Sissy beamed. "Our mother always says a good home-cooked meal with friends is the best medicine for whatever ails you."

"Your mother is a wise woman." Violet raised her water glass in salute to Sissy and Henry.

"Although with the two of you to contend with, I've always been impressed with how calm my mother-in-law is—most of the time." Keith winked at his wife as she stuck out her tongue.

"You are going to give our guest the wrong impression," Sissy said. "Our mother is a dear woman."

"Do you see her often?" Violet avoided her own mother and father as much as possible, which was fairly easy given that they lived in a suburb of Louisville, Kentucky, a nine-hour drive from Northern Virginia.

"No, only once or twice a year." Henry wiped his mouth with his napkin. "Our parents are missionaries with Wycliffe Bible Translators in the Central African Republic. They've been over there for more than thirty years, working on developing a written language for those who speak the Banda, Mid-Southern language."

"Is that where you grew up?" Violet had always wondered what it would be like to live in a foreign country as a child.

"We were both born there," Sissy said. "We lived there until high school."

"You sound very American."

"We didn't when we first came over here." Sissy shrugged. "But the slight accents we picked up have definitely faded over time."

"Did you go to a boarding school? I heard a missionary family at church once say they sent their kids to an American school while they were in some part of Africa." Violet had thought that to be a very hard thing to do, to send away your children while you did God's work.

"Our parents homeschooled us," said Henry.

"That's only because you contracted polio and Mom didn't trust anyone else to properly care for you." Sissy spoke matter-of-factly, but Henry winced at her words.

"Sissy," her husband said, his voice holding a gentle note of warning.

His wife shrugged. "It's not like it's a big secret."

Henry fiddled with the knife beside his plate. To take the focus off Henry and his disability, Violet directed a question to Sissy. "How long will your parents stay in Africa?"

Sissy sighed. "Until their work is done, I think. Mom and Dad are nearly finished with translating the gospels into Banda Central Sud, as it's sometimes called."

"Do you speak the language?" Their childhood seemed very strange to Violet, but it sounded like a better one than she'd had, all things considered.

"I did as a child, but when I moved away to attend high school in the States, I lost most of it." Sissy turned to Henry. "But my brother here is something of a language wizard."

Violet raised her eyebrows. "Really? You speak Banda, what-do-you-call-it?"

Henry smiled, his eyes crinkling in a most attractive way. "Yes, I do."

"Oh, he's being modest," Keith interjected. "Henry is fluent in, what, seven languages? Or is it eight? He's always picking up a new one."

This time Violet let her mouth hang open. "You're kidding me."

Henry ducked his head, another blush stealing up his cheeks.

"Okay, I'll bite. What languages do you know?" Violet leaned on the table.

Henry raised his eyes to hers. "English."

Sissy threw her napkin at him. "You are about to get on my last nerve, little brother."

Henry held up one finger. "Spanish, French, German, Banda Central Sud, Portuguese, and Russian."

"Seven languages?" Violet had no aptitude for languages. Her college French had been a year of torture before she gave up and focused instead on, well, better not dwell on the past.

"That I'm fluent in," Henry added.

Sissy shook her finger at her brother. "What he's not saying is that he also can speak Romanian, Bulgarian, and probably a dozen other languages as well."

"And can he talk to the animals also, a regular Dr. Doolittle?" Violet raised her eyebrows.

Henry laughed. "No, I'm not out communing with the squirrels and raccoons who live in my backyard."

"Good. For a moment, I thought maybe you were some kind of exotic being, but it's nice to know you have your, er, deficiencies." Violet smiled back at him.

"Why don't you two go sit and chat in the living room while we clean up?" Sissy stood, dessert plates in her hand.

"Let me help." Violet rose and tried to take the water goblets, but Keith and Sissy both shook their heads.

"No, we insist. You're our guest. Next time you can help, but for now, please let us take care of it." Sissy disappeared into the kitchen with Keith close behind, his hands balancing several glasses.

"I guess we've been dismissed." Violet turned back to Henry, as he stood with his crutches.

"I've found in most things, it's best to just go along with whatever Sissy wants," Henry said. "Lead the way, if you will."

Violet entered the living room and perched on the edge of the couch. Henry chose a club chair beside her. She worried her bottom lip while he arranged his crutches within easy reach of his chair. She watched his movements, but her mind chewed on a possible solution to a most vexing problem.

"Do you want to tell me what's bothering you?"

She jumped. "Am I that transparent?"

He raised his shoulders. "I'm usually rather clueless about that sort of thing, but you appeared troubled. Your brow was what I think is called furrowed."

"A furrowed brow gave me away?" She smoothed her fingers over her forehead. "I'll probably get wrinkles there if I keep it up. Not that I'm worried about that. Oh, dear. I'm babbling, aren't I?" She shot him a rueful smile. "After all this, I might as well ask you what occurred to me earlier." She sucked in a breath and let it out slowly. "When you said you were fluent in German, does that mean you read German too?"

He nodded, his eyes grave and his expression solemn. "Does this have something to do with our problem?"

"Our problem. Hmm, yes, I think it does." She meandered over to the end table where she had left her shoulder bag earlier. Picking it up, she carried it to her seat on the couch. "I'm sure this is probably nothing but the incoherent thoughts of an old man, but given what's happened with the phone calls, I couldn't help but wonder." Violet reached into her purse and pulled out a book. "It's Mr. Kopecek's copy of your book, *The Stasi in East Berlin*."

She flipped it open and pointed to some pencil notations in the margin before handing the book to Henry. "I think these notes are in German, and I'm pretty sure Mr. Kopecek wrote them. I mean, I saw him with a pencil writing something in this book at Happy Hills."

Violet forced herself to be quiet while Henry studied the page for a few minutes. He turned to read other marginalia before looking at her, his finger on the page, his eyes serious. "Yes, this is written in German."

"What does it say?" She leaned forward, her knees touching his. Maybe this would explain who The Wolf was or why Mr. Kopecek died.

"Nothing much at all. It doesn't make any sense to me. It's all nonsense words and random thoughts with no connection to the chapter at all."

Violet slumped back, disappointment sapping her strength. She had been counting on the book to contain some clue, something to help her find out why Mr. Kopecek died. "So it's just the ramblings of an old man losing his mind."

Henry shook his head. "On the surface, that's what it appears to be." He tapped the book. "But all of my research into the Stasi has made me question the obvious."

Her heart beat faster, and she sat up, her tiredness vanishing as excitement surged through her body. "You think there's something to it?"

"I think we're faced with two possible scenarios." Henry edged closer to her, his voice dropping to a whisper. "Either his mind was playing tricks on him and he wrote gibberish..." He paused, his eyes on hers as the full implication of what he was saying hit her with the force of a sledgehammer. "Or it's in code."

CHAPTER

FOURTEEN

"A little bird told me the maid is spending more time with the professor. I was clear in my expectations. I want them separated."

Iris frowned and swiveled in her chair to place her back to the closed door. She spoke in an undertone, her voice firm despite the thread of unease snaking its way up her spine. "And I told you never to call me at my office on the Hill."

The Wolf laughed softly. "I didn't have time to take the usual precautions. Besides, even if someone found out who was on the other end of the line, it wouldn't raise eyebrows. My company is quite the golden boy on Capitol Hill these days, or don't you read the papers?"

Iris sucked in a sharp breath. "That's exactly why you shouldn't get careless. There's more at stake than raking up the past. There's the future to consider."

"I would have thought you had higher aspirations than a mere cabinet position."

"What is life but a series of steppingstones? Very soon, the current secretary of state will announce his imminent retirement due to health reasons." Iris allowed herself the tiniest smile of pleasure at the thought of being nominated for that post.

"I heard his health is not so very precarious, that perhaps another had a hand in forcing his early dismissal." The Wolf dropped his voice even lower. "Be careful, Iris. A cabinet position comes with more scrutiny than a mere senator. You wouldn't want a reporter or some blogger digging around too deeply."

Iris tapped the phone with her finger. "Oh, I'm not too worried. If I'm exposed, you're exposed, and my crimes were not as treasonous as yours. I wasn't the one betraying my country. That would have been you."

"I'd hate to remind you that your inaction sent dozens of innocent people into the hands of Stasi agents." The Wolf's voice dropped to a silky whisper. "That kind of publicity would scuttle something as important as secretary of state, don't you think?"

Despite her confidence that he couldn't touch her, the shiver of unease turned into a shower of fear, and she swallowed hard. "What's really worrying you? I know it's not my potential post."

"Rainer Kopecek must have hidden something pointing to my identity. I want you to find it and destroy it."

Iris gripped the receiver. "Be careful your paranoia isn't clouding your judgment." Her ire rose at the chances he wanted her to take. "Kopecek wasn't even an agent. Why did you think he was a threat after all these years?"

"Because he's someone who would never forget the face of the man who caused his wife's death," The Wolf growled into the phone. "And because he knew I was the type of man who wouldn't let a loose end like that go. Don't disappoint me."

Iris shuddered and replaced the receiver. Slipping on a sweater as if its thickness would warm her cold bones, she tried to recall when she had become a woman who would willingly lie in bed, metaphorically speaking, with a man like The Wolf. She had no illusions about her own complicity in his schemes. His handsome visage had seduced many a secretary at the United States embassy in West Berlin. Iris herself had not been immune to his charms.

Her discovery of his double identity had been a stroke of pure, dumb luck, a case of being in the wrong place at exactly the right time. Why he hadn't killed her outright was something she had neither the courage nor the curiosity to ask. He had let her live, and she had proven herself first useful, then invaluable to him during the waning days of the Soviet Empire.

Now, decades after their first encounter, he still had the power to get under her skin, although it was less a jolt of sexual attraction and more a feeling of someone walking over her grave. The Wolf might be older, but that didn't mean he was any less dangerous than he had been in his prime. Iris pulled the sweater tightly around her body and leaned back in her chair. She would do well to remember that, even though it meant ruining the lives of two innocent people.

Violet bit her lip. "That's a very kind offer, but—"

"I insist." Sissy cut in. "We have the room, and you need a place to stay."

Accepting Sissy's offer would certainly ease her housing situation, but Violet wasn't sure living with Henry's sister and brother-in-law would be wise. She had kept people at arm's length for so long, the close proximity of sharing a house might breach her defenses. If the Madisons—and Henry, for that matter—found out who she was, they would likely feel she'd violated their trust. Violet paused, trying to make up her mind about the invitation, glad Sissy was on the other end of the cell phone and couldn't see her indecision.

"Besides," Sissy continued, her voice warming, "you'll get to see more of Henry."

Ah, Henry. Violet squashed down the thrill of pleasure the thought of seeing him gave her. Then again, it would be natural for Henry to visit his sister's home. Perhaps it would work out for the best for Violet to stay there for a while, just until she and Henry figured out whether Mr. Kopecek's jottings meant anything.

"Thanks for your offer. I accept."

"Fantastic! We'll expect you this afternoon."

Violet said goodbye and clicked off. She gazed around the hotel room, noting how few belongings she had to pack. From what she had seen of the Madison home, Sissy's decorating tastes ran to the eclectic, which would be a nice change of pace from this bland hotel room and her even blander former apartment.

FIFTEEN

Henry frowned and threw down his pencil. The phrases Kopecek had written in the margins of Henry's book were definitely in German, but the words made no sense, no matter how he translated them. Slipping his arms into his crutch cuffs, he rose and made his way from his study to the kitchen. Maybe a cup of tea would revive his tired brain.

He plugged in the electric kettle and set out the mug and spoon. After leaving his sister's house last night, the idea of a code written in the margins of his book proved too stimulating for sleep, and he'd worked on the translations until well after midnight. Rising at his usual six, he drove to the gym and swam laps, his mind still puzzling over the nonsense words. Unlike writer's block, which usually cleared up after a good night's sleep, the bright light of day hadn't brought any new revelations.

The click of the kettle coincided with the ring tone of his cell phone. He removed it from its waist clip and accepted the call on speaker phone. "Hello, Sissy."

"Dear brother, I have good news for you."

Henry poured the hot water into his cup, dipping his tea bag up and down. "Oh?"

"Violet's agreed to move into our guest room."

Hot water splashed over the cup's rim onto his hand, and Henry bit back a yelp. "Violet's going to live with you and Keith?"

"Yes, isn't it wonderful? Since her apartment was ransacked, she's been living in a hotel, and you know how tiring that can get. We have a lovely empty guest room, and she needs a place to stay. It all worked out for the best."

Henry refrained from asking what *best* that was, given Violet's belongings—and Rainer Kopecek's earthly things—had been vandalized beyond repair. With Sissy, he'd learned to smile and not ask too many questions. "That's very generous of you."

"What else could I do? She's a lovely young lady. Hold on a sec." Sissy's voice sounded muffled, her words indistinct, then she came back on the line. "She's coming over this afternoon, but there's a crisis at the store, something about a wrong order, so I'll be tied up there. I know you don't teach on Fridays. Would you pop over and let her in? I've left a spare key on the dining room table for her."

If it wasn't for the stress he heard in Sissy's voice, he would have sworn this was one of her matchmaking ploys. But somehow, the thought of spending more time with Violet didn't make him want to run in the opposite direction. "I could do that. What time will she be coming by?"

"That I don't know for sure, sometime after lunch." Sissy's voice accelerated. "Gotta go. Oh, I almost forgot. Keith and I have tickets to see the Phantom of the Opera revival at the Kennedy Center, so we won't be back until late." She hung up before he could ask what that had to do with anything, then realized what she had said. He stirred sugar into his tea and added a splash of cream. Dinner alone with Violet would definitely be more interesting than his usual Friday nights spent catching up on his reading.

∽

VIOLET RANG THE MADISONS' DOORBELL AT HALF PAST THREE. WITH A wintry mix drizzling on her bare head, the loss of her favorite winter hat irked her. Why the lining had to be ripped out was beyond her comprehension. She had spent weeks trying on hats before finding just the right slouchie beanie. Since fashions changed so quickly, she would have to start all over again. No one sold slouchie beanies anymore.

The door opened, and her greeting died on her lips when she saw Henry standing there. "Where's Sissy?" She blurted the words before stopping to think. Great. Now he would think she didn't want to see him. Which she did, probably more than she would admit.

Her greeting didn't seem to faze him because he smiled and stepped back to let her move past him into the warm house. "She got stuck at the store, some crisis or another, and asked me to come over."

"I see." Violet stood in the foyer, her meager belongings stuffed into a duffle bag slung over her shoulder, and waited while he shut the door.

When he turned back around, his eyes went to the umbrella she held like a cane. "They didn't destroy your umbrella?"

She glanced down at the old-fashioned instrument, the kind with the hooked handle and long shaft. "This isn't mine. I mean it is now, but it wasn't then."

His brow wrinkled.

"I'm making a muddle of this." She sighed. Nothing had gone her way in a very long time. At the dawn of the new year just a few short weeks ago, she thought her life had moved to the sunny side of the street. Lately, though, she realized that had been wishful thinking. Mr. Kopecek's death, the code in his book, her ransacked and destroyed apartment, and the upcoming anniversary spelled trouble in spades.

"If the umbrella's wet, you can open it to dry out in the laundry room."

She contemplated the accessory. "It's not. I couldn't get it to open. The mechanism must be jammed."

"Why don't I show you to your room, then you can tell me about the umbrella over a cup of something warm. Tea, coffee, or hot chocolate?"

She smiled. "Hot chocolate sounds wonderful."

He grinned back. "Good. You can hang your coat there." He pointed to a coat tree standing by the door. "Put your umbrella here." Another gesture indicated a canister already holding an assortment of colorful umbrellas. "Maybe after you're settled, we can fix the umbrella. The weatherman said on the evening news that you're going to need it this weekend."

After hanging her coat and slipping the umbrella into its place, she followed Henry down the hallway to a room near the back of the house. The sunny yellow walls, bright green curtains, and green-and-yellow plaid bedspread brightened her spirits. "What a delightful room."

Henry nodded. "Sissy has a way with making every room have its own personality. This one always reminded me of spring and daffodils."

Violet turned to him. "That's it exactly."

A blush stole up his cheeks, and he moved to the door. "I'll let you get settled and start the hot chocolate. There's a private bath-room on the left. Come into the kitchen when you're ready."

Violet watched him walk down the hallway, his crutches making a slight thumping noise on the hardwood floor. It must be difficult to have to always need assistance to get anyplace, but he seemed to handle it okay. She shrugged and moved to the dresser to unpack her few clothes. Her toiletries barely filled up one shelf in the vanity of the yellow-and-green bathroom. Sissy had a good eye for color. The touches weren't overwhelming but subtle and soothing.

She left the room, her cell phone tucked into the back pocket of her jeans, and found Henry in the kitchen pouring steaming water into mugs. The scent of chocolate drifted on the air, and she sucked in a deep breath. "Hmm. I love the smell of hot chocolate on a cold, wet day."

"My mom used to fix this on the first rainy day of the summer. It never got this cold in Central Africa, but we still enjoyed it."

Violet took the offered cup, wrapping her hands around it as if she could capture the warmth of Henry's memory. Her own childhood had too much coldness to bring pleasant thoughts. She shook her head in an effort to dislodge her mind from going down that path today.

"On the rare occasion we had marshmallows, Sissy and I used to have a marshmallow eating contest, trying to see who could stuff the most in our mouth at one time and still speak clear enough to be understood." Henry grinned. "I used to let her win every time just to see her cheeks puffed out like a chipmunk. What about you? Do you have any brothers or sisters?"

She stared into the dark brown swirls in her cup. "A brother." Better to not be specific. Less questions that way. "We weren't particularly close."

"Older brother?"

She nodded, her conscious twinging at the almost-lie. Technically, Patrick was older, but only by a few minutes. "We had, um, different interests."

He sipped his cocoa. "Sissy is two years older, but you'd think she was my mother the way she acts sometimes."

"How long have Sissy and Keith been married?" Violet took the opening to steer the conversation away from her background. It was better to not talk at all than to have to dance around the painful truth.

"Nearly four years." Henry frowned. "They want to start a family, but things haven't been moving along as quickly as they'd hoped."

A familiar ache in the pit of her stomach reminded Violet of her own hopes to have a family one day. Patrick's actions scuttled any chance of a long-term relationship. "Sometimes these things take time."

"If there's one thing I've learned over the years, it's that God's timing is not our timing. Let's relocate to the den. Would you mind bringing my cocoa?" Henry led the way into a cozy room off the kitchen and settled into a club chair. Violet set his mug down on the end table. "Thank you. We can make all the plans—and we should— but sometimes circumstances dictate a delay, a change, or a complete overhaul."

Violet sank onto a leather loveseat. "What changed for you?"

"These." He touched the cuff of a crutch.

Violet could have slapped herself for being inquisitive. Of course contracting polio would have changed his life. She started to speak, but he beat her to it.

"I don't mean the polio per se, although that did have a big impact on my mobility." He arranged the crutches on the floor beside the chair. "It's rather a long story, and one I don't tell very often." His brown eyes stared into hers, and she felt as if he caught a glimpse of the pain lurking beneath the surface, of the tension she had lived with for so many years, of the fear of being found out and harassed again.

She cleared her throat. "I'd love to hear, if you want to tell me. My life hasn't gone the way I thought it would, either. You sound as if you've come to peace with the changes." She glanced away. "I haven't, not entirely."

"If my story can be of help, I'm glad to tell it." He leaned back and closed his eyes for a few seconds. "I'd better start a bit further back than the summer I turned fourteen and caught polio as a birthday present. I was very athletic as a child. Sports came very easy to me. I didn't wear these glasses then. Running in Central Africa was heralded above all sports, mostly because everyone could do it and you didn't need any equipment but space, and Central Africa has that in abundance."

Violet kicked off her shoes and tucked her feet underneath her. Henry's words painted a vivid picture of the country in which he grew up. She could almost taste the dust as he described running across the barren land, the hot sun shining.

"Once a month, everyone gathered just outside the village for races, sprints, and distance. You ran by age group and then the winners of each group raced against each other in the final hundred-meter sprint. By the time I was ten, I could outrun nearly everyone in the village, even grown men."

"Did you want to be a runner then?"

"Not exactly. Some of the elders talked in hushed tones about bigger races, country-wide events, that maybe I would bring fame and good fortune to the village." He drank some more cocoa. "My father warned me not to put too much stock in rumors and my own inflated sense of my abilities, but what kid wants to listen to his father? Certainly not me, even as my heart told me he was right."

"What happened?" Violet wondered what it would be like to have such a relationship with one's parent that would trigger such a conversation.

"In June, I ran in my biggest race yet, a regional one. I knew if I did well, I might be considered for training when the next Olympic cycle came along. Central Africa didn't have much of a presence at the games, but the country did send several track and field representatives for the summer games. To make a long story shorter, I won the hundred-meter and two-hundred-meter sprints by a wide margin. My parents weren't convinced this was the right path for me, but I went home dreaming of gold medals."

She had a horrible suspicion she knew what was coming next. "Instead you got sick."

He nodded. "Yes, and it was the best thing that happened to me."

Violet shifted uncomfortably. Patrick's breakdown was the worst thing that happened to her, and she didn't think she would ever see a silver lining in the tragedy. But she couldn't help asking the question, "Why do you say that?"

CHAPTER

SIXTEEN

Henry had grappled with the same question about how polio could be viewed as a positive entrance into his life. Earlier in their conversation, he'd caught a glimpse of deep pain in Violet's green eyes. Now she kept her gaze focused on the rim of her mug, tracing the lip in an endless circle. A quick prayer formed in his mind that his words would be the ones she needed to hear because he suspected her past was even more complicated than his own.

He answered her question as honestly as he could. "I know it sounds strange, but I discovered a love of history as a teenager. I would lay in bed and read. I devoured biographies and histories, especially anything to do with the Soviet Union, which had only recently collapsed. The time I was getting treatment set the course for the rest of my life. If I hadn't been afflicted with polio, I wouldn't have slowed down enough to find out how much I loved history. That led to eventually getting my doctorate and teaching." He paused and sipped his hot chocolate, which had cooled considerably during his recitation.

"I'm glad it turned out well for you, but not every story of adversity has a happy ending." She put her hand over her mouth. "Oh, I didn't mean that your, uh,..."

He smiled as her cheeks blossomed into a soft pink. "I know it might not seem like your typical happy ending since I do need crutches to get around, but there was a time when no one thought I would ever walk again, so I don't mind these." He patted the aluminum poles by his side.

"Didn't you get vaccinated against polio?"

The question everyone generally asked when they found out his disability was caused by the polio virus. "I was, but Central Africa still experienced outbreaks of the virus on a regular basis. The doctors aren't quite sure why I contracted the virus while being fully vaccinated. They think my body didn't store the antibodies as well as it should have, therefore offering little protection against the disease." He shrugged. "Now, you were going to tell me about the umbrella and instead I've rambled on about my childhood."

Violet stared at him for a few seconds, then shook her head, tossing strands of reddish-brown hair onto her still flushed cheek. "The umbrella is Mr. Kopecek's. Apparently, he had lent it to one of the part-time aides right before he died. She had forgotten hers, and it was pouring rain, and staff has to park so far away from the home, she was sure to soak her new boots."

Henry raised his eyebrows. "That's quite an explanation."

She smiled. "The receptionist told me the entire story when she called to let me know the umbrella had been returned and that Ms. Siddons wanted me to come by immediately and take it, since I was Mr. Kopecek's heir."

Her voice caught on the last words, and he remembered how she had talked about Rainer Kopecek like a friend. "How long did you work at Happy Hills?"

"Around four years. I always cleaned Mr. Kopecek's room last so we could visit after I was finished. He read a lot and loved to talk about books. I wish whoever had broken into my apartment hadn't totally destroyed all his books. It was like losing him all over again. Now all I have left is his copy of your book and the umbrella." She paused, her fingers tightening around her mug. "It's funny, but he said something strange about rain in our last conversation."

Henry sat frozen in his chair, his mind racing with the possibility the solution he had been seeking was within his grasp. "*Schirm*."

"What?"

"*Schirm* means umbrella in German. That's the word Kopecek penciled in the margin of several pages of my book."

Their eyes met, and Henry could see the dawning comprehension in hers. Without a word, Violet rose and hurried out of the room, returning with the umbrella clutched in her hand. She sat down, laying the umbrella across her lap.

"What did Mr. Kopecek say exactly?" The feeling they were on the verge of a breakthrough welled up inside him as he gazed at her.

She frowned, wrinkling her nose in a way that made her seem as young as a teenager instead of a grown woman in her late twenties or early thirties. He was never good at guessing women's ages, not that he had much chance to do so. His students seemed younger and younger with each passing year.

"I didn't think it would be this hard to remember his exact words," she confessed. She closed her eyes for a full minute, then opened them. "I'm pretty sure it was, 'Verna loved to walk in the rain.'"

"Verna loved to walk in the rain." Henry's gaze strayed to the umbrella. "Did Mr. Kopecek talk about the weather a lot?"

"Oh no, not at all. In fact, we had a rule that neither one of us would even mention the weather unless it was out of the ordinary, like a snow shower in April or a seventy-degree day in winter." She toyed with the umbrella's shaft. "Which makes his comment about rain all the more extraordinary."

"What do you think he meant?"

Violet sighed. "I don't know what to think. In the space of a week, or rather less than a week, I've lost a good friend, been warned

83

about a wolf, found out I'm Mr. Kopecek's heir, had my apartment completely destroyed, and gotten fired from my job."

"You left out the part where you met a handsome stranger." As soon as the words left his mouth, he wanted to recall them. Now she'd think he was full of himself, and there went their budding relationship. But who was he kidding? She probably just felt sorry for him like all the women he met.

A smile crossed her face. "You're right. It wasn't such a bad week after all."

Her words hung in the air between them, and Henry couldn't help the wide smile stretching across his cheeks. Better steer the conversation back to safer waters. "If Mr. Kopecek didn't usually talk about the weather, and he mentioned rain, and you have his umbrella..." They both stared at the umbrella.

Then Violet laughed. "Surely we are not going to find a hidden mechanism that reveals a secret storage space with a clue. This is becoming rather like a 1930s film noir."

"When you put it that way, it does sound rather far-fetched." Henry tapped his fingers on the arm of the couch. "But then again, we didn't imagine those anonymous phone calls warning us not to wake a wolf."

Violet cocked her head. "What if we're going about this the wrong way?"

"What do you mean?"

"I'm not sure if I can explain it." She paused. "We're assuming Mr. Kopecek is a spy, right? That's what we're both thinking, with the cryptic notes in the margin and the rather scary phone calls."

"Not to mention your apartment being trashed." Henry expected her to agree with him and was surprised to see her shaking her head.

"I'm not sure we can attribute my apartment's destruction to Mr. Kopecek."

"Why not?"

She firmed her lips.. "For reasons I'd rather not say."

"Okay." Henry gazed at her profile, glimpsing a tear trembling on the edge of her lashes before she blinked it away. What kind of pain did those words hide?

"But back to Mr. Kopecek. What if he's not a spy but an ordinary person who's trying to hide something from other ordinary people?"

"I'm not sure what you mean." He was having trouble following her train of thought, mostly because he kept getting sidetracked by a pair of green eyes and silky hair that touched her cheek when she turned her head. His fingers itched to tuck the strand back in its place behind her ear.

She grimaced. "My mother always said I took the long way round to get to my point." She held up a hand as Henry started to speak. "No, let me try again. I think we're making this more complicated than it is. We don't need an umbrella after all. Maybe his words are the clue."

"How can his words be the clue?" Henry tried to think of what she meant but came up empty. "I told you, the notes in the margins of my book don't make any sense at all. It's like reading something Lewis Carroll wrote, all gobbledygook."

She leaned forward. "Exactly. The words are meaningless. Most would discount them as the mutterings of a delusional old man, right? Unless you have a way to decipher his meaning."

He caught some of her excitement, although he wasn't sure for what. "You're saying we have to break the code."

She nodded.

He shifted his position on the couch and reached down to massage his left leg as the muscles bunched together. "But how can we do that if we don't know what code he used?"

"Ah, but we do."

He stopped rubbing his leg. "We do?"

"Yes." She bounced a little in her chair. "I think Mr. Kopecek gave me the code key the last time we spoke."

Enlightenment dawned. It was so simple, it was brilliant. He said in unison with Violet, "Verna loved to walk in the rain."

CHAPTER
SEVENTEEN

Henry slung his messenger bag over his head, adjusting the strap to avoid banging the bag against his crutches. The slight dampness in the cold March air made his legs ache. Standing to lecture during his world history graduate course after lunch had only exacerbated the discomfort. Now at the end of the day, he only wanted a hot cup of tea and a heating pad on his legs. He was nearly to his front door when he saw the figure huddled in the tiny alcove. At his approach, the figure straightened, and he saw with relief Violet's pink cheeks and red nose.

"What are you doing here?" Not quite the greeting he had wanted to give, even if she was the last person he expected to see on his doorstep. Yet another example of why he hadn't found someone.

"I'm sorry. I should have called first. You probably have plans, and I'm in the way." Her words came out in a rush, and she pushed away from the wall to stand in front of him. "Sissy gave me your address, and here I am."

"No, I mean, I don't have plans. You just caught me by surprise." Henry shifted his weight, and her eyes widened.

"Oh, I'm keeping you standing out here in the cold." She pushed back her hair, which had fallen across her face, and moved back to give him access to the door.

He maneuvered his crutches and inserted the key, pushing the door open and crossing the threshold. "Come on in." He moved down the hall and heard the front door close behind him. A quick glance over his shoulder indicated she was removing her coat. "You can hang your coat on the rack."

Without waiting to see if she had done so, he walked down the hall to the open kitchen with a small den to one side. Balancing against the easy chair, he winced as leg muscles tightened. Finally divested of his coat and bag, he sank into the chair and pushed back, elevating his legs and closing his eyes. Something covered his legs, and he popped his eyes open to see Violet tucking the heating pad around his lower limbs.

"I saw it beside your chair and thought it might help ease the pain in your legs." She adjusted the temperature on the pad and warmth spread over his lower limbs.

"Thank you." He sighed. "You have a nice bedside manner."

"I picked up a few tips working at Happy Hills, even though I only cleaned rooms. I put the water on for tea." She touched his shoulder and moved into the kitchen.

He watched her measure the loose-leaf tea into the ball and place it into the teapot, her movements deft. "Why did you work at Happy Hills?"

Her hands stilled for a second before she turned to face him. "I liked the residents."

Frowning, he shook his head. "That's not what I meant. Why did you do the job you did? Not that there's anything wrong with cleaning rooms." He ran a hand through his hair. "I'm making a mess of things as usual."

She laughed, and the sound warmed his heart. "No, you're not. You're right, you know. That job was not utilizing my skills, but at the time, I didn't want to think, so it was perfect." She poured the hot water into the teapot. "If I hadn't, I wouldn't have met Mr. Kopecek—or you."

Henry's mouth went dry at the thought of never having met this vibrant woman for whom he was beginning to care. He accepted the cup of tea she handed him before seating herself on the nearby chair.

Violet balanced the teacup and saucer on her knee. "I felt like I needed a different set of walls to look at for a while."

"I think Sissy and Keith like having you there." He sipped his tea. She had put in just the right amount of sugar and cream, making the Earl Grey Imperial blend perfect, at least to his taste.

"They've been most gracious, but still, it's hard to live in someone else's house, especially when such strange things are happening."

"I understand." He wanted to squeeze her hand and tell her she was safe with him, but who was he kidding? How could he protect her when he could barely stand without assistance? Better leave the knight-in-shining-armor stuff to someone else.

Their eyes met, and he was once again struck by how green hers were. There was something about her that drew him in, that made him want to hold her and whisper everything would be okay. The teacup nearly slipped from his suddenly nerveless fingers, and the moment shattered. Or rather, he told himself sternly, his moment did. He had no way of knowing whether she was attracted to him or just felt sorry for him like so many women he met did. For the first time in a long time, he wanted to be a whole man, one who didn't have to question every look and wonder if it was pity-driven or sincere.

Before he could change the subject, the doorbell pealed. She turned to him, her eyebrows raised in question. "Are you expecting someone"

The grandfather clock in the hallway struck six. "No."

The bell sounded again, longer this time, as if the person on the stoop held it down for several seconds. He started to push up, wincing as his leg muscles protested. The bell pealed again. "Would you mind answering the door?"

"Not at all." She rose and moved rapidly through the kitchen as the persistent caller buzzed a fourth time.

He listened to her footsteps clicking on the hardwood floors, then heard the sound of the front door opening and closing a few minutes later. She appeared shortly after in the kitchen, a floral delivery box in her hands and a smile on her face. "I must say, it isn't every day that a man receives flowers. Do you have a secret admirer, Dr. Silverton?"

He reached for his crutches. "I have no idea."

"Oh, don't get up. There's usually a vase with it." She detached a small card from the outside of the box and carried to him. "Here, you read the message while I attend to the flowers."

He opened the envelope. *Things are not what they seem.* No signature. He gazed at Violet, who had opened the box and pulled out the square vase. "You guessed the anonymous part right."

"Maybe it's one of your students with a crush on you." She picked up the flowers encased in colored plastic and placed them on the counter. "Where are your kitchen scissors?"

He told her, then read the message aloud. "What do you think that means?"

She shrugged. "I have no idea." The scissors sliced through the plastic, and she lifted out the bouquet. Henry saw a riot of white, orange, and yellow blossoms in a mix of varieties that seemed rather out of place together. He picked out a yellow carnation but didn't know the other two kinds. Looking from the flowers to her face, he saw the color drain from her cheeks.

Henry started to push himself up from his chair as she crumpled to the kitchen floor, scattering flowers all around like a Shakespearean death scene.

EIGHTEEN

H enry grabbed his crutches and surged to his feet, dropping the card on the floor. He bit back a curse as the left crutch tangled with the coffee table leg and nearly sent him tumbling onto the couch.

"Violet? Are you okay?" Stupid thing to say, but he had to say something. Rounding the counter, he stared down at her still form lying amidst the orange, yellow, and white blossoms. For a split second, he stood there, unsure of how best to help her without slipping on the petals and falling on top of her.

Dropping his left crutch to the floor with a clatter, he gripped the counter with his hand and eased himself onto the floor, wincing as his knees encountered the flower stems. He reached over and brushed her hair from her face.

"Violet?" Putting aside his other crutch, he leaned forward and shook her shoulders. Maybe he should call 911. His cell phone lay on the counter across the room next to his keys while the handset rested nearby. To reach it, he would have to step over and around her still form. Not a challenge to any able-bodied man, but for him, it might as well have been a minefield of explosives. Flowers covered nearly every inch of floor space between him and the target area.

"Henry?"

He breathed a quick prayer of thankfulness and touched her hand as her eyes fluttered open. "Does anything hurt?"

"Hurt?" She started to push herself to a seated position but stopped when her fingers touched petals. "The flowers." She closed her eyes, and a tear squeezed out of one corner. "It wasn't a bad dream?"

"No. You fainted, I think. Or passed out. Not sure which. Did you hit your head?" He wasn't sure why flowers bothered her so much, making a mental note never to give her a bouquet, not that he would have any reason to send her flowers.

"My head hurts a little, so I must have bumped it." She reached behind her hair and touched the back of her head. "I don't feel a lump, though."

"Let me check." He gently pushed his fingers through her hair and probed the back of her head. The strands of her hair tangled around his fingers, the silkiness of it mesmerizing his senses. He wouldn't soon forget the feel of her cool skin beneath his fingertips or the subtle scent of shampoo overlaying the flowers. She turned her head slightly, and he realized he had been caressing her head. Gently extracting the tresses from his fingers, he withdrew his hand.

"I didn't feel anything." That was an understatement. He felt something, just not a bump on the back of her head. A quick glance at her face showed only a profile, her focus apparently not on him but on the flowers still scattered on the floor. "But I can take you to the emergency room if you'd like to get checked out."

She eased into a seated position, pushing the buds out of the way. "I think I'm okay, just a headache." She sighed. "Do you have any ibuprofen?"

"I think there's some in my medicine cabinet." He paused on his knees beside her. "Are you really okay? I don't know much about fainting, but usually there's a trigger."

~

VIOLET TURNED HER FACE TO THE FLOWERS AT HER KNEES. HER HEAD tingled from the gentle pressure of his fingers. For a moment, she had almost closed her eyes and leaned into his touch, but she squelched that desire, not wanting to embarrass him with her obvious misinterpretation of his kindness.

Reaching for a crushed carnation, she twirled the yellow flower in her hand. It couldn't be a coincidence this particular combination of flowers had arrived at Henry's house with a cryptic card. Someone knew and was taunting her with that knowledge. The silence stretched between them as she debated what to tell him. She was tired of being alone, tired of keeping others at a distance, but she was wary of letting this interesting, handsome man into her life. The last time she had tried that, it had not gone well at all.

He cocked his head and eyed her as if she were dazed. She had to say something. "The bouquet reminded me of something deeply painful." She gathered the flowers on the floor.

He placed his hand over hers, stilling her movements, while his other hand reached over and tipped her chin up so that her eyes met his. The compassion brought tears to her eyes, and she blinked rapidly to keep them from spilling down her cheeks. "If you want to talk, I've been told I'm a good listener."

She nodded at the unspoken invitation to unburden herself. Clearing her throat, she merely said, "Thank you. I, um, it's not something I'm ready to talk about."

His fingers swept the edge of her jaw as he removed his hand, and she nearly caught it in hers to press it against her cheek. This man with his warm brown eyes and gentle and generous spirit, tugged at her heart more than anyone had in a long time. But opening her own heart to him meant divulging her past, and that she couldn't risk. She couldn't bear to have him look at her with contempt and horror.

"I'll get you some ibuprofen." He used the counter to leverage

93

himself up. Then after picking up his crutches, he moved down the hallway.

Violet bit her lip to keep from asking him not to go, reminding herself that she needed to extract herself from his life before she got in too deep. She continued to pick up the flowers, mechanically placing them into some semblance of order. Rising, she found the glass vase included in the delivery, filled it with water, and jammed in the stems.

He stood in the doorway, a pill bottle in his hand. "Here. I wasn't sure if you wanted one or two."

She moved toward him and took the proffered bottle. "I think one will be enough."

"The glasses are to the right of the sink."

She extracted an ibuprofen pill and found a glass. Her hand shook a little as she turned on the tap to fill it halfway with water. The need to tell him everything coursed through her body, but she couldn't give in.

Not now.

Not ever.

Closing her eyes, she choked back a sob. *Get a hold of yourself.*

"Violet?"

She opened her eyes, popped the pill into her mouth, and took a long drink of water. "I'm okay." She'd meant her voice to sound firm, but instead it wavered, uncertainty laced through its tone. Setting the glass down with a crack, she gripped the countertop with both hands, every fiber fighting the urge to give in to the nearly over-whelming desire to be honest with this man.

"Are you sure?" His voice was pitched softly. He had moved across the kitchen and now stood beside her, close enough that if she turned her head, she would encounter the pity in his eyes. At least she thought that would be the emotion, for what else could it be but empathy? No man had ever viewed her with anything else, not after what had happened.

"Yes." Her composure slipped at the expression on his face. Not pity, not compassion, but something else, something she didn't recognize.

He raised his hand, and she watched it as if viewing a film. His eyes never left hers as his fingers pushed back a lock of hair from her cheek. "You have such beautiful hair."

Violet sucked in a breath as her heartbeat quickened and butterflies flew around in her stomach. "Thank you." Her words exhaled on a whisper as his hand massaged the back of her neck. She should pull back to break the gossamer thread drawing them ever closer. Instead, she shifted toward him.

"Violet." Her name on his lips sounded sweeter than honey. "I—"

She placed her fingers on his mouth to stop the words, then removed her hand. "I should go." She should but she didn't want to. "I'm not who you think I am."

"I think you are a very courageous, honest, and compassionate woman." He tugged her closer, and her resistance weakened at the passion sparking in his eyes.

She tried once more to make him understand. "But there are things about me, about my past, I can't tell you."

At her words, he paused, his eyes serious as they scanned her face. "Are you running from the police?"

"No."

"Have you broken the law?"

She shook her head.

"Does this past thing—is it something you did or something you feel responsible for allowing to happen?"

She bit back a gasp at his perception. "I should have known, should have stopped it."

He cradled her cheek, his eyes steady on hers. "We are not responsible for another's actions. If I've learned anything from studying history, it's that." His thumb rubbed her jaw, sending tingles down her spine. "Now, I don't think I can wait any longer."

She yanked her thoughts back to the conversation. "For what?"

"To kiss you."

CHAPTER

NINETEEN

"Kiss me?" Violet breathed out the words in a whisper. It had been much too long since a man had wanted to kiss her. The sensible part of her shouted at her. *Danger! Flee! Now!* But the emptiness in her heart overrode the warning. She wanted to feel cherished, to experience some semblance of normality and affection.

Henry slid his hand from her cheek to intertwine his fingers in her hair. With a soft sigh, she focused on his lips as they moved closer to hers. Yes, it was only a simple kiss—she wasn't deluding herself into thinking it would solve all of her problems—but it would soothe her battered soul and perhaps heal a bit of the brokenness that hid inside the closed-off part of her heart. She closed her eyes and leaned into him as his mouth captured hers. As a tingling sensation raced through her entire body, her breath caught in her throat.

Oh, how wrong she had been. There was nothing simple about his kiss. She had never been kissed so thoroughly by a man. His fingers splayed at the back of her neck, angling her head to the side to fit his lips more closely on hers, yet she sensed that he held himself back in some part, as if knowing intuitively that to press her any farther would be too much, too soon.

As the kiss deepened, she slid her hands up his chest, one hand stopping at his collarbone while the other continued around to his neck. His hair brushed his shirt collar, and she gave into the urge to touch it. As her fingers gently rubbed the base of his neck and flicked through his hair, Henry groaned and lifted his head to rest his forehead against hers, his breath coming in chopping waves.

"I, uh, well." His words tumbled out in a jumble.

She smiled, moving her hand from his neck to rest lightly on the pulse at his throat, which jumped like a jackhammer under her fingers.

He blew out a breath. "I had no idea, I mean, you. I can't think clearly."

"Me, either." She closed her eyes briefly to stop dwelling on the sensation of his lips against hers and the implications such a kiss had on their relationship. What exactly their relationship was would have to be a conversation for another day. Right now, she had trouble remembering her name.

"Violet." He brushed a strand of hair out of her eyes, and she nearly gasped at his tenderness. Had anyone ever viewed at her like that? Her parents had always preferred her brother over her. Even her beloved Granny had distributed more tough love than tender moments. She suspected her brother had quashed any attempts by boys to date her, although she never had any hard evidence.

She pulled back slightly, creating more distance but not breaking the spell completely. "I should go." She glanced behind him at built-in digital clock on the stove. "It's nearly six-thirty already."

"What about dinner? I could whip something up for us here, or we could order takeout." He seemed so hopeful that Violet's chest tightened. She hated to disappoint him, but she needed to go to Sissy's and think, something she couldn't do with him nearby. In the same room with him, her thoughts would center on kissing him again.

Instead, she smiled to soften her rejection. "Could I have a rain check on dinner? It's been a long day."

He nodded and stepped back. "I have to teach tomorrow, and it's my in-office day, so I'll be tied up until dinnertime. How about if I text you in the afternoon?"

"Sounds good." As she turned to leave, her eyes caught sight of the flowers crammed into the vase. She picked up her bag and turned to wave at him. "I can let myself out. See you tomorrow."

He leaned against the counter, his hands braced on either side of him. "Until tomorrow."

She turned quickly before the sexy look in his eyes made her go against her judgment and stay for dinner. Better to focus on the implications of those flowers than her budding relationship with this handsome man, a relationship becoming more tangled by the minute.

HENRY HUMMED AS HE CONTEMPLATED HIS LECTURE NOTES ON THE BERLIN Airlift of 1948, but his thoughts kept straying to the kiss he'd shared with Violet last night. The taste of her lips lingered on his even after a morning cup of tea. The mysterious flower delivery and card couldn't completely dampen his joy, although her reaction to the flowers and her mysterious allusion to her past troubled him. As cryptic messages went, *Things are not what they seem* was fairly standard, more like something found in an old-fashioned detective novel than real life. The anonymous phone calls he and Violet had received flashed to mind. Maybe the same person was trying to scare them from figuring out what Kopecek had written in the book, but that made no sense either. No one else knew about the jottings.

He returned his attention to the notes when a knock at the door broke his concentration again. "Come in."

Juan Delores poked his head inside the room. "Hey, Dr. Silverton. You wanted to see me?"

Henry smiled and motioned to the chair in front of his desk. Juan slung his backpack on the floor and slouched into the chair.

"Thanks for coming by." Last semester, the student had taken his graduate-level Cold War Secrets class about Soviet and U.S. espionage in the 1960s, and Henry had found the young man knowledgeable and eager to learn. "Your master's thesis has something to do with cryptology, right?"

Juan nodded. "Yeah, it's about how modern-day code breakers are using computers to crack secret messages."

"Then I think you're just the person who can help me."

Juan sat up. "You need some help with a code?"

"I think it's a code, but I'm not one hundred percent sure." Henry handed over a photocopied sheet of one of the pages with Kopecek's strange notations and a page with his translation. He tamped down the feeling he shouldn't involve someone else, not with the anonymous phone calls he and Violet had received.

What spurred him to ask Juan to help was Henry's ineptness at code breaking. He'd tried it as a grad student himself, but while he could understand how the Soviets and the United States used codes during the Cold War, deciphering made his head boggle. If he and Violet were ever to find out if Kopecek had even written notes in code, they needed outside help. Official channels would only slow things down and alert the wrong people. Better to keep it as quiet as possible. "The writer wrote in German, and I translated it into English, but either way, the words don't make any sense at all."

Juan studied the German, then the English. "I've been working on codes since I was a kid but never had a chance to take first crack at breaking a real one."

"This could be a wild goose chase and the words only the ramblings of an old man," Henry warned. "Some of his other notations make perfect sense in both German and English."

"If some of what he wrote is clear but these phrases aren't, he could have been writing in code." Juan continued looking at the pages. "I wonder what the key is."

"I think I can help you with that," Henry said. "It's probably, 'Verna loved to walk in the rain.'"

Juan repeated the phrase, his fingers tapping out a rhythm on his knee. "How old do you think the writer was?"

Henry recalled what Violet had said about Kopecek. "In his eighties."

"Then I bet he probably would have used either a symmetric-key cryptograph or a substitution-permutation network."

Henry frowned, his mind sifting through possibilities. He didn't know much about the actual code-breaking work, but he was familiar with the basic ways messages were encoded during the Cold War. "I'd lean more toward the substitution-permutation network, as he most likely learned it as a young man in Eastern Europe."

Juan jounced his leg up and down. "Then it shouldn't be too hard to figure it out, that is, if the key is what you think it is." He folded up the papers and shoved them into his backpack. "This will be a good test for a program I've created to use phrases to decipher other meanings for the coded words. I've been running known codes through the program with success, but the real test will be with an uncoded message and key."

"How long will the program take to run the possibilities?"

"I should have something tomorrow or the day after, depending on how many permutations the phrase creates with the words." Juan stood, slinging the backpack over his shoulder. "Oh wait, the original code is in German, right?"

"That was his first language."

"Ah, then I'm going to need the key phrase in German, too. Using English to break a German code would produce something incomprehensible." He smiled. "At least I think it would. Makes more sense to have both in German."

"Good thinking. It's *Verna liebte, zu Fuß in der regen.*"

"Could you write that down? I'm sure to misspell it."

Henry jotted it down on a piece of paper and handed it to him, keeping his voice as causal as possible when he added, "By the way, keep this a secret, would you?"

Juan winked and lowered his voice. "Of course. Wouldn't want the enemy to find out what we're up to." With a wave, the student left the office.

Henry stacked his notes and slid them into his portfolio, then placed it in his messenger bag. Twenty minutes to get to the lecture hall, and he would barely make it in time despite the closeness of the other building to his office. He picked up his crutches. At least today he had sweet memories of Violet's kiss to accompany him on the journey.

CHAPTER

TWENTY

"Senator Iris Morrison has served for three terms as an independent senator from Wisconsin. She has proven herself to be a woman of integrity and wisdom, navigating the tricky waters of negotiation with grace." President Bradley Myers smiled as he scanned the press room of the White House.

Iris stood beside him, a fixed smile of her own on her face while her mind raced and her eyes scanned the crowd, noting that all the major news agencies had sent representatives to cover her nomination announcement. In the back of her mind, The Wolf's silence nibbled at her pleasure in the moment. The last thing she wanted was for him to scuttle her nomination. She had worked too long and hard for this stepping stone to the White House. Her mother always said she was a girl who got what she wanted, and by Jove, she'd make it to the very top, as the first woman president. Now she turned to shake the president's hand as he introduced her as his nomination for secretary of state.

Later, as she rode in a taxi with her press secretary and chief of staff from the White House back to the Russell Senate Office Building, Iris answered her smartphone without glancing at caller ID. "Hello?"

"You looked lovely up there beside the president."

Iris turned her head and discretely glanced at her two staffers with their heads bowed over their phones. "Thank you."

"Just be careful you don't overreach yourself."

Iris frowned and lowered her voice. "You're the one who's overreaching, stirring up the past."

The Wolf replied in an even softer tone. "Remember you have much to lose, Madame Secretary. Almost as much as I do."

Iris forced a chuckle. "I haven't been approved by Congress, yet."

"Then you wouldn't want to jeopardize that now, would you?" The Wolf's voice dropped even lower.

"You seem to forget what I know."

"Knowledge is one thing, proof another."

"My mother raised me to be a smart woman." Iris paused and snuck another look at the two staffers who appeared oblivious to her conversation. "And as a smart woman, I make sure I have all my ducks in a row."

"Don't threaten me," The Wolf hissed, his anger reaching across the airwaves and driving a stake of fear into her heart. "You have no idea how long my arms can reach."

Iris tightened her grip on the phone and kept her voice level and light with effort. "Oh, I have fond memories of your embrace, darling. Pillow talk and all that is so sweet, don't you think? I wonder how it would sound after all these years."

The caller's swift intake of breath made her smile. Good. He needed to know she was not a woman to be trifled with. "The proof is in a very safe and secure place. Don't bother looking for it, as you'll never find it." She had taken more precautions than usual in hiding the evidence. "Now, it's been so nice chatting with you, but I must go." She ended the call as the cab halted in front of her office building. Iris climbed the steps, accepting congratulations from fellow senators and staffers alike, but her mind stayed on the conversation with The Wolf. She might have won this skirmish, but she had no doubts the next battle would be more fierce and perhaps more deadly.

THE LUNCH CROWD HAD THINNED IN PANERA, LEAVING PLENTY OF EMPTY seats. Violet stirred sugar into her hot tea and snapped on the lid. Sliding into a booth, she plunked down her shoulder bag and placed her cup on the table. She had spent the morning arguing on the phone with her insurance company to file her claim for the damage done to her possessions. After emailing yet another copy of the police report and haggling over the replacement cost of her furniture, the customer service representative finally signed off on the claim, promising the money would be transferred to her account within ten business days.

Sighing, she popped off the plastic lid to cool down the liquid. A nagging ache behind her eyes reminded her of how little sleep she'd had last night as thoughts of Henry and his kiss kept her awake long after midnight. Granted, it had been a long time since a man had pressed his lips to hers, but she couldn't ever recall a kiss that nearly curled her toes. For a few precious moments, she had felt safe and secure, that her future might be brighter than her past. When he pulled back, his brown eyes dark with passion, she panicked and fled with a jumble of words and gestures. On her way out of the kitchen, she threw a look over her shoulder to see him standing in the same spot, a slight smile on his face as if he knew exactly why she rushed out of his house.

Her phone buzzed, signaling an incoming text. She glanced down, glad for the distraction. Henry's number blinked on the screen and her thumb hovered over the read text button for a split second before she pulled up the message.

Where are you?

His refusal to use common texting abbreviations endeared him even more to her. She quickly replied.

Panera drinking tea. U?

Office, grading papers. Dinner tonight?

Violet hesitated. She shouldn't see him, not after their kiss, but she liked him. Really liked him, more than anyone else she'd ever met. If she accepted, she would be committing herself to sharing her past with him. Maybe not tonight, but soon. He deserved to know the worst of her sooner rather than later. But tonight, she would enjoy sharing a meal with a handsome, articulate man.

Sure. Where?

How about the Carlyle Grand in South Arlington?

Love the place! Time?

It's been a long day. Could you come in half an hour?

She checked her watch. Five o'clock. An early night appealed to her as well.

Sounds good. Bye!

She clicked off and took a sip of her cooled tea. Too bad she didn't have time for another stop at Sissy's dress shop to find something a little flirtier than her slacks and sweater. Violet grabbed her bag and tossed the cup into the trashcan. As she headed to the door, an employee approached her with a folded note in his hand.

"Miss? You left this on the table."

Violet automatically reached for the slip of paper, even as she started to say she hadn't left anything. The employee nodded at her and scurried behind the counter to greet new customers. Shrugging, she slipped out of the door and walked to her car. After starting the engine and buckling up, she unfolded the note. Stark, black letters jumped off the page, forming words she could barely comprehend.

Did you enjoy the flowers?

CHAPTER
TWENTY-ONE

A waiter paused by the table, but Henry waved him off. Time enough to order once Violet arrived. If she arrived. Henry tapped his fingers in a mindless rhythm on the table's shiny surface as he waited for her. A quick check of his watch showed that only a minute had crept by since the last time he'd checked. It wasn't like her to be twenty minutes late, not without texting or calling. At least he didn't think she was someone who breezed in ten minutes past an agreed-upon meeting time on a regular basis.

He couldn't wait to see her, and her response to his text had seemed to indicate she wanted to see him, but one couldn't tell from mere words on a screen whether the response was serious or maybe a polite way to brush him off. When she left so quickly after their kiss last night, he had chalked it up to being overwhelmed by the emotions swirling around his kitchen like spices in an Indian curry. He'd certainly been blindsided by the heat of the passion that had seized him when their lips touched. Not one with much experience in kissing, Henry hoped to enjoy the kiss. What he hadn't anticipated was the explosion of desire stirring throughout his entire frame.

He pushed back his sleeve to check the time again. Another five minutes had crept by while he ruminated on last night.

A shadow fell over the table. Violet stood there, her face flushed. Words spilled out even before she slid into the bench seat across from him.

"I'm so sorry I'm late. I, uh..." Tears sprang to her eyes.

"Violet? What's wrong?" He reached across the table to hold her hands but got air instead as she reached into her handbag.

"This." She clutched a piece of paper. "I was leaving Panera right after we texted, and an employee came up to me, saying I'd left this on the table." She extended the slip across the table, then folded her hands together so tightly her knuckles turn white. "Please read it."

Henry opened the paper and read the words printed in black block lettering. *Did you enjoy the flowers?* Glancing up at Violet, he tried to make sense of the note. "I don't understand. Where did you get this?"

"Someone put it there for me. Someone followed me to Panera." She bit her lip. "For all I know, someone followed me here too." She hunched her shoulders as if trying to disappear into the booth's cushion.

"Followed you? Why would someone follow you to ask about flowers?" It didn't make any sense.

"Because the flowers you got yesterday meant nothing to you, but they meant everything to me." She studied the tabletop. "Whoever sent the flowers was sending a message to me through you."

He frowned. The image of Violet's white face before she fainted yesterday evening came to his mind as he reread the note. Tonight, her eyes shone with unshed tears and, hidden in their depths, fear. "I think you need to tell me about the flowers."

She shook her head. "I don't want to get you involved."

He reached across the table to encase her trembling hands in his. "I'm already involved. The flowers were delivered to my house." He started to remind her of the anonymous phone calls they each had received but one look at Violet's pallid face kept the words unspoken.

"There's still time, if we, if I—"

A waiter stopped at their table. Henry nearly shouted at the man to go away, but the waiter appeared oblivious to the tension roiling in the booth.

"Hi, my name is Tom, and I'll be your server." Tom smiled at them both. "May I start you off with something from the bar?"

Henry made a split-second decision. This wasn't the place for a serious discussion. "I'm sorry, but we've changed our minds."

Tom's smile faltered. "Changed your minds?"

Henry slid to the edge of the booth and pulled his crutches out. Tom stepped back as Henry swung himself to his feet. "Yes, we have to leave. She's not feeling well." Indeed, Violet did have a sickly cast to her cheeks and her entire body pulsed with repressed tears.

Tom moved even farther from the table. "I'm sorry to hear that. I hope you'll dine with us again soon."

Henry held out a hand to Violet. "Shall we go?"

She nodded and took his hand, allowing him to assist her out of the booth. He wanted to tuck her hand close to him, but he needed both of his to use his crutches. She followed him out of the restaurant and across the street to the parking deck.

"Wait, I parked in the other garage." She pointed over her shoulder to the garage on the opposite corner.

"I'm right here." He nodded toward his SUV in the first handicapped slot. "Let me drive you to your car." He peered closely at her. "In fact, I'm not sure you should drive. Your hands are shaking."

"I can't leave my car here overnight. I'll be okay." Her voice cracked. "Where are we going?"

The confusion and pain in her eyes tore at his heart. "I don't think you're in the mood for company, so Sissy and Keith's place is out. I'm not sure my place is a good idea, either." He mentally ran through a list of possibilities. "Let's get in my car, and I'll make a call to a friend who might have a good solution, then I'll drive you to your car."

~

VIOLET STARTED THE ENGINE OF HER CAR, THEN BUCKLED HER SEAT BELT. SHE waved over her shoulder to let Henry know she was ready to follow him to Gunther Richter's house in Great Falls. Henry's friend had invited them to have dinner with him at his house. He had assured her it would be safe, as Gunther was in the security business. It was as good a place as any to spill her secrets, but now that she had some distance from receiving the note, she wasn't sure she could tell Henry the truth. Maybe she should share only part of the story.

Her frazzled nerves had been scraped raw by the tension pulsating through her body at the thought someone out there was deliberately taunting her about the past. Above all was the thought that this identity she had painstakingly created for herself had all been for naught and might come unraveled at any time. She wasn't sure she could start over again. Then there was Henry to consider. Henry, who had become very dear to her in such a short time. Would she be able to leave him behind as well? Maybe it was time to face her past and stop running away from it.

She followed Henry onto I-395 North toward Washington, DC. Keeping within sight of Henry's black SUV took all of her concentration in the rush hour traffic. While he'd texted her the address for her phone's GPS, she still didn't want to lose him. A mile or so later, he exited onto Washington Boulevard. Soon he merged onto the George Washington Parkway. Dusk settled over the Potomac River as the road hugged its curves to the left of her. She flicked on her lights in the gloom, suppressing a shiver of apprehension. *Stop seeing ghosts behind every headlight.*

She should be coming up with a plan of how to tell Henry about Patrick. Maybe she could say the flowers reminded her of her brother, who had been sick. True, but not in the way Henry would interpret it, which would cause problems later when he found out the whole truth. She sighed as a dirt-splattered pickup truck inserted itself between her and Henry. Oh, bother. She should have paid closer attention and not let so much distance grow between their cars. In the growing darkness, she squinted to make sure Henry wouldn't exit without her knowing it. He had said they would take the parkway to I-495 before hopping on Georgetown Pike, but she hadn't driven this way in a while and didn't want to miss the exit.

The same pickup swerved into the left lane, accelerating past Henry's Ford Explorer before darting back in front of his SUV. She gripped the steering wheel as the truck hit its brakes and Henry's brake lights came on as well. Tapping her own brakes, the truck move into the left lane and slowed down until it ran parallel with Henry's car.

Something about the way the driver of the pickup was acting made her pay closer attention. She mashed down on the pedal and edged closer to the pickup to read the license plate. One of the charms of the GW parkway was its lack of streetlights, but that also hampered her visual of the license plate, which had a coating of mud like the truck's tailgate.

She couldn't shake an impending sense of doom. Maybe she should get her phone and call the police to report the erratic driver, but she didn't want to take her attention off the road for even an instant.

The truck picked up speed, zooming past Henry's SUV before suddenly changing lanes. Violet screamed as the pickup's tailgate clipped the front left-hand side of Henry's SUV, sending it spinning into the path of her car.

CHAPTER

TWENTY-TWO

Violet hit the brakes and jerked the steering wheel to the right in a desperate attempt to avoid hitting Henry's SUV but couldn't prevent the impact. She slammed her eyes shut as the driver's side of her car crunched into the passenger's side of his vehicle. The force of the crash threw her forward, then back against the seat as the airbag deployed. Another vehicle clipped the tail of her car as it twisted away from Henry's SUV. The sound of metal on metal rent the air as the initial collision triggered a chain reaction in the heavy traffic. She managed to bring her car to a shuddering halt half on the narrow shoulder of the parkway and half in the brambles edging the gravel.

For a moment, Violet stayed perfectly still, her head aching and her shoulder throbbing from the pressure of the locked seat belt. She tentatively moved each of her limbs separately. Nothing seemed to be broken. Thoughts of Henry drove her to fumble to release her seat belt. As her fingers closed over the release button, she strained to see through her windshield—miraculously intact but cracked. However, the crash had aligned her car perpendicular to the road, and she couldn't see his SUV.

One push against her door, and she realized exiting that way would be impossible. Fear for Henry propelled her over the console to the passenger's door, which opened easily. Stumbling into the brush but away from the crawling traffic, she spotted his vehicle a few paces ahead in the right lane, steam rising from beneath its mangled hood. She braced her hand alongside her car as she picked her way through the undergrowth of thorny weeds that grabbed at her legs.

"Miss?" A male voice sliced through the night amidst the jumble of distant sirens, other voices, and car motors.

"Yes?" Violet half-turned to see the man, now a shadowy form on the other side of her car.

"Are you okay?" The man moved toward her.

"I think so." She put a shaking hand to her brow, swiping at her eyes to clear them. Maybe it had started to drizzle, but she had more important things to think about than a wet face. "But I have to check on my friend in the SUV in front of me." Violet resumed picking her way to Henry, which now rested a good fifty feet from her own.

"You're lucky to be alive." While the words sounded right, a hint of something else, something sinister in his voice, halted her in her tracks.

Turning, she strained to see him clearly, her heart thudding in her chest. "What do you mean?"

The man stepped around the hood of her car and stopped a few feet away, his features obscured by the headlights of cars passing behind him. "Watch that your luck doesn't run out." Then he turned and melted into the darkness as an ambulance screamed up to Henry's vehicle and a fire truck blocked off another lane of traffic.

Violet shuddered. No time to think about his words, not with Henry probably hurt, maybe even... No, she wouldn't think the worst. She broke into a halting run to his car as the EMTs arrived at the driver's side door. "Henry!"

A few feet from the car, a firefighter threw out an arm to stop her progress. "You have to stay back."

She stood on her tiptoes to peer over his bulk. "But that's my friend." She brushed sticky tears from her cheek. Another ambulance roared up, its flashing lights momentarily blinding her.

"Were you in the accident?" The firefighter dropped his hand and waved to the newly arrived EMTs. "Over here! Are you hurt?"

Violet swatted away the fireman's question with an impatient flick of her hand and craned her neck. Henry sat in the driver's seat talking to two EMTs. He was alive. Relief rushed through her, and her knees nearly buckled as the tension whooshed out of her. A strong hand under her arm kept her upright.

The EMT kept one hand on her elbow as she bent to place her case on the ground. "Were you in the accident?"

She nodded at the young woman, then focused again on Henry. "I was following my friend." She pointed to the SUV. "Do you know if he's all right? He's talking, but he's not getting out of the car."

"They'll make sure he's okay. It's my job to make sure you're not hurt. What's your name?"

Violet turned to the woman with a frown, unease permeating her entire body. The man's warning flashed into her mind again. *Watch that your luck doesn't run out.* Maybe this woman was his accomplice. She tugged her arm away. "Why are you asking my name?" Violet swiped at her face again. "Why is my face wet?" She eyed the dry night sky. "It's not raining."

"I need a stretcher over here!" The EMT placed a gloved hand under her elbow. "You've a few cuts that I'm going to take care of. Are you in any pain?"

"I have to know about my friend." She took a step toward Henry's car, but the ground seemed to move. Her head wouldn't stop pounding.

Two more medics arrived with a stretcher. The woman EMT gently guided her toward the pair just a few steps away. "Just rest here for a minute."

Violet shook her head even as she sank down on the lowered gurney. "No, I don't want to leave until I know what's wrong with

Henry. Please." She held out her hand in supplication but gasped as the bright flashing lights of the ambulance illuminated her hand. Violet stared at it as the red rotating lights colored it a sickly scarlet.

A firm pressure on her shoulder eased her down on the stretcher. "That's it." The woman EMT motioned to the other medics, who lifted the gurney and pushed it toward the waiting ambulance bay. As her stretcher was placed in the back of the ambulance, she continued to stare at her hand. The white interior lights showed her that the wetness on her face hadn't been rain.

It had been blood.

"I hear it's not a good night to take the GW." The Wolf's voice had a way of saying one thing and meaning another. He didn't suffer fools, and the outcome of the accident wouldn't improve his mood.

"Yeah, traffic is a nightmare." Bryon Smith, aka Dr. Wallace, lit a cigarette as he stood deep in the shadows of the bike path alongside the George Washington Parkway. The police had managed to clear one lane for traffic, which now inched by the accident. A tow truck hoisted the black SUV onto its bed while another hitched a cable to the two-door Honda Accord. He took a long drag on his cigarette, blowing the smoke out in spurts as he contemplated the call he dreaded making.

"I want more than a traffic report."

The man exhaled and flicked the butt into the Potomac River. "I delivered your message to the girl, but the SUV driver had too many people around him." He wished he had lit another cigarette before tossing the spent one.

Silence. It was never a good thing when The Wolf went quiet. Byron rushed to fill the empty space. "She'll stay away from him if she thinks she's the reason for the accident."

Nothing. Byron unzipped his jacket as his body jacked up the heat. "Do you want me to follow up with her to make sure she leaves him alone?"

"No." The word cracked in his ear, and he pulled the phone away. "You have disappointed me."

Byron swallowed hard and mopped at beads of sweat forming on his forehead with the back of his hand. Begging would do little good. The Wolf had no compassion. He ought to know how cold and hard he was. After all, he had carried out The Wolf's compassionless instructions more times than he wanted to remember.

"Don't call me again." The phone signal went dead, and Byron slowly punched the end button before tucking the phone in his pocket. He lit another cigarette and inhaled deeply, then turned to walk briskly down the pathway in the opposite direction of where he'd left his car.

If he hurried, he might have time to put into motion a way for his death to be avenged beyond the grave. He ran over the contingency plan he had put in place for such a time as this. Violet and Henry would be the perfect pawns in his revenge plot. The beauty of it hinged on The Wolf's belief in his own superiority. That arrogance would prove to be his Achilles' heel.

Too bad he wouldn't be around to see The Wolf fall.

TWENTY-THREE

Iris tapped her manicured nails on the polished surface of her desk and stared across at Dirk Jones, a trusted aide since her days in the West Berlin embassy. "You're sure that they weren't hurt too badly?"

Dirk quirked an eyebrow, one of his more annoying traits, mostly because she had never mastered it herself. "My sources tell me the woman has a concussion, stitches from a minor laceration on her forehead, and bruises from the seatbelt and airbag, while the man suffered some minor cuts and a sprained wrist. The man's SUV took the brunt of the impact, but those newer models have side airbags, which absorbed most of the collision."

"And it was a direct hit?" She kept her face smooth. No need to let on how much the news of the accident had rattled her.

"Yes, my man in the car following the woman saw the pickup deliberately smash into the SUV's front right fender. The action spun the SUV directly into the path of the woman's car." Dirk crossed his ankle over his knee, and Iris glimpsed his custom-made Italian loafers.

"Any thoughts on the pickup's driver?"

"My guess? A professional driver. It takes precision to cause such an accident and not get pulled into it yourself."

Yes, The Wolf wouldn't hire amateurs to do the job. "But why cause an accident at all?" She spread her hands over her desk, tidied for the weekend. "What are we missing that he sees? What threat are they to him?" Iris didn't bother to spell out who the *he* was in those questions. Dirk knew The Wolf almost as well as she did and had even more reason to hate him.

Dirk shrugged. "Who knows? Maybe he's getting more paranoid in his old age."

Iris suppressed a shudder. The Wolf had always looked over his shoulder, which was why he was still alive. "If he thinks someone's getting close, you can bet it's true they are. You know he has a sixth sense about being discovered."

"That may have been true in East Germany, but he's been out of the game too long. Maybe he's slipping."

She leaned back in her chair, careful to keep her growing fear under control. Dirk might be the closest thing she had to a confidant, but he had a streak of unpredictability that came into play at the most inopportune times. Geneva had shown her that in spades. An image of a young child, her shining chestnut hair gleaming in the bright sunlight, flitted across her mind. So young to have such a tragic end. "Do you ever think about the old days?" The question slipped out before she had time to think of its implications.

Dirk stared at her, and Iris bit back a smile at his incredulous expression. She wasn't one to embark on a trip down memory lane, preferring to leave the past in the past. But in for a penny and all that. She gave a half smile. "Sometimes I think things were much simpler when we first met. Loyalties seemed so clear cut. Right and wrong had stark differences. Nowadays, friends are enemies, and sometimes enemies are friends. Everything has gotten all mixed up."

He sat in silence for a moment before meeting her eyes. "It's not the Cold War I think about, it's relationships." He paused. "Since you opened the conversation, I've often wondered what would have happened if you and I had..." Dirk shook his head. "But no use talking about regrets now. We've both made our choices."

Iris caught her breath at the bleak look in his eyes. Dirk had always wanted more than she could give him. Her affection for him never crossed into the kind of love he longed to have. Nothing could turn back the clock. If that were possible, Iris would have chosen a different path, one that might have ended her diplomatic career and possibly derailed her political ambitions. But she lived with the decisions she'd made in her youth. She only hoped Violet and Henry wouldn't have to learn such a costly lesson. Bringing the matter back to the accident, she said, "What is it The Wolf thinks they know?"

Dirk relaxed his shoulders, a sign her probing had unsettled him more than he would admit. "Not his identity, or they would be dead."

"He was never one to kill unless absolutely necessary." She tapped her fingers on her desk. "Maybe it isn't what they know, but what they might uncover."

"Do you think Kopecek left them a clue or something?" Both of Dirk's eyebrows shot up like twin firecrackers. "I thought you said he wasn't trained in espionage."

"All this started with Kopecek's death." Iris frowned, her mind going over the sequence of events. "Something about Kopecek has The Wolf on high alert."

Dirk shrugged. "I investigated his background. Sure, he lived in East Berlin around the timeThe Wolf started operating, but as far as we can tell, the two never crossed paths and had no reason to do so."

"We must have missed something." She sighed. "I'll take another look. I still have friends in the Stasi archives. Maybe something will show us the connection."

"It's your sleepless nights, not mine." Dirk stood, stretching to his full height. "Walk you to your car?"

Iris shook her head. "I've got a few loose ends to tie up before I head home tonight."

"Okay, see you on Monday." Dirk paused with his hand on the doorknob. "Be careful. You don't want to be collateral damage."

She waved him off and sat silently until the door closed and his footsteps faded. Then she unlocked a bottom drawer, reached under a stack of files, and extracted a small metal box. Lifting the lid, she stared down at the dull black metal of a SIG-Sauer, calculating just how long it had been since she had fired the eight-shot 9mm handgun. The double-action/single-action gun had been popular with both West and East German police in the 1980s, but she liked it for its smooth action and ability to rapidly fire without a lot of kick back. The gun had stayed inside its locked box for years since the early days of her congressional term. Once she took the gun out of the office, she wouldn't be able to smuggle it back in. These days, even senators had to walk through metal detectors to enter the office building.

She wouldn't think about what happened the last time she'd fired the weapon. Swiftly loading the pistol, she then tucked the gun into the small of her back before returning the box to its hiding place. Good thing she'd worn dress slacks with a belt today. The matching jacket would cover the gun's bump. Now all she had to do was summon the courage to use it.

Byron Smith crouched behind a van to watch Dirk Jones slip into the shadows minutes before Iris Morrison exited the elevator to walk to her car. The senator carried only her purse slung over one shoulder, her pace sure and confident. Never once did she glance around as if suspecting two people monitored her progress across the parking garage to her Mini Cooper. Pure luck had guided Byron here after his conversation with The Wolf. He had arrived just in time to see Dirk enter the parking garage. If he'd believed in a higher power, Byron would have attributed the coincidence to that entity since the very man he sought stood within striking distance. Now, he fought the urge to pray God would allow him enough time to finish what The Wolf's phone call had set into motion.

Dirk melted farther behind a concrete pillar. Byron suspected Dirk wasn't there to keep an eye on the senator, at least not for her protection. From what he knew of Morrison, she could take care of herself. After all, she knew the identity of The Wolf, a secret The Wolf had killed others to keep hidden.

The senator held her key fob in front of her, chirped open her door, and slid behind the wheel. Soon her car zoomed out of the parking space and up the ramp to the First Street SW exit. Byron straightened as Dirk turned and made his way to the South Capitol Street exit. Byron kept Dirk in sight as Dirk turned down a side street. Even on this cool March evening, pedestrians clogged the sidewalks. When Dirk ducked into a small Indian restaurant in the downstairs of his condo building, Byron entered the lobby with a group of residents and rode the elevator to the fourth floor. Relieved that no one else got off on the same floor, Byron moved purposefully down the hallway, stopping before Dirk's front door. Given Byron's particular skill set, gaining entry into Dirk's apartment took only a few moments.

A quick sweep of the condo revealed no hidden listening devices, but he did find three handguns stashed in various places. Dirk was a careful man but not overly cautious, which sometimes happened when a man had been out of the field for a long time. Byron settled on the couch and lit a cigarette to wait for Dirk to come home.

The cigarette had only burned halfway down when the fragrant smell of curry alerted him that Dirk was at the door. As it opened, Byron spoke, keeping his voice level and pleasant. "About time you got home." He stubbed out his cigarette in a saucer he'd filched from the kitchen, wishing he'd had time to finish it, but business came before pleasure.

Dirk slowly shut the door and reached for a lamp, flicking it on before easing into the room. His eyes never left Byron's face. "Mind if I put my food down?"

"Nice and slow. I'm a bit jumpy this evening, so there's no telling what will happen if you make any sudden or suspicious moves." Byron gently patted the Glock on his lap.

Dirk slowly set the food bag on the coffee table.

"Now place your cell phones on the table, both of them. But by the edges, if you please." Byron saw the brief spark of shock as Dirk reached into his pocket and plucked out the work-issued iPhone and the burner cell phone. Byron ignored the iPhone and picked up the prepaid device, checking the call and text record with a flick of his finger. "Sit down and let's get more acquainted."

Dirk sank onto the couch, his hand edging down into the side.

Byron laughed, a hoarse bark of a laugh. "Don't bother looking for your guns. I found 'em all. You had quite an arsenal here. Are you looking to start a war or end one?"

Dirk's lips compressed in a grimace. "Obviously, I should have taken one with me this morning to work."

"Oh, I don't think you would have made it past the Capitol police, not with the tightened security of the Russell Senate Building, and especially not with Senator Morrison nominated for secretary of state." Byron leaned back, striking a deceptively casual pose.

"You seem to know a lot about me." Dirk shifted on the couch, his eyes darting around the room.

"Enough to know who you're really working for." Byron nearly smiled. The man was sweating bullets, and he had hardly begun his interrogation. "Now that we're both more comfortable, why don't you tell me what The Wolf wants you to do."

CHAPTER
TWENTY-FOUR

Henry opened his eyes, squinting a little in the bright sunlight spilling onto the extra guest room of his sister's home. His stomach growled, propelling him to rise even though his body protested. The ER doctor told him to expect more aches and pains this morning as the shock of the accident wore off, but he wasn't expecting every muscle to scream at him as he pushed himself to a sitting position. Pausing to catch his breath, he grabbed his crutches, wincing over the movement. He'd agreed to stay with Sissy and Keith to avoid a fight he saw brewing in his sister's eyes over his care. But the stay would be only for a day or two. He had fought too hard to carve out an independent life. The fact that Violet also had a room in what Sissy was calling her boarding house had nothing to do with his decision.

Slipping his legs into the braces, he snapped the metal joints into place and reached for his right-hand crutch. According to the ER doctor, he would likely not regain full use of his bruised left wrist for a few days.

A knock on the door drew his attention. "Henry?" Sissy called.

"Come in. I'm awake." Henry shifted on his bed, glad to put off standing for another minute.

Sissy pushed open the door and grinned at her brother. "Hello, sleepyhead."

"Hey, yourself. What time is it?"

She pointed to the digital clock on the bedside table he'd forgotten was there. "Ten o'clock."

Henry tried to remember what day it was, but his mind wouldn't cooperate. The doctor said he might be a little fuzzy headed for a day or two from the accident, but surely he knew the day of the week. He sighed as his brain pulled up the information. "I don't think I've slept in this late on a Saturday in a long time."

"Violet's in the shower." Sissy raised her eyebrows. "I'm cooking pancakes and bacon, so you only have half an hour to get spiffy before breakfast is ready."

"Then you'd best get on with it and let me get fresh." He eased to his feet slowly, testing his balance with one crutch. So far, so good.

"I'm going." Sissy gave him a saucy look before exiting his room and shutting the door behind her.

He moved tentatively toward the adjoining bathroom, his gait more awkward than usual. Once in the bathroom, he turned on water, grateful Sissy and Keith had added a handicap accessible bathroom in their downstairs guest room. At least taking a shower wouldn't be too difficult despite his hurt wrist. The warm water eased his sore limbs, and he felt more like himself as he toweled off. Wiping the steam from the mirror, he stared at the large bruise on the left side of his face. Definitely a day to skip shaving.

Forty minutes later, after he'd dressed and managed to comb his hair, he shuffled into the kitchen. Violet sat at the table, her head buried behind the morning's *Washington Post*. Henry collapsed into a chair opposite her.

She lowered the paper and gasped. "Are you okay?"

He settled his crutch beside him and grimaced. "It hurts, but probably looks worse than it feels." He gestured toward her forehead. "You look like you've been in a fight yourself."

She touched the bandage around her head. "I had a worse headache when I woke up this morning, but a couple of ibuprofen took the edge off."

"You two are quite a pair." Sissy set a steaming plate of pancakes in the middle of the table. "Keith will be down in a minute, then we'll eat." She turned back to the stove.

"Hmm, smells heavenly. I can't remember the last time someone made homemade pancakes for me." Violet's tone was light but held a wistful quality.

"Perhaps you need to get out more," Sissy tossed over her shoulder. "Henry makes a mean omelet."

"I'd be happy to cook you breakfast any morning." His cheeks grew hot as the implication of what that could mean dawned on him.

Violet's face flushed too. She ducked her head, busying herself with refolding the newspaper.

Sissy set down a plate of bacon and gave Henry a knowing look. He bit back a groan. His sister could read him like a book, and he wasn't sure he wanted to be that transparent, not where Violet was concerned.

Keith came in, saving Henry from having to pick up the conversation thread. "Good morning." He pulled out a chair for Sissy, then sat himself. "This looks delicious. We'll have to have guests more often." He leaned toward Violet and Henry. "It's the only time she'll cook pancakes and bacon."

Sissy snorted. "Don't you believe him."

Keith said the blessing and passed the platters of food. "Henry, your grad student called and said he had finished the first part of the assignment. I told him you were not in any shape to travel, so he's coming by around eleven."

Henry opened his mouth to ask which grad student, then caught himself. He'd given the Madisons' home number to Juan Delores in case Juan had a breakthrough on cracking the code and couldn't reach Henry at the office or on his cell phone. He glanced at Violet, who stared back at him, a question in her eyes.

His answer to her unspoken question would be brief. "It's his thesis. Juan said he might need some guidance this weekend." That sounded natural. Maybe he could get the hang of espionage after all.

VIOLET SMOOTHED HER HAIR AND PUT DOWN THE BRUSH. SHE LEANED CLOSER to the bathroom mirror and frowned at her reflection. Nothing was going to make her face look any better this morning. The white bandage near her hairline covered the cut, which had necessitated four stitches. She hadn't had a chance to talk to Henry about the accident, as both of them had been tired and mildly sedated on painkillers when Keith had driven them to the house late last night. But now with Sissy at the store and Keith golfing with friends, maybe she could do it before the grad student came over.

While Henry's SUV had been totaled, hers needed extensive body work to make it drivable. Thank goodness the shop had a cancellation and was working on the repairs today. The cost would eat into her meager savings, but Mr. Davidson had said Mr. Kopecek's estate could advance her funds if necessary. Hurrying out of the room, she went downstairs and found Henry in the den off the kitchen, settled back into an easy chair, a book propped on his lap. She paused in the doorway, unsure if she should tell him about the man at the accident scene. Maybe she imagined the whole thing or read a more sinister meaning into his words.

"Hi." Henry smiled at her.

She tried to smile back, but her lips didn't want to comply. The pancakes that had tasted so good a short while ago now turned somersaults in her stomach.

Henry's smile faded. "What's wrong?"

Those simple words broke her resolve. It had been too long since someone had been concerned about her. She moved into the room and sank on the ottoman beside the chair. "I don't know. I mean, I do know but I don't know."

"It sounds serious." Henry slid a bookmark into the book and closed the cover. "Is it about the accident?"

She nodded and took a deep breath. "When I got out of my car to check on you, a man came up." Even in the warm room, she shivered at the memory. Henry's hand covered her clenched ones, and she drew strength from his touch. "He said I was lucky to be alive. Then he said, 'Watch that your luck doesn't run out.'"

Henry repeated the last phrase. "What do you think he meant?"

She swallowed, struggling to put her fear and concern into words. "At the time, I wasn't sure because I was so afraid something had happened to you. But when I was waiting for someone to stitch me up in the ER, the man's words kept repeating in my mind, and it frightened me. I think he had something to do with the accident that wasn't an accident. The truck swerved deliberately into your lane."

Henry frowned. "I don't remember much, but the police told me witnesses saw the truck weaving in and out of traffic right before he hit my SUV."

Violet nodded. "I saw that, too, but the impact seemed deliberate to me because the truck sped away after clipping your vehicle." She turned her hand over and laced her fingers through Henry's. He gave hers a squeeze.

"The police seem to think the driver was intoxicated, but there's been no sign of the truck. The license plate was obscured by mud and no witnesses got a clear view of the driver." He rubbed his thumb over the back of her hand, the gesture soothing and stimulating. "That man at the scene changes things. It means someone followed us, knew where to find us."

A shudder rippled through her body as she wondered if they had been followed back to Sissy and Keith's. "I don't understand why. Why you, why me? Why now?"

Henry tightened his grip on her hand. "There's something

someone doesn't want us to figure out. Before I met you, no one was leaving anonymous messages or trying to run me off the road." Henry paused. "My life was actually a textbook case of a boring academic, which leads me to deduce that somehow, everything must be related to the one common denominator in all of this."

The import of what Henry was saying pierced her conscious. "Mr. Kopecek?"

Henry nodded and released her hand to tick the items off on his fingers. "Your apartment trashed, his rather cryptic letter to me, the notations we think are code in my book, the anonymous phone calls warning us to stop investigating, the flowers, the note to you, and now this accident. Someone doesn't want us to dig any deeper."

"But Mr. Kopecek was so ordinary." It wasn't exactly the truth. She could imagine a secret life beneath the quiet, well-read man in room 202. After all, she lived such a life herself, with none the wiser. Well, almost no one, if the note about the flowers were any indication. Her secret might not stay a hidden much longer.

"Ordinary is the perfect cover for espionage," he said, reclaiming her hand. "In fact, the more commonplace the man, the better the spy, as my research has shown time and again."

Violet stared at him. "I'm sure he wasn't a spy, not a real one. I hear what you're saying, but he wasn't hiding a double life, I'm sure of it. I think he somehow found out about this Wolf, maybe who The Wolf is, and that's why he was killed."

CHAPTER
TWENTY-FIVE

The doorbell rang and both Violet and Henry jumped. She separated her hand from his. She should stop enjoying his attention so much. It would only make things worse when he found out.

"Juan must be here," Henry said. "Would you mind getting the door?"

"Sure." Henry had apparently forgotten that last night, they had been on their way to a quiet, secure spot so she could tell him about the hidden message behind the flowers. In the bright light of day, she was second guessing that impulse. It wouldn't be fair to put Henry in danger as well. At least Juan's arrival had pushed back the hour of reckoning a little longer.

The thought that perhaps this wasn't the grad student but someone sent by The Wolf made her pause before opening the door. Pressing her eye to the peephole, she saw a young Hispanic male, earbuds dangling around his neck and a backpack slung over one shoulder, standing on the doorstep. His entire demeanor screamed graduate student. She shot a prayer for safety heavenward and hauled open the door.

"Hi, is Dr. Silverton here?"

Better to play it safe. "Is he expecting you?"

"Yes, I'm Juan Delores." The young man peered at her face. "Are you okay?" His voice had an edge of concern to it.

She stepped back, turning her bruised face away from scrutiny. "Car accident. Please, come inside."

Juan entered and paused in the entryway while Violet closed the door. "He's in the den." She led the way down the hall, entered the room, and retook her seat on the stool next to Henry.

"Hi, Dr. Silverton." Juan shrugged his backpack off, then froze. He looked from Henry to Violet and back again to Henry. "Man, you two look like you got on someone's bad side."

"Car accident," Henry volunteered.

"That's what she said." Juan jerked his thumb in Violet's direction.

Violet turned to Henry, and mirth danced in his eyes. She smothered an unexpected laugh. This was beginning to take on the manner of a farce.

"Well." Henry cleared his throat. "It was the same accident, different cars. Juan, this is Violet Lundy."

Juan nodded at Violet, then unzipped his backpack and pulled out a laptop. "She in on the secret?"

Violet's breath caught in her throat. Henry hadn't mentioned he'd told Juan about Mr. Kopecek and The Wolf. The more people who knew about what was going on, the more people who might get hurt. Last night's accident had clarified one thing in her mind. These people were very careful and very clever.

Henry sat forward. "Violet was the one who brought the notations to my attention."

Juan's fingers flew over the keyboard. "I think you were right about the code."

Violet forced herself to ask a question she wasn't sure she wanted answered. "You think it is a code?"

"I think it's a double code." Juan balanced the computer on his knees. "The author used a substitution-permutation network to code the message, but when you decipher the words, you have a simpler code. Then you decode the meaning of the second code and have the answer."

Henry sat back, a thoughtful expression on his face. "You were able to use *Verna liebte, zu Fuß in der regen* to decipher the phrases?"

"Yes." Juan read from the screen. "The first phrase decoded translates into *Der amerikanische Blume weiß etwas*. Here, take a look. My German is rudimentary at best."

Juan turned the laptop around so Henry could read the words on the screen. Henry softly repeated the phrase in German, then translated it into English. "'The American flower knows something.'"

"That's what the online Google translator came up with, but it didn't make any sense," Juan said. "What do flowers know?"

"Perhaps he's alluding to the language of flowers." Henry returned Juan's computer. "I think my sister has a book on flower meanings around here somewhere. Would you check the bookcase behind you, Juan? I think it's on one of the top shelves."

While Juan searched for the volume, Violet repeated the phrase over and over in her mind. The American flower knows something. Flowers couldn't know anything. They were only flowers, after all. If Mr. Kopecek had wanted to point to the meaning behind flowers, as the sender had done with the bouquet the other day, he would have listed specific varieties.

Instead, Mr. Kopecek had used the generic *flower*. She turned to Henry, her words tumbling over one another. "He was trying to say someone's name, but he couldn't say her name, so he wrote it in code."

Henry eyed her as if she had done the hokey pokey on the coffee table. "We know it's in code."

Violet waved her hand. "That's not what I meant. Of course I know the phrase was in code, or double code, as Juan pointed out. What I'm saying is *flower* is a code for someone's name." Her gaze traveled between the two men. "You know what I mean. A flower name like mine."

Juan shook his head. "Of course it's a flower name, but which flower name, and what does that flower name mean?"

Henry smiled. "Brilliant. Absolutely brilliant. So all we have to do is find the right flower name."

Juan cut in. "I still don't get it."

"Violet thinks the word flower is code for another woman who has a first name that is also the name of a flower, like Rose or Lily. This is the woman we need to find because she must know something we need to know," Henry explained. "All we have to do is find the right flower name."

"I imagine naming girls after flowers isn't uncommon," Juan said. "How are you going to find this flower woman?"

Violet slumped back. Of course it would be difficult to know to whom Mr. Kopecek was referring.

"Ah, but we mustn't be so easily discouraged. I have some idea as to where to look." Henry grinned at Violet. "I can't believe I didn't think of it myself, it's so obvious."

Now it was Violet's turn to stare back without comprehension. "It's still murky to me."

Henry's posture stiffened, and he slipped into his professorial mode. "We know this must have something to do with the past. Otherwise, why write the code in the margins of a book about East Berlin?"

"He didn't talk much about those days, only about the days when his wife was alive." Violet's mind went back to conversations with Mr. Kopecek. "He did say something once about the walls listening."

Henry raised his eyebrows. "I'm not surprised. The Stasi developed ingenious ways to spy on their own people."

"It's beginning to make sense." Violet worked her lip between her teeth as her mind raced with possibilities. "We should look at Americans in West and East Berlin in the early 1980s with a flower first name."

"Whoa, you two are jumping down rabbit holes right and left." Juan scratched his head. "How did you get from a flower to espionage in the Cold War?"

Henry and Violet glanced at each other. "He already knows about the code," Henry said. "We need his help to decode the rest."

"But it's risky." She pushed her hair back from her face, wincing as she brushed against one of the sore spots on her head. "Look what happened to us last night."

"We don't know if it's connected." Uncertainty filled Henry's voice.

"It is. It has to be." She refused to think her past was solely responsible for the accident.

"You two are kind of creeping me out. What's going on, Dr. Silverton?" Juan moved his laptop to the coffee table.

Henry shrugged at Violet, then turned to Juan. "I should have been straight with you, but it still seemed so fantastical we could be in any real danger. Last night's accident might not have been an accident."

"And Rainer Kopecek's death might not have been because of old age," Violet put in.

Juan stared at them. "You're saying someone killed this Kopecek fellow and caused a traffic accident because of something Kopecek knew?"

"Yes." Violet swallowed down the sudden tears that threatened to overwhelm her at the thought of the kind old man using the last days of his life to write her a coded note. "Mr. Kopecek grew up in East Germany, in East Berlin to be exact. He rarely talked about those times, but we think someone from his past called The Wolf came back into his life in some way or another. We need your help to decode the rest of his message to me."

"The Wolf." Juan blew out a breath. "This sounds like one of those cloak and dagger TV shows my dad used to watch."

"I know it doesn't sound real, but it is, and it's dangerous." Henry reached over and took Violet's hand.

Juan stared at them both. "Are you saying you believe Kopecek wrote clues in code about an East German spy from forty-odd years ago?"

Violet blinked. She hadn't thought that The Wolf must be involved in espionage, but of course, that was the most logical explanation.

"Not just a spy but a double agent," Henry answered.

She gasped as the implication of what that would mean even today burst upon her mind. The statute of limitations never ran out on someone who betrayed his country. That person would in all likelihood kill to keep his secret buried.

"But wouldn't that be a good thing?" Juan waved his hand. "If we turned an East German agent to our side during the Cold War?"

"It would indeed," Henry agreed. "But not if the man who turned went the other way."

Juan's eyes widened. "You mean an American agent who worked for the Soviets, like Aldrich Ames and Robert Hanssen?"

"In a word, yes." Henry squeezed Violet's hand. "If he's escaped detection all this time, then he's someone who has a lot to lose. Your life could be in danger if you help us, so it's only fair that we make you aware of it."

Juan clenched hands. "If I've learned anything from studying history, it's that turncoats do more damage than enemy spies. If there's a double agent who hasn't been brought to justice and I can help, then I'm in. Where do we go from here?"

CHAPTER
TWENTY-SIX

Iris swung her crossed leg, and her high heel shoe slipped down to her toes. She tightened her grip on a burner cell phone, semi-distracted by the low hum of the line as she waited for an answer. So much for German efficiency. She'd been on hold for nearly ten minutes for her contact at the Stasi archives to come back to the phone. A sharp movement of her leg sent the shoe off her toes and onto the thick carpet of the Jefferson Hotel in Washington, DC. Sensitive calls like this one were best done in the privacy of a randomly selected hotel room rather than her Capitol Hill office or home. No telling what might be bugged in those locations.

"I have what you wanted to know," said her contact, his voice gravely from years of chain smoking. In fact, she could practically smell the fumes of his favorite menthol cigarette wafting over the line. Iris permitted herself a small smile. Manfred—not his real name, of course, but after all these years, she doubted even he remembered what his mother had christened him—would not fail her. He owed her too great a debt, and her favor was a simple one.

He coughed, then cleared his throat. "This a safe line?"

"Yes. Tell me." Old habits died hard. Manfred had never trusted cell phones. No matter how much she explained about untraceable phones she used only once or twice—and purchased with cash at locations throughout the Metro DC area—he wasn't convinced. But now wasn't the time for another lecture on telecomm technology.

"In 1982, Rainer Kopecek's wife, Verna Kopecek, requested a visa to travel to West Berlin to visit her dying mother. She went through official channels. Stasi agents verified her mother's condition. Because neither Kopecek nor his wife had caused any trouble before and had no other living relatives outside of East Germany, permission was initially granted for her to travel alone."

Iris nodded, her eyes focused on the rather good reproduction painting of an English hunting scene as she concentrated on the alternate timeline to the one Manfred revealed to her. That same year, 1982, marked the beginning of her association with The Wolf. Something tickled at the back of her mind, but she needed more information to bring it forward. "What month was approval given?"

A pause, and then Manfred answered, "April."

April 1982. Her breath caught in her throat. No, it couldn't be, but it had to be. She'd learned long ago not to believe in coincidence. "Where did the Kopeceks live in East Berlin?"

The answer came more readily this time. "At 23 Grimmstrasse Street."

The cell phone slipped in her hand, and Iris tightened her grip. One final piece of information would confirm her suspicions. "What date was Verna Kopecek's visa approval revoked?"

"Our old friend is involved, isn't he?"

Iris didn't answer, and Manfred sighed. "April 15."

"I don't have to tell you we never spoke." She slowly lowered the cell phone and punched the end button. Manfred wouldn't be offended by her abrupt disconnection, not where The Wolf was concerned. Her mind raced with possibilities as to how Rainer Kopecek stumbled upon that particular operation. Lots of East Berliners lived on Grimmstrasse, many of them crammed into tiny apartments at number twenty-three. She needed more information, but she couldn't afford to tip off The Wolf any more than she had already by shadowing Henry and Violet. Retrieving her shoe, she slipped it on and pushed back the window curtain. She gazed at the White House, its lights blinking on in the early March twilight.

Talking with Manfred brought back those long-ago days when danger literally stalked her every move. A risky business helping prominent East Berliners escape communism and the Soviet Union, but the thrill of outsmarting the Stasi had been more exhilarating than anything she'd ever done. Meeting The Wolf and joining him in his double game only heightened the danger. Becoming his lover had been very foolish and very rewarding, her loyalties and common-sense getting mixed up in the headiness of having a man such as him warming her bed at night.

Now she wished she could slap that naïve girl and tell her to brush off the flirtations and double entendres with The Wolf. No matter what she told herself at the time, it wasn't worth it. None of it. Not when the past threatened to derail all she had worked for, all she had sacrificed. Not when The Wolf wouldn't stay in his lair. She had to find out Rainer Kopecek's connection, but all her old contacts knew The Wolf too well and would likely have their ultimate loyalty to him, not her. Turning from the window, Iris clenched her fists, frustration making her body rigid. There had to be a way. He couldn't win. Not again. Just when she was about to concede defeat and go home, a name came to her. Juergen Schneider.

With decisive steps, she returned to the desk and picked up her cell phone, dialing a number she had only called once before. The call connected and rang in a country house deep in the German woods outside of a tiny hamlet most maps never listed. One ring, two rings. She drummed her fingers against the desktop as she counted the rings. Fifteen, sixteen. Juergen never did like anything more modern than a rotary telephone. Seventeen, eighteen. Surely he would be there. After all, it was the middle of the night. Twenty. Just when she was about to hang up, the call was answered.

"*Guten Morgen*," said a male voice, rusty from disuse.

Iris nearly cried with relief. "*Guten Morgen,* Juergen Schneider."

The old man stayed silent a long time before replying. "Iris?"

"*Ja, es ist mir,*" she replied, slipping back into German with ease.

"*Es ist schon eine lange Zeit.*"

It's been a long time, Iris translated in her head. "I'm calling about a certain friend we have in common."

Another long pause. "If I continue this conversation, this will complete my obligation to you."

"Yes, I understand." Of course, Juergen would confirm her phone call meant she was finally redeeming the favor he owed her.

"Then what do you want?"

Iris told him as concisely as she could.

He sighed. "You don't make things easy on an old man, do you? I wanted to live my remaining few years at peace. What you're asking will bring down the wrath of the one whose name I shall never speak again."

"This information will provide the means for his destruction."

"That's what so many thought before you. He has already killed again to keep this secret buried for all eternity."

A chill swept over Iris. The answer was obvious, but she couldn't help asking the question. "What do you mean?"

Juergen chuckled, a rusty, ragged sound like an unused hinge being forced open. "I may be living a quiet country life, but I still have my ways. Rainer Kopecek's death was not a natural one. I shouldn't think I would have to tell you that."

Iris winced as the dart hit home. "That's why I need to know, need to find proof."

"Proof is what you're after, is it? Security is more like it, Madame Secretary."

"There are other lives at stake, truly innocent ones." She hoped Henry and Violet would stay out of it, but she doubted they would, not after the car accident. She wouldn't in their shoes. In some ways, Violet reminded her of how she was before The Wolf snared her in his game of intrigue and treason.

"Ah, you've grown a conscience since we last met."

"Perhaps." Iris wasn't going to admit she was thinking more of herself than Henry and Violet, but let the old man believe her call was not all about saving her own skin.

"I will do as you ask. Call me again at this number in two days' time."

"Of course."

"*Auf Wiedersehen.*" Juergen hung up the phone before Iris could echo the goodbye.

She ended the call and flipped the phone over to take out the SIM card. Reaching into her purse for a tiny hammer, she pounded the card into bits, then swept the bits into a plastic bag. Rising, Iris tucked the items into her bag and picked up the room key. Time to return home. Within forty-eight hours, if luck was on her side, she'd have something valuable with which to bargain with The Wolf. As she pulled the door closed behind her, she refused to consider what would happen if The Wolf wasn't in a bartering mood.

CHAPTER
TWENTY-SEVEN

In her room at Sissy and Keith's, Violet sorted through the stack of mail she'd picked up from the post office. Thank goodness she had opened a P.O. box instead of having mail delivered to her apartment. But that didn't solve the problem of figuring out where to move. She couldn't impose on Henry's sister and brother-in-law much longer. Somehow, working at another nursing home or senior housing complex wasn't as appealing as it had been three years ago.

An ad circular joined the other junk mail in the trash can. She had canceled her phone and internet service, closed her gas and electric accounts after turning in her apartment key, so most of the mail in the thick stack was generic or come-ons. When she spotted the McCreary Penitentiary return address on the plain white envelope, her heart sank. Better get it over with. She ripped open the envelope and tugged out the sheets of yellow lined paper. A quick count told her this wouldn't be an easy read. Her brother had used eight sheets of legal-sized paper this time.

She sucked in a deep breath and began to read.

Dear Sis,

I'd ask how you are doing, but I already know it's better than me stuck here in this awful place with nothing to do but think about the injustice of it all. Why didn't you send a birthday card? It's not as if you could forget my birthday, given that you share it.

When I told Mom I didn't have your address, she was happy to give it to me. One would think you were ashamed of your brother, the way you try to hide our association. You shouldn't be ashamed, not when you know the reasons behind my actions and how they prove my innocence in these outrageous claims.

The only consolation I have is that the anniversary of my incarceration is fast approaching, which will mean new faces to which to tell my story. I'm sure the news media will want to hear my side of things and will tell it right this time. Five years of lies is long enough. The truth must come out...

Violet skimmed the rest, which was more of the same. Her brother proclaimed his innocence and ranted about the many injustices done to him by those in authority and "fellow inmates who feel themselves superior, but who in reality are not even worthy to breathe the same air as me." Her heart ached as once again, she faced the fact her brother would never own up to his part in the crime that put him behind bars.

His allusion to the media coverage of the five-year anniversary troubled her. He probably had already contacted as many major television, radio, print, and blog personnel as he could to garner as much attention as possible. Violet had spent the last five years hiding her association with him, while he flaunted his unjust imprisonment for a crime he admitted doing but for good reasons. A jury had not agreed, nor did Violet, although their mother had sided with Patrick. What their father thought was anyone's guess, as he had stayed out of the discussions as far as Violet knew.

Her cell phone rang, putting an end to her ruminations. She picked it up and winced at the caller ID. Her parents' number. Great, just what she needed after reading Patrick's letter. She clicked the answer button. "Hello?"

"Why haven't you written your brother?"

Violet sighed. Her mother should have been a crusader, the way she clung tenaciously to a lost cause, namely her son and his wrongful incarceration. "Mom, whether or not I correspond with Patrick is my business, not yours."

As expected, the words slid by her mother like an eel slipping by in the river's current. "You don't know what it's like being cooped up there day after day. He told me he'd written you a nice, long letter two weeks ago, but still nothing from you."

"If you only called to harangue me about my dismal correspondence record, I'm hanging up." Unfortunately, the only way to stop the tirade was to end the conversation cold. Reasoning didn't work with her mother.

"Well, no, that wasn't the only reason I called." Her mother paused, and Violet pictured her straightening the photos of Patrick hanging on the wall in the family room, where her mother spent most of her time. During her last visit home two years ago, Violet had counted the number of photos featuring her brother. Twenty-nine. Of herself? Only one, and it included her brother. If her mother had been able to cut Violet out of that photo without taking half of Patrick's face, she probably would have done so.

Now Violet waited for her mother to come to the point.

"I, that is your father and I, want you to come home for the anniversary."

A prickle of unease snaked its way up Violet's spine. "Why?"

"It's been five years, and we think a united front would be best."

The unease uncoiled into a rattlesnake poised to strike. This wasn't good at all. "Who's going to be there?"

Her mother gave a weak laugh. "Oh, just a few, um, friends Patrick invited."

Violet bit down hard on her lip and tasted blood. Better to bleed than tell her mother what she thought of Patrick's friends. "Which ones?"

"You know Patrick."

"Just tell me."

"Don't get all high and mighty with me, young lady. If you must know, it's Jessica Havens with the CNN crime show. What is it called again? *Justice Delayed.*"

"You'll have to handle that without me. I'm not coming." No way was she going to be party to her mother's attempts to rehabilitate her son's image. Not that a few appearances on a cable television show could accomplish that.

"I can't believe you." Her mother huffed on the phone, her anger at Violet's noncompliance with her plans evident across the line. "It's certainly suspect his own twin won't speak out in his defense."

The words tore off the bandage of a wound so deep, Violet doubted it would ever heal. The closeness she shared with Patrick made his betrayal beyond what she could bear at times. The rift between herself and her mother only exacerbated the jaggedness of the hurt. Now, every phone call with her mother seemed to end with anger on her mother's side and unshed tears on Violet's. She took several deep breaths to cleanse the hurt from her voice. It wouldn't do to let her mother think she had found a chink in the armor Violet wore when discussing Patrick. "I've got to go. I, uh, I love you. Give my love to Dad." Violet ended the call and rubbed her aching eyes. The only thing she wanted to do was curl up under the covers and stay there until this nightmare ended.

HENRY EASED AWAY FROM THE DOOR TO VIOLET'S BEDROOM, ASHAMED AT himself for eavesdropping on her private conversation. He hadn't meant to overhear, but once he realized she was talking to her mother about a brother she didn't talk about, he couldn't seem to move away from the slight crack in the door.

As he hobbled as quietly as he could back down the hall, the tidbits he had picked up swirled in his mind. Her relationship with her mother didn't appear to be very warm, and there was anguish in her voice when she mentioned someone named Patrick. He longed to push open the door and gather her in his arms like a hero from those romances his sister read. But then he would have to admit he had listened in on her side of the conversation, which might squelch any tender feelings she had toward him.

Back in the kitchen, he debated what to do next. He had been about to ask Violet if she wanted to eat lunch and discuss their next steps in the investigation. A friend in the State Department was combing the archives to see if any flower names popped up on the West Berlin Embassy list in the 1980s, but it would take a few days because much of that information was still classified or in boxes in the agency's basement.

His cell rang and he reached for it, glad of the distraction. An international number with the German country code popped on the screen. With a frown, he punched the connection button. "Hello?"

"Ah, Heinrich?"

At the sound of the thick German accent, Henry tensed, wary of a trap laid by The Wolf. He slipped into German with ease. "*Ja.*"

"*Es Kristian Weber.*"

At the name, Henry relaxed his shoulders. "Kristian! *Keine Neuigkeiten?*" His friend, whom he had met on a research trip to Berlin last summer, had been keeping an eye on any mention of Rainer or Verna Kopecek in the Stasi archives, where Kristian worked as a clerk.

"*Ja*, this is why I'm calling." Kristian paused and dropped his voice. "There has been some activity."

Henry gripped the phone tighter, sure whatever Kristian was about to tell him would be a big part of the puzzle they were trying to complete. "Oh? What kind of activity?"

"I didn't want to send it by email, so I'm calling with a—how do you say?—burned mobile."

Translating the German brought a smile to Henry's face. "A burner phone."

"*Ja*, to avoid detection."

The tension roiled back, and Henry stiffened. Usually, the pair corresponded by email, so Kristian using a disposable mobile made Henry uneasy.

Kristian went on. "Someone did a search for our friends in the online in-house archives, the ones not open to the public in general. No new information, but you wanted to know if someone was looking into those particular friends."

Henry leaned back against the kitchen counter, wanting to pace but unable to handle crutches and cell phone at the same time. "When was this?"

"Yesterday."

Interesting. Someone—but not The Wolf, given he seemed to know all there was to know about the Kopeceks already—was delving into Rainer and Verna's life in East Berlin. That in and of itself wasn't particularly sensitive data, so he asked the obvious question. "What else has happened?"

Kristian sighed. "My *onkle*, the one who lives in the woods, has asked a favor."

Henry scrambled to recall what he knew of Kristian's reclusive uncle, but all he could remember were stories from Kristian's childhood which involved a lot of hot chocolate and snowy winter evenings around a giant hearth in a log cabin in the middle of nowhere. "What kind of favor?"

"The kind that can get you killed."

TWENTY-EIGHT

Henry shifted his weight as Kristian's words echoed in his mind. Kristian was no fool. As a young student in the waning days of the Berlin Wall, he had survived the transition from communism to democracy relatively unscathed. Now he ran the cybersecurity system for the Stasi archives, which gave him unfettered access to both classified and unclassified documents. "Why are you telling me this?"

"Because it's time for the truth to come out."

Kristian had a moralistic streak that reared up every once in a while. The man might fight like crazy to keep certain things from Germany's past from marring its future, but he also had his own sense of justice, especially relating to Berlin's divided past. "Which truth is that?"

Kristian dropped his voice to a bare whisper. "My *onkle* told me to look in a particular box buried deep in the archive shelves. The box contained a bunch of invoices and other papers from an old paint factory the Nazis ran in the 1940s, except for one item hidden underneath all those documents."

Henry held his breath, certain this was the break, the piece of information that would flush out The Wolf. "What was it?"

"An old reel-to-reel metal case containing a single spool labeled April 16, 1984."

Whatever Henry had expected, it wasn't a decades-old recording. "Is the tape playable? I mean, did you listen to it?"

Kristian chuckled, a dry sound devoid of humor. "No, I didn't want to know. That's how I've managed to stay employed and alive all these years."

"Then why are you calling me?" Henry deflated, his belief Kristian had stumbled across something related to the mysterious Wolf draining away.

"Because my *onkle* never asks for any favors. He likes to be the one to whom favors are owed." Kristian paused, his voice barely audible as he continued. "And because he mentioned a name I haven't heard in years, someone who shouldn't be talked about at all because he's supposed to be dead."

His heart racing, Henry gripped the phone tighter. "*Der Wolf.*"

Kristian sucked in his breath. "*Ja.*"

For several seconds, both men stayed silent, then Kristian spoke. "I did a very foolish thing before I sent the tape to my *onkle.*"

Holding out hope, Henry said, "What foolish thing?"

"I made a copy and mailed it to you."

Henry blinked, not believing his ears. "To me?"

"*Ja,* to your home, not office. By way of my sister in London." Kristian sighed. "If my *onkle* finds out…. I don't have to tell you this is a dangerous game you're playing. He might be old, but his reach is still long. We must not talk again. I will be in touch if I can. *Lebewohl, mein Freund.*"

"*Abschied.*" Henry disconnected the call and placed the phone on the counter just as Violet stepped into the kitchen. Her eyes had red rings, and his heart ached at the thought of her crying alone.

"Any news?" She stopped in front of him, wrapping her arms around her waist as if she was chilled.

Henry wanted to envelope her in his arms, but the logistics of trying to do so with his crutches kept him frozen with his back against the counter. Better to focus on the new information than dwelling on how she'd felt in his arms when he kissed her a few days ago. "As a matter of fact, there is. An old friend from Germany just called with the news that someone was rooting around in the Stasi archives for information on Rainer and Verna Kopecek."

Violet's eyes widened. "But not our friend The Wolf because he already knows about the Kopeceks."

He nodded. "It has to be someone else."

"Maybe this elusive flower we're seeking?"

"That was my thought too." Henry shifted his position, balancing his crutches better to ease the weight on his legs. Standing too long in one position tended to make his muscles ache. "But that's not all."

She cocked her head. "What else happened?"

Succinctly, he explained what Kristian had told him. She tapped her fingers on her crossed arm as she processed the data. "Someone else is calling in favors related to The Wolf?"

"I've never met Kristian's uncle, but from what little he's told me, the man was a higher up in the Stasi or East Berlin government."

"Do you think it could be the same person who's been rifling through the archives?"

He shrugged. "It would be too much of a coincidence, but then again, stranger things have happened. Are happening."

"That's for sure." She rubbed her forehead.

"Headache?"

"No, I just can't help thinking there's something obvious we're missing." Now it was her turn to shrug. "When do you think Juan will have more lines decoded?"

Henry picked up his phone and scrolled through his texts. "He texted me this morning to say he modified his program and fed in the next two coded phrases." He glanced up. "Not that he said it outright. He insisted on using his own code to talk about the assignment. I think he's enjoying the cloak-and-dagger elements of this a bit too much."

Violet smiled, and Henry returned the smile. He started to reach for her but instead knocked over one of his crutches, sending it clattering to the floor. Before he could start the laborious process of easing down to pick it up, she had plucked the crutch off the floor. She extended it to him, and as he grasped it, he avoided her eyes. The last thing he wanted to see in their depths was pity.

"Henry?"

At the soft sound of his name on her lips, his gaze collided with hers. Pity wasn't what swam in her eyes. Instead, something glimmered like unshed tears. "Yes?"

Violet moved closer until their bodies nearly touched. She laid one of her hands on his arm, the heat from it warming his entire frame. "Would you... I mean. Oh, dear."

With an effort, he focused on what she was saying. Or, more accurately, what she wasn't saying.

She shook her head. "I'm sorry, I shouldn't impose."

She removed her hand and started to take a step back, but Henry brought his hand up to cup her elbow in a gentle hold.

"Yes, you should." He tugged her unresisting body closer until she leaned against him. With one hand on the counter to brace himself, he slid the other up her arm to her shoulders and pressed her toward him. "I might have weak legs, but I think I'm strong enough to hold you."

With a heavy sigh, Violet wilted into his embrace. He pretended not to notice the tears dampening his shirt as he rubbed circles on her back with his free hand. Her head rested in a hollow beneath his chin, and she clutched his shirt as she sobbed. Whatever hurt she had suffered, he was glad she had chosen him to share it.

IRIS FROWNED AND REPLACED THE RECEIVER. IT WASN'T LIKE DIRK NOT TO answer his phone or to blow off work, especially with all the preparation needed for her Senate confirmation hearing to become secretary of state.

She buzzed her assistant. "Richelle, please check with the staff to see if Dirk left any messages."

That task done, she tried to turn her attention to the piles of paperwork on her desk, but her mind kept returning to Dirk's absence. Close to noon, she finally tossed her pen onto the desk and closed the folder. The farm bill markup would have to wait until after lunch and a quick trip to Dirk's apartment.

Iris strode out of her office, instructing her assistant to hold all calls until after lunch. In the hallway, she tucked her worry away and played the politics game with the other senators and staffers she met on her way to the garage. Once in the car, she reached into the glove compartment for her gun. Nowadays she couldn't carry it in the office building, but knowing it was close by in the garage gave her comfort. With the gun out of sight in her handbag, she left the car and walked briskly the few blocks to Dirk's apartment.

Punching in the security code, she took the stairs to the fourth floor and knocked on his door. No answer. She waited and knocked again, harder this time. Still no answer. Iris nearly dropped her keys trying to find the one that fit Dirk's apartment door. Finally locating the right key, she shoved it in the lock and turned the handle, opening the door.

The light breeze created by the door swinging open told her all she needed to know. She might not have smelled the scent since her West Berlin days, but the stench was unmistakable.

Dirk was dead.

CHAPTER

TWENTY-NINE

Bryon Smith threaded his way through the throngs of people milling about on the sidewalk outside Dirk Jones's apartment building. The crime-scene van and police cars with flashing lights blocked the street. The senator's aide was probably dead.

But by whose hand? Dirk's own or The Wolf's?

With Iris Morrison's confirmation hearing coming up, she wouldn't dare sully her hands with murder even if she'd discovered Dirk was in league with The Wolf. She might have blood on her hands, but it was dried.

He craned his neck to see over the heads of the crowd to the front door, which had two beat cops checking the IDs of everyone who attempted to enter. He wouldn't be able to talk his way past them. An older man with a small dog came out and headed toward him. Bryon leaned down and held out his hand to the dog, who trotted up with a happy yip.

"Nice dog you have. What's his name?" Bryon scratched the shaggy pooch behind the ears.

"Sully." The man paused. "The police asked us to take a little walk because he kept barking at all the activity on the floor."

Bryon glanced at the man, then back down at the dog, who had rolled over for a belly rub. "I saw all the cop cars and crime scene van. Someone get robbed?"

The man snorted. "Are you kidding me? They barely send out one officer for a reported burglary. No, the man across the hall from me is dead. He apparently works—correction, worked—for a senator. That woman who's up for secretary of state."

A witness he could pump for information with a little finesse was a godsend and exactly what Bryon needed to stay one step ahead of The Wolf. "How'd he die?"

"I overheard one of the cops say it looked like suicide, but I'm not sure the senator is convinced."

Bryon gave the dog one last scratch and stood. "She's there?"

"She called it in. Sully barked when the senator stopped at the man's apartment door. I took a quick look through my peephole and saw her enter. Sully always alerts me when someone he doesn't know is near our door."

"He didn't bark when your neighbor came home?"

The man shook his head. "No, Sully knew the man. I think dogs are keen to recognizing footsteps or maybe a familiar scent. He never barked when the neighbor came home or left."

"Sounds like a good watchdog." The man must have been out when Bryon had paid Jones a visit, or he might have recognized Bryon.

The owner reached down and patted the animal on its head. "He might be little, but he's the best warning dog I've seen."

"Sounds like he is." Bryon strove to sound causal. "Did he bark last night?"

"Funny you should ask. I tried to tell the detective who questioned me about whether I'd seen anyone or not, but he didn't want to hear about a dog barking in the wee hours of the morning."

"So you think a stranger stopped by the man's apartment in the middle of the night?" Bryon kept his face devoid of anything but innocent curiosity, but inside, it was apparent The Wolf had struck again.

"All I know is Sully started barking about two-thirty and then again at little before three a.m. I told those detectives my dog only barks at strangers, but they weren't interested."

Or the police were instructed not to look beyond the obvious and rule it suicide no matter what evidence turned up. The Wolf had long tentacles that reached into many places.

The man shook his head. "All they wanted to know was when the senator knocked on my door and when she had entered the unit across the hall."

"What did you say?" Bryon hoped the question would keep the man talking.

"That she was in there less than five minutes and that she asked if she could wait in my apartment until the police arrived."

"Did she tell you what happened?"

"Only that the gentleman across the way was dead."

"I hope they can clear this up soon." He stepped back as the man tugged on the dog leash, then walked away with Sully trotting in front.

As the pair turned the corner, Bryon's mind whirred with the knowledge that, despite what the police seemed to think, Dirk Jones had been murdered.

IRIS RUBBED HER TEMPLES TO EASE THE ACHE IN HER HEAD, NOT WANTING TO believe Dirk was dead. Her trusted confidant and aide since her West Berlin days, he had been the only one who knew about The Wolf. The detectives at the crime scene assured her they would investigate his death as suspicious, but she read in their eyes they'd concluded death by suicide.

The scene, the gun, the note all pointed to Dirk taking his own life.

But what the police didn't know—and she wasn't about to tell them—was the envelope she'd found in Dirk's shoe. An old trick, one Dirk had employed to ferry documents many times in the past. After a quick look around the living room, she had spotted the shiny leather loafers next to the couch, as if waiting for their owner to step into them and leave for the office. She would have overlooked them had she not seen Dirk wearing the wingtips. Her aide had been most fastidious about keeping things in their proper place. Leaving a pair of shoes out when he had no intention of wearing them was out of character. His preference for slipping documents between the sole and the liner prompted her to check, and she'd discovered the envelope.

She rested against the back of her sofa, the silent house a balm on her shattered nerves. The envelope lay unopened on her lap. Dirk had been a good friend despite their employer/employee relationship, and whatever the envelope contained, she didn't want it to mar that memory. On the other hand, she needed to know if he had taken his own life or had his life cut short by another.

With a sigh, she carefully opened the envelope, extracting a single sheet of paper and two photographs. One picture showed a young woman with feathered dark brown hair wearing an off-shoulder sweater. She didn't need to turn it over to know the woman's identity. Amy. Tightness in her chest caused her breath to come in gasps. Her finger traced the woman's figure. The other photograph was of the same young woman in a simple t-shirt and jeans, her large sunglasses pushed up and holding back her tousled hair.

Iris turned over the first photo and read the brief inscription scrawled in Dirk's bold handwriting. *Amy, 1986.* The second photo had a similarly short identification, but the name and year had changed. *Allison, 2013.*

Iris's brows tensed, and she flipped both photos over to compare the women. The first one was definitely Amy, but on closer inspection, the second one had a slightly differently shaped face and darker eyes. The two women had to be related. The obvious answer was mother and daughter.

The only problem was Amy had died more than a quarter century ago, according to Dirk.

She shook her head and opened the piece of paper. The letter addressed to her had yesterday's date scribbled in the right-hand corner. She immediately recognized Dirk's handwriting.

Dear Iris,

If you're reading this letter, I must be dead.

You and I have shared many secrets, but there were several I had to carry alone. One was Amy. You knew we were lovers, but what you didn't know was we married secretly for her protection. But in the end, it wasn't enough, and Amy died.

Thus I must apologize with the written word rather than in person. And apologize I must, for I made a bargain with the devil in order to save an angel.

The second secret was Amy had a child we named Allison. I only told one person about Allison's existence because he was the only person who could guarantee her safety. Yes, I handed over my daughter's identity to The Wolf in exchange for her life. He arranged for her adoption by an American couple in Tennessee. She's had a good life, a safe life, one wholly unconnected with me or The Wolf. He kept his end of the deal and I've kept mine by informing him as to your movements concerning him.

DIRK'S BETRAYAL RIPPED THROUGH HER BODY LIKE A BULLET. ALL THESE years, through all the lies and cover-ups, she had never suspected Dirk was working for The Wolf. The one thought that had sustained her during those dark months following The Wolf's supposed demise was Dirk's steadfast loyalty. She would have kept his daughter safe, but even as the thought ricocheted across her mind, it was a lie. Back then, she wasn't as strong as she was now. She might have sold Amy and Allison out if the price had been right. Not for money but for the future. Maybe Dirk did know her better than she knew herself.

She turned back to the page.

I didn't tell him everything, as I owe you my life, but enough to keep his suspicions at bay. This arrangement might have continued but for a man who called himself Byron Smith, one of The Wolf's many minions. Smith came to see me a few days ago, and he knew things about our past, things only The Wolf had known, or so we thought. However, even Smith had stumbled, and now The Wolf was on his trail. I'm not sure if Smith is clever enough to outwit the hunter. If he is, he'll contact you. Listen to him but remain guarded. The Wolf is cleaning house—be careful you aren't disposed of with the rest of the garbage.

Dirk

Iris refolded the paper and tucked the photographs back inside the envelope. She should burn the letter and photographs, but she wanted to keep this last link to Dirk. At least she still had one last gamble to bring The Wolf to heel. If she succeeded, she wouldn't have to worry about The Wolf ever again.

If she failed, she wouldn't worry about anything. Ever. Again.

CHAPTER

THIRTY

H enry stretched his arms above his head and rotated his shoulders. The microfiche room at the U.S. State Department archives had no windows and stale air, as if no one bothered opening the door most days. No surprise, since most researchers accomplished their work trolling through the internet rather than sifting through dusty shelves of microfiche reels. However, staff logs from foreign embassies weren't a top priority to upload to an internet search engine. His friend in the State Department had cleared it so Henry could look at the unclassified personnel lists.

With a sigh, he inserted the next reel, threading it through the machine with practiced ease. Fast-forwarding through the front matter, he slowed and began the tedious task of scanning the list of names associated with the United State's West Germany Embassy during the 1980s. He had already gone through 1980, 1981, 1982, and 1983. A tall stack beside him made him shudder. 1984 had two reels, as did 1985 and 1986. He might not resurface for days at this rate.

As he scrolled the list of staffers, his mind drifted to Violet and their budding relationship. Holding her last night in the kitchen had awakened in him a desire to taste her lips again and cradle her in his arms, whispering sweet words. Those feelings had also stirred a chivalrous desire to walk beside her and keep her safe from whatever troubled her.

Henry jerked himself back to the present, and the microfiche shot forward, sending names flying by at warp speed. Hitting the stop button, he clenched his jaw and reversed the reel. Great, his daydreaming had cost him a lot of time. The microfiche began to pick up speed when a date caught his eye. April 1984.

He stopped the whirring machine and sat back, turning over that date in his mind as he slowly combed through the names of staff at the embassy in that month and year. A name midway down the page jumped out at him. When he cross-referenced where the person worked in the embassy, he was certain he had found their flower.

Picking up his phone, he sent Violet a text to meet him in front of the State Department Library in fifteen minutes. They had taken the Metro downtown together, but since she lacked research credentials, she couldn't accompany him to the library's archives. Instead, she had spent the morning at the Smithsonian National Museum of Natural History.

10-4. Her affirmative reply made him smile.

He jotted down the pertinent information from the microfiche and returned the reels to their respective boxes. After stacking the boxes on the cart beside the microfiche table, he gathered his belongings and crutches. A short time later, he stood on the sidewalk breathing in the crisp March air.

"Henry!"

He turned, then waved at Violet, who hurried toward him, her cheeks flushed and her hair flying out behind her. Henry waited until she stood beside him to speak. "Hello."

She cocked her head and grinned at him. "You've discovered something."

Henry returned her smile. "Indeed I have."

Raising her eyebrows, she put her hands on her hips. "You'd better tell me."

"Okay, okay. Can't a man have a little suspense in his life?"

"After all we've been through? No more suspense."

He laughed. "You're right." He lowered his voice. "I think I've found our flower."

Her jaw dropped for several seconds. Henry started to ask if she'd heard him when she said, "Really?"

"Buy me a cup of tea, and I'll fill you in."

"You wouldn't last too long as a real spy if your information can be purchased so cheaply." She moved to his left and gestured toward the intersection. "There's a Corner Bakery Café on Pennsylvania Avenue."

"Sounds good." Not for the first time, Henry wanted to put his arm around her shoulders or hold her hand. But that was a luxury a man on crutches couldn't afford. He had to content himself with brushing her arm with his.

Soon, they were snug in a booth with steaming cups of pomegranate oolong tea and two cranberry scones. Henry could have simply stared at Violet all day and not grown tired of the view, but her fidgeting told him she wanted to know his discovery.

"Before I reveal the name, I need to tell you a bit of background."

Violet grimaced. "You're not going to get all professorial and launch into a lecture, are you? Because I don't think I have the patience, not when I feel like we're getting so close to figuring things out."

Henry shook his head. "I promise not to pretend I'm at the lectern addressing a group of freshmen."

"Then go forth and background me." Violet accompanied her words with a sweeping gesture of her hand that nearly overturned her tea. With a blush, she wrapped her hands around the ceramic cup.

Henry reached across the table and touched her arm briefly and was rewarded with a smile. "Here goes. After plowing through the early eighties, I came to 1984, which had two microfiche reels. The first one held much of the same as the earlier reels, then I accidentally fast-forwarded through most of February and all of March, stopping in April. That jogged my memory of something significant or at least noteworthy happening in April 1984."

"What happened in April 1984?"

"As you probably know, hundreds, if not thousands, of people defected or tried to defect from East Germany, especially East Berlin, well into the 1980s. In early 1984, a man named Stefan Nussbaum contacted Eric Green, who helped people defect to the United States. But then Nussbaum told Green what he did, and everything changed." Henry reveled in the drama he'd created surrounding the discovery. After all, the story called for just a little bit of showmanship.

"Oh, this is intriguing." Violet broke off a piece of scone and popped it in her mouth.

"Nussbaum revealed he was a nuclear scientist who had worked closely with Peter Adolf Thiessen and others on the Soviet Union's atomic bomb project. Basically, one of the designers of the Soviet's nuclear missile program wanted to come to our side. If successful, it would be the biggest coup of Green's career."

"I can see by your expression he didn't make it out."

"I'm that transparent, am I?" He shrugged. "A little more backstory. Nussbaum was in his 60s, and he wanted to bring his wife of forty years out with him. She, however, always stayed behind the Iron Curtain whenever Nussbaum traveled to ensure he'd return to the mother country."

"This Green fellow had to get the scientist's wife out or the scientist wouldn't defect."

"Exactly. Nussbaum couldn't walk into the U.S. Embassy and demand asylum. It had to be done covertly."

Violet nodded, then frowned. "You still haven't told me what this has to do with our case or whatever we're calling it."

"Patience," he teased, delighted to see a faint blush touch her cheeks. "The defection of such a scientist would have been a devastating blow to the Soviet Union with major repercussions. Of course, the Soviets didn't like any defections, especially from East Germany or East Berlin. The Stasi agents in West Berlin were on the lookout for any meetings between U.S. embassy staff and East German citizens."

Henry took a sip of his tea. "Green had just started the process to bring out Nussbaum's wife when it all went to pieces. The wife disappeared, and Nussbaum suffered what appeared to be a heart attack in a café where he was to meet Green to finalize the details of his defection."

"That doesn't sound sinister. I mean, the wife's disappearance seems too much of a coincidence, but a heart attack at his age, under the stress he must have been under, doesn't shout foul play."

"That's what everyone initially thought." Henry settled back into the booth as the events played out in his mind. "And I'd agree if Green himself wasn't found two days later with a bullet in the back of his head."

Violet gasped softly. "Oh, my."

"Nussbaum's wife turned up in the River Havel a few days after that, an accidental drowning victim, or so the official verdict went at the time. My sources at the Stasi archives say the real cause of death was strangulation."

"This is all fascinating, but I still don't see the connection."

"When I first came across Green's story years ago, it appeared he was just an unfortunate casualty of the Cold War. In my research about the Stasi, I discovered they had several moles inside the U.S. Embassy, ones providing vital information, such as secret meetings between defectors. I began tracing several such 'unfortunate' incidents and uncovered potential double agents." Henry glanced around and lowered his voice. "One I hadn't traced was Green, and when I saw the April 1984 date, I thought I would see if perhaps a staffer with a connection to him also had a flower name."

Violet stared at him. "And you did find such a person."

He allowed himself a small smile. "Yes."

"Don't keep me in suspense. Who was it?"

"Iris Wheeler."

"Iris!" Her face reddened, and she lowered her voice. "That's definitely a flower name. I wonder where she is today or if she's still alive."

Henry leaned across the table and motioned Violet closer with a small wave of his hand. "She is. But she goes by her married name now. Iris Morrison."

THIRTY-ONE

"Iris Morrison?" Violet furrowed her brow. "The name sounds familiar."

"You probably heard about her on the news." Henry gave her a sheepish smile. "To be honest, I didn't know who she was, until I Googled Iris Wheeler while waiting for you."

They were inching closer to the truth, closer to The Wolf's identity. Baby steps, to be sure, but at least they were moving forward.

"She's the U.S. senator from Wisconsin who's been all over the news lately because the president has submitted her name for secretary of state."

"Secretary of state?" Violet tapped her fingers on the table. "A senator? Doesn't sound like someone with a murky past."

"That's what I thought too, until I realized she was one of a handful of lower-level people at the West Berlin Embassy who might have had access to sensitive information. She worked directly for Eric Green when she first arrived there in January 1984."

"I thought you went through January and didn't see her name."

"I did." Henry finished his tea and stuffed his napkin inside the cup. "I called my friend in human resources at the State Department, who pulled up her employment file. She came in January but wasn't officially listed until April because she was first attached to the ambassador's personal staff before transferring to the embassy."

"How sure are you that this Iris Morrison, née Wheeler, is connected with the, um, animal we're seeking?" She didn't want to say The Wolf's name aloud in a crowded restaurant. It still seemed too surreal they would have found their flower so easily.

"I can't be 100 percent sure, but I'd say it's a distinct possibility."

Violet studied his warm brown eyes across the table. He had become very dear to her over the last few weeks. Maybe soon they could have a real date, not one based on solving this mystery. "Then where do we go from here?"

Henry rubbed the bridge of his nose. "That's the tricky part. I think we have two options. One, continue our independent research and compile a timeline and facts for Iris Wheeler in West Berlin. That will take time and tact, as we can't let anyone suspect what we're doing or why. But her cabinet nomination will be in our favor, as more press will be nosing around her life and background. We might just blend right in with all of those inquires."

Violet figured she knew what the second option was but asked anyway. "And the second?"

"One of us calls Iris Morrison and simply asks her."

⌖

THIS WEARINESS OF MINE, MAY IT NOT COME
   From something that doth need no setting right?
   Shall fruit be blamed if it hang wearily
   A day before it perfected drop plumb
   To the sad earth from off its nursing tree?
   Ripeness must always come with loss of might.
   The weary evening fall before the resting night.

. . .

Iris slid a bookmark into the devotional book, *Diary of an Old Soul* by George MacDonald, and placed the book on the end table. She had always loved the simplicity of MacDonald's writing and had stumbled across this gem when she returned from West Berlin. The quiet faith and words of wisdom bathed each entry and soothed her battered soul.

Roger had encouraged her to delve deep into the pages, but she had rarely picked up the book since her husband's death nearly fifteen years ago. If it weren't for his cancer and dying so early in their marriage, things would have been different.

She rose from her favorite reading chair to gaze out of the French windows overlooking a barren garden, still asleep in the winter's cold. She rested her forehead against the cool glass. Her thoughts returned to Roger. He hadn't known everything about her past. She'd wanted to tell him, longed to unburden her heart, but couldn't find the words. Then it was too late.

A knock at the door broke into her reflections. Her head still resting against the glass, she answered, "Come in."

"A visitor to see you, ma'am."

Iris turned. A man stood behind her housekeeper. She sighed. "I told you I wasn't to be disturbed."

The man stepped around the other woman. "I'm afraid I insisted."

She studied him for a moment. In her business, it paid to remember faces. A hard face with a small scar slashed on his left cheek, drawing the eye to a slightly crooked nose. Not a face one would easily forget. "Thank you, Janet. I'll let you know if we need any refreshments."

Janet silently closed the door behind the man, whose slightly raised eyebrows made Iris think he was amused.

"Well?" Irritation sharpened her voice.

"Now is that anyway to treat an old friend?"

"We've never met." Her body tensed as he crossed the room and stopped a few feet from her.

"No, but we have a rather important mutual friend."

Her heart raced as the words of Dirk's letter flashed in her mind. "You're Byron Smith."

His eyes widened for a split second before his face resumed its impassive expression. Good, she had surprised him. If she could keep him off balance, she would learn more than she revealed to him. "And our mutual friend would go by the moniker The Wolf, I suppose?" By effort, she kept her voice light and airy, the tone she'd used to such great effect in West Berlin. Eric Green and others had thought her rather vapid, which suited her just fine. The dumber they thought her, the more information she gathered—and used—to bring low those who had dug their shoes into her shoulders on their climb toward the top.

He crossed to a wing chair and settled himself. She debated keeping the appearance of the upper hand by standing but decided nothing would be gained by such a show with this man. She chose the loveseat, gracefully seated herself, then crossed her legs at the ankles.

"Now that we know where we stand, why don't you tell me why you're here?"

"Dirk Jones."

Iris raised an eyebrow. "He's dead." She paused, considering whether to ask him and deciding it wouldn't hurt. "Did you kill him?"

"The Wolf has always spoken of you with admiration and now I know why." Bryon gave her a mocking salute. "You have a way about you that is most disarming."

She acknowledged the compliment with a tiny nod of her head and waited for him to continue.

"No, I did not kill him. Rumor has it the police are going to rule suicide."

A pang of regret sliced through her that Dirk would be tainted, even after death, with such a mark. "But you don't think so."

"Neither do you."

Iris tilted her head. "Then who ended his life?"

"Our mutual friend."

"By his own hand?" If The Wolf had committed the crime himself, things were more dire than she thought.

Bryon nodded. "He's starting to take risks he's never taken before."

Iris contemplated his words. The Wolf's actions had struck her as a bit erratic, but the crucial questions of why now and what he hoped to accomplish still eluded her. "He's had a very successful career. Why take these chances now?"

"I'm not sure."

Her frustration mounted. The man toyed with her, and she wasn't amused. Not at all. "Why did you come here, Mr. Smith?"

"I think you know why, senator."

Probably his need of sanctuary, now that he had fled from The Wolf's lair. "How do I know I can trust you? For all your talk, you could still be loyal to our mutual friend."

"I assure you, that's not the case." Bryon leaned forward, his eyes hard as flint.

"Words carry less weight than actions." She almost believed him but sensed he wasn't sharing everything.

Bryon reclined into the chair. "Of course. There was one project I was working on concerning two people in whom you've taken an interest."

Iris raised her eyebrows in a practiced gesture of carelessness. "Oh, and who might that be?"

"Dr. Henry Silverton and Violet Lundy."

CHAPTER
THIRTY-TWO

Henry glanced up from the pile of papers on his desk at the knock on the door. "Come in."

Juan Delores opened the door and entered. "Hi, Dr. Silverton."

"Juan, have a seat. Does this mean you've decoded some more?"

Juan slung his backpack on the floor and slouched in the chair across from Henry's desk. He glanced behind him as if checking to make sure the door remained closed.

Henry raised an eyebrow at his covert manner. "Are you okay?"

Juan shifted in his chair and leaned forward, his voice soft. "Maybe we should go someplace else, in case, you know, someone's listening?"

Henry hadn't considered the possibility his office could be bugged. However, after teaching two classes and an evening lecture facing him shortly, his legs wouldn't be up to moving to a new location. Besides, his left wrist still ached after the car accident, and he didn't want to tax it too much. He lowered his own voice, "You might be right, but I'm not physically up to leaving this chair."

"Hmm." Juan closed his eyes, then popped them open again. "I think I have a solution." He tapped on his cell phone and soon the sound of raindrops filled the room. Placing the phone on the desk, Juan moved his chair until it nearly touched Henry's. "If we talk softly, this should cover our conversation."

Henry bit back a smile at the younger man's earnestness, glad Juan was taking his admonishment to be careful very seriously. He wouldn't want something to happen to the younger man. "A good idea. Now, what did you find out?"

"I think I've figured out the rest of the code."

"Fantastic. What is it?"

"You tell me. I didn't want to chance running it through the Google translator, just in case someone was onto me." Juan handed him a piece of paper with two German phrases.

Henry read the first line: *3. Januar, der Washington Post, einen Abschnitt, Seite vier.* "It appears to be a reference to a *Washington Post* article, but not the title, just the section and page number."

Juan nodded. "That makes sense from what I could figure out. Good thing *Washington Post* doesn't have a German equivalent."

"Hmm. We'll have to go to the paper's archives because this doesn't specify which story, and the website doesn't keep the layout version of the print edition up for more than a couple of days. I'll have to do some digging on this one. Let's see if the other one sheds any light." He read the last line: *Nicht der, der er zu sein scheint.* "It means 'Not who he seems to be.'"

"Not very helpful if we don't know who *he* is." Juan sat back, his face glum. "I thought these would be the keys to the whole mystery."

"Don't give up too fast," Henry warned. "Without you, we wouldn't even have this. Let me see where in the book these two phrases appeared." He flipped through Kopecek's copy to the three pages with the codes. Taken sequentially, the flower phrase came first, then the Post article, followed by the final phrase. "Finding the newspaper story will be key to figuring out this final phrase. Once we know who the *he* is or at least have some inkling of who it could be, then we can perhaps figure out who's hiding something."

Henry turned to Juan. "I'll let you know if we find something. Meanwhile, be careful."

Juan grinned as he scooted back his chair and turned off the rain shower on his phone. "Are you kidding? This is the most fun I've had all year." He grabbed his backpack and left the office, closing the door behind him.

Henry sat at his desk. There was no way he'd have time to search for the article today. Reaching for his phone, he sent Violet a text.

Can you get print copy of January 3, Washington Post, A section, page four? See you tonight after my class.

A few seconds later, she replied.

Sure thing! C u later.

He glanced at his watch. Six more hours before he would see Violet again. An eternity. With a sigh, he turned his attention to the stack of papers on his desk.

VIOLET STOPPED AT THE REFERENCE DESK AT THE CITY OF FAIRFAX REGIONAL Library. "Excuse me," she said to the woman typing on the computer behind the desk.

The woman—her name tag read Molly—stopped her task and smiled at Violet. "How can I help you?"

"How long do you keep copies of the Post? I checked the current reading section, but it only goes back a week."

"That depends on what month you're looking for."

Violet consulted her phone. "I'm looking for the January 3rd print edition."

Molly tapped a few keys. "Ah, we have that one in our reference area. Take the stairs, turn left at the top, and you'll see the shelves labeled for newspapers."

Violet thanked her and headed upstairs. On the second floor, she easily found the location of the newspaper stacks and hunted for the right issue. Flipping through the January cubby, she came to the 31st without finding the 3rd. Strange that one particular issue would be missing. She went through the papers slower and discovered January 3rd hiding inside January 6th.

Sliding the front section from the rest of the paper, she carried it to an empty table and spread it out. Page four contained three stories. The top one concerned a ranch in Nebraska battling the U.S. government over range use on federal land. A photo of a man standing in front of a barn, his hand on the halter of a quarter horse accompanied the text. She skimmed the article, but nothing jumped out at her. The second, which ran along the right-hand side of the page, talked about a new cancer drug the U.S. Food and Drug Administration just approved for a clinical trial. Again, nothing of significance that she could see.

Maybe Mr. Kopecek hadn't left them a code to crack. Maybe they were tilting at windmills. Maybe she needed more sleep. With a shake of her head, she returned to the paper to read the final story, a short piece about a cybersecurity company in California.

Calif. Cybersecurity Company Awarded Federal Grant

SAN DIEGO (AP) – The U.S. Department of Homeland Security awarded Vault Cybersecurity a multi-million dollar grant to develop cybersecurity for the federal government. The brainchild of billionaire financier Bob DeLancey, Vault Cybersecurity has grown from a small technology company into a major player in the cybersecurity world.

The rest of the article provided more details on the grant and company. The photograph of a group of Vault Cybersecurity employees accompanied the piece. She started to put the paper down when she noticed the picture again. Four of the five men faced the camera, but one had his face turned away. The photographer had caught his profile only, and the caption identified that man as Bob DeLancey.

Taking the paper to the photocopy machine, she made two copies of the page and returned the issue to the stacks. Then she found an empty computer terminal and keyed in "Bob DeLancey" into Google. Twenty minutes later, she had discovered quite a lot about DeLancey. The most intriguing part was his stint in the State Department during the 1980s. Bob DeLancey had been stationed in Europe during the time of The Wolf. A man with his connections and power definitely had a lot to lose if a shady past came out into the light.

CHAPTER

THIRTY-THREE

Violet stopped at the corner of North Street and University Avenue to wait for the signal to cross the street. The late-afternoon sun slanted its golden rays on the buildings, bringing with it a hint of spring. Only a couple of weeks before March 21st, and already the crocuses were starting to stretch from their winter slumber. She tightened the grip on her shoulder bag and stepped off the curb as the light changed. Suddenly, a man ran at her from the side and yanked her arm, propelling her back onto the sidewalk. Violet hit the bricks hard, pain shooting up her arms. For a few seconds, she couldn't focus on what was happening. Shouts and tires squealing on asphalt mingled together.

"Miss, are you okay?"

Violet stared at the man, a short scar marring the left side of his face. Anger shot the words out of her mouth. "You pushed me down." There was something familiar about him, but she couldn't place where she'd see him.

The man started to answer, but a woman nearby overheard and inserted herself into the conversation. "And it's a good thing he did, young lady. That car didn't even stop as it roared down the street and took the corner. If he hadn't gotten you out of the way, you would have been hit."

Violet gasped, her ire fading at the realization his action saved her. "Oh, my. Then thank you."

The man studied her face. "Will you be all right?"

She tested her limbs. "I think so. Some bruises but nothing too serious."

He nodded. "Be careful. You might not be so lucky a third time." Before Violet could ask what he meant or even his name, the man melted into the crowd and was gone.

Struggling to her feet, she swayed as a wave of dizziness swept over her.

The woman who had spoken before gently took her arm and guided her to a bench. "Here, dear. Just sit down for a little bit. An ambulance is on its way."

"Ambulance? I don't need a doctor. I'm fine, really." Violet winced as she sat, her body aching from the impact with the ground. She lifted her hand and saw her palm had red slashes from her skid over the pavement. Her jacket now sported a rip up one arm, and her jeans had a hole in the left knee. At least the bruises and cut from the car crash had faded before she'd added new ones.

"Is there someone I can call for you?" The woman hovered beside her, her older face a crease of concern.

Violet shook her head. The man's cryptic words and disappearance made her uneasy. Maybe the car's path wasn't accidental. "Did you see what kind of the car it was?"

The woman frowned. "No, it happened so fast. All I know is that it was a black sedan."

A young man with knit cap and a skateboard tucked under one arm chimed in, "It wasn't a car. It was a pickup truck."

The woman turned to him with a hand on one hip. "I think I know a sedan from a pickup."

The young man shrugged and dropped his skateboard onto the

182

sidewalk. "Just saying what I saw." With a nod to Violet, he pushed off, balancing on the thin board with ease.

The woman's insistence the vehicle was a car, not a truck, should have eased Violet's mind, but visions of another dark pickup truck zooming around Henry's SUV flashed across her mind. Before she could ask more questions, an ambulance screeched to a halt in the traffic lane beside the bench, with a police motorcycle right behind it. A paramedic approached, kit in hand. "Miss? May I take a look?"

Violet tried to protest, but in the end, it was easier to let the EMTs do their job. At this rate, she would be on a first-name basis with paramedics across Northern Virginia. While the first-aid responders checked her vitals and bandaged her hands and knee, she provided the scant details to the police officer. The man who had pushed her to safety had left the scene. The woman provided her version of the scene, making no mention of the young man's insistence that the car wasn't a sedan at all, but a truck. Having not seen the speeding vehicle, Violet stayed silent.

Twenty minutes later, she sank into a booth at Starbucks with a cup of Royal English Breakfast to steady her nerves. It was only as the police officer questioned her about the incident did she realize how close she came to being slammed by a car. If the man hadn't acted so quickly, she would have been heading to the hospital—or worse.

Her phone admonished her to "Get Happy." Her mother's number flashed on the screen. Just what she needed. Experience told her to answer her mother's call, but prudence demanded she ignore it. The former won, given her mother's history of repeated calls until Violet answered, her version of not giving up. "Hello, Mom."

"Have you thought anymore about supporting your brother?"

Really, it was like the conversation they had days ago had no discernable effect on the woman. "I already said I wasn't coming."

Her mother sighed, a drawn-out, long-suffering sigh, calculated to bring her wayward daughter to heel. "But I already told the producer you'd be here. It's the only reason she agreed to do the interview."

Putting her head on her hand, Violet counted to ten. Getting angry at her mother only resulted in a longer conversation. "I'm sorry, but you had no right to do that. I will not be on the program or any other show."

"Well," her mother huffed, indignation permeating the airwaves between them. "I think it's pretty shabby that you won't join your father and me in a show of love for Patrick."

Violet stayed silent. The only reply her mother wanted to hear was Violet's capitulation to her scheme. She had learned long ago that silence was the single effective response to her mother's guilt trips. When her mother offered nothing else, Violet said goodbye and disconnected the call. In all the excitement, she had forgotten about Patrick's anniversary—and that Henry didn't know about her past. She would tell Henry tonight before her former life collided with her current one.

HENRY DROPPED HIS BAG INTO THE BACK SEAT OF HIS NEW SUV AND CLOSED the door. As he opened the driver's door, he noticed a flyer and a brown envelope stuck under the windshield wiper. Plucking it out, he glanced at the printed message proclaiming a nearby restaurant to have the best chicken wrap on the block. He tossed it and the envelope on the passenger's seat and maneuvered himself into the car. The drive home took longer than usual with an accident on I-66 East blocking the two left lanes. Waiting to move, he sent Violet a quick text.

Stuck in traffic. Any luck with Post article?

He inched forward before halting again, giving him time to read her reply.

Found & copied page. One possibility. R U coming to Sissy's?

Traffic started moving, so he put down his phone and concentrated on keeping pace with the heavy volume. He didn't have an opportunity to answer until he pulled into his driveway and turned off the car.

Too tired & needed some things from my house. Call you in 10?

Her smiley face response nearly made him put the car in reverse and head over to his sister's, but a cramp in his leg reminded him that resting took precedence over seeing Violet.

Once inside, he settled into his recliner with a heating pad to ease the pain in his leg and sorted his mail. Then he picked up the envelope left on his car. Nothing but his name was scrawled across the front. Most decidedly not with the restaurant flyer. He opened the flap and tugged out a sheaf of papers. Paper-clipped to the top was a short note.

Dr. Silverton,

Thought you might like to know more about your charming companion.

HENRY FROWNED AND REMOVED THE UNSIGNED NOTE TO READ THE FIRST page, which was a photocopy of a newspaper article from the *Louisville Chronicle*, dated five years ago. The headline screamed in dark, thick letters: "Former student kills 18 at Louisville middle school."

The opening paragraph focused on the bare facts.

LOUISVILLE, KY. (AP) – A QUIET MARCH DAY AT KEY MIDDLE SCHOOL was shattered when a gunman entered the building and opened fire in an art teacher's classroom, killing the teacher and all 17 students present. The alleged shooter, Patrick Cunningham, 25, then barricaded himself in the room until police arrived, when he peacefully surrendered.

. . .

Henry skimmed the rest of the article before flipping through the rest of the stack and scanning the headlines. All of the articles, clipped together in chronological order, were about the shooting and its aftermath. The final stories focused on the trial and conviction of Cunningham, who was serving a life sentence without parole in Kentucky.

Puzzled, he started to put the pages back in the envelope when one sheet slipped out and fell to the floor. He picked it up, glancing at the large photograph of Patrick and a young woman. The picture accompanied an in-depth piece about Patrick's upbringing. The photo credit indicated it was from the family. The caption read: *Patrick and his twin sister, Patricia, the summer before the shooting.*

In hands that trembled, he examined the photograph more closely.

The young woman, her auburn hair held back from her face with a headband, was the mirror image of Violet.

THIRTY-FOUR

Violet stared at her phone as if by sheer willpower she could make it ring. Henry texted he would call her in ten minutes, but thirty minutes had passed without a word. She bit her lip. He might have fallen asleep in his recliner after a long day, and she hated to wake him. On the other hand, she was dying to tell him of her discovery and almost accident. Easing back against the pillows on the bed, she shifted into a more comfortable position. Her body ached, and she longed to soak the sore muscles in a hot bath before having an early night of it herself. Maybe she should send Henry the highlights of her day in a quick text, then start running the water.

> *Lots to tell. Found article. Nearly hit by speeding car.*
> *Bit bruised but OK. Taking bath. Talk in a.m.?*

She hit send and hauled herself off the bed to the guest bathroom attached to the bedroom. Turning on the taps, she adjusted the water, dumped in some lavender bath salts, and returned to check her phone. Nothing. With a frown, she stared at the blank screen. Henry must have fallen asleep. Otherwise, he would have replied.

Shrugging, she ignored the niggling feeling that something wasn't quite right and stripped off her clothes.

Once in the bath, she closed her eyes and let the hot, scented water sooth her muscles. But she couldn't relax fully, not with Henry so silent. Her phone sat on the shelf by the sink, quiet as a mouse. Five minutes later, she gave up and toweled off, slipping into pajama pants and a sweatshirt. Maybe a cup of warm milk would help ease her troubled mind.

In the kitchen, she poured milk into a pan and set it on the stove. She had just turned on the burner when Sissy came into the room. Violet tossed her a quick smile before turning her attention back to the milk. "Have you heard from Henry tonight? He isn't answering my texts."

Violet waited a moment, but when Sissy didn't reply, she peered over her shoulder. Sissy simply stood there, her eyes on Violet. "Sissy? Is something wrong?" Violet snapped off the burner and faced the other woman. "Is Henry okay?"

Sissy crossed her arms and glared at Violet. "Is that all you've got to say?"

Violet took a step back at the anger in Sissy's voice. "What do you mean?"

"Was it all a game to you? Some sort of sick fantasy with you as the victim of some nefarious plot?"

"I don't understand what you're talking about."

"Oh, don't you, Violet? Or should I call you Patricia?"

Violet gulped in air as the room started to spin. She staggered back against the stove, sending the milk pan crashing to the floor. Warm milk splashed on her pants, but she barely registered the discomfort. She forced herself to speak. "Henry knows about Patrick?"

Sissy snorted, the sound piercing Violet's heart with its contempt. "Oh, he knows, all right. He knows you've been lying to him about who you are. You're not some poor girl who needed rescuing. You're the twin sister of a mass murderer, a fact you kept hidden from everyone, even those who cared about you." Sissy shook her head. "I think it's best if you get your things and go to a hotel. From what I've read, your family has enough money that you can afford it."

Closing her eyes, Violet hung her head. Her heart ached so bad, she wondered if she was having a heart attack. In a way, she was. Her heart was breaking into a million pieces. "What about Henry?"

"What about him?"

Violet raised her head and locked eyes with Sissy. "What does he say?"

Sissy unfolded her arms, planting them on her hips. "You do not have the right to know anything more about my brother."

Violet stared at the other woman, but Sissy's gaze never wavered. In other circumstances, she would have admired the sight of the big sister protecting her younger brother. Now it only added to her loss, as her own brother had never bothered to protect her at all. The realization stopped the words of explanation from tumbling out of her mouth. Sissy was doing what she felt was best to protect Henry. The love she'd seen between the brother and sister had warmed her heart. She would not be the one to come between them. Violet knew all too well the terrible pain a fractured sibling relationship could bring.

Without a word, Violet stepped over the spilled milk and retreated to her bedroom. After stripping out of her soggy pajama pants and putting on some jeans, she stuffed her clothes and toiletries into two bags, hoisted them over her shoulder, and left without speaking to Sissy again. At least she'd picked up her car from the shop earlier. As the front door clicked shut behind her, Violet let the tears fall and her shoulders slump, her worries weighing heavily on her body. With Henry by her side, she had been ready to face her past, to come into the open. Now, she barely had the strength to make it to her car.

~

"She's gone?" Henry leaned back in his recliner in an attempt to ease his achy body. Sleep eluded him last night, as the hurt of Violet's — Patricia's—deception teased his mind. He cared about her in a way he'd never felt about a woman ever. For the first time, his hopes of a future with a wife and perhaps children didn't seem quite so out of reach. Now those dreams had been smashed to smithereens against the lies of her life, her words, her actions. He refused to think about their kiss or holding her in his arms while she sobbed in his kitchen.

It was only in the dark hours of the morning, alone in his bed with thoughts of her, did he admit to himself that he loved her. God help him, he longed to see her, to believe she did it for a good reason, that her omissions didn't mean she didn't trust him. But above all of his visceral longing swirled one, compelling thought. If she lied about her very name, then what else had she lied about?

"Yes, last night." Sissy spoke in what Henry often thought of as her matron's brisk and no-nonsense tone.

"Did she say anything?" Even in the bright light of day, he was grasping at straws.

"No, not really."

Henry pressed his sister for more details, his desire to know painful information overcoming his common sense to let sleeping dogs lie. "She didn't say anything about me?"

"She asked about you."

"What did you say?"

"The truth, that she didn't have any right to know anything about you."

The indignation in Sissy's voice brought a brief smile to his face. She always protected him, but today, that knowledge didn't bring the warm glow it usually did. Maybe he didn't need her protection. Maybe he could do things on his own without her help. Sure, he did plenty of things by himself, but when it came to male-female relationships, he had allowed Sissy to push and prod him into dates.

Violet had been the first woman Henry had liked despite Sissy's machinations. "Did she say where she was going?"

"No. In fact, she didn't say anything at all. Just packed up her clothes and left." Sissy paused. "You really liked her, didn't you?"

The softness in her voice reminded him of the time she'd given him her worn blue stuffed rabbit when he had chickenpox as a child. "You might say that."

"Oh, Henry. I'm sorry."

"Not as sorry as I am." He said goodbye and ended the call. Violet's text messages from the previous evening flashed on the screen. He had ignored them the night before, too angry to read anything she'd written. Now he scrolled through the messages and shifted positions in the recliner. Her last one brought him upright in his chair.

> *Lots to tell. Found article. Nearly hit by speeding car.*
> *Bit bruised but OK. Taking bath. Talk in a.m.?*

Violet had narrowly escaped being the victim of a hit-and-run, and all he could think about was her not telling him about having a mass murderer for a brother. For a while, he had let his own hurt get in the way of the very real danger she could be in.

His anger at Violet's deception dissipated with the knowledge that someone wanted her out of the way.

Permanently.

CHAPTER

THIRTY-FIVE

"Thank you for seeing me today." Violet sat down across the desk from Mr. Davidson.

"My secretary said it was urgent." The lawyer leaned back and smiled at her, his calm demeanor easing some of her anxiety.

"You had mentioned I might be able to get an advance on Mr. Kopecek's estate." Violet rubbed her forehead. Sleep had not come until the wee hours of the morning. Her room at the budget hotel had been right next to the elevator, so early departing guests woke her up a few hours after she fell asleep. Once awake, she couldn't return to a dreamless state, not when her body and heart ached. The twists and turns the situation had taken made her head ache. If she and Henry worked on it together, they could probably make some headway with the bits and pieces of flotsam and jetsam they had accumulated. Alone, she wasn't sure if she could figure out anything.

She had called first thing for an appointment with Mr. Davidson to see if any money from Mr. Kopecek's estate could be advanced, as her own funds danced along the razor's edge.

"Not to sound greedy, but without a job, I could use the

money. The insurance company keeps promising to deposit the amount for the damage done to my apartment, but I still haven't received it."

"The will still needs to go through probate, but as executor of the will, I can advance you some funds, given the circumstances." He jotted down some numbers on a slip of paper. "Would five thousand be enough to tide you over for a few weeks?"

"Yes, thank you."

"My secretary will draw up the necessary papers and issue a cashier's check. I'll be in touch as soon as the will makes it through probate. Given the size of Mr. Kopecek's estate, it shouldn't take longer than four or five months."

Violet rose. "Thank you."

Mr. Davidson escorted her to his secretary. "Please issue Ms. Lundy a check for five thousand dollars as an advance on the Kopecek estate."

She shook his hand. "I appreciate all you've done for Mr. Kopecek and me."

"Mr. Kopecek thought the world of you," Mr. Davidson said. "He said you were someone he could count on. You meant a lot to him."

She blinked back tears. "He was taken much too soon. I miss him."

"I imagine all who knew him feel the same. I know I do." Mr. Davidson said goodbye and went back into his office.

As Violet waited for the check, she knew at least one person who had known Rainer Kopecek didn't miss him—his murderer. Even without Henry's help, she would see that Mr. Kopecek's killer didn't escape justice.

IRIS CHECKED THE CALLER ID ON HER DISPOSABLE CELL PHONE. THE COUNTRY code for Germany flashed on the screen, and she picked up the call. "Hello?"

"You have received the package?" Juergen's voice sounded crystal clear despite the distance between them.

"Yes, it arrived only a few minutes ago." Iris let her shoulders relax. "Is this the only copy?"

Juergen chuckled. "I do not know, but I can tell you I did not make a copy, nor do I know of any copies in existence."

Iris contemplated the single reel labeled April 16, 1984, nestled in the special delivery box of an international courier company. "That's all I could ask."

"I hope it contains what you were looking for, *fraulein*."

"So do I." If it didn't, Iris had no hope of containing The Wolf and his plans.

"You will forgive me if I terminate this call and our relationship. *Ich wünsche Ihnen viel Glück und abschied für immer*."

As she ended the call and flipped the phone over to pull out the SIM card, Iris mentally translated his last words. *I wish you good luck and goodbye forever.* She would need all the luck in the world if her quest to catch The Wolf were to be successful. Reaching for her iPhone, she started to text Dirk Jones before remembering this was one adventure she couldn't share with her old friend and colleague.

Brushing away a tear, Iris went to a wall of wood-fronted bookcases and opened one set of doors in the far right. No time for grieving, although that was the reason she had given to her staff on Capitol Hill for taking a few days off. There was much work to be done and so very little time. She felt in her bones that the sands of her time were slipping faster and faster away.

Shaking her head at the fanciful turn her thoughts were taking, she fitted the tape easily into the old-fashioned reel-to-reel recording device, a holdover from her West Berlin days. Dirk had teased her about keeping so much outdated equipment, but she had stubbornly refused to part with it. The Stasi hadn't bothered to switch from the reels to more manageable cassette tapes when such technology became more available in the mid-1980s. Personally, Iris always thought it had more to do with not wanting to spend the money on new equipment than the party line of not wanting to embrace Western advances.

Vindicated by having the ability to listen to the decades-old recording, she pulled up a chair and slipped on headphones. One modification she had made to the equipment was to rig up a way to copy recordings from the reel to her computer drive. Having an engineer for a father and being his helper as he tinkered with radios and other electronic paraphernalia had made her more than adept at working with technological gear.

After opening a notebook to a fresh page, she hit the play button and settled down to listen. Thirty minutes later, the tape unwound and Iris removed the headphones. *"Oh meine Güte,"* she uttered, her hand on her throat at the realization of what The Wolf had done.

The words echoed in the silent room. Iris slumped in her chair. No wonder Dirk had chosen to throw in his lot with The Wolf rather than try his luck with her.

CHAPTER

THIRTY-SIX

H enry ripped open the package with the London postmark and out tumbled a small cardboard box and a note.

Es tut uns leid für die Rolle - ich hatte die alte Vervielfäl-tigungsmaschine im Keller zu verwenden, um nicht entdeckt zu werden. Kristain

Translating the note, Henry sighed. Kristain hadn't been able to use a modern duplication machine for the reel he'd found for his uncle, which meant Henry had to find a reel-to-reel recorder in order to listen to the tape. Juan had talked about transferring old cassette tapes to CD. Maybe he had a lead on a company that could help.

His doorbell rang, and he left the reel on the counter to answer it. His mind on the possibilities of how to listen to the recording, he forgot to look through the peephole before opening the door.

Violet stood on the steps, her face wan and her eyes red. "Henry?"

For a moment, he couldn't move, couldn't speak.

Tears filled her eyes and one slid down her cheek. He fought an overwhelming desire to comfort her. No, he was in need of comfort, not her. The hurt from her not sharing about her brother came roaring back, washing over him like a tidal wave and sealing his lips. Maybe if he'd had more experience in male-female relationships, he wouldn't be so mixed up about how to handle this, but he had shared so much of himself with her that the thought that she hadn't been able to tell him about Patrick cut deep. In his mind, he realized how irrational he was being. She might have valid reasons for not blurting out the circumstances about her connection with a mass murderer.

"May I come in and explain?" Her voice wobbled. "Please."

She lied to him, but the sight her standing there looking so vulnerable tugged his heart. The emotion behind the word please broke his resolve to keep her at a distance and thus guard his heart. If he'd learned anything at all from being a student of history was that regret was cold comfort when day dawned.

"Henry?" She asked again, her voice soft and anguished. "Please listen." Her words came faster. "I know you're hurt. I should have told you about Patrick. I was going to the night we met for dinner at the Carlyle Grand. Then we had the accident before I could, and I kept promising myself I would find a good time and somehow never did."

The memory of the accident reminded him of how terrified he had been at the thought of losing her. He was an idiot to push her away, especially now with their investigation pulling them deeper into danger. Hard on the heels of that thought came one that sent him reeling back a step. Someone had sent him the newspaper articles, someone who knew Violet's true identity and had wanted to drive them apart by sharing that knowledge with him.

At his continued silence, Violet sighed and moved her head down, but not before he caught a glimpse of another tear sliding down her cheek. "I shouldn't have come," she whispered.

She had turned to leave before Henry finally found his voice. "No, don't go. Come inside." The tiny flicker of hope in her eyes wrenched his heart. "I'll make some tea and we can talk."

She paused for a moment before nodding and moving past him into the house. In the entryway, she removed her jacket and hung it on the coat rack as he closed and locked the door. "Thank you, Henry."

A flood of nervousness made his hands slip out of the cuffs, then his crutch skidded on the tile. "Don't thank me yet. You haven't tasted the tea."

With a small smile, she allowed him to pass, then followed him to the kitchen. Henry busied himself with filling the electric kettle and plugging it in. Opening a cabinet, he surveyed the tea options. "How about Earl Grey? Seems to fit this rather overcast March day, don't you think?"

"Fine." Violet seated herself at the kitchen table, her arms folded on top.

Henry couldn't think of any small talk to make while the tea brewed, and Violet didn't say anything either until Henry set the tea mugs on the table. As he rounded the table to take the chair opposite her, she spoke. "How did you find out about Patrick?"

He paused and rotated to reach the brown envelope on the counter near the fridge. "Someone sent me these." He handed it to Violet and sat down.

She opened the envelope and spilled out the articles, fanning through them quickly before sliding them back inside. She stared at the hot brown liquid in her cup as if the answers to life's greatest mystery swirled in its depths. The grandfather clock in the hallway chimed the quarter hour as the silence stretched between them. "You read the articles, so you know what he did. It's all true. He killed those children and the teacher, Brenda Evans." She addressed her narrative to the tea, her hands gripping the mug so tightly, her knuckles turned white.

Henry didn't bombard her with questions, instead choosing to wait for her to continue when she was ready. The newspapers had related the facts in stark yet vivid detail. Hurt over the breakup with his girlfriend of nine months, Patrick had come to the middle school where she taught art, checked in at the office, and gone to her classroom. After barricading the door with a bicycle U-lock he had brought with him, he had calmly shot Brenda in the head, then proceeded to shoot all seventeen students in the classroom at point blank range. Then he had scattered the bouquet of flowers he had anonymously sent Brenda the day before over the dead bodies.

"What the newspapers couldn't figure out was the flowers. Why send her flowers if he was planning on killing her?" Violet raised her eyes to his. "The bouquet you received with the cryptic note was a replica of what Patrick sent Brenda. White petunias, orange begonias, and yellow carnations."

Henry gaped at her. "Exactly the same?" He recalled the colors of the flowers but didn't realize the significance. The image of Violet collapsed in a faint on the kitchen floor amidst the yellow, white, and orange blossoms made him shudder. "That's why you were so upset when you saw them."

She nodded. "Not only the combination but the meaning behind the flowers. Patrick picked those particular flowers for a reason. It wasn't a random choice. White petunias mean anger or resentment, orange begonias mean beware, and yellow carnations mean disappointment or rejection."

"It was a warning." In all that had happened since, he had attributed the flower delivery to The Wolf's hand.

"I think so. Someone warning us to beware because we were making someone very angry." She lifted her mug, spilling some on the table as her hand shook. Replacing it without taking a sip, she continued her narrative about her brother. "Patrick didn't include a note with his flowers because he expected Brenda to read their message and apologize for making him angry and for rejecting him."

"And when she didn't, he came to the school to kill her?" He couldn't understand why someone would do such a thing to children because of a broken love affair.

"In a word, yes. My brother has always been a very angry

person." Violet spoke softly. "At least, that's what I thought was the underlying emotion. As a young child, my parents did nothing to correct or control his outbursts. When he got older, his sense that the world was against him bordered on paranoia. He refuses to cooperate with the prison psychologists and psychiatrists, so I doubt he'll ever be diagnosed definitively. I'm not even sure he has a mental illness. Some people are just wicked."

"Did he ever hurt you?" As soon as the words left his mouth, he wished to recall them. What a terrible thing to ask someone about her twin brother. Sissy, for all her faults, would never knowingly hurt him.

Violet pushed up the sleeve of her shirt and held out her arm. Near the elbow, the flesh twisted into a web of lines. "When we were six, he held a lit match to my skin because he wanted to see what happened when flesh burned. He had tied me up first and stuffed a gag in my mouth so I couldn't scream for help. I don't know how long he burned my skin because I fainted from the pain."

Words seemed inadequate to such horror, so Henry reached out a hand and laid it gently on the rough surface on her skin.

"He told my mother I had been playing with matches and burned myself."

Without removing his hand, Henry asked, "What happened when you told the truth?"

A small smile crossed her lips. "What always happened. I was accused of lying and punished."

"But surely..." Henry let the thought trail off when Violet shook her head.

"My mother thought the sun rose and set on Patrick. She hadn't wanted two children, and especially not a girl. To her, having a son as bright and handsome as Patrick was all that mattered. The fact that she wouldn't have had Patrick without me was the only reason she tolerated my presence." She touched his hand briefly before tugging her sleeve back down.

"What about your father?"

Violet took a sip of tea before answering. "My dad traveled a lot on business, gone for weeks at a time. When he was home, he didn't want to be bothered with sibling squabbles. His term. I learned early not to tell him the truth about Patrick."

CHAPTER

THIRTY-SEVEN

Violet couldn't stop the shudder that shook her frame as memories of Patrick smiling his charming smile at their teachers, his manner sad yet loving, as he explained about his twin sister's lying habits. His crafty manipulation, beating her down in order to build himself up, sickened her

"They all believed Patrick over me, and my mother backed him up."

She avoided Henry's eyes, not wanting to see the pity she was sure would be there. For years, she hadn't told anyone about Patrick's cruelty. In the aftermath of the shooting, she finally had a willing audience for her tales but found she hadn't the stomach for telling them. Only when the district attorney said Patrick's defense would likely revolve around an insanity plea did she dredge up the past.

"I tried to warn Brenda about his anger, but she didn't believe me until it was too late." Violet sighed. "Patrick often dropped by the school to visit with Brenda in her classroom during her breaks. She hadn't told the office they'd broken up, so the secretary gave him a pass like usual."

"And he went in there and locked the door." He frowned. "But why kill the kids?"

"Because before she knew he had a gun, Brenda told him to leave because she had to teach 'her kids.'" Violet clenched her hands, remembering how awful it had been to watch video feed from the classroom in court. The school district had installed cameras only that year in every high school and middle school classroom because of gang violence in a few inner-city schools. The film captured his words and actions in the classroom, leaving no doubt as to his intention. "He didn't want her to have anyone but him. Her innocent remark cost her and those kids their lives." Her hair brushed the sides of her face as tears began to fall.

A warm hand on her shoulder only brought more tears. "Oh, Violet. Come here, my darling."

The soft endearment broke the fragile hold she had on her emotions, and she turned into his arms, nestling into his embrace with a sob. Henry rhythmically rubbed her back, his voice a rumble in her ear as it lay pressed against his chest. After a while, Violet gently pushed herself to a seated position, disappointed when he removed his arms from her back as they separated.

"Feel better?"

"Yes." No. She wanted to stay in his embrace forever, or at least a while longer. He was the first person who seemed to understand her. She fished in her pocket for a tissue and blew her nose. She wadded up the tissue, her eyes on her closed fist, tears threatening to overflow again. So many tears shed because of Patrick. She was sick of the emotional see-saw her brother put her through, tired of being second-tier in her own family and having to hide her true identity to avoid the publicity and hatemongers who had terrorized her family after his arrest.

His conviction with a life sentence hadn't stopped the vitriol in the form of letters, phone calls, and drive-bys. Her parents had scrubbed epithets written in bright red paint off their front door and cars. Her mother had given up planting flowers or shrubs in the front yard because vandals always dug them up and left them in tatters on the lawn.

"Violet?"

With a jolt, she came back to Henry's kitchen. "I'm sorry." She tried a smile, but it came out all wobbly. "Lost in the past, I guess."

"Should I call you Patricia?"

She reared back as if he had struck her. "No, please don't. I hate that name."

His eyes widened at the vehemence in her voice, and she reached up to touch his cheek to reassure him she wasn't angry with him. But she stopped herself just in time, her hand in mid-air. He might have comforted her, but that didn't mean he had forgiven her or was ready to resume their relationship. As she started to drop her hand down, he grabbed it with his own and brought it slowly to his left cheek, pressing it there briefly before removing his hand. The slight stubble tickled her fingers, and she spread her hand wider to caress his jaw line.

The air in the room seemed to grow still as her heartbeat fluttered faster. She licked her lips and a spark ignited in his eyes. "My middle name is Violet. I took my grandmother's maiden name Lundy as my new last name." She stroked his cheek. "I legally changed it. Patricia Cunningham is no more."

"Good." He leaned closer to her as his hand snaked around her neck to tangle in her hair.

She could barely breathe as he brought her face closer to his. "Good?" She repeated inanely, her mind starting to focus more on his lips than his words.

"Oh, it's very good." He shifted closer, bringing the distance between them to mere inches. "Because I find I like Violet Lundy very much."

"You do?" Violet smiled, absurdly happy this man liked her, despite her brother, despite her background.

"Yes. Now—" he placed a finger on her lips—"let's stop talking." He followed his own advice by placing his lips on hers.

Violet closed her eyes and moved her hand to his chest as she sank into the kiss. His heart thumped underneath her fingers, tapping in time with hers.

Henry pulled back and she sighed, not wanting the kiss to end so soon. "Violet?"

"Hmm?" Her head nestled onto his shoulder, the heat from his skin warming her cheek.

"I, um." He cleared his throat, a rumbling sound in her ear. "I think I love you."

For half a second, she was sure she hadn't heard him right. Lifting her head, her eyes met his. "You think you love me?"

Tracing her lips with his finger, Henry smiled. "No."

"No?" The movement against her mouth muddled her thoughts.

"I love you."

At his declarative words, the hardened core surrounding her heart thawed in a rush of happiness. Violet reached up and grabbed his finger, stilling the motion. "I love you too." She pressed her mouth to his finger, then cocked her head. "Now shut up and kiss me again."

Bryon ground out his cigarette with the heel of his boot, then bent down, picked it up, and tucked it into his back pocket. Years of working for The Wolf had taught him to leave no trace, a habit that had kept him out of trouble many times over. He itched to smoke another but decided to forgo the pleasure until he ended his surveillance. So far, no one showed the slightest interest in Dr. Silverton's townhouse.

Every few days, Bryon stopped by to check on the half dozen microscopic cameras he'd installed on buildings, trees, and telephone poles to capture the comings and goings of those who passed the professor's house. The digital cameras recorded continuously twenty-four hours a day. He could review the footage remotely on his laptop. So far, he hadn't spotted anyone who didn't belong on the street.

Tonight, he'd stationed himself in the shadows of the shed in Dr. Silverton's back yard, which afforded a clear view into the kitchen through a curtainless bay window. The sight of the two kissing in the kitchen brought a pang of regret. His work had made having a wife and family of his own impossible. It wouldn't do to give The Wolf a weapon to use against him, never mind his enemies, of which there were many.

Bending his knees to relieve the tight muscles from standing in one place, he resettled into the small space between the stone wall and side of the shed. The March air still held a decided nip, as if reluctant to give way to warm spring breezes. Tugging his coat closer, he blew onto his cold hands. The way those two were heating things up inside, another cigarette tip glowing in the backyard wouldn't be noticed.

Pushing thoughts of smoking out of his mind, Bryon mulled over his next step. He'd managed to stay a few moves ahead of The Wolf, but that could change in the blink of an eye. No sense standing out here in the dark. Henry and Violet weren't going to be thinking about Kopecek anytime soon.

He moved silently through the backyard and paused by the corner of the house to scan the street. A couple halted in front of the house next door. Bryon sank deeper into the shadows and waited.

The woman pulled out her phone. "It's the next house."

"Do you want to do the set up here with the house in the background?" The man held up his hand, a small video camera in his grip.

The woman glanced around but seemed satisfied with the quiet street. "Yes, then we'll knock on the door and confront her."

"Rolling in three, two, one." The man pointed a finger at the woman, who turned to the camera with a professional smile.

"Good evening. I'm Sylvia Banks with WUSA-TV on assignment in Alexandria, Virginia, with an exclusive update on the Louisville Middle School shooter story. Wednesday marks the fifth anniversary of the tragedy in which Patrick Cunningham gunned down seventeen students and his former girlfriend, art teacher Brenda Evans." Sylvia gestured to Henry's house. "Inside this house is Patrick's twin sister, Patricia, who has refused to speak about her brother or the shooting. We've just learned from an anonymous tip she's changed her name to Violet Lundy and, until recently, had been living in Fairfax, Virginia, and working as a cleaner at the Happy Hills Assisted Living Facility. This is the home of Dr. Henry Silverton, a close friend."

She stopped talking and asked, "How's that, Jerry?"

Jerry checked the camera screen. "Got it." He lowered the device. "You never told me this was the result of an anonymous tip."

"Because I knew you wouldn't come if you knew." Sylvia fluffed her hair with her fingers.

"I'm not filming another second until you spill the beans. What tip?" Jerry fisted a hand and put it on his hip.

Sylvia shot him a look before sighing. "Oh, all right. Come over here. If they know we're here, it will ruin the element of surprise." She tugged on his arm and the pair edged out of the streetlight and closer to where Bryon stood against the side of the house. "I got a call this afternoon from a reliable source."

"What source?"

She shook her finger at him. "I don't know his name, but he's always given me accurate information, so why should I doubt him this time? And before you ask, he's called four other times in the past year. The National Zoo funding disaster? The tip came from him. Also the scandal about that senator from New York."

"All stories to further your career."

"Why not? If I can get the sister of the convicted killer of one of the worst school shootings on record when no one else has even gotten a 'no comment' from her, you bet management will sit up and take notice." She tilted her head up at Jerry. "And you know you're my favorite cameraman."

"Save the sweet talk for someone who cares." Jerry shifted his stance.

"We good? Because we have only another hour before we miss the eleven o'clock run down."

"Sure, let's roll." The two quietly moved back onto the sidewalk.

The Wolf certainly got around. No doubt his former boss was the anonymous tipster. He had to warn Henry and Violet not to open the door. If Violet's identity was confirmed and broadcast, the ensuing media firestorm would be brutal and possibly give The Wolf time to disappear. Bryon turned his back to shield the light from his phone and sent a text to Henry's number.

Now all he had to do was wait and see if Henry would be smart enough to follow his instructions.

THIRTY-EIGHT

A buzzing penetrated Henry's consciousness, but he blocked out the nuisance to attend to the matter at hand, namely kissing Violet. Her warm breath tickled his lips as she said in a breathless voice, "Henry, I think your phone is vibrating."

He reluctantly eased back, blinking slowly in the bright kitchen light. A quick glance at his phone showed an incoming text. "Unknown number. Now where were we?" He reached for Violet, but she wiggled away.

"Oh, no, you don't." She stayed just out of arm's length, but her eyes danced as she stared back at him.

He started to rise, but his phone buzzed again. Shoot. Whoever invented smartphones obviously lacked a love life. Picking up the device, he hit receive and gawked at the message.

Don't open door. TV reporter on your doorstep. After Violet. Reporter suspects her true identity as Patricia.

Violet's brow creased. "What's wrong?"

Henry opened his mouth to answer but the doorbell rang. "You'd better read this message." He handed her the phone.

Frowning, she accepted the device. "Aren't you going to answer the door?"

"Read it first."

Violet turned her attention to the text and gasped. "You think…" The doorbell pealed again, the caller holding the button down longer this time.

"It can't be a coincidence someone's at my door seconds after this anonymous text arrives." He grabbed his crutches. "We should move away from the windows in case they come around back. The latch doesn't always catch on the gate."

Violet shot him a worried look but followed him to the den with curtained windows. Without saying a word, she secured the drapes together before sitting on the love seat. "Do you think they're still there?"

Henry shrugged off her anxiousness in hopes of easing the tension etched across her face. "I think if we ignore them, they will eventually go away." He joined her on the couch.

She leaned back into the sofa. "That's what I hated the most, all those nosey reporters shouting inane questions at me, at my parents, at anyone connected with the shooting. Everywhere we went, someone followed us. If it wasn't the press, it was a relative or friend of one of the victims."

"It must have been awful." He couldn't imagine living through the aftermath of a mass shooting. The pain in her voice triggered an ache in his heart.

"You don't know the half of it." She picked at the fringe on one of the throw pillows. "During the trial, his lawyers argued he wasn't quite in his right mind. Not insane, mind you, or temporarily insane, just a little bit crazy because he had loved Brenda so much. The jury must have believed he wasn't fully culpable because they gave him life in prison without parole instead of the death penalty."

"Do your parents visit him?"

She nodded. "They make the six-hour drive every month."

"Have you gone to see him?" The vulnerability in her posture as she clutched a throw pillow to her chest squeezed his heart.

"No." Violet gazed at her hands. "I can't. He's..." She stopped and sucked in a deep breath. "You've heard of toxic people?"

"Yes." He'd heard of them but never met one himself, not sure what a person would have to do to be labeled as toxic. After hearing Violet describe her brother and his actions, he understood a little bit better why people distanced themselves from toxic family members or friends.

"Patrick is one of them. I have as little contact with him as possible, mostly because the few times I've written or allowed a phone call, all he did was berate me for not being there for him. He's never once expressed remorse. Instead he feels like the world should have seen what he did as just retribution for Brenda's crime of leaving him."

"I can't imagine what you must have been through, are going through." Words seemed inadequate to convey the depth of his feelings, so he reached over and took her hand, lacing his fingers through hers.

She offered a weak smile. "One day, my mom and I went into a hardware store, and of course, people avoided us and whispered. Everyone acted as if it was our fault Patrick did what he did. My parents do bear some of the responsibility for never curbing his behavior, but they certainly are not responsible for his shooting those kids and their teacher. Those were his actions and his alone, but Patrick was not walking around for people to lash out at, so we were the targets."

With her free hand, she brushed a tear from her cheek, then cleared her throat. "We were only in the hardware store for a short time, but while we were, someone threw red paint all over our car."

"Did you call the police?"

"Yes, but they either didn't show up, or if they did, it was hours after we called."

Henry drew Violet closer to him. With a soft sigh, she settled against his chest, their hands still locked together. "I can see why you left your hometown. What made you pick Fairfax and a job as a cleaner?"

"Fairfax seemed big enough to live unnoticed. As for the job, well, I didn't need a degree, which Violet Lundy doesn't have."

"What would you have done if it wasn't for Patrick?"

"I have a degree in communications and was even scheduled to sit for the Civil Service exam, but Patrick's actions derailed my taking the exam then. After his trial, I left Kentucky and got the job with Happy Hills. No one pays attention to cleaners. It was a good job to disappear into, if that makes sense."

His heart twinged for all the loss and longing in that sentence. Beautiful Violet, running from a past that wouldn't let her go. "Everything went along as planned until Mr. Kopecek died."

"Right." Violet put her hand on his chest. "Sometimes I think I imagined it all. His sudden death, the mysterious way he'd been acting beforehand, the notations in your book that turned out to be in code, the phone calls warning us to stop looking."

"The car accident," Henry supplied, then remembered her text. "Wait a minute, you said something about a near miss in your message."

Violet sat up straight. "I was walking to get a cup of tea after visiting the library. I had the light at the crosswalk and was a few steps into the crosswalk when a man yanked me back onto the sidewalk. Turns out, a car was speeding around the corner and would have crushed me if he hadn't intervened."

Henry stared at her, his pulse racing in a way that had nothing to do with her closeness. "Do you think it was a coincidence?"

Violet frowned. "The speeding car or the man?"

"Both."

Her eyes narrowed. "No, I don't think I do. The man must have spotted the car accelerating. Otherwise he would never have reached me in time."

"So who was he?"

She shrugged. "I don't know, but I'll know him if I see him again. He has a scar on his left cheek." She tapped the corresponding area on her face. "He did say something strange. You know, it reminded of the man who spoke to me after our car accident. Both men referred to my being lucky."

Henry leaned forward. "Do you think it could have been the same man?" If they could just figure out who the players were, they would have a chance at discovering what Mr. Kopecek knew and the identity of The Wolf.

"The night of the accident was dark, and I was pretty shaken. The only thing I can say for certain is that he was about the same height and roughly the same build as the man who shoved me out of the way." She shook her head. "But the description could apply to millions of men."

"What about his voice?" Henry fought to keep the disappointment from showing. It wasn't Violet's fault she couldn't give a better description of the two men.

"He sounded familiar, but I can't definitely place him on the GW the night of our accident."

Another dead end. Or maybe not as dead as he initially thought, given the text warning them of the reporters. Coupled with the man saving Violet from being mowed down by a speeding car, it might just be the break they needed. "You know, I wonder if we haven't acquired a guardian angel."

HENRY SIGHED AS HE PULLED ANOTHER MID-TERM EXAM FROM THE TEETERING stack at his elbow. At least he had a morning without meetings or classes to tackle the tedious task. A sharp knock on his closed office door interrupted Henry's concentration. The sign posted on the door clearly stated he was not to be disturbed. Ignoring the caller, he dug back into his work.

After another rat-a-tat-tat on the door, Henry glanced up in time to see the door handle turning. Alarm barely had time to replace annoyance before Juan poked in his head. "Dr. Silverton?"

With a sigh of relief that it was only Juan, Henry put down his red pen. "Yes?"

Juan eased into the room, his right arm in a sling, and pushed the door closed behind him. Gone was the cocky grad student with the Cheshire grin. His white face creased with pain, Juan gingerly maneuvered himself into the chair in front of the desk.

Henry's relief morphed into concern. "What happened?" A fissure of foreboding snaked its way down Henry's spine as Violet's near miss flashed across his mind.

Juan summoned a brief smile. "Bike accident."

Henry studied Juan's face. The emphasis on the word *accident* reverberated in his head. "But you don't think it was an accident."

"Nope." Juan shifted a bit in the chair and winced. "It's hard to find a position that doesn't make some part of me hurt."

"What makes you think it wasn't an accident?"

"You know my summer job is with a bike courier company in DC, right?"

Henry nodded.

"I know how to handle myself on a bike and how to avoid pedestrians, cyclists, and drivers who are not paying attention to me. Sure, accidents happen, but no way that sedan didn't see me."

Violet had said the car that nearly ran her down was a dark-colored sedan. "Where did the accident happen?"

"At the intersection of Route 123 and Braddock Road near campus." Juan repositioned his right arm, a flash of pain crossing his face. "I was in the left turn lane waiting for the light to get onto Braddock. He came up behind me. Just as the left turn light clicked to green, I heard his engine gun, and the car accelerated way too fast for the turn. I managed to move slightly to the right so the vehicle didn't hit me dead on."

"Any witnesses?" Even as he asked, Henry was certain the answer would be no. This couldn't be random, not after Violet's near-accident two days earlier.

Juan shook his head. "No, at least none who collaborate my account of the engine racing."

"Sounds like you were pretty lucky." The man who had saved Violet's life and possibly warned her after their own car accident had said she was lucky. Somehow, Henry didn't think luck had much to do with it.

"If you call a broken arm, cracked ribs, and bruises lucky."

"I guess I was thinking of the alternative." A shudder ran through Henry as an image of Violet lying on the pavement, her body broken from its impact with three thousand pounds of steel.

Juan studied Henry. "Yeah, I could be dead."

CHAPTER
THIRTY-NINE

The Wolf was getting more aggressive. Violet's near-accident and Juan's close call had happened within two days of each other. Things were ramping up and the frustration of not knowing their enemy was wearing on Henry.

"I didn't take your warning about possible danger seriously enough." Juan gave a wry smile. "I viewed decoding words as merely academic, that it would be fun to play at being a spy. Until yesterday, it was only a game. Based on our conversation, I have no doubt the driver deliberately tried to run me over."

"I never should have gotten you involved." Henry mentally kicked himself for the cavalier attitude he'd had, dragging Juan into their game with a mere warning. In reality, Henry thought the danger would be limited to anonymous phone calls. Even though Mr. Kopecek's death seemed mysterious, they had no proof except their overactive imaginations he'd been murdered.

Juan smiled. "The good news is I had already dropped off the reel-to-reel audio tape at the New for You Studio. The employee I spoke with said it wouldn't take long to transfer it into a CD."

In all the drama about Violet's past, Henry had forgotten he'd asked Juan to find a place to turn the audio tape Kristian had sent into a CD so they could listen to the recording.

"Otherwise, it would have been crushed in the accident, as I fell directly on my backpack." Juan patted his battered backpack on the floor, and Henry noticed for the first time the scuff marks and long rip on one side.

"I supposed that qualifies as good news." Henry wasn't so sure that saving the audio tape was worth Juan's current condition, but the younger man seemed satisfied to have succeeded in his mission.

Juan winced as he lifted the bag to his lap. "I think, though, under the circumstances, you should pick up the CD, which will be ready this afternoon."

"Sure. I'll stop by on my way home. But at the very least, you must let me buy you a new backpack."

"Nah, my sister can sew this up in a flash." Juan shouldered the battered pack and stood. "I've gotten kind of partial to this bag. The only thing I want to know is who's behind all this."

"You and me both." Henry's guilt swelled in his stomach as the grad student limped to the door. "You take care of yourself."

Juan waved in response and eased out of the room, closing the door behind him. Henry slumped in his chair. The uncomfortable feeling in his belly intensified—a snare was closing tighter and tighter around them. If they didn't figure out The Wolf's identity, they might just find themselves caught in a trap with no way out.

IRIS TAPPED HER FOOT AS SHE WAITED FOR THE POLICE LIEUTENANT TO SEE her. A glance at the wall clock revealed she had been cooling her heels for fifteen minutes. She didn't like waiting, never had developed the patience for it. Even as a little girl, she had always found where her mother had hidden her presents for birthdays or Christmas and pleaded to open them early.

"Senator Morrison? Lieutenant Stevens will see you now." A

smiling policewoman in a crisp blue uniform gestured down the hallway.

Iris pursed her lips. This wasn't going to be a pleasant meeting, and she needed to stay calm and cool. She followed the younger woman through a maze of offices inside the Metropolitan Police Headquarters—or the Henry J. Daly Building, as it had been christened after the death of a sergeant killed defending the occupants from an armed intruder. Iris found it odd the way buildings, highways, and places were named after local individuals who died in the line of duty. Perhaps a building would be named after her, once she made her mark as secretary of state.

The police officer knocked smartly on a partially opened door and stepped aside to allow Iris to enter. Lieutenant Stevens stood and moved around his desk with his hand extended. "Senator Morrison. Thank you for coming by. Won't you have a seat?"

She shook his hand briefly. "Lieutenant." Iris skirted around the two chairs in front of his desk, then seated herself. Without giving him time to talk pleasantries about the weather, she dove right into the reason she came. "What is the status of the investigation into the death of Dirk Jones?"

Stevens winced but quickly schooled his face into placid lines. "Senator, we combed over every inch of his apartment and could find no evidence of foul play." He went on to describe the technical methods his team had used to sift through the apartment. Then he paused.

Iris had no intention of speaking until the man had said the words he was dancing around. She fixed a pleasant expression on her face and merely stared back.

He squirmed in his chair at her silence, but gamely went on. "We are ruling his death a suicide and closing the case."

The finality of those words rushed over her, and for a moment, she couldn't breathe. Long years of practice in difficult situations came to her rescue, and she gained control over her emotions. "Dirk Jones would never kill himself."

The lieutenant started to speak but her upraised hand stopped him.

"I know people often do the unexpected or behave out-of-character when it comes to suicides." Her words cracked across the space between them like a gunshot. "I've known Dirk for longer than you've been alive. We've been through hell and back, and there is no way he would take his own life."

A look of pity flashed across his face. Iris tightened her grip on her control. She rose, and he hastily stood as well. "I'll suggest to the police chief you hold off releasing your finding until you've had time to consider all the possibilities."

Iris swept her eyes over the accolades and photos with prominent Washingtonians that covered the office walls. Her gaze stopped on his face. "I would hate for your budding career to be cut short over such a mistake."

With a curt nod, she turned and left the office. Despite his assistant's verbal attempt to stop her, Iris swept by her and exited the building.

Standing in the sunshine of the warm March day, she contemplated her next move. She didn't like threatening the lieutenant, but he needed to be aware of how far she would take it to have Dirk Jones not labeled a suicide. Scrolling through her iPhone, she found the number she was looking for and hit the connection key. A brief chat with the police chief should light a fire under Stevens' butt and quite possibly have him do the real police work that would, if not prove Dirk was murdered, at least cast serious doubt on the suicide verdict. She could do no less for her old friend.

CHAPTER
FORTY

Violet studied the array of boom boxes on the shelf at the local electronics store. Who knew they would have more than one choice when it came to portable CD players with speakers? Apparently everyone hadn't given up on CDs in favor of streaming music on their handheld devices, as the vast selection at this store proved.

"Do you have a color preference?" Henry nodded toward the rainbow of audio selections from orange to red to silver.

"I don't suppose the color enhances the sound." She squinted at the prices. "But I'm not sure having something other than black is worth an extra five bucks."

"They charge more for color?" Henry leaned over and read the prices aloud. "I guess they do."

They glanced at each other and shrugged at the same time. Violet laughed. She could get used to running errands with Henry. Maybe it wasn't outside the realm of possibility they could have a future together.

"The red one, right?" Henry raised an eyebrow. "After all, if we're going to listen to such an important recording, that color seems more appropriate, given the probable content. Even if it's an extra five dollars."

Violet stared at him. "Oh, right." Understanding dawned as well as a sobering reminder of the stakes in the game they were playing. "The Red Scare of communism." She plucked one off the shelf.

They found a register and paid, then walked out into the cool evening to Henry's SUV. Henry glanced around before chirping the alarm to unlock the doors. They climbed in, and Violet placed the carton on the floor, then buckled her seatbelt. "Have you heard from the insurance company about your apartment?"

"No. I knew I shouldn't have gone with the cheapest company, but I suspect getting the claim settled will take a long time."

"At least you have the money from Mr. Kopecek's estate coming to you."

"And I was able to get an advance to help with expenses for now." She sniffed. "I love the new car smell. Have you gotten used to the new model yet?"

Henry put the vehicle in gear. "It's the same model, so there was not much difference from my old one, apart from the car payment. I'm glad you were able to get yours fixed rather quickly."

"I am grateful I didn't have to buy a new one right now, as I doubt I could without a job."

Henry negotiated the turn into his driveway and cut the engine. He opened his door and Violet did the same, grabbing the boom box from the floor of the SUV. Once inside the townhouse, she hung up her jacket on the coat rack, marveling at how quickly she'd become accustomed to Henry's place. Following him to the kitchen, she asked the now familiar question, "Shall I make us some tea?"

"Yes, please. I'll get this unpacked." Henry took the box from her, tucking it under his arm, and disappeared into the study.

She'd quickly learned that despite his handicap, he was perfectly capable of carrying things. Love for this man swelled in her heart.

The song "Smoke Gets in Your Eyes" played on the boom box in the other room, the haunting lyrics capturing her attention, and she hummed along as she filled the electric kettle.

Henry stepped into the doorway of the kitchen and softly sang the first line of the second verse about discovering love. She smiled and sang along with him on the next line about those who love being blind. He glided closer, his crutches a silent partner as he moved across the floor. There was no mistaking the fiery passion in his eyes that made her forget the past and its troubles. As the music swirled around them, he stopped in front of her.

"Ah, Violet. You do know what you do to me." His hand caressed her cheek as his head dipped toward hers.

"Do I?"

His mouth hovered a whisper away from her own and her heart beat faster. "I love you." His hand slid behind her neck and his fingers tangled in her hair, tugging her lips even closer to his own. But still he didn't kiss her. "I think of you when I open my eyes in the morning, and you haunt my dreams at night."

Every fiber in her being shouted at him to shut up and kiss her. Her mind scrambled for the words to respond to his wooing but all she could manage was, "Hmm?"

He chuckled, his breath a warm breeze cooling her lips just before he bridged the remaining distance between them and kissed her. The relief of the contact jumbled with the pure pleasure of feeling his mouth on hers.

The kettle clicked off, signaling the water had boiled. Henry leaned back a fraction of an inch. "The water's ready."

He sighed, stole one last kiss, and stepped back. "We have work to do. By the way, you never did tell me what you discovered about the newspaper clue."

The man drove her crazy, but she loved every minute she spent with him. Violet poured the steaming liquid into the waiting teapot. "I didn't?"

"No." A red flush crept up his face. He resembled an adorable little boy for half an instant. "I, well, got the package, and then we, um, didn't talk about your discovery."

"Right." No need to go over that ground again. She stirred sugar and cream into the cups. "There were three articles on that page. One was about a Nebraska rancher, one about the FDA approving a new drug, and one about a cybersecurity company being awarded a grant from Homeland Security."

"Sounds like the cybersecurity company's the only possibility. Who runs the company?"

"Some billionaire financier named Bob DeLancey." Violet poured the tea into the mugs and carried them to the den, Henry at her heels. "I Googled him. Turns out DeLancey was in West Berlin at the right time, but his dossier listed his position as a low-level State Department employee, kind of a glorified coffee-fetcher."

Henry settled in his chair, placing his crutches on the floor beside him. "Rather circumstantial evidence connecting this DeLancey fellow with The Wolf."

"I thought so too until I realized Mr. Kopecek would probably not know a name. I mean, The Wolf, whoever he is, wouldn't have operated under his real name."

"Okay." Henry sipped his tea.

"It wasn't the article that caught Mr. Kopecek's attention, it was the photograph accompanying the article. I barely noticed it myself when I originally found the right page, thinking the answer must be in the text."

She pulled up the scanned image on her phone and handed it to Henry. "See the man on the far left, with his face turned slightly away from the camera? That's DeLancey."

He studied the photo of the five men from Vault Cybersecurity,while Violet continued. "What's really interesting is when I went online to see if I could find a clearer photo of DeLancey, I couldn't. The handful of photographs available all show his face obscured by a hand or hat or something. One newspaper hinted DeLancey was famously camera-shy, which would explain why his face is in profile."

Pointing to the photo, he gazed at Violet. "If Rainer Kopecek saw this photo, it might have been enough to jog his memory of the man he knew as The Wolf."

She nodded. "Knowing The Wolf was still alive and with even more reasons to want to keep his past quiet, Mr. Kopecek knew he couldn't tell anyone. Who would believe an elderly man in an assisted living facility, whose memory was failing? So he had to write it in code."

Henry placed his mug on the end table, then leaned forward. "This is good detective work."

"Thanks." She grinned, but it quickly faded. "I wish Mr. Kopecek was around to share the news that we cracked his code and got the message he left for us."

The excitement in Henry's eyes dulled, and he covered her hand with his. "I know."

"Now, let's listen to the CD. Maybe the answers we've been looking for will be revealed."

"I pray so." Henry punched the play button and the whip-whip sound of a reel-to-reel tape blared into the room. With a sheepish grin, he lowered the volume.

"Wir haben das Paket bereit zu liefern." The raspy voice that spoke could have been male or female. *"Wo sehen wir es senden?"*

Henry hit the pause button and translated for her. "It appears to be a recorded telephone conversation. The first speaker said the package is ready to deliver, then asked where to send it."

"What do you think it means?"

"If I had to guess, I would say it's someone trying to escape from East Berlin."

"Right. They would talk in code to avoid detection." How careful they had to be, with the Stasi all around and neighbors willing to spy on friends for a better apartment or scented soap. Henry's book had shown her a bit about life behind the Iron Curtain, especially as it was lived by East Berliners. Her heart ached with how hard it must have been for Mr. Kopecek and his beloved Verna to live in such a place.

"*Gut. Der Tropfpunkt wird heute Abend im Tierpark Berlin , nahe dem Südeingang.*" Even in German, the steely sound of the man's voice reminded Violet of the sharp edge of a sword.

"*Wie viel uhr?*"

"*Mitternacht. Komm nicht zu spät.*" The call disconnected with a loud click, then a buzzing sound.

Once again, Henry paused the CD to translate. "The drop location was to be the Tierpark Berlin at the south entrance at midnight. It's a large zoological garden in Friedrichsfelde fairly close to Stasi headquarters." He frowned. "An unusual place for a defector to meet his handler."

"Or maybe it would be safer because the Stasi wouldn't think someone would be brazen enough to try something right under their noses," Violet suggested.

"Possibly. I hope there's more on the tape than the short conversation. If there is, I'll pause every so often to translate." Henry turned the CD on again.

This time, the steely-voiced man called someone else. "Otto, the package is ready, tonight at midnight, Tierpark Berlin, south entrance."

"Ah, how many this time?" Otto had a groveling voice, as if he had breathed in the smoke-filled air of a closed room for far too long.

"Two, a husband and wife."

"How sweet." Otto coughed. "But we will be waiting for them."

"Just make sure they are not able to tell tales."

The stone-cold malice in the man's voice frightened Violet, even though decades separated them.

"Don't worry, my friend The Wolf," Otto said, a bit of glee in his voice. "They will not live to see tomorrow."

CHAPTER
FORTY-ONE

"The Wolf? Are you sure that's what he said?" Violet could easily believe the steely voice belonged to the man with the alias of The Wolf.

Henry nodded. "That's the exact translation."

"It means we have his voice on tape." The Wolf's voice had held her spellbound with its strength, bravado, and undercurrent of terror. Surely this would be enough to get someone to take a closer look at who they suspected The Wolf to be. "Now we have evidence he was a double agent, sending two defectors to their death."

"Perhaps. I'm not sure this evidence would be enough, but maybe there's more on the tape."

Violet eyed the player as if it could tell her the secrets behind the voices on the CD. Henry had tried to sound optimistic, but his facial expression showed he was as disappointed as she in the ambiguous content. "There has to be more. Why else would someone want it after all these years?"

"Only one way to find out." Henry punched the play button and the conversation continued in German, with Henry pausing the recording periodically to translate for Violet.

"And my payment?" The Wolf voiced the question so nonchalantly, Violet wasn't sure he cared very much.

"You are cold-blooded. Sending people to their deaths for money."

"We all have our weaknesses." Silk laced The Wolf's voice, like a shawl covering a woman's shoulders. "Yours seems to be lovely, young—well, we could hardly call them men, not at their tender ages."

"Yours seems to be no loyalty," Otto snapped back. "You have forgotten who is working for whom."

"You're the one who has a short memory." Violet jumped at the sharp retort, even though she didn't understand the words until Henry translated.

Otto sighed. "Send us your invoice as usual." His tone signaled the end to hostilities between the two men, at least for the moment.

"Always with the red tape. Two exterminations by the *Ost-Berlin Schädlingsbekämpfung Unternehmen*."

The other man laughed. "Ah, the old East Berlin Pest Extermination Company. Your sense of humor is a breath of fresh air. You wouldn't believe the dull sods I have to work with."

"I keep telling you double dipping adds spice to an otherwise boring existence." The Wolf spoke with the confidence of a man who viewed himself as invincible.

"I'll leave the intrigue to you, Wolf. Now if there's nothing else..."

"There is." The Wolf's voice cut across the other man's words like a sword cleaving a watermelon. "While I have enjoyed our arrangement very much, I must exit the arena earlier than anticipated."

"Oh? Someone on your trail?" Otto sounded faintly amused.

The Wolf gave a sound that might have been a laugh on a less steely man. "No, but there are some unforeseen complications that necessitate a change of plans."

"So this is to be our last transaction?"

"Of this nature, yes. But I require your services in a different matter."

"What would that be?" Otto said in a very quiet voice.

"I need to disappear."

Iris rubbed her forehead in an attempt to alleviate the pounding headache throbbing behind her eyes. She had been thinking all day of how to use the tape to stop The Wolf, but she had yet to discover a foolproof plan. If only Dirk was here. Together they could lick this problem. Every avenue she started down ended in an unscalable wall. She had to find some way to ensure The Wolf went down while she stayed afloat. But that seemed more and more unlikely.

Pacing to the window in her office, she shoved aside the thick drapes and gazed across at the Capitol dome, shining under the spotlights and full moon. She was so close to attaining her goal. A cabinet position, what she had dreamed of during those long, dreary days in West Berlin. Her association with The Wolf had begun as a flirtation with a handsome co-worker, but she had quickly realized there was more to him under the surface. Her beauty and femininity meant many of her colleagues either ignored her or dismissed her, leaving the field wide open for her to ferret out tidbits of information useful for a spot of blackmail or advancement.

She'd watched him for three weeks to learn his habits and timed her visit to his apartment for when he usually went to the local brothel. However, he must have known she had been tailing him because he surprised her by returning earlier than expected. The fury in his eyes had frightened her. When he'd smiled, her fear escalated. Then he told her what she was going to do for him. She'd wanted to refuse outright, but his flexing hands warned she wouldn't leave alive if she didn't agree.

Their alliance started that very evening. At first, her assignments caused her no loss of sleep. But The Wolf had been toying with her, drawing her ever deeper in the black forest of treason. By the time she'd parceled out what all those messages meant, she had been ferrying potential East German defectors to their death for months.

A shudder ran through her body as memories of the double game in which he had snared her still held her fast. His death all those years ago had freed her, allowed her to forget the past and move forward to a brighter future. She'd left Berlin as soon as possible afterward and turned her attention to politics. None of her embassy colleagues or her family knew the true nature of her work in West Berlin.

Then fifteen years ago, she spotted his face in the crowd at one of her re-election campaign fundraisers. That's when the nightmare began all over again, and she accepted with resignation that she would never be free of him. He would continue to ask, "a simple favor from my dear friend," one designed to remind her of all she owed him.

For years, she had searched for a way to bring him down without exposing herself in the process, but such a path eluded her. She wanted the cabinet position so much she could taste the sweet champagne of success. If only... A line from an East Berliner's diary came to her mind. "Our lives have lost their spirit, and we can do nothing to stop them."

She let the drape fall into place, blocking out the city lights. Maybe a good night's rest would clear her head and she would find the answer in the morning. She logged off her computer and picked up her purse. A knock on the door triggered a gasp. Her staff had gone home hours ago. Her thoughts flashed to the gun in her car's glove compartment.

The door opened just as she reached it, and two tall men in blue suits blocked her way. "Senator Morrison."

She purposefully raised an eyebrow. "It's after hours, gentlemen, but if you'll call my secretary in the morning, I'm sure she can find time in my busy schedule for an appointment."

The men in dark suits took a step toward her and simultaneously flipped open dark blue badge holders, displaying government-issued

ID. "FBI," the shorter one said, causally slipping the badge back into his inner breast pocket and letting her see his gun holster.

Iris determined right then the best way to handle the forced interruption was a charming offense. "How can I assist you?"

The taller man raised his hand. "Senator, if you'll have a seat, the director will be here shortly."

If the director of the FBI was coming, something big had happened. She took a deep breath and let it out in a slow, controlled exhale, concentrating on staying calm. No reason to panic yet. "If the director wants to see me, he should have made an appointment."

The two men folded their hands in front of them and stood silently. Blast them. She wasn't going to be intimidated by a pair of federal goons.

"Gentlemen, please step aside. I'm not in the mood to talk to the director tonight." She headed toward the door, but neither man indicated he had heard her request. "Do I need to call Capitol security, or will you allow me to pass?"

"Good evening, senator," said Harold Channing, the FBI director, as he came up behind the men. "There's no need to play hardball with my men." The two agents moved aside to let him into her office before exiting the room and closing the door behind them. Channing turned to Iris. "Why don't you have a seat? This is a courtesy call, senator."

"If this is your idea of courtesy, I shudder at what your poor mother must think of your manners." Iris held her head high. The head of the FBI in her office late at night was not a good sign. The Wolf must be up to his old tricks. She braced herself for the revelation that would threaten to derail her nomination hearings.

Channing's eyes turned cold. "Senator, we have received some disturbing information relating to your time with the embassy in West Berlin, information that if confirmed, will end your political career and possibly put you in jail."

CHAPTER
FORTY-TWO

Henry slid the *Washington Post* out of its plastic bag and flipped it open. The jarring headline *"School shooter unrepentant"* screamed at him. The lead story chronicled Patrick Cunningham's attempt to justify his actions. Shaking his head in disgust at the man's propaganda, Henry scanned the rest of the front page, and his breath caught at a story just below the fold.

"Shooter's twin sister uncovered"

This would bring unwanted attention to them. After listening to the rest of the recording last night, he and Violet had discussed how they could connect Bob DeLancey with The Wolf. It had been hard to let her leave to return to her hotel a few blocks away from his townhouse in Old Towne Alexandria. He wanted to keep her close, as the sense of danger heightened around them with each new revelation.

Having Violet's new identity out there was going to complicate both their stalled investigation and her safety. He skimmed the first few paragraphs to determine the accuracy of the information.

FAIRFAX, Va. — Patrick Cunningham's twin sister, Patricia, legally changed her name to Violet Lundy and moved away from Louisville after the trial that convicted her brother of 18 counts of murder and sentenced him to life in prison without the possibility of parole. Three years later, Lundy moved to Fairfax and worked as a cleaner at the Happy Hills Assisted Living Home. Karen Siddons, director at Happy Hills Assisted Living, says, "In the workplace, Violet seemed to be a loner, but she consistently showed up on time and did her job. Other than that, there's not much else I can tell you."

The rest of the story brimmed with speculation and innuendo about Violet's reasons for her disappearing act. At least the reporter hadn't dug too deep, as nothing about her recent car accident or apartment break-in appeared in the story. Henry tossed the paper onto the kitchen table with a thump. It must be a slow news day if the discovery of Patrick Cunningham's twin sister's new identity ranked such treatment. Violet would be crushed by the revelation, given how much she had tried to distance herself from Patrick and his poison. He punched in Violet's cell phone number.

"Henry, I'm so glad it's you."

"You've seen the paper. I'm so sorry."

Violet sobbed, her voice coming in bits and pieces over the phone. "Yes, I ordered...a newspaper...with my breakfast. I can't... believe this... is happening. I'm afraid...to leave...my room."

"I don't know what to say." If she were here, he would fold her into his arms and hold her tight.

"I wish you were here." Her voice broke, and she blew her nose. "I'm afraid. Really afraid. You don't know how crazy people can get. My parents received bags and bags of hate mail after the shooting and during the trial. I begged them to move, but they wouldn't hear of it."

He wouldn't let her go through this alone. "I'm calling Sissy right now."

"That's sweet of you, but I can't drag your sister into this. It's not fair to her and Keith. Or you."

Ignoring her words, he focused on ways to keep her safe. "You can't stay in a hotel. I'd love for you to stay here, but I find you too attractive for that to be a good idea."

"You do?" Another sniffle, but Henry swore he could hear a smile in her voice.

"Yes." The simple declaration hung in the air between them, electrifying the invisible bond drawing them ever closer together.

"When you put it that way, if Sissy and Keith will have me, then it might work, for now."

He smiled. "Don't worry about Sissy. I know how to get my way with her."

That brought a hearty chuckle from Violet. "I'm sure you do."

IRIS FOLDED HER ARMS AROUND HER WAIST, TRYING TO WARM A COLDNESS IN her bones that had nothing to do with the temperature. It was all his fault, of course. The Wolf still liked to weave his intricate webs of deception and destruction. He should have picked the Brown Recluse as his moniker, as his actions were more spider-like than wolf-like.

Harold Channing's late-night office visit had smacked more of a fishing expedition with a dash of warning thrown in for good measure. If he had hard evidence, she would have spent the night at FBI headquarters and not here in the comfort of her own bed. Whatever Channing had heard, it was likely rumor tied with a bit of fact to dress it up. Nonetheless, Iris was now prepared for the agents who would sniff around her past.

What worried her more was the tip had to be from The Wolf, which meant he now saw her as a threat. She had little time to get her affairs in order before her adversary fed more damaging information to the FBI about West Berlin. Channing might not know who was behind the veiled allegations against her, but she hoped he still had enough field agent in him to wonder about the timing and source.

The grandfather clock in the study struck five. Iris sighed. She had spent most of the night pacing and thinking. Now that she had listened to the tape, she had called a few more of her old contacts to gather hard evidence.

A slim stack of photographs winked at her from the polished surface of the desk. The photographer had had to stay at a great distance, so the shots weren't as crisp or as detailed as she would have liked, but modern technology could work wonders on pictures these days. Besides, the faces of the two men were clear enough to identify them. An old contact had sent the package to her as requested, but she couldn't keep them here. The Wolf's eyes and ears were everywhere.

Another turn around the room, and the idea came to her like the proverbial apple falling on Isaac Newton's head. It was so simple, so ingenious, she couldn't believe it had taken her all night to come up with the solution.

She would make copies of the old photographs but send the duplicates to someone else for safe keeping, someone who should be able to puzzle out what he had and solve the riddle. She hated to put Violet and Henry in more danger, but these were desperate times.

With quick, sure movements, she went to the basement to gather the hidden bottles of silver nitrate and potassium bromide, along with cellophane. She hadn't thought she would need to use such an old-fashioned way of hiding things in plain sight but was glad she had obeyed her instincts and kept supplies at hand for an emergency. Once back in her home office, Iris pulled a book off the shelf and snapped it open to reveal a hidden camera. Amazing where one could hide tiny cameras, although by today's standard, this one was mammoth.

A slow smile spread over her face as Iris photographed the pictures. With any luck, she would be able to hide the evidence where even her nemesis with all his cunning wouldn't find them before it was too late for him.

CHAPTER
FORTY-THREE

"Our bird had a visit from some dogs last night."

Byron Smith drew in a lungful of smoke and blew it out slowly, ignoring the sun rising over the Potomac River a few feet from where he stood. "The topic of the conversation?"

The former senator chuckled. "I'm retired, if you had forgotten. And I'm not about to risk my pension on overhearing what was said between the top dog and the bird."

"Then why are you calling me?"

"Because we both know this has to end. Better on our terms than his."

Bryon shifted his grip on the cell phone and scanned the area as he headed down South Union Street toward Gibbon Street. A few hardy joggers and cyclists made their way down the trail that hugged the river's coastline on the Virginia side. "Too bad you didn't come to the conclusion when you could have made more of a difference."

"Some of us had a family to consider," the other man snapped.

"Take it easy. I'm not busting your chops. What do you have for me?"

"My sources say the top dog was sniffing around, trying to see if a tip had any truth to it."

"And does it?" Bryon ground out the cigarette with his heel and picked up the butt to tuck into his pocket. He hung a left onto St. Asaph Street, his eyes skimming over Henry's townhouse as he passed.

"As far as the dogs know, the veracity is uncertain. However, I suspect more tidbits will be forthcoming."

The Wolf was making his move on the senator, and Bryon wasn't ready with his countermove, not yet. He only hoped Iris had made provisions of her own for this day of reckoning.

Bryon swore under his breath. "Keep me posted." He ended the call before his contact had a chance to add anything else. The man wouldn't bleat to The Wolf, but he also might not tell Bryon everything.

Pausing at the corner of St. Asaph and Jefferson streets, he pondered his next move. Better to go directly to the top, given the circumstances. Good, a cab moved toward him, and he hailed it. Sliding into the backseat, he barked the address at the cabbie. "935 Pennsylvania Avenue NW."

Time to pay Harold Channing a visit in person, and he knew just how to guarantee entry into the director's office. Keying in a few lines of text, he hit send and settled back against the seat as he used the cab ride to check messages and email.

A glance outside the window revealed clusters of trees where there should have been buildings. "Hey, buddy, why are you taking Rock Creek Parkway instead of Pennsylvania? You're heading in the opposite direction."

The cabbie didn't turn around, and Bryon reached forward to shove the glass partition open a bit more. "Did you hear me? You're going the wrong way."

The cab lurched forward as the driver hit the gas, throwing Byron back. He righted himself as they whizzed by trees with alarming speed. His heart pounding, Byron reached for the door handle and came up empty. The handles on both sides had been stripped off, leaving an exposed bolt that couldn't be turned with a bare hand.

Bryon slid down in the seat, quickly tapping a message out on the cell phone's tiny keyboard. No time to do anything but warn Iris of the danger to come. Ripping the SIM card out of the phone, he eased the window down to toss the items out of the cab.

The driver slowed the cab to turn into the Parrotts Woods parking lot at Rock Creek Trails, but Bryon heard with satisfaction the sound of a vehicle coming from the opposite direction crushing the phone with its tires. At least Iris would be forewarned. Maybe she'd have better luck. After all, she knew The Wolf better than anyone.

The cab shuddered to a halt in the nearly empty parking lot. The driver exited and opened the door. Now the driver was paying attention to him. He climbed out and the driver shut the door, handed him a folded piece of paper, then got back into the cab.

As it screeched away down the parkway, Bryon unfolded the note and read one word.

Traitor.

THE MOMENT HENRY STEPPED INTO THE FOYER OF SISSY'S HOME, VIOLET melted into his arms. Her emotions, rubbed raw by the media coverage of the fifth anniversary, along with her own unmasking, bubbled over into a mixture of fear, relief, and anger. Once more, Patrick and his problems intruded on her life, sucking her in and spitting her out again. As Henry's arms closed around her, some of the tension eased from her body. "I'm so glad you're here."

He relaxed his embrace, smoothed hair away from her face, then took a step back. "So am I."

Her heartbeat quickened as his head dipped toward hers.

"Am I interrupting?" Sissy spoke from behind Violet.

Violet jumped and put a hand to her warm face.

Henry groaned and slipped his hands into his crutches. "Sissy, your timing is, as always, impeccable."

His sister rolled her eyes. "Sorry, but you two can't stand in the entryway all day. Come on, Keith's in the kitchen making tea, and I've just pulled my delicious blueberry scones out of the oven. We need to have a powwow to figure out how to tackle this newest development."

Henry grinned at her as they followed Sissy down the hallway to the kitchen. Violet didn't hold a grudge against the way Sissy had defended her brother, but she was glad Sissy was back on her side too. Once seated at the table, steaming cups of Darjeeling tea and a warm, buttered scone on a plate in front of each of them, Sissy took charge of the conversation.

"I've already apologized to Violet." Sissy laid a hand on Violet's forearm. "I had no right to be so judgmental."

Tears pricked Violet's eyes and she took a discrete deep breath to hold them at bay.

Sissy continued. "I tried to tell myself I was defending my brother, but in reality, I was angry, pure and simple, that you hadn't shared your whole life with us." She glanced at Keith with a rueful smile. "What I forgot is there are things in every life we'd rather not broadcast to the world."

Violet tried to speak, but a lump in her throat the size of Kansas got in the way, so she took a sip of tea to wash it down. "Just because it's hard for me to share that part of my life doesn't mean I have the right to hide it from my friends. And I do feel like you've become my friend these past few weeks."

"I forgive you too." Sissy squeezed her arm. "I'm glad Henry stumbled upon you or you upon him." She cracked a smile. "And me upon you."

"Once again, my lovely wife has revealed her brilliant powers of deduction." Keith broke off a piece of his scone and popped it in his mouth as Sissy mock-scowled at him. "However, we should turn our attention to this latest bit of news."

Henry tapped his fingers on the table. "I'm not sure what we can do. It's all over the news media and blogosphere about Violet's new name."

"There's more," Violet interjected. "My mother called me right after you did this morning to remind me today's the day of Patrick's segment on *Justice Delayed* with Jessica Havens."

"The CNN true-crime show?" Sissy asked.

Violet nodded. "My brother somehow convinced Ms. Havens to interview him." She shuddered. "I don't really want to see the show, but given everything that's happened, we should probably watch it. If I know my brother, he has an agenda all his own."

Keith rose to his feet and grabbed the remote for the small flat screen TV on the kitchen wall. "What time is it on?"

Violet noted the time on her watch. "In just a few minutes."

He clicked on the television, flipped to CNN, then returned to his seat just as the teaser for *Justice Delayed* played on the screen.

An announcer's voice spoke over day-of-the-shooting footage from the middle school. "Coming up next, Jessica Havens talks to Louisville Middle School shooter Patrick Cunningham in his first media appearance since the verdict three years ago. What he has to say may shock you. Stay tuned."

"Why do they always say things like that?" Sissy groused as a commercial for a diet soda played on the screen.

"To get you to watch these ads," her husband chuckled.

Sissy playfully socked him in the arm. "Whose side are you on, anyway?"

Keith captured her hand and brought it to his lips. "Yours, always."

Violet risked a glance at Henry. His attention was fixed not on his sister and brother-in-law, but on her. The warmth in his eyes brought a flush to her cheeks. The theme music to *Justice Delayed* drew her attention back to the TV.

The host stood in front of a federal penitentiary. "Good morning, I'm Jessica Havens." Jessica faced the camera, her blonde hair blowing in a slight breeze. "Today, we bring you an exclusive interview with convicted mass murderer Patrick Cunningham from his cell at McCreary Penitentiary in Pine Knot, Kentucky. Patrick is speaking to the media for the first time since his incarceration three years ago following his conviction of the shooting of seventeen middle school students and his ex-girlfriend, art teacher Brenda Evans."

The camera followed Jessica as she strode toward the entrance. Violet couldn't help but think how much the exterior resembled a school, with its flag poles and portico. The camera panned wider to show the guard tower and industrial strength flood lights, changing the scene from picturesque to somber.

Jessica pointed to her left. "Inside this high security federal prison near the Tennessee-Kentucky border, Cunningham is serving a life sentence without the possibility of parole. Earlier today, I interviewed Cunningham in his cell."

The shot cut to a stark cell with a single bunk, toilet, and sink. Violet bit back a gasp as her twin waltzed into the cell, his tall, lanky figure moving like a rooster strutting into a hen house. He wore his short, dark hair brushed back from his forehead and underneath the prison-issued blue button-down shirt, his arms bulged with muscles she'd never seen on him before. Flashing a smile toward the camera, he seated himself on the bunk as Jessica settled into a metal folding chair probably brought in for the interview.

The talk show host leaned forward, her brows knit together. "Patrick, it's been three years since your trial and conviction. Have you adjusted to life on the inside?"

Patrick crossed his ankle over his knee, the very picture of a man at ease with his surroundings. When her brother acted like he hadn't a care in the world, you'd better watch out. "There are some things you don't adjust to, Jessica. Prison is one of them. But I've found a routine to make the time pass."

Violet's stomach clenched.

"Some say you should have gotten the death penalty."

Patrick's hand tightened ever so slightly, then relaxed. "The jury didn't think my actions deserved death."

"You didn't take the stand during your trial. Why do you want to speak out now?"

Patrick uncrossed his leg. He hunched forward, his forearms on his legs, and loosely clasped his hands. "The truth must come out."

"The truth about what?"

"The proof my attorneys wouldn't talk about at my trial. That's why I'm petitioning for a new trial. Once people hear the truth, I will be exonerated." Patrick's eyes blazed with the fervor of those convinced of their innocence despite their actions.

Violet put her hand to her mouth. She knew the look, had learned to run away and hide as a child when his eyes gleamed like that.

"Patrick, isn't it true you lost your appeal for a new trial?"

He waved his hand as if dismissing her question. "Yes, but now I have new evidence so I can't be held responsible."

"You mean the cold-blooded shooting of those kids and your ex-girlfriend is not your fault?"

"Yes." He pointed a finger at Jessica, who leaned back fractionally. "It's in my genes."

Keith nodded to the screen. "What's he talking about?"

Sissy shushed him as the show's host voiced the question on everyone's mind. "Are you saying you're genetically predisposed to murder?"

Violet wrapped her hands around her tea mug, trying to transfer the last bit of warmth from the liquid to her cold body. Patrick fixated on his own version of the truth, but even for him, this was quite a stretch. A fissure of unease worked its way down her spine. Patrick's very unpredictability taught her that whatever he was going to claim, it wasn't going to be anything she expected.

Patrick nodded. "Exactly. With all of the work on mapping

human genes, my case will provide scientists with concrete data to help them in that quest."

"But no one's isolated a killing gene."

"Not yet, but I think that day is coming, don't you? Then I will be exonerated."

Jessica widened her eyes in the classic expression of astonishment. "But what proof do you have for this so-called killing gene?"

The self-satisfied look on her twin's face punched Violet in the gut. This was going to be worse than the time he had decapitated a stray cat and gutted it in their tree house with a paring knife.

Patrick leaned forward, his eyes fixed on the lens. Violet sensed he was about to speak directly to her.

"My twin sister is as much a murderer as I am."

FORTY-FOUR

As the television program cut to a well-timed commercial break, Henry reached over and grabbed Violet's ice-cold hand. "Violet?"

Violet turned shadowed eyes to him. "Did he say I was just like him? A murderer?"

He rubbed her hand between both of his. "I'm sorry."

"What is he talking about?" Her fingers tightened on his. "Isn't it enough he destroyed my childhood with his lies and sick games? Will he ever leave me alone?" Tears ran down her cheeks.

Henry freed one of his hands and gently swiped the wetness from her face with his thumb. "Darling, I don't have the answers, but I know someone who does." He closed his eyes. "Dear Heavenly Father, you know the pain Violet is feeling right now. Please wrap your loving arms around her and sustain her through this new trial. In Jesus' name, Amen."

"Thank you." She offered him a faint smile.

Sissy cleared her throat. "The show's coming back on."

Sissy, Keith, Henry, and Violet once again focused their attention on the TV as Jessica Havens's image filled the screen. "Your twin sister killed someone?" The camera caught the incredulous look on Jessica's face.

"Don't look so surprised, Jessica." Patrick crossed his arms. "She can be devious. Even as a kid, she spread all kinds of lies about me to cover up her actions."

"But murder is a serious accusation."

Smugness tugged at his lips, turning Patrick's smile into a grotesque Medieval gargoyle. "I know what you're thinking, but I have proof."

Jessica's eyes widened. "Let's hear it."

Patrick settled back, his twisted smile intact. "First, she changed her name to Violet Lundy after the trial and got a job working in some old folk's home."

"How is that proof of your allegation?" Jessica raised her eyebrows.

Patrick continued talking as if he hadn't heard Jessica's statement. "She weaseled her way into the good graces of one of the residents, got listed as sole beneficiary of his will, then she killed him."

Henry's heart pounded. He wanted to shield Violet from what was coming next but was helpless against the relentless lies her brother spewed on national television.

"Does this resident have a name?"

Patrick stared into the camera, allowing his silence to heighten the tension.

"Well?" Jessica persisted.

Patrick turned back to her. "Rainer Kopecek," he said in monotone.

"No!" Violet gripped the table, then stood. She trembled all over.

Henry rose also, using the table to assist with his unsteady gait as he made his way to stand beside her. "Violet, honey, it's okay."

The camera zoomed in on Patrick's face, and Henry quickly turned Violet away from the television. He gently enfolded her shaking body in his arms.

Violet stiffened as the interview continued.

"How do you know it was murder?" Jessica asked skepticism evident in her tone. "Elderly people die for all sorts of reasons."

Patrick rolled up his sleeve. The camera zoomed out as Patrick gestured with his finger as if pushing a hypodermic needle into his arm. "She used an insulin injection."

Henry winced at the sight of a tattooed wolf on Patrick's forearm. The screen faded to black as the station went into another commercial break.

Violet leaned back, her eyes filled with such sadness that his heart ached for her. "What?"

A sick feeling washed over him. It should not have shocked him The Wolf would have a hand in this, but nevertheless, the man's reach and scope of influence ranged much farther and wider than he'd ever considered possible.

Henry brushed back a damp piece of hair. "He said you killed Mr. Kopecek with insulin."

She frowned. "I heard that, but there's more to it, and you're not telling me because you think I need to be protected. Am I right?"

She had come to know him well. Yes, he wanted to protect her, but it would be impossible if she didn't know the entire truth. After all, knowledge was power and to be forewarned was to be forearmed. He mentally gave himself a shake to dismiss the predicable clichés popping into his head. Better to simply tell her what he'd seen and see if she could shed any light on why her brother would have such an image on his arm. After all, it could be a coincidence— not that he believed it for one minute.

"Your brother has a tattoo on his arm." He took a deep breath, knowing his next words were likely to hurt her even more.

Violet's brow furrowed, and he longed to kiss away the worry. "That's not unusual, is it? I thought most prisoners, especially those with long sentences, got tattoos."

"It's not the fact that he has a tattoo that surprised me." He paused. "It's the subject matter."

"What was it?" The trembling in her voice betrayed how close to the surface her emotions were running.

Henry cupped her face in his hands. "The tattoo is an image of a snarling wolf."

~

AT THE SHARP RAP OF THE DOOR, IRIS SIGHED AND PUT DOWN HER RED PEN. "Come in."

Two men in dark suits moved into her office. From their attire and serious demeanor, she pegged them as FBI agents, probably here to arrest her. She remained seated. "To what do I owe the pleasure, gentlemen? Does the director require my presence? If so, he should have come himself instead of sending his boys."

Exchanging a glance with each other, one approached her desk. "I'm Special Agent Wilson and this is Special Agent Graham with the FBI. Senator Morrison, please come with us."

She eyed them and leaned back in her chair, staying silent as she considered her options. The text message from Bryon Smith yesterday afternoon rattled her, but she had never really counted on his assistance. The precautions she had taken should ensure the truth eventually floated to the surface. The photographs resided in her safe, along with a copy of the recording. The originals were in the safest place she could think of, a place not even The Wolf would consider. So now she waited to see what their next move would be, idly reviewing what piece of evidence The Wolf had sent to Director Channing. It could be any number of things, she had no doubt.

"Senator, you must come with us." Agent Wilson moved beside her desk, mere inches from where she sat.

"Why?" Sitting up in her chair, she fixed them with a cool stare. If they thought they could intimidate her with bluster, they obviously had no idea of what she was capable. She had outwitted some of the best agents, East or West, during her tenure in Germany. "Do you have a warrant for my arrest?"

The other agent grimaced slightly before schooling his face back to a blank expression. Good, no warrant. The boys were still on a fishing expedition. Whatever Channing thought he had, it wasn't enough to read her the Miranda rights. Something about the way these two stood alerted her to danger. She wasn't sure what it was, but she had long ago learned to trust her instincts implicitly.

Wilson headed around the back of the desk and reached down as if to grab her arm. In a flash, she stood and pressed a razor-sharp letter opener against his throat. "Agent Graham, if that's your real name, keep your distance, hands where I can see them, or mine might slip."

Iris surveyed the two men. "Graham, you'll place your firearm very carefully on the floor and kick it toward me. One false move, and I won't hesitate to press my advantage on your friend."

Her posture and expression conveyed her meaning perfectly, and the other agent gingerly removed his weapon, laid it slowly on the carpet, then sent it spinning under her desk with his foot. She turned her attention to Wilson. "Now, please take out your gun very slowly."

Wilson reached into his jacket and handed her his gun, she accepted it in her left hand and stepped back quickly, dropping the letter opener on her desk and transferring the weapon to her right hand. With Agent Wilson's gun firmly in hand, she loaded the chamber in a fluid motion, then motioned for him to take several steps back.

Then she pressed a buzzer on her phone to call her administrative assistant. "Richelle, call the Capitol police. And send Charles in here right away."

Eyes on the two agents, she hefted the gun in her hand. "Back in my day, we had to make do with an eight-shot, 9mm handgun. This has much better balance, with, what, fifteen rounds?"

Neither man said a word.

A knock at the door drew her attention. "Come in."

The door opened and Charles, the head of her security detail, stepped inside. The two men spun and dashed toward the door, shoving Charles aside.

"Stop them!" Iris ran after them, her heart pounding with the adrenaline of the chase. She hit the door to the corridor, but they charged toward to the stairs. Charles dashed past her and was gaining ground when a legislative assistant, her arms full of folders, blundered into his path. Charles tried to move around her, but instead ended up knocking the folders to the ground and the assistant along with them.

Iris dashed back to her office.

"Senator? I have the captain on duty on the phone." Richelle held out a receiver.

Iris put the gun down on the desk and snatched up the phone. "This is Senator Morrison. Two men in dark suits are heading down the east staircase. They must not leave the building."

"Senator, you know how many men in dark suits pass through this building every day." The captain's voice, with its slightly bored inflection, grated on her nerves.

She had to get a wise guy on the line when every second counted. "Yes, but these two men are impersonating FBI agents. They may be armed."

That shook him out of his torpor. "I'll do my best, ma'am." He hung up, and Iris turned back to her staff.

Charles stood in the doorway, huffing slightly. "I'm sorry I couldn't catch them. Who were they?"

"I don't know. I only know they weren't FBI agents as they claimed." Iris turned back to Richelle. "Please get FBI Director Channing on the line."

"I'll go talk to the Capitol police." Charles left the room.

"I have the director on the phone," Richelle said.

Iris crossed the room on wobbly legs, glad she'd worn a pantsuit with flats today instead of a skirt paired with high heels. Richelle handed her the receiver. "Director Channing, did you send two agents to my office today?"

"No, I did not." The director paused. "But I'm guessing two such men appeared at your office."

"That's correct. However, they weren't quite as stiff and solemn as your agents are, so I avoided leaving with them."

"Are the men still in the building?"

"I'm sure they're long gone by now. My head of security is conferring with the police now." Iris held little hope the men would be caught. The Capitol police could have easily missed them, especially if the pair split up and left separately with different groups of people. "You'd better send some agents over to see if there are any clues to who these men were. They would have had to show ID to the guards to get their guns through security."

"A name, even a false one, would be better than nothing," the director agreed.

"What about a gun?"

"I'm not even going to ask how you managed to separate two armed men from their weapons," the director said with admiration in his voice. "I'll send Special Agents Monroe and Talbot over right away."

She thanked the director and hung up the phone. With a practiced gesture, she dropped the magazine from the Glock and slid the action back to pop the bullet out of the chamber. Locking the slide back, she visually checked to ensure the weapon was unloaded and put the gun down on Richelle's desk. When she finished, she saw the entire office staff staring at her.

"You're a woman of hidden talents, senator," said Bill Lummons, her chief of staff.

Iris inclined her head slightly in acknowledgement, then raised her eyebrows as she gazed at the rest of her staff. "Now that you know I can handle a gun, why don't we get back to the real reason we're here and serve our constituents by doing our jobs." Her words effectively broke up the group. "Richelle, two FBI agents will be along shortly to collect the weapons and bullets as evidence."

"More agents?" Richelle wrinkled her nose in confusion.

"The two men who fled were imposters." Iris strode to her door, tossing over her shoulder, "Tell Special Agents Monroe and Talbot I'll be available to speak with them after they've finished interviewing everyone else." She went into her office and closed the door, slumping back against it.

Dear Lord, that was a shave too close. The next time, The Wolf would not make the same mistake.

CHAPTER
FORTY-FIVE

"You don't know Patrick." Violet paced the kitchen, her hands slashing the air. She thought herself safe from his machinations with him behind bars, but still his torture continued. She wanted to pray, but it had been too long since she'd had a relationship with God. After all, He had allowed Patrick to enact his terrible retribution. "This is his revenge for my ignoring his summons to appear on the show and sing his praises."

Henry's eyes filled with concern. The dear man wanted to help ease her burden, but Violet had no idea what he could do. The program had ended its segment on Patrick with an interview with their parents, who reiterated that their son shouldn't be locked up for the rest of his life. Thankfully, their appearance was brief. She wasn't sure she could handle hearing her mother's one-woman crusade on her son's behalf. She'd read about mothers who favored firstborn sons to the exclusion of all other children, but what those books and articles failed to capture was the heart-wrenching pain it caused the other children. To never share anything of substance with her mother hurt worse than not having a mother.

Sissy cleared their mugs from the table. "What I don't get is how Patrick knew about this Kopecek man."

Henry frowned. "I think his death was mentioned in the obits on the Fairfax City Patch website."

His sister set the mugs in dishwasher. "I don't mean the fact he's dead, but how he knew Violet worked at the nursing home where Kopecek lived."

Keith chimed in, "Sissy's right. That sort of information wouldn't be public knowledge. My college roommate worked for the correctional system one summer and he said inmates had extremely limited access to the outside world."

Violet's heart pounded in her chest. "I didn't think about that." His eyes reflected the same fear they knew exactly how Patrick acquired these details.

"Someone must have sent him the information." Keith spoke the words Violet had been thinking.

"Who would do such a terrible thing?" Sissy wiped the counter with a sponge. "I mean, telling your brother where you worked and even your new name is not too bad, but the person must also have provided the details of Kopecek's death, right? How else would Patrick tie it to you?"

"I don't know." Violet struggled to keep her voice even.

Henry placed his hand on her back and rubbed gently. "Right now, we have more questions than answers."

Sissy threw her husband one of those meaningful looks spouses give. "I need to check in at the boutique. Keith? Don't you have a meeting this afternoon at the office?"

"Yes, better get back." Keith paused at the doorway. "Remember, we're here for you, whatever you need."

Violet nodded, her voice constricted by the welling of emotion. She wasn't even family, and yet Keith and Sissy treated her better than her own.

"Thanks, that means the world to us," Henry said.

She and Henry stood there side by side in the kitchen until the front door open and close behind Sissy and Keith. She introduced the subject she had been avoiding since seeing Patrick's tattoo and hearing his accusation. "It's The Wolf, isn't it? He's somehow gotten to Patrick, convinced him a genetic predisposition triggered his murderous tendencies and I share this same gene because I murdered Mr. Kopecek."

Henry shifted on his crutches to face her. "The Wolf has a much broader reach than we thought, if he could contact your brother in prison."

"What will happen now?" She wanted to crawl into bed and stay there until all of this blew over, but she couldn't with The Wolf on the prowl and Patrick weaving his lies from prison.

"We have to consider The Wolf might have also sent information to the police about Mr. Kopecek's death. You told me it seemed suspicious to you."

Violet closed her eyes, running the sequence of events right before and after Mr. Kopecek's death in her mind. "Wait a minute. There was the doctor who signed the death certificate."

"Did he say something was not as it should be?"

"No, just that he wasn't the regular doctor. Siddons, the director, hadn't seen him before."

"Do you think Siddons had anything to do with his death?"

She shook her head. "The woman looked after her own skin, but I don't think she would do anything illegal."

"If it was an insulin shot, then it will likely be undetectable now."

Violet wrinkled her nose. "What do you mean?"

"If they decide to dig him up, they won't find any evidence to harm you."

Violet stared at him. "They won't find anything. There's no body to exhume."

"No body?"

"He wanted to be cremated." Violet swallowed the lump in her throat at the memory of Mr. Kopecek's funeral. "I scattered his ashes in the Potomac River."

"Then I guess we'd better hope there's nothing to tie you to his death."

"I can't imagine what it could be, given everything of Mr. Kopecek's except your book was torn apart by a crazed burglar." Violet shuddered at the memory.

"Somehow, I doubt that will stop The Wolf from trying if he thinks it will be in his best interest."

"What should we do next?" She tried to keep the quiver from her voice but failed. Her brother's declaration had cut deep. All she wanted was to keep Henry safe, but even that seemed an impossible task, given The Wolf's tendency to be one step ahead of them.

"What we should have done a few days ago. Find out from someone who was there at the beginning." Henry laid a hand on her shoulder and gave it a gentle squeeze. "Call Senator Iris Morrison."

IRIS SWIVELED IN HER LEATHER CHAIR AND TOYED WITH THE LETTER OPENER. The day's personal mail lay unopened on her desk, a neat stack of letters and envelopes. In half an hour, Dr. Henry Silverton and Violet Lundy had an appointment with her. She had almost declined to see them but decided it would be safer if someone else knew her secret. It was past time to delve into the past, a place she tried not to think about too much these days.

The late afternoon sun slanted through the long windows on the left side of her office, but her thoughts weren't on the early spring weather. She put the letter opener on her desk and ran a finger down the small scar on her neck. The day she acquired the scar had been a day much like today, one with a warm breeze carrying a hint of spring across West Berlin. She had decided her future in politics meant she would need to disassociate herself from The Wolf. Even in private, he demanded to be called by that moniker. Ridiculous, really, how a grown man set so much in store by his code name...

· · ·

APRIL 28, 1986

The Wolf called her name as she stood on the street corner waiting for him. She turned and smiled. It wouldn't do for him to guess her intentions, not when he was always the one who left. She had lasted longer than any of the others, but she was under no illusion that she was the only girl in his life. A man with his appetites wouldn't stick to just one woman.

"Hello, darling." He kissed her cheek, and she breathed in the smell she associated with him—cigars and cheap wine. Those scents mixed with the aroma of damp wool from the morning's rain.

"Hello yourself." She hooked her arm through his, and they strolled down the street toward a little café they frequented. While they waited at the corner for a break in traffic, a car screeched to a stop beside them, and two men jumped out. One grabbed him, the other her, forcing them both into the vehicle. She was shoved to the floor with The Wolf landing on top of her. A dirty blanket thrown over them triggered a coughing fit that brought tears to her eyes. Firm pressure from a pair of feet kept The Wolf's body pressed down on hers.

The jerking of the car twisted her insides into knots, and she tried not to retch. For several hours, the car drove around. With each jounce, The Wolf's body bumped into hers. Neither of them spoke until the car shuddered to a stop and the blanket was lifted off.

"Get out." The voice, harsh, guttural, spoke German like a native.

Iris waited until The Wolf unfolded himself from on top of her, then she scrambled out and found herself standing on the banks of a river, probably the Havel, which bisected West Berlin. The driver stayed in the car while two other men stood waiting for them to get out of the vehicle. Darkness had fallen, but a full moon provided enough light to see two of their captors' faces.

"You know who we are?" The taller of the two men standing outside addressed The Wolf in perfect English.

"I think so." The Wolf pushed his hands into his pants' pockets.

Iris swallowed hard and stayed quiet. This wasn't quite how she envisioned the night unfolding.

"Then you know what we want." The taller man nodded to his companion who struck The Wolf in the midsection. He doubled over with a grunt and fell to his knees. The taller man watched as his comrade proceeded to hit and kick The Wolf for several long moments.

Iris couldn't stand it anymore. "Stop it!"

The taller man turned his gaze to her. "Do you want to take his place?"

Iris bit her knuckle as the cold, hard stare from those brown eyes bore into hers, and shook her head.

"*Gut,* because Bruno's not known for his way with the ladies." The man lit a cigarette, inhaling the smoke and blowing it out as if he sat in a café with a newspaper spread on the table in front of him.

"Please, he's had enough." Iris fisted her hands as Bruno delivered another well-placed kick to The Wolf. "What do you want?"

"He knows what we want. And he'll give it to us." The taller man nodded at his companion, who produced a switchblade that opened with a snick. But instead of thrusting the blade into The Wolf as she'd expected, Bruno grabbed her and put the blade to her throat.

"Perhaps now your companion will tell us what we want to know," the taller man said, his tone as pleasant as if offering her a cup of coffee.

The Wolf lifted his head and locked gazes with Iris. "The list is in my pocket."

With a smile all the more sinister because of the way the moon lit only the lower half of his face, the taller man leaned down and extracted a piece of paper from the inside pocket of The Wolf's jacket.

The knife at Iris's throat leaned into the soft flesh and a trickle of blood ran down to her coat collar. With effort, she kept her attention on the taller man, who unfolded the piece of paper and scanned the list. He nodded once and tucked the paper in his coat pocket. "*Ihn zu töten.*"

Kill him.

Iris screamed. "Don't!" But the man holding her removed the blade for an instant before slashing the knife downward into her flesh. Blood spurted from her neck as he shoved her from him. She slumped to the ground, one hand clutching at her wound. Her eyes on her lover, she could do nothing as Bruno thrust the knife into The Wolf's side with one fluid motion.

The life she longed for, a life of political power, was slipping away like the blood flowing from the man with which she had betrayed her country. For what, she couldn't recall now. First, perhaps, it had been the thrill of leading a double life, the intoxication of an affair with a man as dangerous as The Wolf. The money definitely soothed her conscience, not that she'd thought too hard about the lives lost because of her infatuation with pretty things. She might have been trained in how to kill, but she'd never seen anyone murdered in front her.

The driver exited the car and walked to where The Wolf lay on the pavement. As he and Bruno picked up the limp body, she seized her chance and pushed to her feet, pressing the scarf tighter to her neck to staunch the bleeding. A quick glance inside the car showed the keys dangled from the ignition. She'd only have one opportunity, and her timing had to be perfect. The two men kept their focus on the prone Wolf. As they bent to pick up his limp form, she shifted closer to the car, keeping her body low to the ground. The men with their burden came between her and the tall man.

When they had nearly reached the riverbank, she eased open the door, slid across the seat, and slammed the clutch down with her left foot. She twisted the key and the car roared to life just as the pair dumped his body into the river. Throwing the car into first gear, she gunned the engine and sped down the street, flicking on the head-lights. A gunshot shattered the passenger side mirror, but a quick turn of the wheel onto a side street took her out of the line of fire. She drove as if being chased by demons to the American embassy.

And safety.

PRESENT DAY

Iris remembered the chaos her appearance had created. The soaked scarf and tale of murder on the banks of the River Havel had shaken the small American contingent, especially when she mentioned the list. It wasn't until days later she found out it contained the names of all American operatives undercover in East Berlin. Some had already been shot, execution-style, before they could be alerted to the danger.

She had recovered from her wound and left West Berlin, relieved at having no loose ends related to her association with The Wolf. His reappearance in her life hadn't been as disruptive as she'd initially feared until her Cabinet appointment and the death of Rainer Kopecek ripped open old wounds. That's why she had taken certain precautions, ones she hoped would point the finger directly at him should anything happen to her.

But enough woolgathering for one day. Time to turn her attention to her personal correspondence. A glance at her watch showed she had just enough time to wade through the rest of the mail before her appointment with Henry and Violet.

With a sigh, she picked up the letter opener and began. Some senators liked their staff to prioritize their mail, leaving them to read only correspondence from major donors and other political office holders. She preferred the more hands-on approach, at least as it related to actual mail. Her junior staff read and routed the hundreds of emails that came into her office, printing out the ones requiring her personal attention.

Seventeen minutes later, she picked up the final piece of mail, a 9 X 11 brown envelope marked "Personal." Slitting open the flap, she tipped it over, and out fell a second envelope with the flap unstuck.

Frowning, she pulled out a birthday card. Strange to receive one seven months early. She opened the card and gasped at the color photo taped inside. Bryon Smith, his neck at a grotesque angle, stared up at her with vacant eyes from a bed of leaves. Iris slammed the card on her desk and gripped her hands together to stop their trembling.

She had tried to get in touch with Byron after receiving his text, but her replies went unanswered. Knowing how The Wolf operated, she wasn't entirely surprised at his death, but nothing prepared her for such gruesome confirmation.

Looking up, she stared at the blurred shadows advancing across the carpet toward her, but no matter how many times she rubbed her eyes, the images remained distorted. The room grew fuzzy, and she blinked to bring it back into focus. A rasping in her throat alarmed her. With unsteady hands, she reached for the phone, but instead knocked it off her desk.

She tried to cry out, but the words refused to surface. Pushing herself to her feet took nearly all her remaining strength, and she only managed one step before paralysis overcame her.

As she fell forward to the floor, her last thought was she would have made a very good secretary of state.

CHAPTER
FORTY-SIX

Henry and Violet moved slowly up the ramp to the Delaware entrance at the Russell Senate Office Building on Constitution Avenue. The late afternoon sun slanted across the U.S. Capitol behind them, throwing long shadows. Violet shielded her eyes. "I didn't think it would be so easy to get an appointment with the senator."

"Maybe she knows why we're coming and wants to talk about The Wolf. She knows something, I'm sure of it." He hit the handicap button for the entrance to the building.

Violet followed him through the doors and stopped with him at the security checkpoint. "That's a pretty big maybe." Nerves made her voice squeak a bit. If Henry noticed, he said nothing. Another reason she loved him.

The line moved at a languid pace, and Violet suppressed a sigh. No sense in bellyaching about the Capitol police officers doing their job in screening visitors, not with the Capitol Hill riot of January 6, 2021, a not-so-distant memory. Finally, they reached the front, and she handed over her purse for a search and went through the body scanner. Henry took a few minutes longer because his crutches set off the alarm, so he had to be wanded by an officer. After clearing security, they made their way to the elevator and rode to the fifth floor.

"Which office is Senator Morrison's?" Henry waited until she exited the elevator car before following.

Violet consulted her phone, which displayed a map of the building. "She's in room 519, at the far end of the hallway to the left." She led the way down the polished marble hall, surprised at the quietness permeating the area. The door to 519 stood open, but when they entered, instead of the bustle of a busy senator's office, silence greeted their arrival.

"Hello?" No one replied. The empty reception desk sent a wave of unease down Violet's back. The very air seemed to shout something wasn't right.

"Where could everyone be?"

Violet shrugged.

"Her assistant asked for my email when I made the appointment, so let me check to see if they had to cancel at the last minute." Henry moved to one of the chairs lining the wall near the door and sat down to pull out his phone.

She tapped the smooth top of the desk, trying to keep her impatience in check. They were so close to finally finding some answers, and now this delay.

"There's nothing from the senator's office." Henry pocketed his phone.

"I don't like this. I'm going exploring, just a little."

"Not without me, you're not." Henry stood on his crutches.

Violet turned to the right and moved to a larger outer office with another empty office chair. Beyond that, a partially opened door beckoned. Swallowing her growing fear, Violet turned to Henry. "I don't have a good feeling about this."

"Me either." He inched closer to the open door. "Should we go in?"

She nodded. "Much as I want to turn and hightail it out of here, something tells me we can't, not without seeing what's going on." With a deep breath, she pushed the door wider and stepped inside. At first, nothing unusual caught her eye. Then, as she advanced across the Oriental rug, she saw a high heel shoe laying on its side. Stifling a cry, she said sharply, "Call 911."

"Does that belong to...?" Henry didn't complete the sentence.

Violet inched closer and peered around a club chair to see the body of a young woman on the floor. Violet dropped to her knees and grabbed the woman's wrist to check for a pulse. The coolness of her skin and absent heartbeat chilled her to the bone. "I thinks she's, uh, dead."

"The senator?"

Violet forced herself to look at the woman again, recalling Iris Morrison's short cropped salt-and-pepper hair from their research. This woman had dark, curly hair. "No, not Senator Morrison."

Henry left the door open as he made the call from the assistant's desk. She heard him connect, then decided to see if the senator was in the room.

Heart pounding, she sidestepped the body to move to the massive desk centered near the back wall. With a deep breath, she peered over the top of the desk, taking care not to touch or disturb anything.

Violet gasped.

Iris Morrison, senator from Wisconsin and presidential Cabinet appointee, lay on her back with her mouth slightly open and her eyes staring blankly at the ceiling.

HENRY GRIPPED THE RECEIVER AND SPOKE TO THE DISPATCHER IN A controlled voice despite his anxiousness. "My name is Dr. Henry Silverton, and I'm in Senator Iris Morrison's office at the Russell Senate Building on South Capitol Street. There's a dead body in the office, a young woman."

Violet stepped out of the senator's office, closed the door behind her. Her ashen complexion and glazed eyes revealed Iris Morrison may also be in the room.

He mouthed to Violet, "Is the senator dead too?"

She nodded and folded her arms across her chest.

"Sir, is there anyone else with you?"

"Yes, Violet Lundy. She came with me to see the senator."

She folded her arms across her chest and hugged herself.

Henry overrode the dispatcher's question. "Listen, you need to send someone now. There are two dead women in there, one of which is Senator Morrison."

"Sir, calm down. Are you saying Senator Morrison is dead?"

With a sigh, he tried to make her understand the situation. All he wanted to do was hold Violet in his arms. "I only saw the first body when I came out of the office to call 911. Violet checked the rest of the room and found the senator. Yes, both are clearly deceased."

"Units are on the way. Please secure the room until the officers arrive."

"Okay." Voices suddenly drifted to them. With a quick glance at Violet, he turned his back to the door and completed the call with the dispatcher. As he hung up the phone, a man with tousled hair and black-framed glasses came into the room, his attention focused on the thick batch of papers held in his hands.

"Richelle, would you please give this to the senator?" He stopped. "Who are you?" He swiveled his head around and eyeballed Henry. "Where is Richelle?"

Violet uncrossed her arms and straightened, her tone shaky. "I believe Richelle's with the senator." Her voice shook. "But you can't go in there."

The man narrowed his eyes. "Who did you say you were? And why are you blocking my entry?"

Henry answered. "I'm Dr. Henry Silverton and this is Violet Lundy. You can't go in there because the senator and a young woman, Richelle presumably, are dead."

The man's jaw dropped. "What are you talking about? How can they be dead?" He tried to reach around Violet for the door handle, but she stayed firmly put.

"We've called 911," Henry interjected hurriedly. "The police are on their way, and the dispatcher said we shouldn't let anyone in the room until they get here."

The man opened his mouth to protest when another man sauntered in, his eyes on his phone, thumbs tapping away. "Hey, Jack. Did you give the senator the marked-up transportation bill yet?"

The second man stopped short at the sight of Violet guarding the door with Jack beside her. "What's going on?"

"She won't let me past to see the senator." Then Jack pointed to Henry. "Because he says the senator and Richelle are dead. He's called the police."

The other man blinked several times in rapid succession, then pocketed his phone. "I'm Senator Morrison's chief of staff, Bill Lummons. Who are you and what's going on?"

Henry told him succinctly what they had discovered.

Bill listened and only asked a couple of questions. "Right. Jack, you wait at the outer door for the police to arrive, and do not say anything about this to anyone. If someone asks, say the officers are coming to talk about security at the senator's fundraiser this weekend." Jack left in a huff.

Bill picked up the phone on Richelle's desk. "Susan? Please come to Richelle's office right away."

The three of them waited for a few seconds before a woman approached the desk. "What's up, Bill?"

Bill filled her in "Start working on a statement for the press."

Bill started for the door to the senator's office. Violet put up a hand to stop him. "The dispatcher instructed Dr. Silverton to keep everyone out of the senator's office until help arrives."

"Who has to know?" Bill countered. "I just want to peek inside."

"No. I'm sorry." Violet crossed her arms. "Besides, you can't see anything until you're practically at the senator's desk."

"Now listen." Bill started forward. "I am her chief of staff. I have every right to go in there."

Henry grabbed his arm as he passed, his elbow keeping the crutch from falling. "I understand you want to see for yourself, but we can't let you in there. The women are dead. There's nothing we can do for them now except assist the police by making sure the crime scene isn't compromised, which will facilitate finding their killer. "

Susan held up from her phone. "Jack just texted. The FBI's here."

CHAPTER

FORTY-SEVEN

Violet pulled the takeout out of the plastic bags and breathed in the savory smell of pad thai and yen tafo. She'd fallen in love with the sweet, spicy, sour, and salty yen tafo, which had become her go-to dish when ordering from this local restaurant. "Where are your plates again?"

"In the left-hand upper cabinet next to the fridge," Henry called from the den.

She opened the cupboard and took down two plates. The FBI had kept them at Iris Morrison's office for hours, asking the same questions over and over. Why did they want to see the senator? How did they discover the body? What had they touched?

Bill Lummons had solved the mystery of where the staff had been when Violet and Henry had arrived. The chief of staff for Senator Baldwin, the other Wisconsin delegate, was retiring after forty years on the Hill, and Senator Morrison had encouraged everyone to attend his going-away party. Both Richelle and the senator had planned to join them after finishing a letter the senator wanted sent out in the last mail pickup of the day, but no one noticed when they didn't show.

As for how both women had died, Violet hadn't a clue, but she agreed with Henry the circumstances pointed to The Wolf, directly or indirectly. Her stomach growled as she scooped the meal onto plates. It was after nine o'clock. No wonder she was hungry.

"Here you go." She handed one plate to Henry and put the other down on the coffee table. "How are your legs?"

Henry grimaced. "Spasming, but the muscle relaxer will help."

"Spasming? I don't think that's a word," Violet teased, trying to take his mind off the pain. He had been so stoic, standing throughout the questioning as one of the agents grilled them on the details of their visit. The entire office had been labeled a crime scene, and they were instructed not to disturb the furnishing or other belongings, which translated into no place to sit. To make the situation even more physically taxing, after they'd been questioned, the agent advised them to wait in the hallway until cleared to leave the scene, but they were overlooked for more than an hour.

"Maybe not, but that's what it feels like." He settled the plate on his lap. "Shall I say the blessing?"

She nodded and bowed her head. Praying over meals was something she'd gotten out of the habit of doing. However, Henry's prayers had a more intimate quality to them, as if he truly believed God heard him. In the past few weeks, she found herself wanting to believe in a God she had thought had forsaken her after Patrick shot and killed those kids. The prayers her father said over family meals had tended toward the generic, very bland, and impersonal.

"Heavenly Father, we come before you tired and hungry, not just for food, but for your peace and wisdom. Please bless our meal. Guide us and keep us safe from harm. Amen." Henry unfolded his napkin. "I had no idea that a Thai restaurant was so close."

She smiled. "I guess the old adage you learn something new every day is true." She forked succulent noodles into her mouth. They ate in silence for a few minutes, and Violet savored the quiet almost as much as the food. It was hard to find someone who could

272

be comfortable with not talking, with letting the hush settle over them like a shawl, cozy and warm.

Then the doorbell rang, shattering the calm atmosphere like a gunshot through a plate glass window. Violet jumped and lost her grip on the plate, which tumbled over and onto the floor. The doorbell pealed again.

Henry moved as if to rise, and she shot out her hand to stop him. "You stay there." The bell sounded longer, as if the caller kept his finger pressed on the button for several seconds. "I'll go see who's so insistent at nine-thirty this evening, then I'll take care of the mess."

She stepped over the plate on the floor and marched to the door. A thunderous knocking greeted her arrival in the foyer. She peered through the peephole. Two police officers stood side by side. Leaving the chain latched, she eased open the door. "Yes?"

The taller man asked, "Violet Lundy?"

"What is this about?" She intentionally avoided a direct answer.

He took a step forward. "Are you Violet Lundy?"

The directness coupled with the icy stare of his dark eyes sent her heart racing. "Yes."

"Open the door, ma'am."

The muscles between her shoulders tightened. "Forgive me for asking again, but I'd like to know what this is about first?"

"Ma'am, we're Alexandria police officers. We're here to serve a Fairfax County warrant for your arrest."

FORTY-EIGHT

Violet froze, her body filling the small space between the partially opened door and its frame. Her heart pounded in her ears.

"Violet?" Henry called from the den.

She pressed her hand to her forehead. Surely this was only a dream, and she would wake up soon.

"Ma'am?" The taller officer stepped closer, his voice bristling with authority. "Please step outside."

It was the suggestion to leave the sanctuary of the house that jolted Violet out of her stupor. Her brain kicked into high gear. Her encounters with the mysterious Wolf had taught her nothing was as it seemed. "I'd like to read the warrant first."

The two policemen exchanged glances, then the spokesman shrugged and tugged a piece of paper from his shirt pocket. She took the slim piece of paper and skimmed the words. *Warrant for the arrest of Violet Lundy for the murder of Rainer Kopecek.* It certainly seemed official, but she wasn't taking any chances. She handed the paper back to the officer.

"You need to come outside." He stuffed the paper back into his pocket.

Violet craned her neck to see around them and spotted a police cruiser parked at the curb, its blue lights flashing. She leveled a gaze at the officers. "I need to verify you're who you say you are. I've had some threatening phone calls lately. Would you mind waiting here while I make a call?"

"I'm sorry, ma'am, we can't do that." The lead officer didn't say it unkindly, but his voice brokered no negotiation.

She bit her lip and tried anyway. "What if I make the call with the door cracked, so you can hear and see me?"

The two officers exchanged glances. Violet wished she could interpret their unspoken communication.

"Please, I'm truly not trying to pull anything." Tears sprang to her eyes.

"Is everything okay?" Henry spoke behind her, and she jumped.

Violet longed to throw her arms around him and hang on for dear life. She would have to settle for a quick conversation. "Henry, there are two officers here who say they have a warrant for my arrest for the mur...." She choked on the word, but then managed to spit it out, "murder of Mr. Kopecek."

The shock in his eyes mirrored the sick feeling in her stomach. "They're from the Alexandria police but the warrant is for Fairfax. County. Would you call the Alexandria police to see if it's true?"

Henry laid a hand on her shoulder as he peered around her to see the officers.

"It'll be okay, sweetheart," he whispered in her ear before addressing the officers. "I'm Dr. Henry Silverton, owner of this home. Would it be okay if I make the call while Violet stays right here?"

The lead policeman gave his consent, and Henry withdrew his phone, using the voice assistant to call the Alexandria police non-emergency number.

She hugged herself and wondered when this nightmare would end. Ever since her brother had made his outlandish statement on national TV, she had been half-expecting this scenario. Her sole comfort was there couldn't possibly be any evidence because she hadn't done anything wrong. Since Mr. Kopecek had requested cremation, no proof of murder could be fabricated.

Henry touched her shoulder.

She couldn't turn around, didn't want to see his face as she asked, "Is the warrant real?"

"Yes."

Closing her eyes, she sucked in a breath and said to the officers, "I have to close the door to slip the chain off." Suiting actions to words, she pushed it in and removed the chain with surprisingly steady fingers. Opening the door again, she stepped back. "I'll need to get my jacket and purse."

The lead officer nodded to Henry while sidestepping around him. "I'll come with you."

The policeman's partner stayed at the front door with Henry while the officer followed her to the kitchen. She grabbed her jacket from the back of the chair and her purse from the tabletop. Slipping her arms inside, she buttoned it.

The officer gestured for her to precede him to the front door. Once there, she halted. "Do you have to handcuff me?"

The taller officer studied her for a long moment, then shook his head. "No, it's not required, but I do have to read you your rights."

Violet listened to the familiar litany of the Miranda warning. She was innocent but she was still scared. She could almost feel The Wolf's sharp claws reaching out for her, ready to pounce and devour her. Somehow, he'd gotten to Patrick and fed her brother the information for his outrageous claim on television. Now the shadowy figure had managed to trump up enough false evidence to convince police to arrest her.

The officer finished with her rights and placed his hand on her arm. "Let's go."

"Where will you be taking her?" Henry asked.

"To central booking at the Duke Street Precinct." The officer

277

tugged her toward the door. "But she'll only be there for processing. The Fairfax County prosecutor has arranged for her extradition to their jurisdiction."

Violet threw an anguished look over her shoulder to where Henry stood, phone in hand, looking as bewildered as she felt. But there was something else in his eyes. Anger on her behalf, and that bolstered her confidence. It both warmed and comforted her to have someone like Henry on her side.

"Don't say anything, Violet. I'll have a lawyer waiting at the Fairfax County jail. Remember, I love you," Henry added as the officer propelled her through the door.

Henry's words resonated during the short ride to the police station and subsequent finger-printing and booking. She kept his face firmly in her mind during the humiliation of a strip search and placement in a holding cell.

As the metal door clanged shut, Violet slid to the cold cement floor and cried, ignoring the taunts and sneers of the women in the cell with her. Deep inside her heart, she prayed for help from the God she had become nearly convinced wasn't interested in her. *Dear God, please give me strength to endure this.*

VIOLET PLACED HER HANDS ON THE DULL METAL TABLE BOLTED TO THE FLOOR and tightly interlaced her fingers. She took a deep breath and let it out slowly. Twenty minutes ago, a female Fairfax County police officer had led her to this small, windowless interview room and deposited her there to wait for her attorney.

She shifted in the hard plastic chair, the blue cotton pants and top rubbing against her skin. After a few hours at the Alexandria lockup, she'd been transferred and processed again at the Fairfax County Adult Detention Center and placed in the general female population. At least she had snagged an upper bunk for the night and managed to get a little sleep. But the lack of privacy and noise of the place with its hundreds of inmates grated on her already frazzled nerves.

The door opened and a tall woman holding a briefcase, her brown skin a warm glow that cheered Violet considerably, entered. She chatted with the officer who had brought Violet to the room, laughing at something the policewoman said. Once inside, the other woman eyed her up and down before sitting across from her.

"My name is Laverne Demaris. Dr. Silverton has retained my services on your behalf."

Tears welled in Violet's eyes at the mention of Henry. How she wished he was the one sitting across from her.

"I'm sorry I couldn't get to see you last night, but it was after ten p.m. by the time I found out exactly where you were, and the cells were locked for the night." Ms. Demaris sighed. "I can see you've had a rough night of it."

Violet cleared her throat to stem the flood of tears threatening to spill over. "Did Henry tell you what happened?"

Her lawyer nodded. "He filled me in on everything." The other woman met Violet's gaze. "And I do mean everything, including a certain someone who has, shall we say, animalistic tendencies?"

Ah, so Henry had told her all about The Wolf and their suspicions. "What about my relative?"

"We'll have more time to talk later." Ms. Demaris raised her eyebrows. "Now we only have a few minutes before the detectives and prosecutor come in to interview you. First, I read the charges but have yet to see the evidence. Second, you will answer in as few words as possible and stick only to the facts. No speculation, no embellishments. Third, you will stop talking immediately if I lay my hand on your arm. Are we clear?"

Violet let out a pent-up breath. "Yes. And thank you."

Ms. Demaris snorted. "Don't thank me just yet. Wait until I've obtained your release from this place."

A knock on the door sounded. "Come in." Her attorney rose to move to Violet's side of the table.

The door opened to admit a lanky man wearing a dark suit and an older man with his tie askew and a salt-and-pepper beard. Each man carried several file folders, a well-known tactic of law enforcement interviews Violet had seen before when being interviewed about Patrick in the days following the shooting. Most of the time, the interviewers didn't bother to open the folders.

The older man spoke first. "Ms. Lundy, I'm Detective Travis Sullivan. This is Commonwealth Attorney Andrew Smith, from the prosecutor's office."

Ms. Demaris introduced herself as Violet's counsel and everyone found a seat. Detective Sullivan announced the session would be recorded and pointed to a mounted video camera in the upper right corner of the room. He then listed the date, time, and each participants' full name.

"Ms. Lundy, do you know why you're here?" Detective Sullivan asked, his voice as cordial as if asking Violet if she liked ice cream.

"No." Violet had no idea why they thought Mr. Kopecek had been murdered and what evidence they could possibly have since his body was cremated.

Detective Sullivan leaned forward. "You have been charged with a very serious crime, that of first-degree murder. Here in Virginia, that carries a mandatory sentence of twenty years to life in prison. Do you know what first-degree murder means?"

Violet shook her head, and folded her hands on her lap, relaxing her shoulders to appear at ease, tactics she'd picked up to cope with all the police interviews she went through following Patrick's arrest.

"It means the murder of Rainer Kopececk was premeditated on your part. In other words, you planned to kill him."

"What proof do you have that my client killed Mr. Kopecek?" Ms. Demaris interjected smoothly.

"We have evidence pointing to Ms. Lundy's guilt," the detective retorted.

"Such as?" Ms. Demaris's tone implied she had no doubt as to the scurrilous nature of such evidence.

"We don't have to lay it all out for you right now," the prosecutor snapped.

Ms. Demaris smiled in a way that made Violet glad the woman was on her side. "Now, gentlemen, you know that without proof, you have no case. From what little I've heard so far, you are banking on a confession to bolster your so-called evidence."

Smith pressed his lips together in a firm line but said nothing. Detective Sullivan continued, "Ms. Lundy, or should I call you Ms. Cunningham?"

Violet had known the police would know her former identity but hearing this peacock of a man call her Ms. Cunningham riled her like red flag being waved in front of a bull. "My legal name is Violet Lundy."

Detective Sullivan nodded. "Yeah, I think I would have changed my name if my twin brother had shot up a classroom full of youngsters."

"What my client's brother did has no bearing on this case," Ms. Demaris jumped in, her voice as icy as the frozen tundra. "Do not bring it up again."

Violet wanted to hug the woman. Ms. Demaris was like a pit bull defending his bone, just the kind of lawyer a person in Violet's position needed in her corner.

Detective Sullivan picked up a piece of paper from his open folder. "You worked at the Happy Hills Assisted Living Facility in housekeeping for three years, is that right?"

"Yes." Violet remembered her attorney's admonition and kept her answer short.

"Why?" the detective asked.

Violet frowned. "I don't understand the question."

"Why would a woman with a college degree work at a job clearly beneath her skills?" Detective Sullivan clarified.

"I needed a job that didn't require me to explain why Violet Lundy didn't have any work history. The cleaning job fit the bill." Violet thought back to her first months at Happy Hill, the hard work easing her sleep at night. Slowly, her conversations with Mr. Kopecek brought her back from the haze she had been living in since her brother's conviction.

"With the added bonus of getting close to lonely old men in the hopes they would make you beneficiaries in their wills?" Detective Sullivan added.

Violet ignored his tone and implication. "No."

"Do you have any facts to back this up or are you on a fishing expedition?" Ms. Demaris said, her voice sharp.

"Fact one," Detective Sullivan said, leaning forward and jabbing his finger at Violet, "you were named sole beneficiary of Rainer Kopecek's will. Fact two, Kopecek died unexpectedly. Fact three, you inherited a sizeable fortune from Kopecek."

Violet nearly laughed aloud but managed to keep her mirth in check. Whoever had supplied the facts to the police had certainly covered a host of possibilities. "First of all, I had no idea I was in Mr. Kopecek's will. Second, the physician who examined his body found no evidence of anything other than natural death due to old age. Third, I would characterize Mr. Kopecek's estate as modest, not sizeable."

"We have affidavits saying you inherited half a million dollars from Mr. Kopecek. When our subpoenas come through, we'll have the evidence from his bank accounts to back it up." Smith shuffled some papers. "And also that you buttered up the old man by spending time with him after your shift ended."

Violet counted to ten to hold her anger in check at the implication she spent time with the sweet old man just to weasel her way into his will. "Mr. Davidson, Mr. Kopecek's attorney, will tell you I had no idea I was the beneficiary."

"It sounds like you've been listening to gossip, Detective Sullivan. Better to have gotten your facts straight before making an ill-advised arrest." Ms. Demaris's voice was amused.

"There's also the manner of Mr. Kopecek's death." Detective Sullivan set his jaw \in a stubborn line.

"Do you have any evidence Mr. Kopecek's demise was anything but natural?" Ms. Demaris's eyes were hard.

"We will once we get our order to exhume the body." Detective Sullivan replied. "Then we'll look for extra insulin in the body tissue."

Violet closed her eyes briefly, then opened them. "You can't."

Detective Sullivan smirked. "Our request is before a judge as we speak. There's nothing you can do to stop it."

Violet shook her head. "I didn't mean you couldn't get the order. I meant you couldn't exhume the body."

"Why not?" Detective Sullivan sat back, crossing his arms, a smug smile marring his countenance.

"Because there is no body." Violet looked from the detective to the commonwealth attorney. "Mr. Kopecek's will stipulated he was to be cremated, and he was."

FORTY-NINE

"I'd say your case has completely collapsed," Ms. Demaris said, her confidence easing the ache between Violet's shoulders. "Is there anything else before I put my motion before a judge asking all charges of this spurious allegation be dismissed immediately?"

"Wait a minute," Detective Sullivan snapped. "Just because we don't have a body doesn't mean she didn't murder Kopecek for his money. Besides, her own brother said she killed the old man."

Ms. Demaris sat back and steepled her fingers. "Gentlemen, I'm surprised you hadn't done your homework, instead of relying on innuendo and the word of convicted mass murderer."

"It wasn't just the brother," exclaimed Smith. "We have a detailed letter outlining exactly how Ms. Lundy killed Mr. Kopecek."

Ms. Demaris raised her eyebrows. "I think you two need a lesson in elementary evidence procedure. Letters do not constitute proof of a crime. It can launch an investigation, but I'm shocked you managed to convince a judge to write out an arrest warrant on such a flimsy basis." She shook her head. "This is shoddy work, even for you, Smith. What hard evidence of a crime do you have with no body, no real motive, and no witnesses?"

The commonwealth attorney and detective exchanged glances.

"I see, you were banking on a confession and circumstantial proof that has simply vanished now, hasn't it?" Ms. Demaris stood, snapping her briefcase closed. "I expect all charges against my client dropped immediately, and her release within the hour. This interview is now over. Please send a copy of the recording to my office pronto."

The detective entered the time before snapping off the video recorder to end the session and the two men stood. The prosecutor spoke first. "Ms. Demaris, I'll have the paperwork sent over as soon as I return to my office."

"I'll wait while you call your secretary to start the process. I don't want my client to spend another moment in custody than she has to." Ms. Demaris tapped her foot while Smith pulled out his cell and called his office. Satisfied with his end of the conversation, she turned to Violet. "You'll be out of here in two shakes of a lamb's tail."

Sixty-three minutes later, Violet walked out of the detention center dressed in her own clothes. Ms. Demaris was waiting for her in the lobby. "Better?"

"Yes." Violet sucked in a lungful of cool, damp air. "It's unnerving to be confined to an area you cannot leave." She touched the attorney's arm. "Thanks for your help."

Ms. Demaris laughed. "You're welcome. It helped, of course, that there was zero evidence. Sometimes I wonder how people get as far as they do in life. Those two numbskulls have always taken the path of least resistance when it comes to gathering evidence."

"Why are they still employed?"

"Because there are criminals out there even stupider than those two, which means they get it right often enough to keep their bosses happy." Ms. Demaris motioned to Violet to walk beside her.

"Ah." Violet breathed deeply again, not able to draw in enough fresh air.

"I called Henry to let him know you would be released soon with all charges dismissed. He wanted to come, but he had a conference call with his department scheduled earlier this morning, and I wasn't sure how long the paperwork would take. May I drop you somewhere?"

"Thank you. I should call Henry first." Violet pulled out her cell phone and dialed his number. She couldn't wait to hear his voice.

"I'm out, Henry," Violet said as soon as he answered his phone.

"Praise the Lord! Ms. Demaris said things had worked out. How about you come over for a celebration brunch? I have all the fixings for western omelets."

Violet brushed away a tear. "I can't think of anything I'd like more."

HENRY EXTRACTED THE MAIL FROM THE BOX BESIDE HIS DOOR AND TOOK THE bundle inside, careful to close the door as softly as possible. Violet had fallen asleep on his couch in the den after their brunch, and he hadn't the heart to waken her. Instead, he'd draped an afghan over her and left her snoozing. He couldn't believe what she'd been through, arrested for murdering Mr. Kopecek and spending the night in jail.

Instead of heading back to the kitchen, he went into the front room he had transformed into a library with floor-to-ceiling book-shelves and a pair of cozy chairs with floor lamps for reading. Once seated in his favorite chair, he flipped through the stack, dumping catalogs and junk mail into the recycling bin on the floor beside the chair.

When he finished sorting, all that remained were a few charity mailings and a postcard showing a magnificent castle with snow covering the ground and holiday garlands above the windows. A quick glance at the postcard revealed no return address, only his name and address on a computer-generated label. No message at all, not even pre-printed information about the castle.

The DC postmark told him nothing to pinpoint the sender's identity. There were more than half a million people living in the city, with hundreds of thousands of commuters coming in from Maryland, Virginia, West Virginia, and Pennsylvania to work.

He sat lost in thought, trying to come up with a plausible—or implausible—reason for someone sending him a blank postcard.

"Henry?"

With a start, Henry bit back a yelp as Violet came into the room. "You scared me."

"Sorry." She yawned. "You should have woken me."

She stretched and her blouse pulled tightly across her chest. His eyes lingered for a second, then he caught himself and followed her upraised arms to her tousled hair. The urge to kiss her nearly overwhelmed him, followed by the thought that if she were his wife, he would wake up to this look every day. His cheeks warmed and he ducked his head to keep Violet from commenting on his expression. He wasn't sure he could adequately explain the direction his thoughts had taken.

"Whatcha doing?" She sank into the opposite chair and ran her fingers through her hair.

"Doing?" *Watching you, wanting to kiss you, wishing I had the guts to follow through.* He shifted and some of the mail slid off his lap onto the floor. "Uh, going through the mail. I forgot to get it yesterday."

"Anything interesting?"

Henry handed her the postcard. "Just this, although it's more along the lines of intriguing."

She noted the picturesque scene and turned it over. "No message?"

"Nope. No clue as to who sent it, especially with the label being printed from a computer."

She ran her fingers over the smooth surface. "Seems awfully strange to get a blank postcard. It must mean something."

"But what?" He shrugged. "There's no message to decode."

"Maybe that's why amateurs so often fail at spy games. We don't have a devious enough mind to come up with what a blank postcard could be saying to us." She held out the card to Henry.

Tucking it into a book on the end table by his chair, he reached for his crutches and stood. "The FBI called while you were sleeping. They want us to come down to headquarters to go over and sign our statements about finding the senator yesterday. Do you feel up to going now?"

"I nearly forgot they wanted us to come downtown. Finding Iris Morrison's body seems so long ago now." She rose and smoothed her hair back from her face. "I wish I could shower and change clothes. I'm kind of tired of being in these, although they're better than the awful prison-issued attire." She shuddered.

"Come here, my love."

With a shy smile, she took a step closer.

Henry let one crutch drop back against the chair and tucked his hand around the back of her neck. He leaned his forehead against hers. "I'm so sorry you had to go through that."

"Me too."

"I wish there was a way for me to make it all disappear from your memory."

A saucy grin spread across her face. "Well, there is one thing..."

He raised his eyebrows. "Ms. Lundy, I do believe you're asking for a kiss."

"You know me so well, Dr. Silverton." Violet sighed and swayed closer, her eyes drifting closed as his lips descended onto hers.

Henry allowed himself the very real pleasure of holding the woman he loved in his arms, wanting to never let her go.

CHAPTER

FIFTY

Violet cinched the belt on the cherry-red merino wool dress. The color was probably a tad too bold for a meeting with the FBI, but the dress was the only thing Sissy had left at Henry's townhouse besides baggy jeans. After her experience with local law enforcement, she needed the confidence such a dress gave her.

"Are you ready? The taxi's waiting outside," Henry called up the stairs.

"Coming!" She pirouetted in front of the floor-length mirror in the guest room once more to be sure everything was in place, picked up her handbag, and went downstairs.

Henry whistled as she turned the corner on the landing. "Wow, you look, um, delicious."

Violet held the handrail as she descended. "Good enough to eat, huh?" She laughed, happier than she had a right to be, given the circumstances. Lately, her thoughts turned with more frequency to what life might be like when this was all over.

He blocked her movement toward the front door by stepping in

291

front of her, a gleam in his eyes that warmed her all the way to her toes. "Maybe I'll just take a little nibble, to tide me over until lunch."

She grinned as he pretended to bite her neck, then gasped as his lips grazed a sensitive area. "Henry!"

A honking car horn brought his head up. "Saved by the bell."

Opening the door, he shooed her out and followed, locking it behind them. Violet resisted the urge to look behind them on the drive over but the prickly feeling of being watched wouldn't leave her. On the drive to FBI headquarters, they talked of inconsequential things, not wanting the cab driver to overhear anything related to their suspicions about The Wolf, but to her own ears, their conversation sounded more stilted than natural.

Once on the sidewalk before the J. Edgar Hoover building's handicap entrance, she turned to Henry. "To tell or not to tell what we think is happening, that is the question before us now." A quick glance around showed the sidewalk teeming with office workers and tourists. The Wolf or his spies could be anywhere.

"If we tell, how much do we tell?" he replied as they made their way up the ramp to the double doors.

"And," she added as she hit the automatic door button, "will they believe us if we do?"

Waiting in line for security clearance, Henry said, "Hey, don't be nervous. We'll be safe enough inside FBI headquarters."

"I wish I could shake the feeling we're being followed or watched, but I'm probably more on edge after spending last night in jail." She gave him a smile as they went through the metal detectors.

Once past security, the pair gave their names to the receptionist and asked to see Special Agent Monroe or Talbot. The woman nodded, then gestured toward the spacious lobby where they could wait. "I'll let them know you're here."

"Thank you," Henry said. He nodded to a bench against a wall. "I need to sit. Too much standing yesterday."

"Sure." She stood near him, too restless to join him on the bench.

After ten minutes of waiting, she sank onto the bench beside him. "What's taking so long?"

He shrugged. "Important government things, I guess."

She sighed and tapped her toe impatiently. Another ten minutes went by while they amused themselves by making up stories about the people passing by their line of sight.

At the half hour mark, a man in a dark blue suit approached them. "Ms. Lundy? Dr. Silverton?"

Violet and Henry rose in unison. "Yes."

"I'm Special Agent Douglas." He smiled. "If you'll follow me, I'll take you up to see Agents Monroe and Talbot."

Soon, Violet and Henry were seated in a small, windowless conference room. After asking if they wanted coffee or something else to drink—to which both replied water would be welcome—the agent left them alone.

"Do you think they have this room bugged to hear our conversation?" Henry whispered to Violet. "Or have I been too immersed in the Stasi and their underhanded methods and now see intrigue where there's merely a bland landscape." He pointed to a muted watercolor of a mountain with the sun setting just over the peak that adorned one wall.

She stifled a giggle. "Maybe the recording device is hidden in the dreadful dried flower arrangement in the center of the table."

Henry leaned forward and pretended to examine the object without touching it. "Perhaps, but I'm guessing it's tucked into the sprinkler right above your head." He sat back. "A microphone could be concealed inside its housing without anyone being the wiser."

They shared a grin as the door opened and the two men Violet had seen yesterday came into the room, each carrying a file folder and two bottles of water. They once again introduced themselves and showed their badges, then handed Violet and Henry each a water bottle, reserving one for each of them.

Agent Monroe took the lead. "We'd like to go over your statements before you sign them. We often find witnesses recall more details after some time has passed."

"Before we do, what exactly happened to the senator?" Henry asked.

The agents exchanged glances. "We're not at liberty to say."

"Do you have a suspect in the murders?" Henry squeezed her hand under the table.

"Why do you say murders?" Agent Talbot pounced on his word choice.

Henry gave them a hard stare. "When a senator and her assistant both die around the same time, murder is not a far-fetched conclusion for any reasonable person to draw."

"That may be, but we're here to go over your statements and recollections." Agent Monroe turned to Violet. "Did you see anything out of place when you discovered the bodies?"

"I'm not sure. Let me think about it." She closed her eyes, willing her mind to bring up the grisly scene. First she saw the assistant's legs, her bare right foot and high heel shoe lying on its side. Then the woman, lying on her side, clutching something. Violet opened her eyes. "She was holding a piece of paper—the assistant, I mean. In her left hand, nearly under her body."

Agent Monroe raised his eyebrows and opened the folder to jot down a note. "That's a pretty important detail to leave out of your statement yesterday afternoon."

Violet frowned. "I didn't remember until right now. I've never seen a dead body before, at least not like that." She took a deep breath. "I guess it rattled me more than I realized."

"But that's not entirely true, is it, Ms. Lundy?" Agent Talbot leaned across the table. "You saw plenty of dead bodies, didn't you, the day your brother gunned down a classroom full of seventh graders."

CHAPTER
FIFTY-ONE

Violet expected them to look into her background, but the words brought back memories she'd tried hard to forget. Crime scene photos showing bloody bodies of children lying in heaps on the floor haunted her dreams from time to time.

"What has that to do with the senator's death?" Henry shot back, his voice hard.

Some of the tension seeped out of her shoulders. At least now she had Henry on her side, and that made all the difference between what happened after Patrick's arrest and today. Before the agents could reply, she interjected, "No, I did not see what Patrick did, not apart from the news footage or from the photographs the police shoved in my face afterwards. I wasn't at the school." She choked back tears and continued, "I didn't see those children or Brenda in person."

Agent Monroe raised his eyebrows. "Patrick Cunningham is your twin. I find it hard to believe you knew nothing of his plans. Maybe you were the brains behind your brother's actions."

"And maybe I did the same thing with the senator. That's what you're really implying, aren't you?" Anger sizzled in her blood at their smug implications.

"Now hold on." Agent Talbot held up a hand. "You have to admit it's rather suspicious the twin sister of a mass murderer finds herself first on the scene of a murdered senator and her aide."

"Maybe," Henry said, "but maybe it's a distraction taking you away from the real killer."

"Perhaps," Agent Monroe conceded before turning to Violet again. "Why did you change your name?"

She twisted the cap off her water bottle and took a sip. The interview had barely begun and already her energy lagged from the questions, so repetitious of the ones she'd endured in the police interrogation room hours earlier. Now she had to try to explain the unexplainable. "Have you ever run into people who don't like what you do? Made fun of you because of who you are?"

The agents shrugged, nearly in unison. "Not everyone loves it when the FBI comes calling," Agent Talbot offered.

"Right, but they don't usually get too nasty about it, do they? After all, you have the power to arrest them or make their lives uncomfortable." She recapped her water. "But imagine, if you can, living in a small town where everyone knows everybody. One big happy family. Then throw in a horrific shooting, lots of dead children. Add one unremorseful young man who didn't kill himself afterwards but instead proclaimed loud and clear they had it coming because their teacher had the audacity to break up with him."

She had their full attention at least. If she could only relate to them some of what she went through, what her parents went through, in the days following Patrick's actions, then they might stop looking at her as if she was tainted by her association with a kid killer. Lacing her fingers together to stop them from shaking, she went on. "People you thought were your friends suddenly turned and literally ran in the other direction if you passed them on the street. Terrible words were constantly spray-painted on your house, and the police didn't do anything, wouldn't come out, wouldn't take a report, nothing." The injustice of it all strengthened her voice. "The whispers followed you everywhere you went. At the supermarket, clerks refused to ring up your groceries or dropped your eggs on purpose, then walked away when you asked for fresh ones."

She studied each agent in turn. "Then multiply that by one hundred—no, by one thousand—and you might begin to see what life was like as Patricia Cunningham. So yes, I changed my name, legally distanced myself, and moved away. I wanted nothing to do with my brother after what he'd done, but I stayed through the trial because that's what you do for family."

The agents didn't move for several seconds after she finished, then Agent Talbot spoke, "I see." He consulted a folder on the conference table. "Why were you going to see Senator Morrison yesterday?"

Violet sat back, exhausted, and allowed Henry to reply.

"To talk with her." Henry sounded confident and not in the least bit intimidated by being interviewed at FBI headquarters.

"Did you have an appointment?" Agent Monroe picked up the questioning.

If she hadn't been so tired, Violet might have found it interesting the way the pair switched off roles, one being the aggressor, then the other. No strict good cop-bad cop with this duo. But she felt put through a wringer.

"Yes." Henry and the lawyer had mentioned the best way to stay out of trouble with authoritative figures was to answer questions in as few words as necessary. He'd told her that was one tidbit he'd picked up while working on his book about the Stasi. While she had blown it with the explanation about her name change, she saw the wisdom in his advice as he handled the inquiries.

Agent Monroe glanced at Henry, then slid his gaze to Violet. "It wasn't written down in her appointment book."

"When we called, we spoke directly to Senator Morrison, who said she had time yesterday afternoon to see us." Violet took a deep breath to steady her voice.

"What did you want to talk with her about?" Agent Monroe asked, his eyes as hard as Virginia clay in winter.

"To ask her if she knew someone." Henry took Violet's hand and gave it a squeeze. She wished she felt as confident as he did in the justice system. In her experience, the people who ran it could be just as petty and vindictive as anyone.

"Why do I get the feeling you're stonewalling us?" Agent Talbot snarled, his demeanor changing from easy-going to hard-as-nails interrogator in a split second.

Violet shrunk back in her chair, her hand clutching Henry's, hard.

Henry cocked his head, his expression serious yet open. Violet could detect no fear in it. "I'm answering your questions."

"With the barest minimum of replies," growled Agent Talbot.

"I didn't realize my answers needed to be a certain length to fulfill the question asked." Henry's voice had acquired a slight edge of steel in it. Violet hadn't seen this part of him before and she liked feeling protected by this man.

"Who did you want to ask her about?" Agent Talbot asked Henry directly.

Violet answered instead. "I met someone at an assisted care facility where I worked who had a connection with the West Berlin Embassy back when Iris Morrison worked there."

They wanted to introduce Rainer Kopecek's name to the agents in the hopes that perhaps someone from the FBI would follow up, ask questions they couldn't ask about his death. But they also needed to keep The Wolf's potential involvement a secret because they still lacked confirmation of his identity. The Wolf was chasing them, but he probably would not strike to kill unless they proved a direct threat.

"What is this person's name?" Agent Talbot poised his pen above a notepad.

"Rainer Kopecek." Violet spelled the last name for the agent. "Mr. Kopecek recently died, and in going through his papers, I discovered the senator might have known him a quarter century ago." This was the tricky part, couching her words so the agents wouldn't ask to see the evidence connecting the two. She didn't think a coded message about a flower would impress them.

Agent Monroe stopped jotting notes. "Weren't you arrested for his murder yesterday?"

Information certainly got around in law enforcement. "Yes, but all charges were dropped this morning. As I'm sure you know." Now it was her turn to raise an eyebrow. "There was, is, absolutely no basis for such a charge in the first place, as my attorney pointed out. The prosecutor agreed and the case is no longer pending against me."

Agent Monroe smiled slightly. "It was a rather slipshod investigation. Definitely not like we do things in the FBI." His tone turned brisk. "Why did you think the senator would want to know about the death of someone she hadn't seen in years?"

"In my experience in working at the home, the older a person gets, the more they want to connect with people they knew in their youth. Mr. Kopecek often reminisced about his time in Germany." That was true, but she had deliberately left out that it was East Germany and East Berlin of which he had spoken.

Agent Monroe leaned back in his chair. "Did the senator know Kopecek?"

Violet shrugged. "We didn't get a chance to ask her."

"Why did you want to see her yesterday?" Agent Monroe asked. "The chances of her having free time were pretty nil, don't you think?"

"That's why we called to ask. It was our good luck she was available." Henry took over. "When we came across her name, we wanted to let her know as soon as possible. Several weeks had already passed since Mr. Kopecek's death. We didn't want to wait any longer to talk to Mrs. Morrison."

To Violet's relief, the agents seemed satisfied. A knock on the door interrupted them, and Agent Talbot answered it, conferring in a low voice with another man, who handed him a folder. Talbot returned to his seat and talked to his partner in a whisper.

"It appears the senator was looking through her mail right before she died." Agent Talbot gazed at Violet. "You mentioned seeing envelopes and papers scattered on her desk and office floor."

"That's right." Violet wondered where they were going with this. Surely nothing in the senator's mail could incriminate her in Iris's death.

"There were several pieces of mail on which we haven't been able to identify the sender. Would you mind taking a look at these copies to see if you recognize anything?" Agent Talbot opened a folder and extracted a few pieces of paper.

"Sure, but I would think the senator's staff would be more helpful. I didn't know the senator at all." Violet tried to keep the overwhelming feeling of danger from coloring her voice. *Slow and steady. Answer them slowly and steadily.*

Agent Talbot laid a photocopy of a typed letter in front of her. Violet skimmed what seemed to be a form letter requesting Senator Morrison's appearance at a fundraiser in an unspecified city. "I haven't a clue."

He took the sheet from her and handed her another. She read a diatribe against the state of the economy and a plea for help from an unnamed constituent. Then Agent Talbot slid a third piece of paper to her.

She picked it up and gasped. Staring back at her with lifeless eyes, his neck at an odd angle, was the face of the man who had saved her life from the speeding car.

CHAPTER
FIFTY-TWO

"Violet? Are you okay?" Henry gripped Violet's hand.

She wiped her cheeks of tears but didn't reply.

Henry glanced down at the photograph Violet held in front of her but didn't recognize the obviously deceased man.

"Do you know the man in this photo?" Agent Talbot's tone of urgency came across as sharp, whether he intended to or not.

"He's dead." Her voice revealed a tremor, and it was all Henry could do not to gather her in his arms.

The agents exchanged glances, then Agent Monroe spoke. "Yes, he is. His body was found in Rock Creek Park early this morning. If it hadn't been for the owner of a runaway dog searching for his pet, who had chased a squirrel deep into the woods, the victim may not have been discovered so quickly."

Violet let out a shaky breath. "I don't know his name, but he saved my life."

"What do you mean?" Agent Monroe clicked his pen and poised it above the open file.

Violet related the near-miss with the speeding car and the man who pushed her out of the way in the nick of time. "I wanted to thank him, but he simply vanished into the crowd."

To think the man who had pulled her to safety had his neck broken days later chilled Henry to the bone. Violet shot a questioning look at Henry, but he gave a discreet shake of his head. They wouldn't muddy the waters by revealing her suspicions this was the same man who had spoken to her after their car accident.

The agents questioned her about the near-miss for a few more minutes until she couldn't tell them anything else about her encounter with the dead man.

"Where did you get the photo?" Henry voiced the question that had been niggling at the back of his mind since the agent had showed the photograph to Violet.

"It was among the opened mail on Senator Morrison's desk yesterday. Any thoughts why she received it or who sent it?"

Violet shook her head.

The agent turned to Henry. "What about you?"

"I have no idea."

Another knock on the door interrupted the interview. Agent Monroe rose to confer with an older woman who motioned him to leave the conference room. The two reappeared almost immediately, and Agent Monroe introduced the newcomer as Special Agent Millicent Duffy.

"Thank you again for coming in to go over your statement," said Agent Duffy, her tone calm. "We just got back the preliminary autopsy report on the senator, and we're hoping your recollections can help us narrow down the timeline and catch her killer."

"You're sure the senator and her assistant were murdered?" Henry hoped he'd masked his shock. It was one thing to speculate the two women had been killed deliberately and another to have their belief confirmed. Plus, their suspicions the senator knew The Wolf in East Berlin were more likely to be true now her death was labeled a murder.

"Yes." Agent Duffy looked at her colleagues. "I'm afraid Monroe and Talbot weren't at liberty to reveal this earlier as we didn't want to compromise the investigation, but our public liaison office will release the cause of death at a press conference in half an hour, so we can share the findings with you now.

"Iris Morrison was killed by anthrax." Agent Duffy sat back in her chair after delivering the news.

"Anthrax." Henry remembered the Amerithrax case that terrorized the DC area a week after 9/11 in which anthrax-laced letters killed five people and infected seventeen others. He ran a finger under his collar at the thought the deadly substance had been in the same room as him and Violet. Maybe they had been exposed. His pulse ratcheted up to high speed before he realized the other agents in the room wouldn't be so caviler if he and Violet were contaminated. "But how?"

Agent Duffy replied, "There were traces of the poison on the photograph and more on a birthday card and plain brown envelope."

"This photograph!" Violet reared back from the photocopy of the picture.

"Yes, the original of course," said Agent Talbot. "That's a copy of a photograph of the photograph. We need to determine who he is to help us uncover who sent the deadly missive."

"Was the assistant also killed by anthrax?" Henry asked.

"Yes." Agent Duffy looked at Henry, then Violet. "We've been able to determine the anthrax had been altered only to be deadly upon contact, not airborne, so you should be safe from any effects of the spores. Just as a precaution, you will receive a dose of ciprofloxacin before you leave today."

Whoever had killed the senator and her assistant hadn't wanted to cause collateral damage. Henry filed the thought away to examine more fully later with Violet.

"I know you've done this several times, but if you could describe the scene as you found it once more, I'd appreciate hearing it directly from the source," Agent Duffy said to Violet.

"Okay, I'll try." Violet closed her eyes and went over the sequence of events once again.

Agent Duffy interspersed questions as her narrative continued, then turned to Henry. "Dr. Silverton, would you please go over your movements and observations?"

As succinctly and accurately as possible, Henry recounted his version of what happened yesterday afternoon from the moment when he and Violet had arrived at Senator Morrison's office until FBI agents secured the premises.

"I think that wraps things up for now." Agent Duffy smiled at Henry and Violet. "Thank you both for your time and candor." She stood. "If you think of anything else, please don't hesitate to call either Agents Talbot or Monroe. I'll send in my assistant with the ciprofloxacin."

As she exited the room, Agents Talbot and Monroe handed Henry and Violet each one of their business cards. "We appreciate your coming in."

"It's the least we could do," Henry said, shaking hands with both men, who then extended their hands to Violet.

A young woman with blonde hair pulled back into a ponytail entered with a bottle. "Here's the ciprofloxacin." She turned to the two agents. "Agent Duffy said you should have your dose now too."

She shook out four pills and handed them around. Henry pushed down a fissure of fear as he downed the pill along with Violet and the two agents. He had seen the bottle and the pills appeared familiar, as he had taken ciprofloxacin before. His paranoia about The Wolf's reach had him seeing a boogeyman behind every gesture.

The agents escorted Henry and Violet to the elevator bank. Agent Monroe punched the down button. "I'll take you back downstairs. Security doesn't like it when visitors wander the building."

Agent Talbot nodded his goodbye in the hallway and disappeared around the corner.

The elevator arrived, and as the trio stepped inside the empty car, Agent Monroe said, "I'm sorry if Agent Talbot was a bit rough in there."

Henry would have characterized his demeanor as more strident than a bit rough, but neither he nor Violet said anything. A quick glance at her face revealed strain around her mouth and eyes. This afternoon's interview had been more stressful than anticipated.

"The senator's death from anthrax has the entire agency in an uproar," Agent Monroe continued. "As you might imagine, because of her upcoming confirmation hearings, there is immense pressure to solve this quickly."

Henry opted not to engage the agent in conversation, but he wished they could have mentioned The Wolf's potential involvement in the senator's death. However, that would have necessitated a lot of explanation that might come across as implausible rather than true. For now, The Wolf would have to be kept under wraps, at least until they had more solid evidence of his current activities.

But they were saved further ruminations from Agent Monroe as the car bumped to a stop on the lobby level and the doors slid open. Agent Monroe stepped in the doorway and held out his hand. "Thanks for coming in. We'll be in touch if we have any other questions."

Henry, then Violet, shook his hand and left the car.

Heading toward the exit, Henry glanced at Violet. "I'm glad it's over."

"Me too." Violet punched the handicap button and watched the door swing open.

Henry hurried after her into the bright March sunlight. A light breeze carried a hint of spring in its warm undertones. "I don't know about you, but I need something soothing to drink to decompress. How about a cup of tea before going home?" Henry paused to point to a café down the street.

"The best offer I've had all afternoon." Violet smiled at him as they headed to the café.

At the café, Violet moved toward the counter. "Why don't you grab a table while I get the tea?"

Henry nodded his acceptance and moved toward a booth in the back while Violet placed their order. He slid into the booth and noticed someone had left a copy of the day's newspaper on the bench. Arranging his crutches, he picked up the paper to scan the headlines.

He'd only gotten as far as the middle of the front section when Violet approached the table with two mugs. "What kind of tea did you get for us?"

"White oolong, which will go wonderfully with our wild Maine blueberry scones." She placed the steaming cups with steeping tea bags on the table.

Henry frowned up at her. "I don't see any scones."

Violet laughed. "I couldn't carry everything at once, silly. I'm going to get them now."

When she returned with a plated scone in each hand, Henry folded the newspaper and laid it on the table.

"I couldn't resist these. They just came out of the oven. All the talking made me hungry." She bit into one. "This is heavenly."

The two enjoyed their tea and scones in silence for a several moments. With each sip of the hot liquid, some of the tension eased in his shoulders. Ever since he'd met Violet, he had been off balance, his head spinning with the mystery and the suspense of their investigation, not to mention the lovely young woman across from him who had become very essential to his life.

His love for her only strengthened his resolve to uncover the identity of The Wolf and end this game of cat and mouse so he could concentrate entirely on wooing Violet.

FIFTY-THREE

Violet wished they could enjoy their tea like the other couples sitting at nearby tables in the busy café, but stopping The Wolf once and for all kept her from relaxing completely. The rigid set of Henry's shoulders showed he too couldn't leave all that had happened to them over the past few weeks behind.

"What are we going to do?" She finished her scone and wiped her mouth with a napkin.

Henry put down his mug and reached for her hand. She gladly took his in her own. His warmth and strength gave her courage. "When Mr. Kopecek died, all I could think was I'd lost my one real friend. Then there was the break-in, your book with Mr. Kopecek's strange notations, the phone calls, the car accident. The coincidences are piling up way too fast for them not to be connected."

"And we can now add the deaths of the senator, her assistant, and this other man who might have been involved in the car accident and your near-miss." Henry frowned. "Before, those things could be explained away, but a rising body count can't be. If it's not The Wolf, someone else is playing a very serious game."

Violet reached for her cup of tea and knocked a section of the newspaper on the floor. "I'll get it." She gathered the pages. Refolding them into the Metro section, a name in a memorial notice caught her eye. She sucked in a breath.

"Violet? What is it?"

"This memorial notice." She tapped the paper. "It's for a man named Dirk Jones." Her eyes met Henry's across the table. "He was the longtime aide to Senator Iris Morrison."

"When did he die?"

She skimmed the brief paragraph. "It looks like sometime last week. His memorial service is today."

Henry pulled out his phone. "I'll bet there was a longer obit a day or two after his death. Let me see if I can find it on the *Washington Post* website."

Violet smoothed the paper back into order. Tension climbed up her back onto her shoulders and neck. This aide's death couldn't be an accident.

"Here it is." Henry cleared his throat. "Dirk Jones, longtime aide to Senator Iris Morrison, died of an apparent suicide in his apartment last night. According to police, Jones, 59, left a note outlining his intentions. Jones and Morrison met overseas when both worked for the U.S. Department of State at the West Berlin Embassy in the mid-1980s."

"It all leads back to West Berlin." Violet hadn't expected the connection to be quite so clear, but it appeared both Iris and her aide had been in West Berlin during the time The Wolf operated. Their deaths—one suicide, one murder—must mean they knew something about the mysterious man who had caused so many already.

"I think we can attribute his demise to The Wolf as well." Henry finished his tea. "It's time we told the authorities about all these seemingly disconnected things. It's getting too dangerous to keep our speculation to ourselves."

"I agree. But who?" Violet shoved her hands through her hair, her fingers tangling in the long strands. "I don't know who we can trust or even who would believe our story. All we have is a hunch and circumstantial evidence pointing to The Wolf's identity. For all we know, the Bob fellow isn't who Mr. Kopecek had in mind when he wrote code. If it's even a code. We could be chasing our tails, going in circles, and trying to solve a mystery that's not really a mystery."

Henry frowned. "You don't believe that, do you?"

She shook her head. "All I believe at this point is too many scary things are happening to us and around us. I'm frightened. We could be next on someone's hit list." Violet took a deep breath and let it out slowly in an effort to steady her voice. "And I don't want to lose you."

"I don't want to lose you either." The passion in his eyes sent a shiver down her spine.

"If I were the heroine in a suspense novel, I'd whip out at a plan to convince the authorities of my reasoning and trap The Wolf to boot." She squeezed his hand. "But then if I were only a character in a book, I wouldn't have met you, so I guess we'll have to muddle through like amateur sleuths."

"We haven't done too badly so far." Henry reached for his crutches. "But we can do something constructive book heroes and heroines often do when they're stuck and that's review what we know and what we need to find out. Maybe it will help us see if we have enough to make a case that everything's somehow connected." He stood.

"You mean write it all down on a notepad?" Violet slid out of the booth and gathered their mugs and napkins.

Henry smiled. "Yeah. Since we're talking about old school spying, why not old school paper and pencil? Ready?"

With a nod and a heart a bit lighter than before, she deposited their trash in the bin and put the mugs in the plastic tub while Henry maneuvered around the closely packed tables. Surely going over everything again would make things become clearer and give them a sense of where to go.

"Shall I call a cab?" She shielded her eyes from the mid-morning sun while scanning the busy street.

"It might be dicey this time of day since it's inching toward rush hour."

"No worries." She threw him a grin as she put her thumb and forefinger between her lips and blew a piercing whistle. A yellow cab at the light a half block away flicked its lights at them.

Henry gaped at her. "Where'd you learn to do that?"

Violet laughed. "Oh, I'm a woman filled with surprises." The cab pulled up beside the curb. She opened the door and slid inside, scooting over to make room for Henry. She gave the cabbie Henry's address as he placed his crutches across the floor and closed the door.

The cab merged into heavy traffic. "My grandfather taught me to whistle," she volunteered. "He tried to teach Patrick, but my brother didn't have the patience to learn."

"You are a handy woman to have around."

"Am I? Then maybe you ought to keep me around."

"Maybe I will."

His words unintentionally reminded her of the seriousness of their predicament. "I've dragged you into this mess."

"There is some good in all this, you know." Henry put his arm around her and hugged her close.

"And what's that?" She snuggled down onto his shoulder, breathing in the clean, crisp scent of him and the security she felt sheltered in his embrace.

He dropped a kiss on her temple. "It's brought us together."

She angled her head to look him in the eye. "There is that." Laying her hand on his cheek, she stretched up and kissed him. The rest of the cab ride, the two said nothing but simply held each other close.

All too soon, the taxi braked in front of his townhouse. Henry exited the cab while Violet paid the driver. Once inside and settled in the den, she steeled herself to focus on the investigation rather than on Henry's close proximity. The longing to kiss him again kept muddling her thoughts, but she managed to inquire about writing implements to keep them on the task at hand. Which was writing a list, not exploring his lips.

"There are pencils and pads of paper in the desk." Henry eased into his recliner.

She quickly found pencil and paper and settled onto the loveseat. "This feels like one of those snappy 30s comedies. I'm half expecting Cary Grant to walk through the door." For emphasis, she licked the end of a pencil and poised it above a fresh pad of paper. "Shall we start with the facts?"

He nodded. "Maybe in chronological order?"

"Very organized. I approve." She closed her eyes to think back to the beginning, less than eight weeks ago, then opened them. "It all starts with Mr. Kopecek's death."

CHAPTER
FIFTY-FOUR

Henry tried to keep his mind on the list, but he continued to be distracted by the strand of hair across Violet's cheek. Instead of brushing it back behind her ear, which is what he wanted to do, he pulled his focus back to the matter at hand. "Did you write down the doctor who signed Mr. Kopecek's death certificate?"

Violet nodded as her pencil moved across the page.

"I received a letter from Mr. Kopecek telling me The Wolf is alive." Henry ticked off the events on his fingers. "Then your apartment is trashed."

"Third, we met for coffee, where you told me about the letter." Violet gave a soft smile that took his breath away. "One of the last things Mr. Kopecek said to me was about wanting me to find someone special. If it hadn't been for his death, we wouldn't have met. So in a way, he did bring us together."

"Which is another reason we owe it to him to expose The Wolf's identity, since Mr. Kopecek died because he knew who this traitor was." Not for the first time, Henry wished he could have met the old

313

man. By Violet's accounts of him, he had been someone who had a lot to share.

"Okay, back to our list." Violet rested the end of the pencil between her lips, a gesture Henry found endearing.

In fact, he found a lot of her quirky mannerisms delightful, like the way she bounced on the balls of her feet when excited or how she flicked her hair back when concentrating on something.

She tapped her pencil against the notepad. "What came next?"

"I think it's the anonymous phone calls we each received warning us about The Wolf, followed by the dinner at Sissy's, where you show me my book with Mr. Kopecek's notations." He squared his shoulders and cleared his throat, causing her to look up from her writing. "Then I deduced those jottings might be in code."

Violet raised her eyebrows. "You sound a bit smug."

"Sorry, I thought it was rather brilliant of me." He shrugged, attempting to appear suave, but he must have come across like a crippled James Bond, given the laughter in her eyes.

She stuck out her tongue and went back to her notes. "Maybe, but I figured out the key to the code."

"Then I receive those flowers and you fainted because it reminded you of your brother."

Violet held up her left hand. "Slow down. I can't keep up."

Henry watched as she frowned in concentration over the pad of paper. The urge to kiss her wrinkled brow nearly overpowered him but he managed to tamp down the feeling and continue with their list.

"Okay, caught up. What's next, the car accident?"

"Yes." The reminder of how close they had both come to being killed on the GW Parkway yanked his thoughts from romance back to reality. That had been the first time he'd realized how serious things had become. They were amateurs, stumbling and bumbling about, chasing a Cold War ghost, one that officially didn't even exist.

But making this list should help them find out how to stop The Wolf. "Then Juan gave us the first possible decoding of the message."

"Which was *The American flower knows something.* We're pretty sure that referred to Iris Morrison." Violet tucked the errant strand of hair behind her ear. Her brow furrowed. "Now we might never know for sure. I can't believe she's dead, murdered right before our arrival."

"I can't either." Henry wanted to reach out to wrap an arm around her shoulders, but his position in the recliner didn't allow for such spontaneous gestures. Just as well, since they should stay on task. He shoved the thought a diversion might be quite pleasant and revisited the events in his mind to see where they were chronologically. "But before we zeroed in on Morrison, one of my German contacts alerted me to a recording that might be relevant to my research."

"But it also turned out to have information about The Wolf." She sighed. "This list is getting longer, but I'm not sure these pieces really fit together."

"We might as well finish it. Maybe the pattern might reveal something we've missed once everything is on one page."

"Perhaps." Violet wrote as she spoke. "Then you and Juan decoded another clue, which led me to the possible name of The Wolf. Bob DeLancey."

"And right after that, you're nearly run over by a car, but a man pulled you back just in time. This man very well could be the same one who spoke to you after our car accident. Then he turned up dead in Rock Creek Park." That the man had apparently been murdered so soon after his altruistic move was unnerving. No doubt the two events—Violet's near-miss and the man's murder—were connected. But seeing the words on paper only highlighted how coincidental their evidence linking these events together was.

She tucked her feet underneath her and leaned back against the loveseat pillows. He smiled at the cozy picture she made. "Don't forget our anonymous text warning about a TV reporter who had discovered your new name."

Violet took a few minutes to document the information. "Okay, keep going."

"Juan had a hit-and-run accident on his bike after dropping off the tape. I get the CD, and we listen to a double agent we assume is The Wolf selling out potential defectors to the East Germans."

She put down her pencil and stretched her fingers before picking up the writing instrument again. "We can't forget Patrick said on national TV that I killed Mr. Kopecek, plus he has a wolf tattoo on his arm."

"Then we try to confront the senator, but instead discover her body. You're arrested on suspicion of murdering Mr. Kopecek, but the charges are dropped. We find out from the FBI Morrison and her assistant were murdered with anthrax and discover it was administered via a photo of the dead man who saved your life." Henry rested his head against the back of his chair, glad the university was on spring break and he could concentrate on helping Violet rather than teaching students about Cold War history.

The list only proved how much they didn't know. How on earth did he expect they would uncover the identity of a man who, by contemporary accounts, was dead more than four decades? They were chasing rainbows or rabbits or whatever people chased without catching it. If it hadn't been for those anonymous phone calls and the murder of the senator, her assistant, and the man who saved Violet's life, he would have real concerns he was imagining things.

Violet finished writing. "Whew. Those all can't be coincidences."

"No, they can't." He closed his eyes to concentrate. There had to be a connection, something that tied them all together. If they could figure out what, they would have a better chance of convincing the authorities of The Wolf's existence. "What do they have in common?"

"The Wolf is behind it all."

He opened his eyes. "What does it mean? I mean what stirred up The Wolf today and not forty years ago?"

"Four decades ago, everyone thought he was dead." Violet pointed out.

"But don't they still? In all my research on spies during that time period, I only uncovered whispers about his existence that ended in his death. No one ever hinted he might be still alive. Why would The Wolf kill Mr. Kopecek? And we do think he did, right?"

"I don't see who else could have done it."

Henry drummed his fingers on the arm of the chair. "Why has he gone after us with threatening phone calls, car accidents? What happened to set off this particular string of events?"

Violet's right hand shot up, and her pencil dropped to the floor. "Wait a minute. I didn't think anything of it at the time. In fact, I completely forgot about it until now."

"What?" Henry jerked his recliner back to a seated position.

"Let me make sure I have this straight in my mind first." She bit her lip.

The blood thrummed in his veins as he waited for her explanation. Just maybe, this recollection was the break they needed.

"A week or so before he died, Mr. Kopecek asked me about cell phones."

"Cell phones?" Henry wasn't sure what mobile devices had to do with The Wolf.

She nodded. "Yes, he asked if one could call anywhere in the world with a cell phone. Basically, I told him yes, but it also depended on what type of calling plan you had. I briefly explained you could call all over and not pay extra for long distance."

He slumped back in his chair. Cell phones. "Oh, I thought you were going to say he might have called The Wolf."

Violet's hand shot up again. "Wait, I'm not finished. A day or two before he died, Daura said something to me about lending Mr. Kopecek her cell phone a few times. She said he told her he liked to play a game on her phone."

Henry struggled to hide his disappointment in the story's end. "He liked an app on Daura's phone? I don't see the..." He leaned into the conversation. "You think he did more than play a game on the phone. You think he called The Wolf."

CHAPTER

FIFTY-FIVE

Violet grinned at Henry, pleased he'd made the same connection she had. Mr. Kopecek's phone call quite possibly pushed The Wolf out of his lair. "Now all we have to do is review Daura's call records and see if there's a number she doesn't recognize."

"But how?"

"We ask Daura to take a look." Violet reached for her phone.

"You think she'll give it to you?" Henry shifted in his recliner.

"Won't know until we ask." She pulled up Daura's number in her phone contacts and hit call, then speaker so Henry could hear the conversation.

The phone rang half a dozen times before Daura picked up. "Violet?"

"Daura, how are you?"

"Girl, I'm doing okay. Hold on a sec." A short pause ensued while Daura murmured something inaudible, then the aide's voice came back on the line. "What are you up to?"

"I need a favor." Violet held her breath. Surely the authorities would have to at least hear them out if they presented evidence of a connection.

Daura laughed. "Why am I not surprised? Go ahead." Her voice sounded as pleasant as the sea breeze of her home country in the Caribbean.

"You lent Mr. Kopecek your phone to play a game a few times the week before he died, right?"

"Yes. I miss that sweet man." Daura sighed. "They don't make gentlemen like that anymore. Although it sure was funny watching him swipe candy into bunches."

Violet dabbed a stray tear from her cheek at the memory of Mr. Kopecek hunched over Daura's phone, his full concentration fixed on the tiny screen. She cleared her suddenly clogged throat. "They sure don't. I was wondering if he might have made a call from your phone."

"A call?" Daura's voice sounded incredulous. "I wasn't aware Mr. Kopecek knew how to use a cell phone."

"As you said, he was old-fashioned, yet there was a cunning streak in him." Now that Violet knew a bit more about what he must have gone through in East Berlin, she wasn't at all surprised he managed to fool Daura into thinking he didn't know how to make calls. "Remember the way he used to thwart Siddons about her rule of no candy in resident rooms by hiding M&Ms in his soap dish?"

"Oh, Lordy, I remember." Daura chortled. "But since I have unlimited data and calling, I wouldn't have noticed an extra phone call, even if he had made it."

Violet gathered her thoughts. She wanted to be truthful and still protect Daura from The Wolf by not giving away the true reason for her call. "Do you think he might have called a distant relative or friend? If he did, they should be notified of his passing. I didn't think about it earlier, what with his dying so suddenly and the will and all."

The tricky part was not alarming Daura or triggering any

curiosity with her next question. "Would you mind looking through your call records to see if there's any numbers you don't recognize?"

"Hang on, and I'll scroll through. That is, if my seven-year old son hasn't inadvertently deleted them when I've let him play with my phone." Daura's voice faded. There were several clicks, then silence as Daura placed her on hold.

Violet turned to Henry. "We might be in luck."

"Violet?" Daura's voice came back on the line.

"Yes?" *Lord, please let this be what we've been waiting for.* Violet had been praying a lot more since she met Henry than she had in the years since her brother's conviction.

"There's one number I don't recognize, an outgoing call made on January twenty-seventh, around one p.m." Daura chuckled. "I remember now. That was the day one of the residents spilled orange juice at breakfast all over my clothes, and I had to change into something without pockets. Since Mrs. Smith hates seeing my phone—calls the things 'rectangle demons'—I always try to keep it out of sight when I help her with lunch. Without pockets, I figured I'd leave it with Mr. Kopecek, seeing as we pass his room on our way to the dining hall."

"What's the number?" Violet nibbled on her lower lip. They were so close, she just knew it.

Daura rattled off the number with an unfamiliar area code and Violet jotted it down on the pad. Daura said, "Hope it's a relative or friend of Mr. Kopecek. I always hate it when a resident dies so completely alone."

"Me too." Violet stared at the ten digits on the page.

"You take care of yourself. It's not the same without you here."

"It wouldn't have been the same for me without Mr. Kopecek. Thanks again for the help, and it was good to talk to you. Bye." Violet ended the call. "Do you think we should dial it?"

"Let's do a reverse look up online to see if anything pops up first."

"Good idea." She laced her fingers together to keep them from shaking as Henry pulled his laptop across his legs. "Ready?" At his nod, she read off the numbers.

His fingers flew over the keys before hitting the enter button. A moment later, the tension around his mouth alerted her the news might not be what they expected. "You won't believe what came up."

"Try me." Her heart pounding, Violet stared at him.

"It's the main number for Vault Cybersecurity."

Her mouth fell open. Even though she had half-expected this outcome, to have their suppositions confirmed boggled her mind. "Bob DeLancey's company." Violet let out a breath she hadn't realized she'd been holding. "It's a slim piece of evidence. So what if Mr. Kopecek placed a phone call to the main number of a large company? All DeLancey has to say is he never spoke with Mr. Kopecek. Who would believe an old man in an assisted living facility could get through to the president of a multi-billion dollar cybersecurity company?"

Henry's focus shifted to the laptop. He clicked some keys, his attention riveted to the screen. "Not just any cybersecurity company, but one with a large portion of its funding from federal contracts, including ones with the U.S. Department of Homeland Security and the U.S. Department of Defense."

Her stomach churned at the thought a man who had so callously betrayed his country now had a hand in protecting its cybersecurity. "Could explain why he's not anxious for his past to come to light now. He'd lose those contracts and probably his company."

"What if that's not all he'd lose?"

She raised her eyebrows. "What else is there?"

"If a man was willing to betray his country once..." The implication of his unfinished thought jolted her.

"Then he might do it again." Once a traitor, always a traitor. Certainly The Wolf was someone not to be trusted.

"Exactly."

Swallowing hard, she wrapped her arms around her middle as a chill that had nothing to do with the setting sun invaded her body. "I'm scared, Henry."

"Me too." He set his laptop on the coffee table and moved over to sit next to her on the loveseat. "But I know someone who isn't afraid."

Violet wished she could be so confident. Part of her still struggled with why a loving God could allow such evil to flourish in the world, but seeing how natural Henry lived his faith made her realize how shallow her own faith had become. She wanted to change that going forward. She reached for his hands. "Will you pray for us?"

With a squeeze on her hands, he nodded and closed his eyes. "Heavenly Father, we come before you humble and needy. We're in need of your protection, and we're grateful you would give it to us, if it is your holy will. Please guide us as we seek justice for Mr. Kopecek, Senator Morrison, Richelle, and the unidentified man in the park. Thank you for all the ways you have kept us safe thus far. We rely on you and your mercy to help us find the answers we seek. In Jesus's name, Amen."

"Amen." Violet brushed tears from her eyes. "I'm sorry. I've become quite the watering pot lately."

Henry pulled a handkerchief from his pocket and wiped her damp cheeks. "Good thing I'm a true gentleman and carry a hand-kerchief."

"Yes, that's what I like about you."

With a wicked gleam in his eye, he leaned closer. "Is that all you like about me?"

Violet bridged the short distance between them and briefly kissed him on the lips. "No. I like your kisses too." She followed that statement by demonstrating just how much she enjoyed kissing him.

FIFTY-SIX

enry put down his fork and groaned. "I had no idea a meal with kale could taste so good."

"I'm glad you liked the sautéed kale." Violet grinned at him. "I see your culinary education needs updating. There are more things to greet your palate besides green beans." She rose to gather the plates and waved off his attempt to help. "No, I've got this."

As she cleared the table and loaded the dishwasher, he smiled inwardly. Each moment he spent with this gorgeous, sweet woman made him fall deeper in love with her. It wasn't just the way she looked or the fact she didn't view his handicap as a hindrance. It was how she had faced hard things and not become bitter, keeping an optimistic outlook.

"Everything's done, so I guess I should leave." She stood at the table drying her hands on a kitchen towel. "If I stay any longer, I'll fall asleep again. My reputation won't survive another night under your roof."

He stood, sliding his hands into his crutch cuffs. "You should probably leave. It's not easy being a gentleman knowing you're just down the hall at two a.m."

"That sounds a bit, um, racy, Dr. Silverton. And here I thought missionary kids were so straitlaced." To his delight, a blush crossed her face bringing a light pinkness to her cheeks.

Stepping toward her, he slipped his hand free from his crutch and cupped her chin in his palm. "Ah, but you see, there's always a danger some of the native practices have rubbed off on us. You never know when I might pay your father a bride price and carry you off to live in my hut and pound grain for my supper." He kissed her lightly on the lips. "Now, I'd better call you a cab. You're much too tempting."

HENRY DROPPED THE PAPERS ON HIS DESK WITH A SIGH. HE HAD THOUGHT with Violet safely ensconced at Sissy and Keith's home, he would be able to concentrate on his book. His due date was fast approaching, and he had yet to finish the last six chapters. Writing usually consumed his entire brain, but lately, he found himself daydreaming about a pair of green eyes and auburn hair, not to mention those luscious lips. If he wasn't careful, he'd start penning odes about Violet's loveliness and not write another word about East Germany.

Maybe he should call her to make sure she was okay. After all, it had been a few hours since she phoned to let him know she had arrived safe and sound. That would set his mind at ease, and he could return to his book. Satisfied with his rationale, he dialed.

"Henry? What's up?" The welcome in her voice warmed him from the crown of his head to the soles of his feet.

"Nothing, just checking in on you." He settled back in his chair and propped his feet up on his desk.

"Ah, I see. Writer's block."

"What are you talking about?" He bristled. "I'll have you know

I've written exactly—" he squinted at the laptop—"fifty words since you left."

"Fifty words? That's progress indeed." Her soft laughter tickled his ears.

"I've been a tad distracted."

"And I'm not even there."

"That's the problem. Maybe if you were here, I would be able to work." Henry knew it for a lie the moment he said it.

"We both know you would not be working if I was there."

"We do?"

Violet sighed. "Yes, and while I wish I was there too, it's really for the best. You're a very tempting man, Dr. Silverton."

He grinned. "Do tell."

"No more. That's all you're getting out of me tonight. You're becoming too puffed up for your own good as it is."

"How are you entertaining yourself tonight while I slave over my book?"

"I'm reading your book, or rather, I'm jumping around reading bits of Mr. Kopecek's copy of *The Stasi in East Berlin* in the sections where he made notations."

"Finding it interesting, I hope." Henry held his breath.

"Yes, actually."

He deflated like a limp balloon. "Must you sound so surprised?"

"Oh, it's not your writing, silly man. That's marvelous. I was just puzzling over how far we've come in the spy world."

"What do you mean?" Henry put his feet back down, knocking off a research book he had been reading. He leaned down and picked up the tome along with the blank postcard tucked into its pages.

"About how spies from both sides used technology to create even smaller and more far-reaching listening devices. But my favorite has been reading about the microdots. I can't believe how much information—documents, photographs, etc.—could be contained on a small dot the size of a pin head. Pretty amazing stuff when you think about it."

"Yes, it is." He started to toss the postcard into his overflowing inbox but turned it over to look at its scene of the castle in winter. Snow blanketed the trees and turrets creating a fairytale setting. He blinked hard. What he had at first glance taken for an English castle was the famous German Neuschwanstein Castle. He must have really been distracted by Violet to have missed identifying the picture earlier.

"Henry? Have I've lost you to your book? That's a good thing and all, but should I hang up now?"

"My love, you're right. I'd better go and try to finish more of this chapter. I love you. See you in the morning." Better to follow this lead on his own before mentioning it to Violet.

"I love you too. Sweet dreams."

He disconnected the call and stared at the postcard. Now that he knew the picture was of a German castle, he had to take a closer look at the rectangle piece of cardboard. He saved his work and closed his laptop before placing the postcard on his desk.

Rummaging through his desk drawer, he pulled out his magnifying glass and held it above the postcard. Inch by inch, he examined very bit of the photograph. Nothing. Turning it over, he scanned the blank back side. Not even a description of the castle marred the surface. When he got to the stamp, Henry stopped as Violet's words rang in his ears: *"I can't believe how much information—documents, photographs, etc.—could be contained on a small dot the size of a pin head."*

He carried his magnifying glass and postcard to the kitchen, then set the items on the table and filled the kettle with water. Heating the water seemed to take forever, but finally he had enough steam to carefully loosen the stamp. Painstakingly, he removed the stamp bit by bit. Laying it aside, he focused his magnifying glass on the small rectangle of space now revealed. He sucked in his breath when he found the three tiny dots, each indeed the size of a dressmaker's pin, clustered in the upper right corner of the postcard.

CHAPTER

FIFTY-SEVEN

Henry peered through the microscope at one of the microdots. The image blurred but soon came into view as he fiddled with the fine focus adjustor. The photographed document didn't make sense at first, but as he read the German words, he realized it was a copy of a bank statement showing large transfers of money from the East German department of transportation to one Bob DeLancey for Pest Management at the Strausberger Platz subway station.

Pest Management was what The Wolf and his East German contact had called their exchange of defectors for cash on the phone recording. Because of its busy terminal, Strausberger Platz also was a popular spot for Stasi agents to swap information or hand off tailing assignments, providing another link between The Wolf, Bob DeLancey, and the Stasi. One more piece of the puzzle clicked into place.

He slid the second microdot under the microscope. It showed a split photo of a man holding a gun to the back of a woman's head, then in the second half of the photo the woman slumped on the ground with the same man standing over her. Henry swallowed hard at the sight of the smoke curling from the barrel of the pistol. The man's face was clearly visible in the first and second photos. The resemblance to the recent picture of Bob DeLancey in the *Washington Post* was uncanny.

The third microdot was a typewritten letter dated only a few days ago. He read the salutation and bit back a gasp.

Dear Dr. Silverton,

I'm hoping you are as bright as your books seem to indicate, and that you will be able to fully comprehend the documents I've included with this letter. The first document shows Bob DeLancey, currently president and CEO of Vault Cybersecurity, was formerly a U.S. spy-turned-traitor during the last years of the Cold War in West and East Berlin. You probably know him by his code name, The Wolf. A man who was presumed to have died in late April 1986 on the banks of the Havel River. I believed the story myself, as I had been selected to view his execution that day.

However, a chance encounter fifteen years ago brought us face-to-face. Since the reunion, I've been dancing a delicate waltz surrounding the truth of his past, which would not only bring him down but destroy a very comfortable and powerful life I had built for myself, a life I enjoyed very much. Over the years, I consoled myself that I was doing good as a senator and would have even more opportunities as secretary of state.

But then Rainer Kopecek died. His death brought The Wolf out of his lair once more, perhaps for the last time. You might not know the connection between Rainer and The Wolf, but I do. The Wolf knew Rainer had seen him long ago in a place The Wolf had no business being—at the Tierpark Berlin delivering two people to Stasi agents, who subsequently killed them. But it wasn't until Verna Kopecek tried to escape East Berlin that The Wolf took his revenge and betrayed her. Her death silenced Rainer as effectively as if The Wolf had killed him instead.

I believe Rainer contacted The Wolf recently, and everything bubbled to the surface. My complicity in The Wolf's schemes, through feigning a blind eye to his existence, stared me down and demanded I make amends before it was too late. And so I did. From that point on, I kept an eye on you and Violet Lundy. I gathered the last bit of proof of The Wolf's betrayal and hid it in a safe place. But in the end, The Wolf proved too strong for me. He killed my fellow agent and best friend, Dirk Jones, although the police ruled his death a suicide. I found evidence to the contrary, but none I could provide at the time because of the ramifications such information would have on my career. Bryon Smith, who did The Wolf's dirty work, recently helped me—and you—too.

Now, though, my time is running out. My betrayal and part in letting so many who sought to escape from the Iron Curtain to die yards from that freedom will be my legacy rather than the good that I've struggled to do in the years since. But I'm ready to own up to my sins and to say I'm sorry. As amends, I will provide evidence of The Wolf's betrayal, as well as mine, for you see the two are intertwined together as tightly as a vine around a tree branch.

I had a feeling The Wolf would revert to his old tricks—can a man who betrayed so many resist the lure of outwitting his country once again? —and I found information that will implicate The Wolf in a plan to sell cybersecurity secrets to our old enemy, Russia.

You will find the proof secreted away in the one place The Wolf will never think to look—in the National Cathedral. I left a package there with the cathedral dean, who is an old friend. He will give it to you or Ms. Lundy only. Take it to the authorities but be careful of whom you trust. The Wolf has many powerful friends. Godspeed, Dr. Silverton. And may you bring the truth out into the light and dispel the darkness once and for all.

Iris Morrison

CHAPTER

FIFTY-EIGHT

Violet shivered and pulled her coat tighter around her as she glanced up at the magnificent façade of the National Cathedral. "The weatherman wasn't kidding when he said frigid air was returning to DC. Yesterday was balmy compared to today's temperature."

"This cold front isn't fooling around." Henry glanced at the main doors. "Let's try through there to see about talking with the cathedral dean." He consulted a piece of paper. "The Very Reverend Dean Withers."

"The Episcopals certainly have interesting clergy titles." Violet tugged open the massive oak door and held it open for Henry to pass through first. "What exactly is a cathedral dean?"

"He's the top guy at the cathedral, kind of like its president." Henry moved through the door, adding over his shoulder, "I hope he's available."

"Me too." Maybe the decision to time an arrival at the cathedral to coincide with its ten o'clock opening rather than calling for an appointment wasn't the best idea after all. She turned to Henry. "I have the uncomfortable feeling that time, as they say, is of the essence."

Once inside, she paused to let her eyes adjust to the dim interior. A woman with a name tag pinned on her right lapel approached. "Are you here for a tour? One will be starting in the nave shortly."

"No," Violet said. "We're here to see the Very Reverend Dean Withers."

"Oh, I see. Do you have an appointment?"

Violet shook her head. "A friend, the late Senator Iris Morrison, suggested we talk with him on an urgent matter."

At the mention of the senator's name, the docent's demeanor changed to one of solicitousness. "Her death was so very tragic. May I offer my condolences?"

"Thank you," Violet said softly.

"Let me see if the reverend is available. I'll just be a moment." She moved a few feet to a small table and pulled out a telephone cleverly hidden behind a stack of books.

Violet couldn't overhear the quiet conversation, but the woman soon returned with a smile. "The dean has a few minutes to spare this morning. Take the hallway to your right and turn left at the end. His assistant James will be there to escort you the rest of the way."

Thanking her, Violet and Henry went down the hallway indicated and turned left to find a man dressed in a dark grey suit standing there.

"You're here to see Rev. Withers?"

Henry nodded.

"This way," the man said.

Violet, with Henry behind her, followed the man through a door and into an aisle with offices on either side. At the end, the man knocked on a door and opened it. "Reverend Withers, these are the friends of the late Senator Morrison."

The man with silver hair rose from behind an ornate desk as they entered. "Come in and have a seat. Any friend of Iris's is always welcome here. Her death was so unexpected and tragic."

"Yes, it was." Violet sat beside Henry in one of the two matching chairs as the reverend reseated himself. She leaned forward. "My name is Violet Lundy, and this is Dr. Henry Silverton. We understand the senator left a package for us in your care, and we'd like to collect it." She'd agreed with Henry that a direct approach would be best, but based on the reverend's raised brow, maybe a subtler approach would have worked better.

The reverend gazed at them for several long seconds. "May I see some identification?"

"Of course." Violet dug into her purse and retrieved her wallet, flipping it open, and extending it across the desk to show Withers her Virginia driver's license.

Henry also presented his ID for the reverend's perusal. Withers carefully examined each document, eyeing Violet, then Henry, before handing back their wallets.

"Thank you." He steepled his fingers. "How did you know the senator?"

Violet relaxed a bit as his demeanor softened. She exchanged glances with Henry, then answered. "We never actually met her."

The reverend nodded. "Iris told me you hadn't been introduced. She was very troubled when she dropped this off in my care. She often came to visit me, but this time, she said the sins of her past were coming due."

Sorrow colored Withers' blue eyes. "Iris was a woman of many secrets, some of which I don't think she had the courage to shed light on given they had been kept in darkness for so long. Now that she's gone, I think it's past time those secrets become known."

Tears stung her eyes at his words. The Iris Morrison she had been chasing all these weeks had suddenly become more real in this moment than she had lying there dead on the floor of her office. Violet reached over and slipped her hand into Henry's.

Withers leaned back. He unhooked a set of keys from a clip on his belt, then swiveled his chair away from the desk and unlocked a

335

bottom drawer. He extracted a small leather satchel and held it in his hands.

"When did she leave this with you?" Henry asked.

"The day before her death." Withers shook his head. "I could tell something was deeply disturbing her, and I encouraged her to tell someone about her troubles, even if that someone wasn't me. But she insisted she would be all right."

The reverend passed it across the desk to Violet. "Use this wisely." He released his grip.

Violet grasped the buttery leather satchel. "We'll try." Her posture stiffened. "I'm afraid this information will not be kind to the senator's memory."

Withers smiled, but it didn't reach his sorrowful eyes. "I might not know what's in that satchel, but this I do know for certain that truth is always redemptive, even when it cuts deeply. Iris wanted the truth to finally come out, whatever the cost to her reputation."

"Thank you for honoring her wishes." Violet got to her feet and waited for Henry to join her.

"Please be cautious. I sensed danger was never far from Iris, and sadly that was proven to be case." The reverend stood. "May God go with you."

"THAT'S QUITE A STORY." LAVERNE DEMARIS SAT BACK, HER EXPRESSION AS blank as a freshly washed chalkboard. "But given how the events played out pertaining to Violet's arrest, I'm inclined to think your conclusions are probably spot on."

Violet wished she knew what the attorney was thinking behind her dramatically bright-red framed glasses. Because Ms. Demaris had been instrumental in securing Violet's release from police custody, Violet had agreed with Henry the lawyer was the logical person to go to for advice on how to approach law enforcement with their theory and evidence. Luckily, they had been able to see Ms.

Demaris right after their meeting with the reverend because of a cancellation in her schedule.

Henry nodded. "You can see why we've been hesitant to go to the authorities. We're not sure who would believe us, and we don't want to tip off The Wolf too soon."

"This is a rather precarious situation, one that must be handled with due diligence. Given how The Wolf arranged for your arrest, we must expect he has a contingency plan in place for his exposure." The attorney swiveled in her desk chair. "I see two courses of action. One, we arrange a meeting with Agents Talbot and Monroe to lay out all your evidence."

"The downside is they might not believe us," Violet said.

"Or they call DeLancey directly, tipping our hand," Henry added.

"A very real danger, I'm afraid." Ms. Demaris tapped her polished red fingernails against the edge of the desk momentarily, then sat forward. An unspoken level of enthusiasm danced in her brown eyes. "The second option is to trap The Wolf."

Violet gulped. It was one thing to assemble evidence. It was quite another to try to gain a confession out of a man who betrayed his country without a qualm. "This is a man who has killed at least three people, probably four."

"Five," Henry interjected. "Iris's letter said she was sure The Wolf had killed Dirk Jones as well, and the evidence in the box from the reverend appears to confirm more deaths going back to his time in East Berlin."

"So many lives lost." Violet blinked back tears, then took a deep breath. "This isn't a game. We're not professionals, and the lives of others are at stake. Specifically ours."

The lawyer's expression turned sympathetic. "I have a few friends who work in cybersecurity. Let me see what I can find out about Bob DeLancey. We need to keep you both safe."

"We appreciate that. Right, Henry?" Violet nudged Henry, who appeared lost in thought.

"Yes, of course," he finally stammered. "Thank you."

Violet turned back to Ms. Demaris. "We've not been able to find out much beyond the public info gleaned from the company website and news articles." Maybe once they knew more about DeLancey, they would be able to figure out their next step in bringing him to justice and preventing him from selling more secrets to Russia. "What should we do in the meantime?"

"You have a timeline. You have evidence," Ms. Demaris restated from earlier conversations. "What you don't have is a way to present it in a coherent way that weaves in your conclusions."

Violet bit her lip as she considered their next step. "Maybe we should put together some sort of presentation with the highlights."

"Exactly." Henry snapped his fingers. "We use visuals and text to explain it in a logical manner." He turned to the lawyer. "You have more experience with law enforcement. Would something like this work?"

She arched one of her eyebrows and pursed her lips. "Given the amount of information and the time jumping from four-plus decades ago to now, it would help show how the pieces fit together."

Henry leaned across the desk to shake her hand. "Okay, we'll get started right away."

Violet followed suit and extended her hand to Ms. Demaris, whom she thanked again for making safety a priority.

Henry echoed the sentiment as he stood, then tucked his arms into his crutches.

As Violet followed Henry out of the office, Ms. Demaris called after her, "Please be careful. I'll do what I can to keep you safe, but if you two are right, your lives are in danger."

CHAPTER

FIFTY-NINE

"Thanks for checking." Henry ended the call and turned to Violet sitting across from him at the kitchen table, a steaming cup of tea in front of her. She seemed so natural there in his house, her hands wrapped around his china. He was going to have to do something soon to keep her around on a more permanent basis, something that would happily get his sister to stop setting him up on blind dates. A mental image of their shocked faces when he told them his plan made him smile.

"Quarter for your thoughts?"

"Huh?" With a jolt, Henry dragged himself back from a most pleasant daydream and focused on Violet, who watched him with her head cocked to one side. A hot flush stole over his cheeks, and he hurriedly went on before she commented on what must surely be his very red face. "You're willing to spend more than a penny?"

Violet smiled. "The way you were concentrating, I figured it must be worth more than one cent."

Had she guessed the direction his thoughts had taken? No matter, they had other things to do before he could properly address

339

their future. "I was thinking about what Ms. Demaris said relating to her fishing expedition into Bob DeLancey."

"The friend who works for the Department of Homeland Security shutting down her inquiry?"

Henry nodded. "That friend said told Ms. Demaris, and this is a direct quote, 'You don't mess around with Bob DeLancey, and if this is who you're asking about, I'm ending this call right now.'"

"Wow." Violet raised her eyebrows.

"Yeah." His burner cell phone rang before he could comment further, and he checked caller ID. "It's Keith. With his connections at the National Security Agency, I asked him to check out DeLancey as well." As he hit the answer key, he realized how far he had come from writing about espionage to living like a spy, complete with his own prepaid TracFone to foil eavesdroppers.

"Keith, I'm here with Violet. Let me put you on speaker so we can both hear." Placing the phone on the table, he punched the speaker button.

"Hey, Henry and Violet."

"Hello, Keith. Did you get any information on DeLancey?" Violet asked.

"The background on DeLancey is pretty standard corporate bio stuff. There's definitely an undercurrent of you-don't-mess-with-DeLancey out there, but beyond a few whispers without substance, there's nothing concrete to say against him."

Henry sighed. "That's what we're finding out too." Why he thought he could outsmart one of the deadliest traitors of the Cold War, he had no idea. Better stick to writing about history than attempting to live it.

"This is definitely one man nobody wants to rile, so please be careful." Keith's voice had a very serious tone that chilled Henry.

"Thanks, we will." He clicked off the phone, but it immediately rang. "It's Juan." Henry answered and put the phone on speaker. "I have Violet here with me, and you're on speaker."

"Hey, Violet. Listen, I found out something interesting." Juan's voice crackled like the sky before a thunderstorm exploded.

The excitement Henry heard made his own heart pound. What Juan said next could be crucial. "Don't keep us in suspense. What did you discover?"

"Bob DeLancey will be in Baltimore on Thursday to receive a life-time achievement award from the Cybersecurity Hall of Fame for his contribution to the field of cybersecurity."

Henry met Violet's eyes across the table and saw in them the same growing anticipation coursing through his body. "So The Wolf is coming to us."

"Maybe we can use this to our advantage," Juan said.

"Are you suggesting that we confront him at the ceremony?" Violet scrunched up her nose in the endearing way she had when concentrating, making Henry want to kiss the pert appendage.

Henry shook his head to bring his thoughts back to the matter at hand. "Not confront so much as ambush with data, not bullets. Right now, The Wolf has been three steps ahead of us. We need the element of surprise to hit him with the evidence we've amassed."

"You mean show our hand in front of an audience." Violet leaned forward, her eyes intent on Henry.

Henry nodded. "Juan, we've been compiling a kind of presenta-tion on The Wolf showing the evidence and connections we've gathered."

"Ah, I see what you're getting at, and it might just work," Juan said.

"I think we can guarantee the attendance of the FBI." Henry shot Violet a wry smile. "We're well acquainted with a few who might stop by with the right incentive."

Violet raised her eyebrows. "So we hijack the ceremony and present our own findings?"

Both men answered her simultaneously, "Yes."

VIOLET SMOOTHED HER SKIRT OUTSIDE THE FOUR SEASONS HOTEL IN Baltimore.

Henry leaned over and kissed Violet lightly on the cheek as they paused to wait for Juan. The National Cybersecurity Hall of Fame award ceremony would take place after a sit-down dinner, which would start in half an hour. "Nervous?"

"A little." Violet adjusted her sequined blouse. Thank goodness Sissy helped her pick out something suitable from her store for the swanky black-tie ceremony. Violet couldn't remember the last time she'd gotten this dressed up and been escorted by a handsome man. "I feel more like Cinderella going to a ball, although since I've already met my prince, I'm more interested in nabbing a killer."

"So I'm your prince, am I?" Henry wiggled his eyebrows, managing to look adorable in his tailored tuxedo. Henry had explained Sissy had insisted on his buying a tux years ago for some of the faculty events for which he was required to put in an appearance. Violet had to side with Sissy. The custom-fitted tux certainly looked wonderful on him.

"Don't change the subject. We have a job to do." Violet spoiled her stern tone by raising her eyebrows at Henry.

Juan bounded up the steps. "Okay, ready?"

Violet nodded. "As ready as I'll ever be."

"Do you have everything you'll need?"

"Yep." Juan adjusted the cuffs on his rented duds. "I'm off. I'll send a text after the presentation's been uploaded." He melted into the crowd as Henry and Violet moved up the stairs.

Once inside, signage directed them to the ballroom off to the left of the entrance. Waiting in line as security guards waved portable metal detector wands around each guest and association personnel checked tickets, Violet once again breathed deeply in an attempt to calm her nerves. So far, everything had progressed like clockwork. Last-minute tickets had been obtained through Keith's connections, the presentation had been polished, a plan had been concocted, and the FBI contacted.

"Do you think everything will go according to plan?" Violet said in a low undertone as they moved at last into the ballroom and scanned the tables for their seats.

"Probably, but maybe not." Henry walked beside her, the narrow aisles between the tables making navigation with his crutches more difficult.

Violet spotted their table in the back tucked next to a waiter station. Oh, well, probably best they weren't in the thick of things. She waited until Henry had come around beside her before pulling out her chair and sitting down.

"Don't worry." Henry patted her hand.

"Do I look worried?" Violet had thought she was doing a good job of keeping her concerns about the evening from leaking out to Henry.

"Probably not to anyone else, but you get these little lines between your brows when you're uneasy."

Violet wasn't sure if she should be pleased or upset he'd noticed something unflattering.

He winked at her as if he'd read her mind. "It makes me want to pull you into my arms and kiss you until you're not worried anymore."

Some of the tension drained away at his words, coupled with the love in his eyes. Definitely flattered. "If I didn't know any better, I'd say you are flirting with me, Dr. Silverton." She kept her tone light, as more of their table filled in.

Henry draped his arm around her shoulders and leaned closer to her, his lips brushing her cheek as he whispered, "Relax. We've done all we can do."

"You're right." Violet craned her neck to see if she could spot Special Agents Talbot and Monroe in the milling crowd. "Have you seen our friends arrive yet?"

"Darling, I'm sure they won't be late."

Violet tilted her head in acknowledgement. "I'm sorry to be such a nervous Nellie," she said softly.

He trailed his fingers across her shoulder, his attitude entirely one of a man enjoying being out with his date. "I, for one, plan on enjoying spending time with the beautiful woman I love.

Violet tried to let go of her worries and enjoy being with her handsome escort, but her mind simply wouldn't cooperate. "This might be our only chance to expose the truth and stop all this death." She nibbled at her lower lip. "I can't settle down. What if we don't succeed? What if we do, and he gets away anyway and more people die?"

"That's a lot of *what ifs*," Henry said. "Ms. Demaris agreed this was the only viable option. She informed our friends, who said they would attend. We have to trust everything will work out okay."

"I'd rather know for sure that it will." Violet shivered at the risk they were taking to lay out their entire case before an audience of cybersecurity experts. So many things could go wrong, and the potential for more innocent lives being lost tied her stomach in knots.

He rubbed her back. "I know. But at least after tonight, it will be over, one way or another. Either our quarry will be arrested, or he will simply disappear. Either way, we'll have exposed him, and he will have no reason to come after us."

"Unless he wants revenge." Violet couldn't help but recall the photograph of The Wolf standing over the dead woman with a smoking gun in his hand and a look of pure satisfaction in his eyes. This was a man to whom human life was cheap. "From everything we know about The Wolf, revenge is his specialty."

Henry took her hand in his. "I would allay all your fears if I could, but I can't. There's only one person who can do that." He bowed his head.

Violet nodded as Henry quietly prayed for their evening.

"Heavenly Father, I ask that Your will be done tonight. We thank you in advance for the way you'll answer our prayer. Amen." He'd barely said *amen* before his phone buzzed, indicating a text. "It's from Juan. All systems go."

Violet started to reply when the emcee called everyone to their seats and dinner service commenced. Somehow, she managed to make small talk with the six other couples at their table. Much of the conversation revolved around the spinach-and-goat-cheese salad, Beef Wellington and baby carrots, and a lovely sea salt and caramel cheesecake dessert.

Finally, the main event was at hand. Henry squeezed her hand as the lights dimmed and the head of the National Cybersecurity Hall of Fame stood at the podium.

"Now for the moment we've all be anticipating, the induction into the National Cybersecurity Hall of Fame of this year's recipient. While we usually have more than one selected for induction, this year we decided to honor a single inductee because of the huge contribution he has made to cybersecurity. Ladies and gentlemen, please turn your attention to the screens for a closer look at our Hall of Fame inductee, Robert DeLancey."

The president of National Cybersecurity stepped aside as the presentation began playing on screens stationed on each side of the podium. Only it wasn't the association's film.

Violet grabbed Henry's hand as their presentation rolled on. An off-screen announcer intoned, "Robert 'Bob' DeLancey started his career in security as a young staffer with the United States' West Berlin Embassy during the Cold War." A group photo from 1980s West Berlin Embassy with DeLancey flashed on the screen.

"DeLancey quickly became a favorite among the ladies." Another photo showed Bob surrounded by three adoring women, including Iris Morrison. "But there was another side to DeLancey few people saw. For DeLancey wasn't just any embassy staff member. He was a bona fide spy for the United States government."

Up on the dais, Violet saw the man in question stiffen beside the president of National Cybersecurity.

A staffer came up to the president and bent down to whisper in the president's ear. Then the other man moved rapidly toward the back of the room, his phone to his ear. The fact this wasn't the right film had been noticed. Violet prayed they would have enough time before someone pulled the plug.

"What very few people knew at the time was that DeLancey was also a double agent, spying on the United States for the East Germans." Another photo showed a dead man on the ground, a bullet hole clearly marked in his forehead. "DeLancey was responsible directly and indirectly for the deaths of more than thirty dissidents who tried to escape to the West from East Berlin during his tenure at the West Berlin Embassy. His code name, The Wolf, described his modus operandi perfectly." A list of names appeared on the screen with a line drawn through them, along with dates and monetary amounts to the right of each name.

DeLancey shifted in his chair but stayed seated, his face a shade paler to her eyes. A quick glance around the room showed most attendees riveted to the screen, with a few talking amongst themselves. Up on the dais, Agent Monroe moved into position behind The Wolf.

The recording Henry had received now played, with another voice translating the German words. While the recording played, an invoice from the fake pest management company was on screen, with a side-by-side translation. A photograph of a young couple with a baby came next, with their dates of death at the hands of the Stasi for trying to escape. The dates corresponded with the invoice.

Then the photographs Iris had sent appeared on the screen, followed by the announcer saying, "DeLancey faked The Wolf's death in the late 1980s and reinvented himself as a successful cybersecurity expert. With contracts with the Departments of Defense and Homeland Security, DeLancey has access to highly sensitive documents and data. Evidence points to his being involved in selling our security secrets to his old employer, Russia. Isn't it time to finally stop this man known as The Wolf?"

The screen faded to black, and the lights rose. A rumbling built in the room. DeLancey stood up with a cocky smile, his eyes surveying the stunned crowd with a coolness that chilled Violet's blood. This was the man who had betrayed his country without a second thought.

"I'm assuming this wasn't quite the presentation you had planned," DeLancey said with a wave to the association's president, who had rejoined him on the dais. "I'm not sure what happened, but whoever made that film should receive an Academy Award for taking creative liberty with the facts."

Special Agent Talbot moved through the crowd to stand in front of DeLancey. "The only facts we're concerned with are those that implicate you."

Special Agent Monroe took up position behind the man. Agent Talbot flipped open his badge and held it up for DeLancey to see. "FBI Special Agent Talbot. You're under arrest, Mr. DeLancey."

For a moment, DeLancey didn't move at all, then a slow smile stole across his face. "Under what charge?"

Violet gripped Henry's hand. The man's insolence showed how secure he thought he was, which was how a man with many powerful friends would behave. Even now, cornered, he exuded such a calm confidence many in the room likely doubted his guilt.

"Treason."

CHAPTER
SIXTY

Henry sat back as Violet placed a tray of steaming coffee and tea mugs on the low table in his den, then handed round the drinks. She made a lovely hostess for their guests, Agents Talbot and Monroe and Ms. Demaris. The last week had been filled with more questions than answers after the dramatic arrest of Bob DeLancey. Henry hoped many of those questions would finally be resolved.

"Thanks for coming," Henry said as the lawyer and agents settled back with their beverages. "We're eager to hear more about what's happened since DeLancey was taken into custody." Ms. Demaris couldn't promise full disclosure from the FBI, but somehow, she had convinced the agents to agree to an informal gathering.

"We kept looking for updates in the newspaper or online, but it's like the arrest never happened," Violet added.

Henry had assumed the arrest and subsequent federal investigation would continue to make front-page news, but while the events at the awards ceremony made a huge splash in the newspapers and cable news shows, the interest lasted only through the first twenty-four hours. Now, all the news pundits had their attention focused on a sex scandal concerning a New York Democratic senator and an aide working for a Republican congressman from Illinois.

Agent Talbot set down his cup. "In a way, that's true."

Henry frowned. "What do you mean?"

"The administration wants this to go away quietly, without a lot of fuss," he answered.

"Without a lot of fuss!" The words exploded out of Henry with more force than he had intended. "People are dead because of that man. He's probably still selling secrets to Russia and who knows who else, and all the government wants is to sweep it under the rug?"

Agent Monroe held up his hand. "That's not quite what my partner meant." The two agents exchanged glances before Agent Monroe continued. "It means the administration doesn't want to drag old scandals through the press right now, not with an election cycle coming up in November. The situation is being handled in a way designed not to exacerbate things."

Henry shook his head. "It sounds to me like a lot of double talk for letting a man who has betrayed his country fade quietly into the darkness rather than shining the light of truth on his misdeeds."

"I can see how it appears to you." Agent Talbot leaned forward, his expression earnest. "But I can assure you, Bob DeLancey isn't getting away with murder. He's going to jail for a very long time." The man paused to sip his coffee. "Because of your evidence and the proof left behind by Senator Morrison, we have enough to ensure he will not draw in a breath of free air again as long as he lives."

"He's made a plea bargain then?" Ms. Demaris interjected. "Life in prison in exchange for keeping quiet?"

The agents shifted slightly and once again looked at one another before Agent Monroe replied. "All I can tell you is the government is satisfied with his admission of guilt. He will not be a free man."

Henry narrowed his eyes. He hadn't been reading transcripts of Stasi interrogations for years not to recognize an avoidance measure. He was sure the agents were telling the truth. They just weren't telling the whole truth.

But before he could voice his concern, Violet beat him to the punch. "What aren't you telling us?" She gave each agent a hard stare. "What exactly did DeLancey admit to doing? What kind of deal did he make?"

"I'm not sure this falls into the scope of your need to know." Agent Talbot set down his cup.

Henry had had enough. He wanted answers, not put offs. "With all due respect, Agent Talbot," Henry interrupted, "without us and the evidence we uncovered for you, you wouldn't even have a murderous traitor in custody. So I think we deserve to know everything." He made eye contact with Violet. "We nearly lost our lives getting this information. Rainer Kopecek did lose his, and it's because of him and his courage to take on The Wolf that we have stopped the sale of more security secrets to Russia. So yes, I think you do owe us more than pat answers."

Violet reached over and squeezed his hand. He interlaced his fingers through hers as he waited for the agents to reply.

After several seconds, which seemed like an eternity, Agent Talbot cleared his throat. "Okay, but this can't leave the room. Bob DeLancey confessed to setting up contact with Russia to sell cybersecurity secrets related to U.S. military data. That alone would bring a minimum sentence of ten years."

"What about the deaths of Rainer Kopecek, Iris Morrison, and the others?"

Agent Monroe shook his head. "He says he had nothing to do with those recent deaths, and there's no hard evidence to connect him to any of them."

Henry pounced on his word choice. "What about the deaths of people connected with him in East Berlin?"

"Those he claims were related to his efforts to, and I quote, 'stem the tide of communism and secure America's future safety,'" Agent Talbot said.

"Did you believe him?" Violet asked.

"Not a word." Agent Monroe said. "But while we have evidence from the senator showing he had a hand in those Berlin deaths, we can't prove it wasn't as he said it was."

"Surely there are records to show otherwise," Violet protested, her voice pleading. "It isn't right he'll get away with murdering all those people."

Henry tightened his grip on her hand. "I imagine there is evidence, but not enough without eyewitness testimony."

Agent Talbot nodded. "For now, he's agreed to plead to the lesser charges of wanting to sell secrets to the Russians. But not actually having sold said secrets, we can't charge him with treason. Only intent to commit treason."

Violet's shoulders slumped. "After all of our work and Mr. Kopecek's death, the man responsible only gets a decade behind bars. And how do we know we'll be safe even when he's in prison? He's proven he has a long reach."

Henry longed to pull her into his arms and kiss away the pain in her voice, but that would have to wait until their company left.

"At this point, the government has all the evidence you uncovered, so I don't think there's any danger for you two," Agent Monroe said.

"You said he wouldn't draw another fresh breath of freedom." Henry locked eyes with Agent Monroe. "What did you mean?"

The man got to his feet with a smile. "I'd advise you to keep abreast of the news."

CHAPTER
SIXTY-ONE

Violet clutched the *New York Times* in her hands as she climbedthe the steps to Henry's house. The newspaper's front-page headline had caught her eye when she stopped to pick up some scones at a coffeehouse near Sissy's home.

Germany demands extradition of Bob DeLancey

German government requests he stand trial for Cold War-era crimes

This must have been what the FBI agents referred to yesterday. Bob DeLancey wouldn't have any more freedom for his crimes, despite the lenient—at least to her eyes—plea bargain. The Germans must know something of DeLancey's past if they were requesting the extradition of an American citizen.

She rang the doorbell and tucked the paper underneath the pastry box. When Henry opened the door, she bit back a laugh at the sight of the *Washington Post* front page in his hand, a similar headline gracing the space above the fold. Gesturing to the paper, she said, "Unbelievable."

He nodded as she slipped inside, shutting the door behind her. "I know. So much for a quiet handling of the situation."

"Yeah." She sighed. "I still look over my shoulder every time I walk down the street, thinking I'll see DeLancey or one of his goons coming after me." She shivered, and Henry touched her arm briefly before continuing down the hallway to the kitchen. Once there, she set the box and newspaper on the table and seated herself at the kitchen table while he finished brewing tea.

"Have you heard anything else about Patrick's involvement?" Henry placed the full teacups on the table.

She wrinkled her nose. "Agent Monroe called to tell me the guards tossed Patrick's cell after his interview and found several entries in his diary referring to letters signed 'The Wolf' that provided the basic outline of Mr. Kopecek's murder along with my supposed guilt."

"We thought there must be a connection, and Patrick's notations prove it, at least to us."

"At least it was unrelated to his wolf tattoo. He's had that one for several years." She sighed. "I can't believe how meticulous DeLancey was, is, in his dealings. It took a lot of effort to figure out who I really was, track down my brother, and plant those seeds. Although to be honest, I don't think he had to try very hard to convince my brother I too had murderous tendencies, not when it played so well into his own sick game of blame-everyone-but-myself-for-my-troubles.'"

"What are you going to do now?" Henry set the cream and sugar on the table and took his seat.

"I don't know." She stared into the amber liquid as if it held the secrets to the rest of her life. "Before, when I didn't have a mass murderer for a brother, I wanted to go into civil service. Now I have no idea what I want to be."

Henry reached across the table and squeezed her hand. "Might I make a suggestion?"

Violet gave a little laugh even as her stomach flip-flopped at the serious expression in his eyes. "Sure. I can use all the suggestions I can get at this point. I can't live with your sister and brother forever." They had spent so much time figuring out The Wolf's identity and trying not to get killed that she had pushed off thoughts of the future.

With most of the loose ends tied up, her future was all she thought about. While Henry said he loved her, that was a long way from him wanting to rush into a relationship, especially with someone who had a murderer for a brother. Better to keep talking to avoid thinking about how lonely such a future would be without Henry. "The good news is the insurance finally paid the claim on my apartment trashing, so I have a little money in the bank. But that's all I have, and—"

Henry leaned over and placed his finger over her lips, effectively stopping the flow of words. "If you don't mind, I'd like to tell you what I think you should do with the rest of your life."

She nodded, her heart in her throat, making it difficult for her to breath, much less speak. With the barest whisper of pressure, he traced the outline of her mouth before removing his finger. It took every ounce of willpower she possessed not to put her own fingers to her lips to implant the memory of his touch.

"You are the most extraordinary woman I've ever met. You have faced adversity with calmness, helped uncover a spy-turned-traitor, and, most important of all, at least to me, captured my heart." Henry gazed at her, eyes bright with love and promise.

The tightness in her chest eased at his words and expression. Maybe her future wasn't as bleak as she thought it might be. Maybe she would find a new purpose in life. Maybe she shouldn't have drunk the tea so fast. The caffeine was making her pulse do funny things, like beat faster. "You have my heart too."

He grinned. "I know."

Drat the man. Why did he have to sound so cocky and sweet all at the same time?

"Which brings me to my suggestion. What if you took on the biggest challenge of your entire life?"

She blinked. This non-sequitur seemed rather out of line with his previous words. "Challenge?"

His brown eyes crinkled, and he leaned closer. "My sister says I'm quite the challenge to live with, but given how well you've managed so far, do you think you might be up to it?"

Violet frowned. Was his ability to walk deteriorating more than she realized? Was he asking her to be his aide, like she had been at the assisted living facility? Tears sprung to her eyes. She surged to her feet, desperate not to let him see what she thought the direction of the conversation was going. All the talk of love had been nothing more than a smoke screen for his true intention. "I don't think I am."

THE SHARPNESS OF HER WORDS CUT INTO HENRY LIKE A KNIFE SLICING through bread. Somehow, things had taken a turn into the surreal, and he had to get the conversation back on track. "Violet?"

She glared at him, tears spilling from her eyes. "If you want someone to help you, you should call an agency!" With a toss of her head, she picked up her still full cup of tea and carried it to the sink.

Henry sat stunned. Agency? What was she talking about?

"I can't believe you'd think I would want to...." She shook her head and paced toward the kitchen doorway.

Panic raced through his body at the thought she might be walking out of his life forever. "Wait!" He struggled to his feet, knocking over one of his crutches and losing his balance. With a grunt, he fell to the floor.

"Henry?"

Henry shot open his eyes and saw Violet bending over him. "Violet?" He pushed to a seated position, his back against a kitchen cabinet.

"Are you okay?" Her soft hand touched his cheek, and he crushed it to his face with his hand.

"Please, don't go. Please. I couldn't bear to not have you in my life. I love you."

"I wasn't leaving." She settled down on the floor in front of him, her hand still resting under his on his cheek. "I just can't be the person you want me to be. You love me, but not the way I need to be loved."

Henry frowned, his head spinning, whether from the fall or her nearness, he didn't know. He had to convince this woman to stay with him. "I thought you loved me."

She sighed and smoothed a strand of hair behind her ear. "I do love you."

"Then why can't we have a future together?" The frustration he felt bubbled up and the words came out harsher than he intended.

A sadness crept into her eyes, and the sorrow tore out his own heart. "Because I love you." Her voice trembled. "I can't accept what you're proposing as our future."

He closed his eyes again. She loved him, and he certainly loved her. The ancient and modern poets certainly had it right. Love was indeed a complicated thing mere mortals couldn't deem to understand. He opened his eyes and reached up to stroke her cheek, his fingers gliding over the soft skin.

"I don't understand," he said softly. "If we love each other, why can't we get married?"

She froze, her entire body as still as a statute. "What did you say?"

He threaded his fingers into the hair at the nape of her neck. "I'm asking you to marry me."

Violet stared at him for a long moment, one in which he thought he would need to repeat the statement. Then she roused herself as if from sleep. "You want to marry me?"

He nodded, and in case she didn't understand the movement, added, "Yes, I want you to marry me and live here with me. I don't want to face the future without you by my side. As my wife."

Violet touched his cheek with her hand. "I thought you were asking me to come take care of you."

"Take care of me?" Henry furrowed his brow. "Well, I guess I am in a way. That's part of being married, right? That we take care of each other."

She leaned closer and put her forehead to his. "I thought you meant as an aide, like Daura at the assisted living facility."

"As an aide?" He chuckled, then kissed her gently. "Most certainly not what I had in mind. Granted, I'm not the easiest person to love, and I can't promise you a smooth path in life, but I can promise to love and cherish you all the days God gives us together."

"That sounds like a very good promise to me."

He smiled at her as his heart lightened. "Then you'll marry me?"

"Yes, I'll marry you." Violet barely got the words out before Henry claimed her lips as his own. When he drew back slightly, she added in a breathless voice, "But we'd better make it sooner rather than later, as I find I've become rather fond of your house."

With a tug, he pulled her onto his lap. "I think a short engagement can be arranged."

"Good." Violet traced his mouth with her fingers. "I've never wanted a fancy wedding."

"As long as you're there, it doesn't matter to me either." Henry captured her face between his hands and brought his lips near hers. "As long as there's a wolf centerpiece."

She shuddered. "Don't even joke about it."

He apologized with tiny kisses along her jawline.

"I want to walk down the aisle to you while *Concerto No. 2, Op. 21 for Piano and Orchestra: I. Maestoso* by Cyprien Katsaris performed by the Los Angeles Philharmonic with conductor Carlo Maria Giulini and pianist Krystian Zimerman plays."

He pulled back a fraction. "Very specific."

Her eyes filled with tears. "Mr. Kopecek said the recording was the last Christmas present he ever gave Verna. He talked often about how much she enjoyed listening to the record. I'd like to honor him by having it played at our wedding."

Henry nodded. "A fitting way to honor the man who brought us together."

She smiled as he used his thumbs to brush a few tears from her cheeks. "Thank you."

He returned her smile, then dropped his gaze to her lips. "Now, if you don't mind, I think I'd like to kiss my fiancée." As their lips met, Henry silently thanked God—and Rainer Kopecek—for bringing this vibrant, wonderful woman into his life.

THE END

COMING IN FALL 2022...

Book Two in The Cold War Legacy

The Dark Atonement (Seshva Press LLC)

A translator and a medical researcher team up to find a long-lost scientist with an innovative cancer treatment.

German translator Lena Hoffman thought her grandfather died years ago. But the unexpected arrival of a cryptic postcard seems to indicate otherwise. As Lena delves into her grandfather's past and uncovers information about him and his cancer research work in East Germany four decades ago, she unwittingly puts her own life in danger.

Dr. Devlin Mills works as a cancer researcher at the National Institutes of Health and lives across the hall from Lena, although they've never formally met. But when Lena is nearly run down by a vehicle, Devlin finds himself thrust into the role of protector. As their lives intersect, the pair find themselves in a race to discover the whereabouts of her grandfather—and whoever wants to silence him—before the past catches up with the present.

ABOUT SARAH HAMAKER

Sarah Hamaker has been spinning stories since she was a child. While she's had two traditionally published nonfiction books, her heart is writing romantic suspense. You can find a list of her books, listen to her podcast, "The Romantic Side of Suspense," and connect with Sarah on her website, sarahhamakerfiction.com, or on these social media platforms:

Amazon Author Page: https://www.amazon.com/-/e/B002TIARBS
BookBub: https://www.bookbub.com/profile/sarah-hamaker
Goodreads: https://www.goodreads.com/author/show/1804799.Sarah_Hamaker
LinkedIn: https://www.linkedin.com/in/sarah-hamaker-7295a01/
Pinterest: https://www.pinterest.com/hamaker0041/sarah-hamaker-fiction/

OTHER BOOKS BY SARAH HAMAKER

Dangerous Christmas Memories (Love Inspired Suspense)

A witness in jeopardy...and a killer on the loose.

Hiding in witness protection is the only option for Priscilla Anderson after witnessing a murder. Then Lucas Langsdale shows up claiming to be her husband right when a hit man finds her. With partial amnesia, she has no memory of her marriage or the killer's identity. Yet she will have to put her faith in Luc if they both want to live to see another day.

Deadly Diamonds (Seshva Press LLC)

The race to find missing diamonds puts a widow in danger.

Three years ago, Dulce Honeycutt's life imploded when her husband died after a robbing a jewelry store and her 18-year-old son, Kieran, landed in prison as an accessory. The uncut diamonds were never recovered, and when rumors fly that she and Kieran know where the gems are hidden, their lives are in danger.

Veteran insurance investigator Miles Sharp believes Dulce knows more about the diamonds than she's revealing. But as the attacks on the beautiful widow's life multiply, he struggles to maintain his professional objectivity. Is Dulce a victim or is her story a sweet web of lies?

Illusion of Love (Seshva Press LLC)

A suspicious online romance reconnects an agoraphobe and an old friend.

Psychiatrist Jared Quinby's investigation for the FBI leads him to his childhood friend, Mary Divers. Agoraphobic Mary has found love with online beau David. When David reveals his intention of becoming a missionary, Mary takes a leap of faith and accepts David's marriage proposal.

When Jared's case intersects with Mary's online relationship, she refuses to believe anything's amiss with David. When tragedy strikes, Mary pushes Jared away.

Will Jared convince Mary of the truth—and of his love for her—before it's too late?

Mistletoe & Murder (Seshva Press LLC)

Alec Stratman comes home to Twin Oaks, Virginia, after his Army
retirement to contemplate his reentry into civilian life. Instead he's greeted
with the murder of his beloved Great-Aunt Heloise.

For Isabella Montoya, the loss of Heloise Stratman Thatcher goes beyond
the end of a job. Heloise had encouraged Isabella to follow her dreams and
helped fund her studies. Now, accused of her mentor's murder, Isabella is
scrambling to prove her innocence.

Since his great-aunt had written glowing letters about Isabella, Alec is
unwilling to believe the police's suspicion of the former housekeeper.
Instead, he works to help clear her name.

Will Isabella and Alec be able to navigate the secrets that threaten to derail
their budding romance and uncover the truth about Heloise's death before
the killer strikes again?

Protecting Her Witness (Seshva Press LLC)

A family in danger...a U.S. Marshal sworn to protect.

U.S. Marshal Chalissa Manning has been running from her past and God for most of her life. When she meets widower Titus Davis and his son, Sam, her well-built defenses begin to crumble. But someone is targeting Titus and Sam, and it's up to Chalissa to both protect them and to find out who is behind the attacks.

As the threats pile up, will Chalissa be able to keep the family she's grown to love safe?

A finalist in the 2022 Selah Awards, romantic suspense category.

A finalist in the 2022 HOLT Medallion, Best Book by a Virginia Author category.

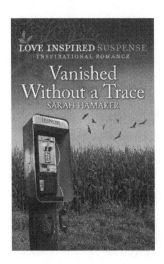

Coming in July 2022...

Vanished Without a Trace (Love Inspired Suspense)

A missing person case. A new clue. And a fight for survival.

After nine years searching for his missing sister, attorney Henderson Parker uncovers a clue that leads him to Twin Oaks, Virginia—and podcaster Elle Updike investigating the case. Partnering with the journalist is the last thing Henderson wants, until mysterious thugs make multiple attacks on both their lives. Now they'll have to trust each other...before the suspected kidnappers make them disappear for good.

Made in the USA
Columbia, SC
02 January 2025

50983041R00207